THE PLACE WE CALL HOME

THE PLACE
WE CALL HOME

Faith Hogan

An Aria Book

Cover design: Charlotte Abrams-Simpson

Typeset by Silicon Chips

Aria
c/o Head of Zeus
First Floor East
5–8 Hardwick Street
London EC1R 4RG

www.ariafiction.com

'There is no place like home…'

Dorothy in *The Wonderful Wizard of Oz*
by L. Frank Baum

Prologue

Miranda

This place. This place, Miranda thought, as she looked across the bay, it was in her bones. From here, Ballycove had not changed, Miranda walked along this path for more years than she cared to remember. It grew only more breathtaking. Far out across the land, beyond the winding river, she could see the glitter of the sea and beyond, she could make out the shadow of Donegal's rugged coastline two counties winding away in the far north. Miranda imagined that beneath the scrubby banks, shingle pebbles glittered in the low evening sun and in the deep of the water, she fancied a lifetime of memories were stored. So many of her memories played out against this riverbank.

Today, the air murmured into a timely heartbeat of the water's current. It whispered a familiar chant. It always calmed her, walking along the river's edge. Sometimes, it was hard to believe that so many decades had passed since she'd spent her summers along this sunny path. Today, as always it was exhilarating in its freshness, a landscape forever shifting and still its fabric remained the same for all time. The grey-green hills beyond the village were surely smaller than in her childhood, as though the weight of time had obliged them to crouch just a little lower with each passing year. Still, they stood, stony and sturdy, their lines of time a testament to their ability to keep Ballycove safe from winter storms.

The water, glittering blues and greens that reached much further than the eye could see, was as timeless as it was unending. It fed families and took fathers, sometimes it seemed with equal generosity and ferociousness. Miranda thought it had never looked more beautiful than now, but then she smiled, because no matter when she walked along this path, she thought the same. She stopped for a moment on the little track, cleared by goats and the chases of foxes and rabbits when no-one else was looking. Miranda had been looking forward to this walk all morning. She had to set things right. It was time.

And now, thinking of her own family, she knew that there was only one thing for it. She would have to pull them all together and lay the foundations for a new beginning.

I

The Past

Miranda Reilly clambered up the hill slowly. The heat made her cotton dress damp against her back, and the stitching cut into her narrow shoulders and arms. It was a size too small, but her mother insisted that another year could be knocked out of it. Her discomfort was heightened by the box of vegetables she carried in her arms, heavy and cumbersome and her excuse to escape the fraught atmosphere of home. It was worth being out of breath to make this short journey.

Most days, she ambled up to old Mrs Bridgestock's cottage on an errand of some sort. It was only a short distance really, but it was such a delightful place it might as well have been in the next county, so far removed was it from the bleak tone of her upended home. It seemed to Miranda that Mrs Bridgestock could be the oldest person in the world. She wore her dresses long and black. Her hair, white and held with pins, framed her soft and lined face in the same fashion as it had some fifty years earlier in the wedding photo that sat on the sideboard. Although Mrs Bridgestock wore the marks of age in her stooped shoulders and slow walk, the woman in the photograph, staring lovingly at the man next to her, would always be who she truly was. There was that same generous glint in the old lady's eye and no-one ever called but they weren't offered the little her cupboards held to bolster them for whatever might come next. Miranda sometimes marvelled at the treats the old lady had put aside for her visits.

She eagerly made her way forwards now, thinking of what they might share today and how they might sit and talk about how things were when Mrs Bridgestock was a girl. As much as Miranda dreamed of living in this cottage one day, she aspired to growing into an old lady like Mrs Bridgestock – although she'd never admit this to another living soul.

In the distance she could just about see the chimneys of Bridgestock Cottage peep above the wall of ash and rowan trees that shaded the farmhouse from winter winds and prying eyes. It was a lazy morning on the cusp of summer and Ballycove welcomed the sun as it did everything else that came its way, balancing a languid acceptance with reluctant eagerness. In truth, it seemed to Miranda Reilly, that the only thing that this village had greeted with any great excitement had been the return of her father a few weeks earlier. The whole village turned out to welcome back Harry Reilly – after four years of war and six of convalescing. In a place that Miranda knew only as St Hugh's, some nameless doctor that her mother couldn't thank enough had set him on the journey home. The sun didn't shine that day, but flags blew vigorously on the breezy afternoon wind and the whole street lined out to greet the returned hero. Funny, how things can turn out so differently to how you expect.

Miranda wiped a tear from her eye now. She would not cry. Instead, she leaned forward and lifted the latch of the heavy gate that kept cattle away from what had once been a lovingly tended kitchen garden. She and her mother had spent the last ten years waiting for her father to return; honestly, Miranda had a feeling they'd both given up any hope. The village had learned after the Great War not to expect good news; her mother didn't say it, but they both knew, World War Two was no better. If anything it had turned out even worse.

While Miranda's father was away, her mother had considered herself lucky each time a telegram arrived in the village and it was not addressed to her. They spent years of hoping the postman would pass their door. And then it was as if they were washed through with shocked relief, gushing and exhilarating all at once when they learned he was convalescing; shell-shocked, but coming home.

Just then, she spotted the postman, coming along the path opposite, his black cap bobbing jauntily beyond the hedge. He would make it to the cottage first and that was unfortunate, because she knew that it meant Mrs Bridgestock would not have so much time for her today.

Miranda sighed as she made her way along the narrow track, worn down by her own feet on her daily visits here. She made it to the door just as Postie Kavanagh propped his bicycle against the grainy windowsill and smiled when he patted her head as though she was a friendly sheepdog. She dropped the box of vegetables in the darkness of the hallway and slumped down on the step at the front door of the cottage. She would sit for a while before making the journey back to the village. There was no rush, only more chores her mother had dreamed up to keep her out of mischief. It was summer holidays and it seemed as if the days stretched endlessly. Her walk back was meaningfully languid and slow – it was preferable to hanging lines of washing out or, worse, being made to scrub the front steps.

Out here, just a mile from town, the only building nearby was the old woollen mills. It loomed ever higher above her as she moved back towards Ballycove. It was as much a feature of this place as the mountains or the river, a grey monolith, reaching and sprawling, its chimneys forever churning out a reminder that its work was never done. Blair's woollen mills – there was something about it, Miranda thought. She slowed down to gaze at it through the thick hedges that sheltered the river from it and perhaps it from the river life that might seek out shelter where it would not be granted willingly.

One way or another, the Blairs kept her whole family. Her mother took in laundry for the Blair family, and Lady Blair paid far more than she should for the small amount they now had each week. Her father might work there too. No-one else would give him a chance because he had come back so strange. Lord Blair had been shell-shocked in the first war so Lady Blair had said she understood better than most what it must be like. Her mother said it was a good thing the Blairs were Presbyterians – their own lot might not be so full of social conscience.

She pushed thoughts of her father from her mind then; not today. It was too nice to spoil it with things she could not change. It was a bright and sanguine day, where the breeze played with her dark hair, a soft warm caress as she moved along the banks and towards the hump-backed bridge that would lead her across to the side of the river that backed on to the mills.

Although it was not the first day of the holidays, it seemed to Miranda that her summer began that day, when she met Richard Blair. He was sitting idly on the bridge, his legs hanging over it while he skimmed stones down river. A boy, perhaps a year older than herself, he was fair-skinned to her tan, blue-eyed to her green and his hair was somewhere between a very light brown and a dark blonde, whereas Miranda was so dark, she might have been a gypsy child roaming about the roads. He looked at her with a mixture of mischief and camaraderie.

'Hey,' he said as though he'd been waiting there for her to come along. It was early yet, full of promise; one of those long hot days that seem like a dream when they're over. Miranda had already spent what there was of it trying to put distance between her father and herself. Instead, she'd offered to bring vegetables to old Mrs Bridgestock who couldn't leave her house because she was a martyr to the gout.

'Hello,' she said spotting his icy blue eyes squinting against the sun while at the same time they picked out flashes on the water beneath him. Miranda had never seen this boy around before and Ballycove was small enough to know everyone. Then she remembered she'd heard her mother say the Blairs had guests, back for summer holidays with a boy not much older than herself. 'On holidays, are you?' she asked hopping up on the bridge next to him.

'I am,' he said, flashing a shy smile and handing her a flat stone to skim across the water's surface.

'Good shot,' she said as she watched an elongated hopping string of splashes along the water's rim. She threw her own and it almost matched his, and she smiled with satisfaction when she saw a glint of admiration in his eyes for her skill. 'Are you staying with the Blairs?'

'Yes, they're my grandparents. I'm here for the whole summer long.' He nodded towards the trees and she presumed he meant the big house, Blair Hall.

'You're really good at that.' She nodded towards the river where another flat stone scudded efficiently across the water's surface.

'Thanks.' He laughed then. 'Richard Blair.' He held out a hand formally. 'Very pleased to meet you.'

'Miranda Reilly,' she said, swinging her legs across the bridge to get a better angle on her next skimming stone. 'Delighted, I'm sure,' she said to match his formality. Then she remembered the time. She needed to get back or her mother would surely have organised a search party. 'Aren't you a bit old to be skimming stones?' she said to make fun of him, throwing one last shot along the water.

'I probably am really. There's not a lot else to do here at the moment. I'm looking forward to getting my fishing rod out. My grandfather is letting me borrow his old punt, but I'll have to do a bit of tidying up on it first.' He jumped down from the bridge and began to walk with her.

'I'd love that... fishing on a boat in this weather. It sounds like heaven,' Miranda said. Trips on boats were few and far between, since most of the boats were fishing boats and they had no room for children who just wanted to sightsee. 'I could help, you know, get it ready, if you wanted,' she said, unsure of what that would entail, but if it meant getting a few boat trips it would be worth it.

'Ah, I'm not sure that's really the kind of thing a girl would be any good at...' He turned now, smiling at her. There was no animosity in his words. 'You know, painting, it's all very messy and it's damned tricky work.'

'Huh, I'll have you know, I've probably done a lot more painting than you have.'

'I'm sure you have, but this is proper painting, not flowers in vases or fruit in bowls.' He bent down, pulled a bunch of cardinal flowers and handed them to her. He laughed then but his eyes were kind.

'That's not proper painting...' she began, because there was one thing that living without her father had taught her over the last few years and that was how to be practical. Each Christmas it was her job to run the paintbrush around the edges of doors and windows, skirting boards and tiles. She had, her mother always said, an eye for detail.

In the distance she heard a church bell ring out and felt a stab of panic. She'd been gone much too long. The short jaunt had turned into not only a long ramble, but stopping here, with Richard Blair, had also robbed her of time when she should be getting back if she didn't want to be grounded for the rest of the summer. That notion made her heart sink. She couldn't imagine being shut up in their little cottage with her father for days on end. 'Where's your boat anyway?'

'Down along the river.' He jutted his thumb forwards. 'Of course, it's locked away in the boathouse on the estate for now, but tomorrow...'

'I know it.' Miranda wouldn't particularly want to admit that she knew most of the old outhouses along the riverbank. She had explored every place she could make her way into. The little boathouse, musty and empty, had given her shelter when she was caught out in an unexpected downpour once on her way back from a day spent tadpoling on the bank.

'You do, do you? Well, I'll be there first thing tomorrow, so if you're at a loose end you'll know where to come, won't you!'

'You're making fun of me,' she said as she hoisted herself up over the gate that blocked this lane from the main road.

'Me? Never.' He smiled and she was suddenly aware that they were standing there watching each other for a little too long.

'Well, I should be getting back,' which of course, was an understatement.

'I suppose that we'll be bumping into each other again,' he said diffidently then he scudded his final flat stone along the top of the river. 'See you soon, Miranda,' he shouted as he made his way in the general direction of Blair Hall.

The following day, Miranda arrived at the boathouse just as Richard was pulling back the huge doors. With the morning light flooding the little shed, it seemed much brighter and less eerie than when she came here before. Now, she could see it was a very old building, home to two boats, one – Richard's little punt – slept silently beneath a great blue cloak. He pulled back the cover and resolutely ignored the sorry-looking remains of a red and white sailboat in the corner.

'Hi,' she said shyly as she slipped around the door.

'Fancy seeing you here.' He was lining up a couple of rusting tins of paint, but there was no way of knowing what they contained without opening the lids. 'Come to watch me work, have you?' he said kindly.

'I thought I'd help you,' Miranda said with more confidence than she felt.

'Oh, I can't see you helping here. It's all...' His words stopped when he caught her eye, as though he was thinking that he might jolly her along. Then he turned back to the bench, taking up one of the paint cans again. Miranda spotted a big old screwdriver and she grabbed it, quickly levering open the first can before moving on to the next, aware of Richard at her back watching her silently.

'Well done, maybe you'll be able to assist me after all,' he said, surprise lilting his voice.

'We're in luck,' Miranda said on opening the final can. It was almost full of varnish, a slightly more vivid colour than the faded tone of the little boat that lay stretched out in the sunshine coming from the doorway. She set to stirring it up with the screwdriver so that soon the lumpy years of disuse were being broken into the liquid. 'Have you found some brushes?' she called to him.

'Well, I have, two, but really...' He held up a wide brush that would quickly cover the whole boat in a first coat and a second, narrow brush that would work well on the darkened rims and around the decorative patch that held the boat's name. Miranda handed the heavy can of paint across to Richard.

'Here, you start with this and I'll have a look at the others.' She nodded towards the three remaining cans. She picked out the most vibrant red and began to stir it up also. Richard was running long, milky strokes along the belly of the boat, which seemed to dry in before he had time to wet his brush for the next. 'It's going to take a couple of coats; the wood is really thirsty,' Miranda said as she knelt down to begin painting around the rims.

'Oh dear, you can't… you mustn't…' Richard began, but he faltered as he watched her delicately apply the fuchsia-coloured paint evenly and precisely along a fine line, giving the body of the vessel immediate definition.

'What's that?' She smiled at him, enjoying his surprise.

'You're actually…' He was embarrassed now, looking across at his own messy work by comparison. 'Well, you're actually very good.' They set to work then, each of them painting their own allotted space, working around each other and chatting happily as they went.

'Some day, perhaps when I have more money, I'll resurrect the old girl again,' he said wistfully as they sat back against a rock later that day looking at the sailboat that would spend another year in darkness.

'Doesn't anyone use it any more?' Miranda asked looking up at what was once a pretty sailboat.

'It was my grandfather's but he hasn't sailed in years. Not likely to now, either.'

'Oh,' Miranda said and she wasn't sure what else to say. She thought she knew everyone in the village of Ballycove, but she couldn't ever remember seeing Richard's grandfather. Surely, she would have remembered him, if she had. She knew his grandmother, a homely-looking woman, with silver flecks through hair that must have once been very close in colour to Richard's.

'He's not well mostly,' Richard said as he caught a few large drips of varnish hanging from the base of the boat. 'The war,' he said making a face, 'the Great War? It did something to him and he's never really been right after it.'

'Same as my dad so.' Miranda exhaled. It was the first time she'd actually admitted to anyone that her father was not right. 'He came back a month ago and he hasn't spoken two words to me since.'

'They used to call it shell shock, from all the loud bangs, but I don't know... my grandfather was an officer in the trenches, listening I suppose to others over his head dropping bombs around his ears.'

'It had to be scary as hell, I suppose,' Miranda supplied. 'He must have been very brave.' She knew the value of hearing something good about her own father.

'Yes, I suppose he must have been. He hardly ever leaves the estate now, hasn't for years, and can't bear to go beyond it.' Richard Blair shook his head as though he could hardly understand it.

'I can't imagine staying put all the time; of course, our house is a lot smaller than Blair Hall.' She laughed now to cover over her nervousness – the last thing she wanted was to make him feel as others had done to her. 'My dad can't stay still at all. Sometimes, he goes off walking at odd hours, even in the middle of the night and when he's home, well, he's never really there, if you get my meaning.' The sadness in her voice was as much for her mother and her father as it was for herself.

'We're a right pair so.' Richard Blair smiled, a lopsided movement of his lips that didn't quite reach his eyes, and Miranda could see in it something of her own experience of happiness always restrained by some unresolved emotion. Over the last month, this halter on her emotions had risen up in her. It was love mixed with fear and guilt and whatever other sentiment she was supposed to feel at any point. It was hard to feel unbridled joy when you were carrying such a sadness about your heart all the time. 'Here.' He searched in a satchel that had been cast carelessly along the bench and handed her a thick sandwich. 'You can have half of mine.' He opened a tall flask that smelled of something between sugar and coffee. 'My grandmother makes the best hot chocolate,' he said smiling at her before pouring them a cup each.

'What about this?' She pointed towards the name on the side of the boat, which was facing them now. 'Funny Girl,' she whispered softly. 'Wouldn't it look great in the red?'

'Perhaps it's what we could call you?' Richard said as he angled a long and gentle gaze in her direction. 'No?' He smiled then, blushed a little, and went back to his sandwich. 'See if you can't paint around it and then we can decide later. There's a nasty shade of yellow as a second option.' He wrinkled his nose. It took almost the whole day to get the boat ready and it would take another day to dry it fully. 'We're lucky, the sun will dry it out quickly. We could be out catching our first fish tomorrow afternoon,' he said.

'I've never been properly fishing before...' Miranda looked back at the huge, expensive looking rods that stood sentry inside the boathouse.

'Well, perhaps I'll show you how...' Richard said with a lazy smile.

When they finished patching and painting, they took their rods along the bank and Richard set up Miranda, holding her steady and working with her hand over hand, his arms around her until at the same moment, they both seemed to realise the intimacy of the situation. Then, they dropped their lines just for fun. Richard had a jar of fresh worms dug up the day before and stored in the cool darkness of the boathouse, saving them for his first trip out on the water.

The day was hot and hazy and the water shimmered, a musky blanket attracting flies just close enough so the salmon nosed towards the water's top. Too many silver salmon jumped up, tantalisingly close to them, but none of them lured by the measly bait on offer. Miranda lay back on the soft grass, enjoying the sounds of summer all around. The river was home to every water animal from frog to stoat and each rustle in the undergrowth suggested the proximity of something teasingly uncommon.

'Probably river rats.' Richard laughed when the grass swished with the bristling sound of something small and fast-moving.

'Don't say that, it could be anything – it could be a fox, or a squirrel, or a…'

'Badger?'

'Goodness, I hope not. Billy Bonner had his leg broken by one last year and you should see the scratches, all the way along his legs, urgh!' She shivered at the thought of it. She moved over a little, on the grass.

'No-one warned me when I came to Ireland, I was in danger of losing life and limb.' Richard was laughing at her now.

'It's okay, I don't think you need to worry; for one thing, I'm not sure they just attack random people and for another…' She looked out at the water for a moment, the line catching her attention, and then she looked back at him again.

'What, for another?'

'Well, Billy Bonner, who wouldn't want to teach him a lesson?' They both laughed at that and Miranda felt a creeping sense of freedom, the familiar tug of loneliness and worry fading from her as though it was releasing her lying there on the warm bank with Richard Blair – perhaps they would be best friends yet?

2

Miranda

Miranda stopped a moment, watching as a seagull swooped with precision into the water beneath her. She would walk to the cliff edge and back. It was less than a mile, and for many years, she had walked it easily, but these days, she was in the habit of moving more slowly, more thoughtfully. A fall at the end of last summer had left her with little more than bruises, but it set off a series of pains and aches that managed to slow her down whether she liked it or not.

In her mind, Miranda connected that fall with her almost heart attack. It reminded her that time was passing, she was getting older, and she did not have forever stretching out ahead of her. Not that she wasn't still a busy woman. Miranda had no intention of sinking into old age anytime soon, but maybe she was coming close to being able to put some time aside just for herself. She was no longer a young woman and still sitting at the helm of the family woollen mills. Perhaps she didn't travel as much as she used to, but her eye for detail was as sharp now as any young thing and her instinct for colour and trends had only honed with experience.

Miranda loved the mills. Ada accused her of loving them more than she had her own family, which of course was typical of her eldest child. Miranda believed Ada wanted no more than to make an old woman of her mother and to take over the reins of the family business. But Ada lacked vision. Ada's strength was in saving, cutting and snipping. There would be no sentimentality, no thought to the men and women whose lives were linked for decades with the Corrigan family through working in the mills.

Ada was a tiny woman, in so many ways. She had always been a little sparrow hawk, with fine shoulder blades and delicate features in her pinched face. She wore her hair such a dark colour that it looked as if it might have been dipped in blue-black ink and it sat in a neat halo gently curled inwards around her head. She always wore a string of pearls at her neck and tweed suits of varying weight depending on the season. She was the quintessential bookkeeper, but she would make a poor leader. It was just a pity she could not see this for herself. She was forty-eight this year and her measured approach to life meant that she'd spent nearly five decades squeezing the good out of everything so she was left with only what had little value to her.

Of course, she cared for her mother; she had been the first one to the hospital when Miranda fell last year. Ada arrived, her eyes filled with concern, her slightly too high voice demanding the very best care for her mother. Poor Ada – Miranda was only relieved that she hadn't brought along Tony. The arrival of Anthony Jackson might have just about finished her off, Miranda thought at the time.

Miranda took a deep breath. This place, the scrubby greens – surely there were more than just forty shades? The earth that could be brown, grey or black or any colour in between depending on the mood of the tide and the sky above, had been the reason why the mills had survived. Maybe it was why Miranda was walking here today. This place had inspired her when Paddy Corrigan died leaving her with a business on the brink of bankruptcy, a cottage on the edge of collapse and a family about her that she promised a better life than the one she had known herself.

Miranda had taken inspiration from the landscape around her to create an award-winning collection of products that had the good luck to resonate with customers from New York to Beijing. The first year had been hard, but she persevered enough to set them back on track and it took ten more to establish the Corrigan Mills as an international brand to rival the other big Irish exports of whiskey, pharmaceuticals and Guinness.

Even now, when Miranda looked upon the stained silt of the riverbank, she could see the tints that dominated woollen blankets that sat everywhere from the White House to Downing Street. Ada, for all her acuity in the accounts department, lacked that vision. It was a passion and Miranda wished it fervently for her daughter, because she believed it brought with it an unbridled joy that Ada so badly needed to make her into the woman Miranda hoped one day she might become.

Callie had it. Combined with her raw talent, it was what had made her youngest daughter into the worldwide success she had become. Miranda worried about Callie, probably more than she should, but she knew that Callie's life in London was not as simple or as rosy as it looked. She worked hard, too hard in Miranda's opinion, and that left far too little time for anything else. Of course, her youngest daughter had managed to net all of the trappings of a successful life, but like her mother, material things counted for little to Callie who was as happy raking out the garden as she was standing on the red carpet of some glitzy event.

Miranda sighed; time seemed to collide on her more often these days with the past almost as clear as anything in the present. Callie Corrigan was born on a sunny day that seemed to herald the arrival of spring although it was late autumn. Miranda smiled, remembering Paddy had been busy in the mills that day, trying to shore up the old machines that were already running on prayer as much as engine power. It was an exercise in sentimentality as much as prudence. Miranda knew they could purchase new looms and weaving machines. They could fill their factory floor with computerised gadgets that would save them money in terms of wages and probably other overhead costs.

But the truth was, Miranda liked things as they were and she knew that Paddy loved them too. She appreciated the crashing of the loom, the smell of the yarn, the greetings from people like Tom Walsh, whose father and grandfather had all carried out the same job before him. She loved the gleam of the metal. When she ran her hand along the nameplates, she adored the feeling that, in some way, she was connecting with the generations who had passed before her and managed to keep the mills running while the world around it too often lost its way.

No, she would not be letting go of the old for something sleek and humourless. Even though Tom would frown when

Big Betty stumbled, he would shake his head and mutter, but his smile of kindliness was priceless as he'd nudge the old machine into productivity once more.

Her husband, Paddy, had been neither a mechanic nor an engineer, but he was a man with a good brain and an interest in tinkering with things until he got them right. He worked away on many a black night and hummed quietly while he set about maintaining all the machines in the mills. She loved to watch him, as his big hands caressed the machines as much with tenderness as with strength. In the end, he crafted a series of replacement cogs, bobbins and timers and they had over the years, in their way, helped Miranda and made her forget that she was carrying the weight of so many futures in her hands.

Unfortunately, their son Simon was nothing like his father. Simon had grown up with that innate ability to seem as if he was pleasing everyone while setting out only to please himself. If Miranda worried about any of her children, it was Simon who had caused her the most sleepless nights over the years. She feared that Simon would never grow into the man she'd always hoped he'd be. Instead, it seemed he was doomed to crave a lifestyle that his modest income would never match in the way he hoped. He was destined never quite to meet the mark.

Ada once said he hadn't managed to find a woman to marry who might keep him in the financial state he obviously felt he deserved. Miranda thought he was becoming played out – middle-aged. No matter that he had his hair carefully tinted or that he spent his time between the gym and God alone knew where else to cling on to the looks that Miranda couldn't decide were a blessing or a curse. It was inevitable that age would win out in the end. It was a cruel way to think, but Simon was the also-ran of the family. He'd had the most wonderful opportunities and somehow, between his own mismanagement, fate and idleness, they had slipped through his fingers.

These days he hung about between the mills and Dublin, never quite fitting in to either. Once, Miranda had blamed herself – perhaps if the mills had consumed her less – but of course, she knew that Simon's life had little to do with her and everything to do with Simon. Neither of his sisters had fallen into the same way of life. The girls were both hard workers, both committed to things outside of themselves. Simon was committed only to himself and his own leisure. He was still a sandy-haired blue-eyed boy in his own imagination, but the truth was, he was almost forty-six and he'd never stuck at anything long enough to make a decent stab at succeeding.

Simon had lunged from one golden opportunity to another, aching after far-off fields, but harbouring no desire to work his way towards them. If he'd been born into the Blair estate a generation or two earlier, he'd surely have picked a wealthy wife and had done with it, but Simon was a Corrigan and unfortunately, for him, there was no title to back up his notions of grandeur.

A light whipping breeze cajoled Miranda from her thoughts – it was a recent doctor's appointment that set her mind racing across the possibilities around the future of the mills. It really was only at the end of a very long day that Miranda allowed the consultant's words to sink in. It was months ago now, but she remembered his voice, a generous inflection that seemed too harmless to ring within her ears this long. He was nice, soft-spoken, but it didn't change the fact that she had heart valve disease. Probably had it for years – that was the truth of it. Her symptoms weren't new, they were just heightened.

That night, if it hadn't been for the fact that Ada was with her, Miranda would have done as she always did – sat it out until the dizziness and pain passed. It was Ada who phoned for an ambulance and maybe it was just as well. Better to know, Ada said; Miranda had spent years blotting it out. Well, if it hadn't killed her years earlier, what was the point in having it seen to now?

'You're a very silly woman.' The doctor smiled at her and she knew he had enough charm to get away with words like silly, even with old women like herself. 'Any pain—' he looked up from the pad before him '—*any pain, at all*, even the slightest niggle,' he said again to emphasise, 'I want you back here again.' He smiled at her then and, somehow, the fact that he was letting her go home, made it seem like it wasn't quite so serious. 'We will be monitoring you, visits to the GP, tests and bloods, but really, my sense is that you could take care of this without any interventions.'

'Interventions?' She smiled at him.

'Surgery,' he said. 'The medication to lower blood pressure and reduce cholesterol is going to be a lifelong companion, but if we can get by without surgery, I'd be much happier.'

'And so say all of us.' Miranda smiled at him.

'No funny business now. It's time to take things easy, smell the roses, if you like,' he said. They'd already talked about her garden and some of the winter borders, she'd admired, on the approach to the hospital.

'But I can still work?' She leaned forward.

'You can go about all the things you've always done, just take everything a little slower, a little easier, less stress and more rest. If you do that, you have a good life ahead of you.' Perhaps he didn't mean to make the words sound ominous, but to Miranda, it felt as though there was an alternative and it was one she'd rather not dwell on.

She was hardly ancient. She was young enough to enjoy life, old enough to see through any nonsense. It wasn't news to her. She was wise enough to know she couldn't go on forever, but the truth was, she wasn't sure what would happen to the mills if she just called a halt. The mills were more than just a business and more than just her life's work; they were the lifeblood of the small community that she loved. The mills were a part of this landscape, almost as much as a mountain or the river. They were one hundred and fifty years old soon. It really was something. Miranda wanted to stay for that landmark. She wanted to guide the mills into their second wind.

Perhaps it was too much to ask. The only alternative or, at least, the only one that seemed to be available to her at present was Ada as the new general manager. It wasn't that Miranda didn't love her daughter. She truly did, but it didn't take a genius to see that Ada was not the daughter to take over the mills. On the other hand, who else was there? She couldn't ask Callie to give up a glittering career in London for a backwater like Ballycove; she wouldn't do it.

Callie had made something quite spectacular of her life. She'd risen to the top of an industry that rarely made stars of outsiders, but Callie had talent. It had always been there, from early childhood when she'd sold blackberries, to those first tentative designs she'd pored over in her art classes at school. That familiar whisper lingered at the back of her heart again – if only there had been grandchildren. She was too old to regret things she couldn't change.

The real problem, Miranda knew, was that she loved all of her children, but the truth was that they were all so very different. Each of them brought joy in their own ways, but there was no denying that Callie brought a little more than the others. She should have had the conversation around the future of the mills years ago. It had been too easy to put it on the long finger. Ada was, in her own mind, the natural successor and perhaps it would be only fair to hand it over to her – after all, she'd been loyal and hardworking and even if in Miranda's opinion she hadn't stayed in Ballycove for the right reasons, well – at least she had stayed.

Still, in passing on the mills, Miranda knew that there was a responsibility not only to her family, but also to so many other people whose livelihoods depended on the business – and had done for generations before. And that was the crux of her worry: it would be easy to pass things along to Ada – but Ada would run the mills in a highly cost-effective way and that would be to the detriment of so many good people that Miranda knew would find it impossible to get work anywhere else in Ballycove.

No. Miranda would have to remain at the mills until the end of the year, see out the celebrations and figure out some way of keeping everyone happy, while ensuring the future survival of the mills. These were the thoughts that filled her mind as she made her way home from the mills each evening. They niggled her more often these days than ever before, perhaps because she had a feeling that time was drawing closer.

3

Ada

Her mother's secretary looked at her as though nothing was less likely to happen. Ada had always thought of her as a sappy little thing, trotting about after Miranda as though she was following a great leader. They'd been discussing the forthcoming arrival of the decorators. Darina was given the task of organising alternative office space where necessary as the decorating was done in each area. Now, Ada suspected the power may have gone to the girl's head.

'So it will only be for one day; they'll begin your office on the Sunday, but it may be that they run into Monday morning and of course, you may not be keen on working with the paint fumes still so fresh.'

'Well, I won't have much of a choice, I suppose,' Ada said in her usual can-do sort of way.

'Miranda has said that anyone who is without a desk can fill in on the shop floor.' Darina's eyes were glued determinedly to her clipboard and so she missed the expression that fell across Ada's face.

'I hardly think that includes me. Really, Darina, I'll just move in alongside Mother and…' Ada stopped in her tracks, because in the girl's expression she saw something that quelled her notions of sharing the huge glass-walled office that overlooked the rushing river falls beyond.

'No, no, we can't be that badly stuck that you have to go sharing with Miranda. Leave it with me and I'll speak with her and see if there's something else that can be arranged,' Darina said, obviously not prepared to have strong words between them, but on clear orders around who was who in the pecking order of things.

'Don't worry, Darina, I will have a word with Mother,' Ada said curtly and turned her attention back to the rows of figures on the screen before her. She didn't look up again until the door softly clicked behind Darina. Then she sat back on her chair and sighed. This office was the one she took over when she came back to work in the mills. It had been part of the long cutting room, once.

Of course, now the cutting was done differently and not only space, but also time was saved and so the profits were greater. There was also more mill floor space available. These days, what had once been industrial storage along with the drying room had been taken over by a visitors' centre, a craft shop, an artisan restaurant and coffee shop. Corrigan Mills was a must-see on the map of every tourist who ventured beyond Dublin. A visit here was more than just learning about the craft of weaving and woollen goods, it was a cultural experience.

Miranda had been very clear about what she wanted this place to be. Long before there was a tourist trail in the 'Wild Atlantic Way', her mother had welcomed wealthy

Americans, Japanese and Europeans to the woollen mills. She sold them not just car rugs, but an Irish experience that was rich enough to pass by word of mouth and make the mills more successful than they'd ever been before.

Ada looked across at the same view that she'd looked at for almost twenty-five years. It was a lacy network of branches, reaching up into the grey morning sky. In a few weeks' time, small green buds would begin to push through and then, later, her view of the car park beyond, full of tour coaches and cars, would be obscured by shiny bright beech leaves. She would watch as the leaves turned golden and later ochre before they disappeared in spiral flight to the ground, leaving her alone with those lacy branches once more.

She picked up the phone and dialled through to Miranda's office. 'Mother.'

'Ah, Ada, how are you today?' Miranda's voice was warm and golden and Ada wondered how she managed to keep that warmth all these years.

'I've just been talking to Darina.'

'Yes, dear, she's here with me now.'

'You don't really mean that you want me to...' Ada stopped; she was not having this conversation with Darina listening at her mother's elbow. 'Shall we go for coffee this morning, if you are free for half an hour?'

'Ada, that would be lovely – say, eleven?' Miranda sounded as though she was checking her diary. That was the difference between them: Miranda had a diary of people to see and organise and lead, whereas Ada just had a computer full of spreadsheets and an end-of-year accounts date to worry about.

'Eleven is fine,' Ada said ringing off. Suddenly there were so many things that she needed to talk to her mother about. First off was the redecorating. After all, Ada thought, what was the point in her choosing accent colours for this office, when ultimately, sooner rather than later, she would be moving to Miranda's large executive office? Surely, now that the painters were coming in, it was as good a time as any for some sort of handover. After Miranda's health scare a few months ago, it was time to start thinking of cutting back, even partial retirement. She was over seventy for heaven's sake; there were so many other things she could be doing with herself.

Ada closed her eyes. She would come at it from that angle. She would talk about her fears for her mother's health. She could bring up that terrible time back in the hospital; she could remind her of what the consultant had said. Perhaps she could suggest some new hobbies or interests for her mother. Maybe she could travel or do some worthwhile community volunteering.

Miranda was already ensconced in the coffee shop when Ada arrived at eleven. She was dressed as always in her rather theatrical, in Ada's opinion, way. She wore a brightly coloured shawl draped softly across her shoulders and an enormous pendant at her neck. Her hair had softened out to a steely grey over the years, but her eyes still danced mischievously and her expressive features had held their definition, if softened somewhat by the passing years. She had been chatting to an old couple who had taken a table in the furthest corner, so they could look down and across the river while they drank their tea.

'That's old Willie Peterson and his wife – don't you

remember them? He started off in the cutting room here, then he was the church sacristan for years. Their son—' Miranda closed her eyes for a moment, trying to remember the name '—Colin, he was in school with you…'

'Yes, of course, Colin Peterson.' But Ada didn't remember old Peterson who'd once worked in the mills. As to his son, she didn't care for Colin Peterson thirty years ago and she cared about him even less now. From the back of her memory, he was a shadowy, short fat boy, who suffered with mild acne and a stutter in primary school.

'Colin Peterson,' Miranda said wistfully. 'I met him a few months ago. Wouldn't have recognised him. He's all grown-up now.'

'He's my age, Mother, of course he's no longer wearing short trousers,' Ada said flatly.

'I suppose he is, but like you, he looks – younger than…' The words hanging between them might have been 'younger than Tony,' who had fallen into middle age as though he'd sat back in a large armchair and allowed it to engulf him, which perhaps, he had. 'Working in fashion, these days.'

'So, he's gay?' Ada said – no point beating about the bush.

'No, the very opposite – I'd say he's the most un-gay man I've met in years. Fighting off the fashion models, the last time I saw him.' Miranda smiled now and Ada knew she loved to see the underdog come up trumps. 'He's exporting to the Emirates among other countries these days, made a fortune for the linen people up north.' She smiled again, as though she knew something that Ada would never grasp. 'Yes indeed, made even more for his own pocket, I don't doubt.'

'Well, that's nice,' Ada said mildly because at the end of

the day, she had no interest in Colin Peterson. 'Anyway, I didn't ask you for coffee to talk about any of that.' Ada sat forward slightly in her chair. 'I've come about the offices.'

'Oh, have you, indeed?' Miranda said wryly and she popped the last piece of cracker into her mouth and chewed with satisfaction while she watched her daughter. The action made Ada even pricklier, because she suspected that her mother thought she already knew what Ada wanted to say.

'Well, yes. I've been thinking. We redecorate the offices, what, every five years or so?'

'Yes.' Miranda nodded. 'Apart from touching up here and there when it's needed.'

'The thing is I think we should be realistic about things.' Ada took a deep breath. 'You're not as young as you were and I worry about you, coming in here every day. It's not as if you're doing a token job. Jetting off around the world, meeting with buyers and suppliers – and I know, it's a cut-throat business; it has to be terribly stressful at this stage in life.'

'Are you saying you don't think I'm up to the job any more, Ada?' Miranda's usually warm voice had a current of irritation within it.

'No. Of course not, you've been great. Look at this place; it's thriving. But I'm saying that you've had a health scare. I'm saying that the consultants, even after the second opinion, said that you needed to slow down a little. I'm saying that there's a lot of living left to do yet and you're not making the most of it. You have a garden you love, things you must want to do beyond here, and your friends.' Ada knew that her mother had more friends than she had herself. She was known as a generous host and had an army of loyal friends, whereas well, Ada was just – Ada.

'I think I'm the better judge of what I'm fit for than anyone, don't you?' Now, Miranda's eyes matched her voice and Ada knew her mother well enough to know it was time to tread very carefully.

'Oh, Mother, please, don't be angry with me. I'm just saying that you're very special to all of us and you gave me a huge shock. The last thing I want is some supplier pushing you into intensive care because he won't meet you on a price.'

'I hardly think that's likely.' Miranda's words were icy cold. She looked up as the Petersons passed, wished them well on their way and then returned her gaze to Ada. 'Do you want to know what I think?'

'I...' Suddenly Ada wasn't so sure that she did. Anytime over the years that Ada had brought up the subject of the mills, her mother had managed to brush her off. In Ada's mind, she was the natural successor – there was no-one else, but Miranda was a different story. There had never been any promises made and even now, today, after all these years, Ada knew better than to push her mother too far.

'I think that with that accountant's brain of yours, you looked about this building and thought, why decorate twice in five years when maybe you could decorate once. I think, you thought that sooner, rather than later, you'd be ensconced in my office and in order to save money, better to paint it a drab grey now rather than when you eventually took the reins.' Her voice rose as though she was asking a question.

'I...' There wasn't time to gather herself and all Ada had

to fall back on in any situation were her analytical mind and her ability to reason practicalities. 'What's so wrong with trying to save the business money? I fail to see what's so wrong about actually doing my job. I am, after all, the financial controller – it's my job to look after the pennies and when I see an opportunity to make a saving, of course I'm going to bring it to your attention.'

'Oh, God, Ada, really?' Her mother sat back in her chair, as though she'd long given up trying to teach her daughter the rudimentary skills required for a simple job that still eluded the child.

'Yes really. Someday, you're not going to be here.' The words were out before she could help it. Actually, it wasn't until she saw the look on her mother's face that she realised she'd said something wrong. But wasn't that half the problem? Hadn't it always been the problem? Ada knew, even if they never spoke about it, her mother believed she lacked empathy, that she would measure out the mills in euro and cents, that somehow her emotional weighing scales were out of sync.

Of course, her mother would not mention that now – it was all tied up with things that happened far too long ago. Ada had been happy to bury events of that awful time under her cool, controlled veneer, even if it meant that sometimes she wondered, looking back, if she'd done things another way, perhaps her life might have turned out very differently.

'How nice of you to remind me.'

'It's the way of the world. I'm just saying why would you want to spend your every waking hour in this place when there is so much more to do beyond it?'

'I might ask the same of you.'

'What?' The word came out as a screech and Ada found her colour rising too high up in her cheeks. It was her new thing, hot sweats and sleepless nights; they came with the territory of oncoming menopause.

'Well, as I see it, you are letting your life slip by far more than I am. Look at you, almost fifty years of age and what have you got to show for it? You spend your day considering figures and ignoring life.' Miranda's colour had risen and her voice had dropped so low that Ada realised she was leaning forward to listen, and then Miranda exhaled. 'Look at us, fighting over a lick of paint – what are we doing?'

'Of course, you're right. I'm sorry, I just worry that it's all too much.' Retreat had always been Ada's only form of attack. She knew her mother well enough to know that she wouldn't win in a war of words with her. And she wasn't sure she wanted to; after all, the consultant had said, quite forcefully, that stress really was not good for her heart condition.

'I know, darling, but you mustn't, you really mustn't. Sometimes I think you do far too much worrying for everyone. It's as if you're carrying all of our worries about with you.' Miranda reached across and took her daughter's cold hand. 'Right, no more talk of painters or saving money today, okay?' Miranda sipped her coffee thoughtfully.

'Fine.' Ada hated herself for sounding like a child.

'Let's talk about something cheerful, like what we might do to celebrate one hundred and fifty years of the mills in operation.'

'I suppose we'll have to have a party,' Ada said. She wasn't much of a party animal. 'Although that's probably more Callie's domain than mine.' It was true, her younger sister Callie was regularly photographed leaving all the best fashion parties in London.

'Yes, well, I'm sure she'll be here for our little celebration of the mills, but she certainly won't have time to organise it,' her mother said softly.

'You've already set a date?'

'Well, tentatively, only just about…' Miranda looked a little defensive. 'I haven't started to organise anything yet; I mean it's only…'

'No, nor should you. Get some of those girls in the shop to do all that. You can't be overloading yourself, Mother. You have enough to do already; if anything you should be cutting back…' Ada stopped herself from rattling on; her mother's expression was enough to let her know she was talking herself into dangerous territory once more.

'Maybe you'd like to take on organising the celebrations?' Miranda said quietly, but they both knew, Ada wasn't a party organiser. If anything she avoided parties like the plague – organising one would be so far beyond her comfort zone it sent her into rivulets of stress-filled sweat just thinking of it.

'We could hire someone in… Couldn't we?'

'I thought you wanted to *save* money?' Miranda was laughing at her.

'Well, I do, obviously, but I know how much this anniversary means to you,' Ada said softly. 'I want it to be the best it can be.'

'God, if Callie was here, she'd have it done in a flash and it would be just fabulous…' Miranda mumbled, but it was a fleeting thought, rather than some underhand criticism, even if that was how it felt to Ada.

'No, well, she's not and we all know she's far too busy

in London being fabulous herself...' Ada hated the sound of bitterness in her own voice. It was unreasonable and it was unnecessary. She caught a flash of pity in her mother's eyes and that only added to her misery. The mere mention of Callie depressed her. She had always been so perfect and, clearly, their mother's favourite.

Ada ran her eyes about at the familiar scene: the restaurant girls all working away behind the splendid banqueting counter. She took in the mossy walls that looked as if they'd been painted in velvet, the distressed wood, the thick-planked floor, the aromas of fresh herbs and spices colliding between the restaurant and the discreet infusers that sat in hand-crafted potter jars throughout the mills. Ada knew without a shadow of doubt that if her mother could have picked between them years ago, Callie would have slipped into her shoes already. Miranda had said it, not in so many words, but it was what she meant. It seemed that Ada had thrown a perfectly good life down the river to adjust balance sheets day after day in the hope of one day being the captain of this ship. It rankled that somehow her sister was always wordlessly deemed the natural successor – albeit one who would never take the throne.

'Ada.' It sounded sharp. 'You're not listening to me. I wasn't putting you down – I know you're up to your eyes with everything – I was only daydreaming out loud.' Miranda pushed away her cup and saucer. She had lost interest in the coffee. Something had fallen like a ghost between them and they both knew it. Callie – the daughter who could do no wrong was making her presence felt even when she wasn't here.

'Anyway, who knows what will happen between now

and then…?' Miranda smiled. It was funny that at this stage in her life she fostered a kind of eternal optimism that there was always something good around the corner. Callie was the exact same and it had always grated on Ada's nerves – well that and the seemingly endless perfection of the life she'd made for herself as far away from Ballycove as she could get.

4

Callie

Callie Corrigan held out the painting – it was quite beautiful, but more than that, it struck her that it was the generosity of spirit that touched her most. 'Darling, it's too thoughtful,' she said kissing him softly on his cheek.

'Oh, it's arrived, has it?' Dennis looked at it, propped on the narrow drinks shelf with the sun shining on it so it picked out the blues and purples in the hilly background mountains. 'I just thought of you, when I saw it. You're always going on about the *old country*... so...'

'You make me sound like a dislodged refugee. Do I really go on about it all that much?' Callie laughed then, a tinkling uncomfortable sound, because Dennis had never seen Ballycove, although she would have loved to share its beauty with him. She walked over to the painting once more, a small gold engraving on its back announced it came from Bridgend Gallery. 'How did you find it?'

'Oh, one of those boring exhibitions one has to turn up to. It's always the same thing, but then... they said that was the West of Ireland.' He pointed at the painting. 'I thought it was rather splendid, in a kitschy sort of way, and maybe you'd like it – perhaps you can find somewhere to hang it?'

'I love it,' Callie said and she did for so many reasons as well as the fact that it reminded her of home. 'Actually, I might drop in there, one of these days.' She fingered the gallery's stamp, thinking it might be the perfect place to pick up something for her mother.

'I really wouldn't bother,' Dennis said quickly. 'I got the best they had when I picked that up for you.' He smiled lazily.

'I'm sure you did, darling,' Callie said, setting the painting back once more against the wall. 'As to this weekend?'

'Oh, pain, but I'm going to have to cry off, I'm afraid, nothing to be done about it.' He made a face and from it she knew that his decision was already made. They had made these plans months ago; as far as she was concerned, they were sacred. It was rare that they had a chance to get away together for two delicious days with their closest friends and no fear of any rumours flying about the office afterwards.

'But, Dennis, you hate London in the summer.' Callie wondered why he was so dead-set against going north. 'You've always hated it.' Then she softened; she shouldn't be so hard on him. His life wasn't easy, trying to balance everyone that expected so very much more of him than he could ever truly give.

'Well, maybe I've changed my mind,' he said and his voice held that impenetrable coolness that made her fear if she continued this conversation, she might drive a wedge between them. 'Anyway, the board are meeting on Monday and there'll be entertaining and... I have responsibilities, you know.'

'Of course,' Callie said flatly. How could she forget? 'Well, perhaps I'll go on my own, I mean, if you're going to be...'

'Fine,' he said cutting the conversation so she was left feeling as though she'd missed a step. She watched him for a moment, glancing back at the pages before her when she caught his eye. There was something different about him, as if an invisible door had closed stealthily between them over the last few weeks and if not talking about it was the coward's way out, she could convince herself that she was being cool, urbane, sophisticated. It was why Dennis had fallen for her in the first place after all.

God, but there were times when she just wanted to drop the act; because it was, for the most part just that – an act. She was being the person he wanted her to be. In the beginning, she convinced herself that he needed her like this. He certainly admired her. She was cool as ice, no strings, no melodrama. She welcomed him when he turned up and didn't cry when he left. She was so sure that someday he would walk away from his empty marriage. *Someday* still hadn't arrived and it was almost ten years later.

Somewhere along the way, she grew into the idea that this was how it would always be and she no longer hankered for anything more official between them. Callie had fallen in love with Dennis Wade and there was nothing she could do about it. If she had to spend a lifetime sharing him with his cold-hearted wife, then so be it. Veronica would never agree to a divorce and since she owned the very bones of Dennis and paid both their wages, there seemed little choice but to carry on.

'Do you need anything?' She lowered her reading glasses over her nose. 'Before I leave, for Monday? The board meeting?'

'No, I shouldn't think so,' he said looking at her now with those light grey eyes. He really was the most beautiful man she'd ever met. At forty-eight, he was older than Callie. She liked that he was more mature; it made her feel in some strange way just a little safer, as though he would always know the right path. His dark hair was flecked with silver threads about his temples now, but he stood straight and walked with the kind of confidence that Callie had only ever known in movie characters before she met him. He was always impeccably turned out. His clothes somehow never seemed to wrinkle, fade or age and he dressed with a timeless style that had little to do with fashion and everything to do with taste. 'No, you head along to your weekend fun and I shall just make the best of things here.' He smiled at her with the kind of grace that should have made her feel better, but somehow only added to her unease.

Callie walked back to her own executive office, a creative tasteful hub at the top of the Theme Empire. She'd put it all together herself, one of the joys of being The Boss. Her rise to the top of one of London's oldest fashion houses had been impressive and at the same time hard won. Callie had brought little from Ballycove apart from her talent and a smattering of Irish luck that seemed to land her in exactly the right place at just the perfect time. All she had needed was the opportunity and her predecessor at the helm of Theme had given her that.

They'd met as much by accident as luck. The day Jack Britten had tripped over her stall of handmade jumpers and scarves had turned out to be the best day of both their lives. He 'discovered' a fresh new talent just when the Theme brand had almost fallen into the abyss of golfing jumpers and walking socks. Callie Corrigan thought all her birthdays had arrived at once when he commissioned her to design a line to appeal to a new Theme customer.

Of course, she obliged and then impressed him even more with her ability to strike a deal and sell a hundredfold the original numbers produced. Callie was everything that Theme needed. She was fresh-faced, energetic and filled with the kind of enthusiasm that made short work of the old hold-you-back outlook. Theme had, with Callie Corrigan, got a new lease of life. Jack Britten called it a *Rebirth*; London Fashion Week called it *Magic*. The board of management didn't particularly care if it was alchemy or not, but they certainly loved the numbers and so Callie was welcomed to the fold and neither had looked back since. Sometimes, she sat back in her minimalistic office and felt like she should pinch herself. This evening, however, it all felt a little ordinary.

It was Dennis, of course. It was the way he didn't seem to mind that she would be spending an entire weekend in the country without him. Time was he couldn't bear her to go to lunch with a good-looking supplier in case she'd be lured away from him. Callie had very much enjoyed that. A faint smile passed across her vermillion lips at the memory. She sighed, remembered that she mustn't judge; after all, poor Dennis did not have the easiest of lives. At least she could drop out of London for the whole weekend and there wasn't one person to stop her, not really. She was as free as a bird, whereas Dennis, well it seemed like he would never be free. Veronica would always make demands of him. She would use every dirty trick in the book from emotional blackmail to downright threats to hold on to him and if she knew about their affair, she would probably sack them both on the spot.

Mind you, even Callie had to admit, theirs was the worst-kept secret in London. The fashion scene was notoriously bitchy and every other person you met just wanted to gossip all day long. Callie blamed it on the fact that this industry made people expendable. Once a model had walked for three or four shows, most were tired faces and there was always a younger, newer version waiting in the wings. At forty, Callie knew she became a virtual dinosaur; Dennis was old enough to be grandfather to some of the girls at this stage. And as for the designers, most only wanted to stay long enough to save for their trip to Paris and take with them a portfolio that would impress any house at all so long as they had a couture line.

She reached into the streamlined closet and pulled out her soft Italian leather handbag. She adored this bag; the stone-coloured leather was so luxuriant it might have been velvet. Inside it was lined with the softest of silk and had pockets for just about every item she needed so there was never any risk of clutter. Callie hated clutter. She tried to make everything in her life clutter-free. She liked things orderly, neat and tidy. The only exception to that was her relationship with Dennis. There was nothing well-arranged about that.

She dropped her phone into one of the slim folds and

caught the scent of the leather – it still smelled new. It was a gift from Dennis, from two seasons earlier, but with a price tag that ran into an annual minimum wage, the normal dating rules hardly applied. She placed her jacket across her shoulders, shoving any irrational fears about Dennis to the back of her mind. Then she switched off the long-arm lamp and the various table lamps from a central switch before closing her office door.

The building was almost empty, only the cleaners working their way to the bottom floors kept lights on, all the better to make sure that everything was spotless for the following week. She walked past them, vaguely aware of the admiring glances from young girls who only dreamed of one day having a life that might be anything like hers.

Outside, the evening was warm and balmy. Her friends Stella and Archie would be leaving London in an hour. She decided to call them and let them leave without her. She really wasn't in the mood for a country house and a lot of Hooray Henrys trying to fill her with gin so they might get lucky. Instead, she would go back to her town house on Chester Square, open up the doors of her lovely living room and listen to a download of something soothing while sipping through her own supply of Connacht Whiskey as the sun set low over the acres of London chimney pots that stretched off towards the middle of the city.

Sometimes, sitting in her back garden, with the smell of turned soil and the aroma of the whiskey, it felt like she was back in Ballycove. She could pretend she was sitting outside her mother's cottage, with the sun falling down dappled through the huge ash and slender rowan trees. Sometimes, it brought a twinge of loneliness over her; she had always meant to go back, after all. London, when she came here, was supposed to be a gap year. An adventure before she settled into real life – funny how things work out. If it hadn't been at first for Jack Britten and now for Dennis, well, who knows what might have been her future.

Callie had a feeling that if she'd never been the darling of the London fashion scene, she'd have been quite happy to go back to Ballycove and see her designs brought to life on the homely yarns and hues of the old woollen mills. She smiled now at the sudden bout of homesickness that could still, after all these years, creep up on her. It was silly, of course; she'd settled for London – how could she possibly go back to Ballycove now?

She caught sight of her reflection in a window, liked that she was every bit the successful fashion executive. Every inch of her appearance from her glossy dark hair to her perfectly cut suit gave the impression that she was a city girl who had become a knowing woman. She was happy with who she was and, mostly, she was happy with where she was. And even if there were times when she thought about the salty smell of the Atlantic Ocean, she had earned her place in this vast city and she was proud of it.

Turning into Claremont Avenue, she felt herself, just for a moment, almost pulled along with the crowds into the Underground. The smell of hot and sticky workers descending into its reeking depths clung to her, maybe more because she so detested it. She walked on a little further, holding her breath, before once more breathing in the heavy fume-filled air. She crossed the road to the trendy vegan eatery that had opened up a few months earlier. Her fridge was filled with groaning emptiness, save for a few bits and pieces she might have cobbled together to entertain at the drop of a hat. Perhaps she'd pick up a bottle of their house wine. Maybe later, she'd phone Dennis and let him know she'd stayed in London for the night. And then again, maybe not.

On Chester Square, Callie believed that everything here had just a little more of all the nicer bits of London, if that was possible. Here, the houses were just a little older than the rest. They seemed a little grander, their windows slightly larger, their front doors painted in the gayest of London colours. The gardens, all well-tended, were filled with summer flowers. It seemed to Callie that every season was the best. But, if there was a best month, in any season, it had to be June. This evening, as she walked along, the smell of woodbine drifted in her path. Roses of every shade of pink and red stood against all-natural laws of gravity. Their blooms seemed much too heavy for their stems. Borders bursting with azaleas, alliums, peonies, geraniums, dahlias and so many more plants than Callie couldn't remember the names of. The flowers bursting with colour reminded her for the second time that day of her mother.

Miranda had spent a lifetime cultivating her garden. Callie had always been the child at her side for endless days spent on their knees, digging out or planting in. Even now, in winter rain or summer sun, when she went back to Ballycove, they spent their time either in the garden or the small conservatory that was little more than a potting shed. Callie had, even then, been so different from her serious, bookish sister. Ada was the clever one; perhaps it was only right that she was the one who would carry on the tradition of the mills. After all, she had married and settled for Ballycove while Callie had managed to move through her twenties and almost to the end of her thirties cutting her ties and hardly looking back, so blinded was she by the pace of her own career and the bright lights of London.

Callie decided, as she ran up the perfectly tiled steps to her lovely home, that she would ring her mother this evening. She would shower and change into her beautiful Japanese silk pyjamas. Later she would eat her dinner to the strains of Ella Fitzgerald or perhaps Amy Winehouse in the back garden. After that, she would sit back on her reclining summer chair and phone Miranda to catch up on all the goings-on in Ballycove and check to see if there had been any more plans made to celebrate the anniversary of the family business.

'I can't believe it's one hundred and fifty years.' Callie echoed the words back to Miranda.

'Yes, and we're still here; still Corrigan Mills and doing rather nicely too, if that doesn't sound too cocky.'

'Oh, Mamma, you above all people couldn't sound vain if you tried. Now me...' Callie laughed. She would never indulge in such self-deprecating humour at work; there were far too many people only waiting to take shots at her already.

'Callie, I'm afraid if Ballycove knocked one thing out of you, it was vanity.'

'You'll have to make it a very special celebration, pull out all the stops. I mean, to think that the mills have been in business for a hundred and fifty years, well it's a big achievement.' Callie was thinking of all the new start-ups, even since she'd been in London, that had gone to the wall over the last decade.

'I think so too. After all, it's something that a lot of families in Ballycove have invested in. You know, we have a youngster here now whose great-great-grandfather worked in the mills, and the family haven't missed a generation since.' Miranda's voice was soft with affection for the people who'd worked in the mills over the years.

'That's marvellous; really, it's something to make something of…'

'Well, he's only in on Saturdays, he's still in school really, but when he told me who he was… well, I couldn't not offer him a job.'

'Oh, Mamma. Sometimes, I wonder how you ever made a penny.' They both laughed at that, but they knew too that when it was called for, Miranda had taken tough decisions and she'd faced down not only hungry bank managers, but avaricious competitors too.

'Well, I'm not sure how much I made, but I'll tell you this, when I hand this place over, it'll be in a much better shape than when I took it on.' Miranda's voice dipped then and Callie had a feeling there was more that she wanted to say, but time and distance put an invisible seal between them.

'That goes without saying,' Callie said to even things off.

'Aren't you doing anything tonight then?' Her mother knew well enough that Callie normally had a full and exciting social life. She was invited to all the best dinner parties; the connections that she'd made over the years meant she was never short of diverting social invitations.

'Oh, you know how it is, sometimes it's just nice to sit in the back garden and watch the swallows play in the evening sun.' Miranda understood exactly the pleasure in activities like this; Ada on the other hand would think she'd turned into a simpleton.

'It must be therapeutic after a busy week at Theme,' Miranda said softly. 'You work so hard.'

'Hmm, and I wonder where I inherited that habit from.' They both laughed again. 'Now, never mind me, what about you? Stop hedging and tell me how we're going to celebrate this big birthday at the mills?'

'Well, as a matter of fact, I was going to ring you next week with exactly that in mind...' Miranda suddenly sounded like a woman half her age and Callie could imagine her all fired up with grand plans to give the village a day or night to remember. 'So, it's really in autumn, but I know, it's probably the worst possible timing for you with work...'

'Mamma, you must think I'm running all of London. It's a party, at the weekend; of course I'm going to be there. I'm going to put it straight into my diary on Monday morning and book my flight first thing tomorrow morning.' She would ask her assistant to book it, but really, it was the same thing – Callie hadn't organised travel for herself in a couple of years. At this stage, her assistant was far better at making sure everything was as hassle-free as possible than she was.

'You could bring someone...' her mother ventured softly, 'you know, if there was someone special.' Callie had never told Miranda about Dennis. It wasn't that she was ashamed of him, or that she feared Miranda judging her or even taking against him. Actually, when Callie thought about it, there was really no reason why she shouldn't have told her mother, except – well, she just hadn't. It had more to do with Dennis than it had with Miranda. Of course, Miranda would worry about Callie having her heart broken, that was quite natural, but her mother was no prude. She may not promote affairs with married men, but she advocated love and she never judged. Callie knew that much for certain.

'Oh, Mamma, I'm afraid I'm going to have let you down once again. It looks like you've raised a confirmed spinster, but at least you have one darling son-in-law.' Anthony Jackson was hardly a catch, but he was steadfast and loyal and he suited Ada, even if neither Callie nor Miranda would ever quite understand what she saw in him.

'Yes, indeed I have,' Miranda said ruefully and then with a burst of enthusiasm: 'Still there must be plenty of eligible men in London, if you suddenly decided you needed to sign up for the whole *in sickness and in health* stuff.'

'Darling, Mamma, believe me, in London there are fewer men I'd be interested in than anywhere else on earth,' Callie said a little too wryly. Everyone assumed men who worked in fashion had to be gay; it turned out only ninety-nine percent were. 'I'll be there as your plus-one, if you'll have me.' They both laughed at that.

'So, I can count you in.' Miranda was back to the business in hand. She was on a mission to organise the best birthday party ever seen in Ballycove. 'I'm so glad; it seems like an age since you've been back.'

'Christmas, I was home for the holiday.'

'Only just though,' Miranda said wistfully. 'But it was good fun, wasn't it?'

'It was. I was sorry to have to leave, but I really couldn't not go when Stella had booked my flights and accommodation. You know I adore the piste; winter just wouldn't be the same without a couple of bumps and sore muscles.'

'Oh, don't say that. I'll wager that like everything else in life, you probably ski more gracefully than anyone else in the party.'

'Well, I wouldn't go as far as all that, but I do my best.'

'I'm glad you got there, even if we did miss you dreadfully when you left.'

'Liar, I'll bet you didn't have time to think, what with the craft fair and then the January sales and you still had Simon.'

'Ah, yes, Simon...' her mother said and Callie could almost hear her drift off into her thoughts again.

'You're not worried about him again, are you?'

'No, I'm afraid; he's too old for me to worry about him now. I've taken your advice and cut the apron strings.'

'Well, it's probably a relief to him in many ways; he wouldn't want you worrying about him either,' Callie murmured thinking of her older brother who still clung onto the lifestyle of someone much younger and richer than he was ever likely to be at this stage.

'I might bequeath him to Ada in my will, something new to fuss about and mollycoddle when I'm not around any more.'

'Oh, Mamma, you're really terrible.' They were laughing again and it reminded Callie just how much she missed spending time with her mamma. When she rang off, she wished she was headed home now, for a week at least. Christmas seemed like such a long time away. *The start of summer in Ballycove, what could be nicer?* she thought as she sipped her icy drink to music from an era long before her own.

5

The Past

The emptiness of the ocean, beyond the river's mouth, beckoned in its vastness to offer some consolation – as though it was a doorstep to a world beyond. In those rare, soundless moments, Richard too enjoyed the profound tranquillity when it seemed like time stood still and all the worries in the world could find no purchase on that little boat. Soon, they had a routine of sorts. She would get all her chores out of the way before most of the other children had even stepped out their front doors. She raced to Mrs Bridgestock, back again to their little cottage and hung out any washing her mother had ready for the clothes lines. If she was allowed, she would use the heated iron on simple laundry like the Blairs' linens and the hotel napkins; it was a way of spending time and talking about mundane things that didn't rattle the delicate atmosphere in ways they couldn't handle. Her mother held her tight to her each time before she left the house, as though fastening her in some way and guaranteeing her safe return again.

Each day, the sun seemed to rise even higher in the sky. One warm day followed another, as though the summer would never end. Miranda thought, as she sat on the little punt, the anchor down and their rods cast off across the sides, that this summer had gone on forever. Even here, on the lapping water – their bellies full of jam sandwiches and ginger beer that Mrs Blair packed for both of them – Miranda felt as happy as she figured it was possible to feel. It was as if her body had been sedated, so thoroughly that the numbness reached right into her soul.

The spinning of a line pulled her from her thoughts, so she sprang up just in time to catch her rod before it landed on the water; such was the ferocious wrench on the bait. Richard too held tight onto the rod. He had come up from behind, his arms about her, helping her to wrestle in her prize.

'It's a whopper,' he yelped, excited by the possibility of what lay ahead. They struggled with that fish for almost twenty minutes, reeling him in, letting him take the bait when it seemed like he might twist away from them and finally, landing him in the enormous net Richard had taken from the boathouse, just in case. 'I've never seen such a huge salmon,' he said. They were both lathered in sweat but his eyes sparkled from the exertion and excitement of the catch. They were giddy with the exhilaration of their labours. 'You might have a record weight there. I'd say he's as big as anyone has ever taken from the river.' He was shaking his head, staring down at the huge silver fish that took up two seats on the little boat.

'Don't you mean *we* might have a record weight?' Miranda smiled at him. 'I couldn't have landed him on my own and I wouldn't have been out here at all if it wasn't for you.' Even if there had been no salmon, it was good to be out of the house and the overbearing reach of her father's silent melancholy.

And so, there was another thing to mark that summer out. Richard Blair and his boat, catching the heaviest salmon ever recorded on the river and long hot summer days filled the remainder of the holidays. When Miranda made her way to Mrs Bridgestock's cottage each morning, she told her all about these things, sharing the experience with the old lady who had not so long ago been her only escape from home.

Miranda set off back towards the village again. She had to call into the local shop to pick up some groceries for her mother before she was due to meet Richard for their fishing trip.

'So, I hear you're knocking about with Richard Blair these days,' Paddy Corrigan said as he parcelled up her shopping in brown paper.

'He's bringing me out to fish for mackerel later today,' Miranda said and regretted it almost immediately. Everyone knew that meant at least making their way to the end of the river and out, far out into the choppy sea beyond. She hadn't told her mother, half afraid the worry of her daughter on the open sea might finish her off completely.

'Well, as long as that's all he's planning on,' Paddy said counting out her change carefully. He was a reedy, dark-haired boy who took his job at the grocery shop very seriously. Everyone knew that Paddy Corrigan would make something of himself; already he had the walk of a man who was aware that every moment counted. Miranda sighed in relief that he hadn't managed to catch her slip. 'This will probably be my last time parcelling up your shopping for you, Miss Reilly.' He always made fun of her, in a way she suspected he didn't with the other kids who came to pick up groceries for their mothers.

'And why's that? I suppose you're too important now to be serving the likes of me.' She laughed at him.

'No, it's not that. Haven't you heard?' He pulled the top ends of the bag apart and began to fold down the heavy brown paper in a neat line. 'I'm going to work in the mills, starting tomorrow morning.'

'Really, but I thought you loved it here. Everyone says you're…' Miranda felt a little colour shoot up into her cheeks. The last thing she wanted was for Paddy Corrigan to be getting ideas above himself. 'Well, that you seem to enjoy it here so much.' It was true, but she also heard the rumour that if the shopkeeper's son, Danny Cleary, didn't watch out, it would be Corrigan above the door in a few years' time. 'I can't imagine you want to settle for a job in the mills.' She was thinking of her father and the job he had waiting to take up. It wasn't much – sweeping around the grounds – but even so, Harry Reilly had not managed to face turning up to begin this simple job. It didn't matter so much to Miranda, although she felt it would be nice to see him getting out of the house and going to work like the other fathers all along their road.

'Well, I suppose it depends on the job, doesn't it?' He smiled and tipped a penny bar into her hand playfully. 'Mr Blair himself has asked me, so I'm afraid I won't be here to keep you stocked up in boiled sweets and chocolate squares.' He was shaking his head now, but still smiling at her and she wondered if he too was just extra nice to her because her father was a little soft and they were all such a pity, no matter how much her mother tried to cover it over.

'Well, maybe they'll get someone here who'll be a little lighter-handed on the weighing scales.' She smirked at him, though she doubted they'd get anyone half as nice as Paddy. Paddy was a few years older than Miranda, not many, but he'd gone straight into the local shop as a messenger boy when he was still at school. It seemed to make him grow up faster than the other kids around. Still, for all his dedication, it was only in the last few months that he'd been promoted to the more important duty of assisting at the counter.

'Hah, I'll have them well warned about your sweet tooth and if you keep gobbling up those sugar mice, you won't have a tooth left in your head.' He was laughing now. 'Anyway, you mind yourself out there with young Blair. He's not local, doesn't know the water, and you don't know what kind of notions he'll have, heading off every day with a young girl like yourself.'

'Oh, Paddy, you're funny, what kind of notions? Won't we be in the middle of nowhere, sure…?' Miranda looked at him and saw a patch of red seep up from his neck to his face. His grey eyes shot towards the door where an old man stood, watching up and down the street as if something momentous might happen – in Miranda's opinion, there was nothing less likely. 'Anyway, I'd better be away back to my mother with these for now.' The exchange left her feeling a little uneasy, but she couldn't quite put her finger on why. 'Good luck, tomorrow,' she called as she made her way out into the sunshine.

After that, the summer rumbled along slowly and eloquently, even if Miranda felt as though she only ghosted through it. Miranda thought the sun shone a little warmer and for longer each day as she made her way down to the slipway, where Richard Blair had pulled in his little boat the evening before. They would bring fruit and bread – sometimes, if it was in the larder, some chicken, or ham or boiled eggs – and head off out around the coast. Richard teased her, saying his grandmother was only so generous because she had a soft spot for Miranda.

Most days they found somewhere to drop anchor and fish for hours on end. It was a summer of burned limbs and seemingly endless idling days, which Miranda dreaded coming to an end, knowing all too well that falling back into a routine of normality would be even more pronounced after such a marvellous holiday.

'I shall be going back to school soon,' Richard said one day as August was drawing to a close. The sun was dancing off the water and the stillness stretched across the harbour, with only the occasional lift of the boat on the waves to interrupt the tranquillity. 'I'm dreading it,' he said hoarsely.

'Really, boarding school and London? It all seems like a great adventure.'

'Does it? Well, it's not. I'm miserable as hell in London. My parents are always taken up with something else, and I've never really fitted in at my school. The boys are all football mad or camped out in the library.'

'I'm sorry,' Miranda said, catching the despair in his voice. 'Maybe it'll be better this time round.'

'I hardly think so. I envy you, staying here, all the time. Being able to walk along the river, come and go as you please, you know, just being normal.' He shook his head.

'You're normal too,' she whispered.

'Here, I am, yes. But back in London, I'm like that salmon; a fish out of water and it's only getting worse all the time. I've begged my mother to let me stay with grandmother, but she says my father is not having it. There are expectations to be met.' He raised his voice, perhaps mimicking his mother.

'There are other ways to look at it, you know.'

'Oh, I'm not discounting that I have three square meals a day, a very comfortable bed to sleep in and someday, the opportunity to go to Cambridge and fall into what is regarded as a privileged life.'

'But?'

'I want to be here.' He waved his hand towards the water. 'This place feels like home to me and I don't want to leave.' He shook his head and stared out into the water for a while, lowered his voice.' Even more so now we've had such a smashing summer.' He took a deep breath, stood up tall in the boat and made it wobble slightly, then looked far out to sea as if he might one day set the boat in the direction of the evening sun and be happy to put as many miles between himself and London as it was possible to manage on this tiny boat. 'At least I am coming back again next year.' He smiled at that, as though the thoughts of it would sustain him in the meantime. 'My grandmother is looking forward to that already.' He smiled then and pushed against her.

'I'm glad, the thoughts of next summer being like this will keep me going when the days grow dark here and Master Moylan is droning on about how to make sense of some piece of ancient Irish poetry.' She laughed then, a little relieved that they were talking about this. 'To be honest, I've been thinking about that a lot,' Miranda said. 'I'll miss this, getting lost each day away from the village.' They'd become firm friends, but more than that, there was a connection between them that seemed to stretch further than companionship. Miranda marvelled that from strangers at the start of summer, such a firm friendship could result. 'I didn't want to mention it. It seemed like it might bring it even closer if I did.'

'Considering, you know, you being a girl—' he was teasing her now '—I've enjoyed spending the summer on the river with you,' he said softly and suddenly she was aware of just how closely they were sitting on the boat.

'I…' Her breath caught for just a second and she looked into those familiar blue eyes. 'I've been so happy… Richard,' she said at last.

'Miranda.' He broke his gaze away from her, for a moment, stretched his breath so it seemed to reach all the way out across the sea before them.

'Yes, Richard?'

'I…' he said gently and he reached towards her and kissed her gently on her cheek, then pulled back very quickly, embarrassed and flustered. 'I… I'm sorry, I don't know what I was thinking. It was…' he started, couldn't quite meet her eyes.

'Don't be.' She leaned forward and kissed him back lightly. Then they broke apart in a fit of giggles.

'I really like you,' he said then leant towards her and kissed her lips, holding her there for a moment. When he let her go, they stayed, looking into each other's eyes for just a while longer. 'I've wanted to do that since that first day when I jumped off the bridge.' He laughed now.

'Really?'

'Yes, really,' he said, smiling now at his own shyness.

'So, why didn't you?' she asked.

'Well, I wasn't sure if you'd kiss me back and to be honest, I was afraid that if you didn't then I'd mess everything up.'

'I think I would have, well, after I got over the shock.'

'Would you?' he asked, then the sound of a bite on one of the rods snatched his attention away and soon they were hauling in a line of mackerel each and if not forgetting about that moment, at least moving away from it for now. Later, as they pulled the boat up on the shingle, he murmured something under his breath.

'What?' she said, a little out of breath from the exertion.

'Funny girl,' he said smiling at her. When they had stored the boat safely beyond the reach of the tide, he sat against it and she dropped down beside him. 'I shall miss you, funny girl.'

'When do you go back to school, really?' She had to know now, had a feeling it must be very close. The village school opened in two weeks' time, so it stood to reason that a boarding school would probably open up a little earlier.

'It was meant to be in a week's time, but my father telegrammed to say they'd be here early tomorrow,' he said quietly.

'So soon?' She hadn't expected it to be time already.

'I'm afraid so,' he said, looking at her now. 'But perhaps I could come back again at Christmas,' he said then, as though trying to convince himself as much as her, but there was a desperateness to his tone that she supposed meant it was unlikely.

'Of course; although I can't see us doing much fishing then.' She smiled.

'No. But, we could go tramping about the lands. My grandfather has guns – ever been shooting?'

'Never,' Miranda said, scrunching up her face. 'I'm not sure I could, I mean, hunting ducks or rabbits or whatever it is you shoot.'

'Yes, I'm not mad about it either, but it wouldn't matter, as long as…'

'As long as, what?'

'Well, as long as we can spend time together,' he said quietly.

'It sounds as though your parents are going to pack you up and whisk you away before they even set foot in the Hall.' She laughed, but the sound dried out when she looked into his eyes.

'That's the thing, I suppose, knowing that my parents really are Londoners. My mother comes out in a rash at the mere mention of Ballycove…' He sighed.

'Well, we will have to make the most of what's left then, won't we?' she said now as cheerfully as she could manage.

'Maybe I should have mentioned it before, but I just didn't want it hanging over us for ages and of course…' he smiled at her now '…I did want to get a kiss off you before I left.'

'You're a silly bugger, I might have kissed you more if you'd told me sooner.' She laughed then – a funny sound, mixed with the sadness of parting from him.

'I'll write to you. Will you write back?'

'Of course, just put the address on your first letter and you can expect plenty of news from Ballycove,' she said, smiling determinedly.

'Right, well, I probably should be heading home for dinner.'

'Me too,' Miranda said, lingering for just a moment too long, but then Richard hopped out of the boat and waded towards the slipway, pulling it behind him.

'I wish you could come and help me put the boat away later, but...' He bent his head down sadly. They both knew that Miranda's mother would have a litter of kittens before she'd let her daughter outside the door after teatime.

'I wish I could too.' She leant in towards him then and kissed him on the cheek and he pulled her close, throwing his arms about her and holding onto her as though his life depended on it. He felt hard and smooth all at once against her and smelled of their day on the sea, mixed with his own unique scent. 'I will miss you, when you go.'

'I'll miss you too and everything about this place,' he whispered into her hair and then pulled back and held her at arm's length. 'Go on now, or you'll have us both crying and it's no good turning into a cry-baby now,' he said making it sound as if all they had to do was laugh and things would be so much better. 'Go on, now,' he said gently and she knew that waiting any longer would be harder for both of them.

She moved from him delicately and walked back up the beach, only looking back to where he stood when she got to the end. She blew him a kiss before running home, keeping the tears that burned at her eyes in check until she got home.

6

Simon

Simon Corrigan turned over his paper. He couldn't quite relax today, and it seemed as if the whole world was conspiring to make him jumpy and irritable. It was why he'd taken himself out of his flat leaving his half-drunk tea on the draining board, and headed towards the city with no actual plan in mind. Well, that wasn't strictly true, even if he tried to convince himself otherwise. His feet brought him along the path in a definite direction and while he could argue that he was feeling peckish and that brunch was uppermost on his mind, the truth was he knew with certainty that he would end up on Jury Street just in time for elevenses. Simon wasn't sure if it was just his imagination, but he fancied that even the city had an air of optimism about it this morning.

He passed by art galleries, rare book stores and expensive trinket shops, and it seemed to him that each one was peopled by staff who acknowledged him through their front windows with a smile. High over the roofs of Dublin, brilliant white seagulls cruised as if it was a summer's day and far off in the distance a bright pink helicopter buzzed like an ornate butterfly for a time before him.

Simon was hardly a man to look for signs, but if he was, he considered that today could be that one day in his life when things finally began to flow his way. Honestly, he thought, it was about time. It was all very well his mother owning the most famous mills in the country and Callie his younger sister being the toast of the London fashion lovelies, but Simon wanted his own taste of success. Why, even Ada – well, she could hardly be called a failure – she had managed to secure a life of middle-class satisfaction with her mundane husband in their comfortable bungalow and her role as the financial controller in the family firm. Simon had never wanted a life so ordinary, but now that he was sailing towards the heavier end of his forties, it didn't seem like quite the life sentence that it once so truly was.

He'd had his chances, over the years. There had been lots of girls, most of them from the very best families, but none of them it seemed content to settle for a man who clearly had no intention of seeing his way into profitability without the bankroll of a generous father-in-law to boost his lifestyle. So, the wealthier daughters had, over time, fallen into marriage with more ambitious, industrious men and Simon had been left to play the field – what a pity he realised too late that rogue players had a sell-by date.

Simon pulled his scarf closer about his neck. It was colder than he'd thought and this scarf, a gift from the mills, generally was enough to keep him cosy when he wore it with his smart sports jacket. He caught sight of himself in a gleaming window as he passed. He looked good, he worked out, took care of himself and, let's face it, he was hardly stressed. He had his sandy hair touched up regularly to replace the silver strands with gold. He lived well, thanks to wealthy friends and an ability to put off any thoughts of stability. Rather, he was blessed with a disposition that believed, doggedly, even in the face of all that might lead another man to doubt – that his ship would surely come in.

There was no hesitancy in his ability to conjure up a life, at some distant future point, where he would be extremely wealthy and of course well connected – he'd been cultivating the latter attribute all of his adult life. So far, the financial ship had lost its course it seemed. Not that he hadn't had a serious stab at a couple of ventures and, at least, he could argue that the failure of each one had somehow been down to other people. Simon had been involved in a number of different industries while knowing little or nothing about any of them. He had managed to sink a substantial amount of his mother's money into an ill-fated oil exploration company in the Indian Ocean – and still, he could almost smell the money that had just gone awry when the company he'd been in partnership with had gone belly-up.

Nor, it could be argued, was it his fault that quite a number of his oldest friends almost lost their shirts when he'd managed to talk them into investing in an import business from China. That particularly disastrous business had fallen thanks to a mix-up in currencies and insurance. Since then, Simon knew, he could not ask any of his friends to invest in a new venture. It was quite out of the question.

He ambled up to a little coffee shop, just a few doors down from one of the oldest jewellery shops in the city, pushed open the door into an aromatically warm room. He ordered an espresso and took a seat looking out on the street beyond. Checking his watch, he knew that even glancing at the paper could be enough to foil his plans; so instead, he kept his eyes trained on the footpath outside. At precisely eleven thirty, he heard the sound of sharp heels on the path and then with the predictability of spring following winter, the door next to him was pushed open and a familiar figure entered, dressed in grey and looking more stressed than he'd ever noticed before.

'Gabby, over here, Gabby...' Simon called out to the woman. When she looked around, her eyes rested on him with an unreadable expression.

'Simon... Simon Corrigan, is it really you?' She squinted at him now, narrowing not only her eyes, but it seemed every facial feature that could be pinched. 'What on earth are you doing here?' She nodded to the girl behind the counter who set about readying her order.

'Yes, yes, it's me...' he said getting up and moving towards her smoothly. He held her shoulders and kissed her cheeks, first one and then the other, before holding her at arm's length to look into her face again. 'You look wonderful. What have you been doing to yourself? Don't tell me, John Dempsey has been looking after you so well that...' Then he stopped, noticed that tell-tale shadow cross her eyes.

'No. No. Enough about me – I think I look wrecked; how could I look anything else?' she said, a little of the certainty he remembered from years earlier depleted now that life had knocked her about a bit. 'What on earth are you doing here?' she said and took the coffee from the girl at the counter. Simon swiftly handed over a ten-euro note to pay for it, waving off the change, so the girl got the best tip of the day – probably from the one customer who could afford it least.

'Nonsense,' he said waving towards the seat next to him. 'Join me; you can't be in that much of a rush... for old times' sake?'

'Oh go on, no-one's going to miss me for a few minutes, I suppose,' she said flopping into the seat next to him. 'So, *what are* you doing here?' she asked him again.

'I'm due to meet someone in half an hour and I was walking along here, saw this place and thought of you. I didn't for a moment think you'd still be coming in here – it used to be Regan's back when...' He let his words drift. There was no point going back to the days when he occasionally turned up to work just across the road from here until, of course, the banking industry fell and he was the most expendable head to cull. 'So, you're still there, plugging in the hours in the old family business...'

Simon actually knew all this. He had run into Gabby's ex-husband only a week earlier. John was shacking up with some new girl now and Gabby had been left on the scrap heap with all that lovely money she'd made and inherited over the years. Simon had always liked her, maybe more because of the huge fortune she was worth. He figured she'd always had a soft spot for him and, he reasoned, perhaps a visit from a forgotten friend might do the old girl good. After all, he was good company and he could tell her all about his plans to invest in shares that were a guaranteed winner. Simon reckoned he was born to it. For heaven's sake, what was there to lose when you had insider information?

'Yes, I'm afraid it's the same old, same old, for me. Still in the jewellery business...' She smiled sadly. 'Still coming in here for coffee to shake the business out of my hair for ten minutes.'

'Well, there's something comforting in the predictability of that, I suppose,' Simon said kindly, but he could see her eyes held an expression that told him she was crying out for something that was more than what she had.

'It's predictable all right,' she said bitterly. 'So bloody predictable my husband could manage to carry on an affair for a year and a half without raising a question because he knew exactly how to go about it without me ever hearing a word.'

'Oh, Gabby, I'm so sorry, I didn't realise and just then...' He shook his head, trying his best to act as convincingly upset as he could. 'You and John are... you've split up?'

'I thought it was common knowledge. He seems to have taken all our friends in the break-up.' She scanned the floor as if it might provide some new answers for her.

'No, I hadn't heard a thing.' Then he sighed. 'God... if it had been a decade ago... eh?' He managed to make his voice sound wistful.

'Excuse me?' She peered at him now, over her coffee cup, the note of incredulity too hard to miss, but Simon was on a mission and he knew, setting out, it was not one for the faint-hearted.

'Well, back then... you and I...' He looked down at the spot she'd found so interesting just a moment earlier. 'You must have realised that I always liked you?' he said looking at her now.

'Oh, Simon, stop it.' Gabby batted him away, but there was a ring in her voice that couldn't conceal her delight at this unexpected flattery. Of course, they both knew that there would never be anything between them. If there had been a time, it had passed, but that didn't matter, not now. For now, Gabby Dempsey – broken-hearted wife, heiress to a fortune – felt that she was fancied, at least. It might not be love but for this moment, here in a little coffee shop that had probably seen her as miserable as she was likely to be, that was enough to lift her spirits.

'So, what about you?' she asked after they giggled at the idea of what might have been that stretched out on unsaid words between them. 'Have you met anyone or are you still Dublin's answer to Rasputin?'

'Well, I was hardly ever that.' He laughed now. 'But of course, I did date a lot of different girls around that time, but none of them serious.'

'And now?'

'I've met someone new. It's different, she's…'

'Younger?' Gabby shook her head at the expected predictability of it all.

'No, actually, she's American, so it's difficult to… well she has her career over there and of course, I'm here so…' He shook his head. He was marking time; there hadn't been anyone significant in his life for as long as he could remember. There was no girl, but the last thing he wanted to do was break old Gabby's heart – all he wanted from her was an investment of five hundred thousand euro, if he could get it and if not, he'd be happy with anything above fifty grand.

'And you, Simon, what do you do now?'

'Same, really, the same as I've been doing since I left here. I invest in businesses, bring them along, sell them on… you know, every cloud and all that…' He smiled assuredly then, because he was fairly certain that no-one would have told Gabby that he had hardly done a hand's turn in five years. Still, it was true, he was a speculator and if he'd had cash in his pocket, there was no reason why he wouldn't have done exactly as he'd said. 'Actually, that's why I'm here today. I have to meet an investor…'

'Oh?'

'I shouldn't say too much, probably, because…' He shook his head solemnly.

'Oh, go on… you know I can keep a secret,' Gabby said sipping her coffee.

'Well, actually, John wanted in on this deal. I wasn't the one he talked to, but he approached one of the other investors and…'

'My John, I mean, John my ex…' She looked at him. They both knew John didn't have two cents to rub together. He'd been living off Gabby since they were in college. John owned a small catering firm that just about netted enough to call it a profit.

'Yeah, of course, I assumed when they said it, that you must have heard about the…' He rubbed his fingers together. He wasn't lying exactly; they would make a killing on this. It was a sure thing. He was positive; this was the windfall he'd spent his whole life waiting for. The only drawback was he hadn't the financial wherewithal to grab this opportunity; that's why he needed Gabby. 'But as to John, well he was late to the table and I figured, it wasn't as if he was ever particularly motivated by money anyway, so we turned him down.'

'I see,' Gabby said, turning over a million different possibilities in her calculating mind. 'As it turns out, I'm not sure how he'd come up with more than the price of his lunch break – I haven't made things easy for him.'

'Couldn't blame you there, he must have been crazy to… well, no doubt he'll come to his senses before too long. Let's hope by then it's not too late for him.'

'Too late?'

'Well, you're not going to hang about forever, are you?' Simon said, enjoying seeing her sense of pride swell up just a little.

'No. No, of course not.' She looked out at the street again. 'It was nice seeing you, Simon, really nice,' she said. 'I'm sorry that John and I weren't investing in your company – I think I'd quite like working with you again…'

'I'd like that too,' Simon said and he held her gaze for just a little longer than he knew he should. 'Anyway, I'd better get going.' He made a bit of a show of looking at the expensive wristwatch that had been a gift a couple of Christmases earlier. This from a girl whose daddy didn't think twice about forking out for a timepiece that was the price of a decent-sized family car. 'We should keep in touch.' He handed her one of the lavishly-crafted business cards he'd had made a year earlier.

'That would be good,' Gabby said, pulling out a card from her own wallet. 'You never know what's around the corner.' Everything about her seemed to be a million times lighter than it had been when she walked through the door earlier.

'You never know,' Simon echoed as he kissed her cheek tenderly before setting off to retrace his steps back to the flat at a much quicker rate than he had arrived.

That Gabby Dempsey would be his main investor, Simon

had absolutely no doubts. It wouldn't take a lot to talk her into coming in with him and it was a grade-A opportunity to make money. He was due at the Embassy Club at nine; drinks and dinner for one of the boys as part of his final nights of freedom before he tied the knot at the weekend.

He decided to give Gabby a couple of days to stew – it never did any good to appear too eager. He had a little while before he had to sign on the dotted line and make any firm financial commitments to getting the ball rolling. He would enjoy his last few days of idleness – not that he intended to flake himself out in any business – ever. Then, perhaps, after the weekend, he'd ring Gabby, mention to her that his main investor had been unable to find the cash and that he was giving her first refusal before he contacted John, but it would have to be done quickly, because there were contracts involved – that would do it nicely.

Simon Corrigan smiled to himself. It was a self-satisfied creasing of his mouth – if he hadn't come up with this plan, he'd have been left with only one option – going back to his mother cap in hand. He was mightily relieved not to have to do that particular little journey.

Miranda had coughed up last time, to clear his bad debt, and the time before that she'd lost her investment. She was not a woman to make the same mistake again. There would be no money from his mother, not for this nor for any other idea – of that Simon was quite sure.

7

Ada

Ada Corrigan had worked at the mills long enough to know when the tide was turning. And yes, she was devastated by her mother's obvious withdrawal of support for her. But of course, she reasoned later, her mother was not a young woman and while she currently held all the cards, the simple fact was, much and all as Miranda may not want to admit it, there was no-one else to take over.

Of course, she knew, it was foolish to be so upset about such a small comment. Her mother had every right to wish Callie was home to visit more often. Perhaps she had a right to wish she could take some of the work off her shoulders also, but Ada felt childishly jealous at the whole idea of it. Why should Callie be the only one her mother had faith in to organise that party? She had been so devastated.

A small voice whispered to be sensible. This was just hormones – an overreaction. She was at that peculiar stage, about to move into a new phase in life; sleep was elusive, she felt tiny surges of heat overtake her normally disciplined body – she was not herself – she was menopausal even if she wasn't going to admit that to anyone else.

She had no idea when she sat in her car where she would go, where she would end up most worryingly of all, indeed if she ever wanted to come back to Ballycove. Her life suddenly seemed so small, so utterly inconsequential. A weaker person might have been tempted to do something foolish. The cliffs at Mount Kennedy were, after all, only a stone's throw from the village. She could have driven there in ten minutes from the factory. How many more had taken that lonely route up those winding hill paths and left behind the life they could no longer face?

She had thought about it, she should admit that, to herself at least. But, quitting – and that would be quitting on the grandest scale – well, it was for failures and Ada never saw herself as a failure. By anyone's standards Ada Corrigan was a success. She had remained married – not always easy – to Anthony for over twenty years. Even if their marriage had seemed empty for as long as she could remember, Ada had stuck it out. If it came down to blame, no-one could cast a stone in her direction. She'd all but cattle prodded Anthony into making some kind of effort, so much so that now, when he put on a clean shirt, it almost felt like a hollow victory.

Sadly, even if he whisked her off to Barbados to renew their vows in a beach wedding, she would feel it was an empty gesture. She would know it was born only of the nagging she'd done for years. In some ways, she was thankful for the menopause; it was an excuse to just give up.

Her husband, it seemed, never listened. Anthony

wouldn't understand, and even if he did, when he tried to be sympathetic, honestly, with his lack of empathy, she wanted to bury his head deep in his LCD screen and leave him there. When Ada was not upset, she knew they were not all that different to each other – she with the mills, Anthony with his sports programmes – but they managed to keep things going. Somehow, he'd saved her and perhaps she'd saved him all those years ago.

Today, she didn't want to think about all that. Today, she wanted to think only about herself and wallow for a while in what it looked like her life might become. It was the inevitability of it all – was that a reason to be so upset? Ada thought it was reason enough.

Her job – well, of course she was a success. She never missed a day at work, the mills were a model of accounting efficiency and she always looked and sounded the part. She drove a new Mercedes for God's sake. How much more do you need to tell the world you are successful?

For her mother, it seemed it was not enough. Ada knew she would always pull the short straw in her mother's affections compared to Callie, and so when Ada walked out the door of the mills, she really did not know what to do or where to go. She certainly could not go home to Anthony.

She had to get away from everything and she had nowhere to go. She couldn't very well drive into Ballycove and bawl her eyes out in the front of the car. Nor was she going to head into one of the two local pubs and drown her sorrows. That was the trouble with small towns and neighbours who cared too much about what went on in other people's lives.

Ada stood in the local pub once a year, when she delivered a sponsorship cheque to the local football team. Twice, if they happened to win a match of any importance – which they hadn't in about five years.

So, she drove out of the mills, miraculously reversed through stinging tears without any idea of how close she came to shaving the rear bumper of her car and just kept driving. She bit back the tears as she drove back through Ballycove, almost ploughing through some poor unfortunate old man as he crossed near the local school. His warnings and waving hands held no import for her. Ada kept driving.

She left the town behind, drove determinedly on past the turn-off for Rowan Drive. Maybe she half considered Anthony, sitting there playing candy crush or solitaire while he followed some American sports team or wrestling match on his beloved television. She drove on past the winding coast road, setting herself onto the motorway, exits flying by at frightening speed. If she kept on going she'd be at Dublin airport in a few hours; Belfast in two more. Thank God, some part of her thought, thank God, she didn't have her passport in her handbag.

Instead, she thought about booking into some anonymous city B & B, or maybe a travel lodge on the outskirts of the city. She could book in somewhere, curl up on a freshly made bed, surrounded by the reassuring sounds of strangers, pull a blanket over her head and cry as though she'd lost her most precious possession. She needed to be somewhere people did not know her, just for now. She switched off her phone; at least that was a start. For the first time in her life, she craved the obscurity that eluded her in Ballycove.

So, she kept on driving. Soon, she needed coffee, she needed to go to the toilet and she had almost cried herself out. She pulled into a service station on an unfamiliar road, filled her car with petrol and ordered a greasy breakfast roll and coffee. She sat in her lovely new Mercedes, surrounded by huge trucks, devouring the comfort food she had deprived herself of for too long to remember. Ada was strictly a salad and nuts woman; for years, the only exception was a neat scone in the mills coffee shop and that was just to please her mother, more than anything else.

It was as she was sitting there, covered in crumbs from the crusty roll, that Ada spotted two blackbirds perched on a railing just at the edge of the forecourt. They seemed to be sitting quite amicably, watching the world go by, and Ada was struck by them, not because of their orange beaks, or their confidence near the huge trucks, nor because of their obvious affiliation to each other. No, rather she was struck by them, because she knew that within them was something she was missing in life. Her mother and her sister would look at those birds and gain immense pleasure from just watching them, whereas Ada could not find even the slightest hint of joy to brighten a dark day.

She kept her eyes on them for quite some time, waiting perhaps for the pleasure to arrive, but nothing happened. Then, unexpectedly, a large truck driver opened his window and threw the remains of his sandwich towards them. Ada watched as the two birds dived towards it and she wondered if they'd fight over the ready meal. Then, out of nowhere, a jackdaw swooped down, picked up the goodies and swept off so fast that even the two blackbirds seemed trapped in rigid shock. Ada heard a small throaty laugh come from somewhere inside her and she had a feeling that in that moment she had learned something.

Had she been, like those loyal and boring blackbirds,

sitting for the last twenty-five years waiting for her mother to cast aside that precious morsel? And worse, was there, somewhere, out of her line of vision, a jackdaw waiting to swoop in and gather up her prize? Ada sat for a long time in her car on that garage forecourt. The blackbirds disappeared without her even noticing, but in many ways, they would stay with her for a very long time.

The strong heat of the day was beginning to disappear when she decided to make her way back to Rowan Drive. She would be late arriving home. She doubted that Anthony would even notice.

It was a surreal drive back to Ballycove. Ada felt as though she had taken the visors off her mind. Everything seemed to be so much clearer than ever before. The landscape around her held a kind of crispness that hadn't been there earlier. Her mind was sharper, even her fingers tingled with a kind of awareness she'd never known was possible. She reasoned with herself: no-one was going to take the mills from her. For one thing, who else actually wanted them? She counted them off in her mind. Not Callie, that was for sure.

Callie, her brilliant, vivacious, successful sister would never settle in a backwater like Ballycove now. It was far too provincial for her for one thing and for another, Callie enjoyed a life where she never worried about what people thought – mainly, Ada always believed, because no-one knew exactly what she was up to. Callie had, since she left Ballycove, lived most of her private life, well, privately. Of course, there were glittering awards and celebrity parties, where she was caught on camera for glossy fashion magazines entering or leaving various London establishments to celebrate fashion parties. And, of course, the world and her sister knew about her success at Theme and the various plaudits she'd garnered over her career.

But her actual private life? That was very much kept under wraps from everyone. Ada hadn't a clue if Callie had a boyfriend or a partner or if she was, as Ada suspected, too long in the tooth for anyone to be bothered about by the time it came to settle down. No, Callie would not want to come back here to live in Ballycove and run the mills forever more amen.

And then there was the notion – and this more than anything scared Ada – that Miranda might consider an outsider for the role. That was the thing about having a board of directors. Ultimately, the Corrigan family could remain at the helm of the mills, but with a general manager in place. Ada would spend the rest of her days playing second fiddle to some young hotshot blow-in and she just wasn't having that.

Ada shook herself out – she really was letting her imagination run away with her. She'd never been a woman to bow down to these silly notions before and so now, she knew, the way her mind was racing had more to do with menopausal stress than it had with anything else. Miranda would not hand the mills over to someone else; she would ask the only person she could ask – Ada. The rest of her family were scattered about the place and her eldest daughter was, when all was said and done, the only one with any real interest in the mills anyway. This thought calmed Ada considerably.

So, she knew, there was no way around it; to feel a little better about herself, she would have to take action. But what to do, that was the question. She would sleep on it.

She would go home, slip into her lovely familiar bed – she cast aside all notions of Anthony snoring his way through the night. She would sleep on it and she would come up with a plan to put things right.

It was later than usual when she arrived at the cul de sac. She parked in the drive, not so carefully as she would have done before; rather, she pulled up with the kind of swagger that comes from finally realising that she was the master of her own destiny. For the first time in her life, Ada realised that she could make her own future and she was not going to be beholden to the benevolence of her mother or wait for fate to deal her the hand it so chose.

'Ada,' Anthony called when she opened the front door, 'where were you?'

'Oh, I got delayed,' she said and noticed the smell of slightly burned beef pouring out of the kitchen. 'You're cooking?'

'Well, yeah. You weren't here, so…' He didn't look at her, but she wondered if perhaps he knew. Then she realised, he couldn't know. How could he? There was nothing to know, just a wobble of anxiety at a throwaway remark by her mother over a cup of coffee.

'Very good, well, you might want to check it now, it could be burning,' she said turning towards the stairs. She needed to take off her work clothes, peel away the day just gone.

'I'll have it on the table in five minutes,' he called after her before heading back into the kitchen. Burnt offerings. Perhaps she should be glad that he had cooked; after all, it should be reassuring to know that if she wasn't there, he wouldn't starve. To be fair, she'd never worried that he would. He was handy with the mobile phone and doubtless would be quite happy to live on takeout food every night of the week and if he became tired of that, he'd never turn his nose up at a pack of pot noodles.

'So, how was work?' he asked uncomfortably as they sat at the kitchen table. It was the first time he'd seemed interested in the mills since she could remember.

'I think you know how work was, Anthony,' Ada said flatly.

'I was talking to Miranda,' he admitted.

'Oh, did she ring?' Ada's mood suddenly lifted.

'No. You were late and I couldn't get you on the phone so I tried the cottage instead.'

'Oh?' she said.

'She said that you'd left the mills in the morning and they hadn't seen you since.'

'That's right.'

'So, what happened – did you have a row?'

'I wouldn't call it a row, exactly,' Ada snapped. It was so much harder to come back from a row than a heated discussion or a minor disagreement.

'That's what she said.'

'Good.' Ada looked at the plate before her. Cremated beef, soggy potatoes and very tragic green beans – it was not good. 'Actually, I ate earlier,' she said, pushing the plate away.

'Right.' Anthony's appetite seemed to have deserted him too, which was unusual. 'She said that you spoke about the anniversary celebrations.'

'Yes.' Ada reached for her bag, took out a slim case that held five cigarettes. She did not smoke, normally, not really, but she allowed herself one cigarette a day. She'd already had a two weeks' supply since seeing that bloody jackdaw. She picked out a cigarette, held it for a moment, then lit it and inhaled deeply. 'We had words, oh, sod it, Anthony, I had been hoping to suggest that she might cut back a bit, think of retiring...'

'And she said that she wasn't ready yet or...' He was picking his words, not quite making eye contact. God help him, but he was trying, in his own inadequate way, to be supportive and had it been just a few months earlier, Ada knew, she'd have been over the moon. But something had changed. The goalposts in her life had been moved – or had they been removed? It suddenly felt as though she was no longer sure of the rules. She wasn't even sure if there were rules any more and that threw everything Ada Corrigan knew up in the air.

'Anthony, my mother is not a young woman. Who knows what goes through her head? But the simple fact is, she can't go on forever and she won't go on forever. We have a big celebration to organise this year for the mills' one-hundred-and-fifty-year anniversary and there's a lot of work to do, perhaps it's already too much for her.'

'So, everything is all right?' he said and suddenly Ada saw her husband for what he actually was. He needed her to get this job as much as she wanted it. Not because they needed the money; the rise in salary would be negligible. Miranda had never been motivated by money and Ada had pressed a higher income on her, as much because it validated her own rather than because her mother wanted it. Anthony needed her to get this job because without it, he wouldn't know how to console or support her and with it, things could just trundle along on the path they had both expected and planned for.

'What do you think?' She rounded on him, but then stopped, because she knew he was just worried about her, perhaps, in his way, about both of them. He didn't deserve to have her take out her bad mood on him. 'I'm going to lie down for a while,' she said then, getting up and leaving him sitting at the kitchen table, for once with a sink full of dirty dishes and no intention of lifting a finger to clean them.

Neither had Ada any notion of lying down and falling asleep. She had much more serious things to think about. Her life had been rattled around in the space of one cup of coffee, but at the same time, somehow, instead of feeling that it was the disaster that it should be, she actually felt in an odd way... liberated. Perhaps it was shock or nerves or just extreme stress, but the whole day seemed to have melted into something sublime.

After all these years of sticking around and showing up, Ada had caught in her mother's off-guard wistfulness the truth that Miranda clearly had no idea what the future held for the woollen mills. And this was the thing that had knocked the air from her lungs – Ada had a sinking feeling that if Callie walked back here in the morning, her mother wouldn't think twice about handing over the mills to her. The only thing was, she knew, Callie would never give up the life she'd made for herself in London – would she?

8

Miranda

Miranda waited at the only set of traffic lights in Ballycove. It was good to be on the journey home after her day. Somehow, she knew that it had been a less than satisfactory day, although she couldn't quite mark out why that was. She suspected it had something to do with her conversation with Ada. God, Ada. Her oldest child, she could be so precious at times. Even the merest mention of Callie and it could drive her mad with jealousy. In the past Miranda was always so careful but not so much now. Since her heart attack, she had started to think she would try to tread more solidly on ground that for too many years she'd walked on softly. Calling a spade a spade was Ada's approach to life. She wasn't so good at hearing the same spade being called exactly what it was.

Miranda sank further into her little car, enjoying the feeling of warm evening sunlight on her arms. The radio droned a dull ongoing conversation just beyond her interest, but then the arrival of a young man, walking towards the supermarket opposite, caught her attention. He was tall and fair, with broad shoulders, slim hips and the familiar gait of a man she'd known years before. Richard Blair. His eyes held that same deep blue. Something in his smile had his spirit too and he raised his hand to acknowledge her as he passed.

He couldn't possibly have recognised her. It was, she knew, just one of those friendly gestures of small towns that make everyone a neighbour and charm visitors who do not understand. Miranda found herself waving back, a nostalgic, slow movement of her hand, clogged up by memories and wistfulness. Then he was gone, disappearing into Mr Singh's supermarket, and Miranda caught her breath for a moment.

It could have been forty years earlier; he could have been Richard Blair, all those decades ago, popping to the village for some trivial thing. Miranda felt a small chill rush through her. She tried not to think of that time, but seeing him jolted open a door to memories that normally she managed to keep tightly locked.

The changing lights caught her eye and she pushed the gearstick into first before taking off slowly towards Bridgestock Cottage. In her rear-view mirror, she spotted Imelda Mooney – the village gossip – hurrying along the street behind her. She ducked into Mr Singh's and Miranda sighed audibly. No doubt by tomorrow everyone in Ballycove would know all about the intriguing stranger in town.

At the end of town, Miranda was just about to turn off onto the narrow road for Bridgestock Cottage when she thought about that man again. She knew she couldn't just drive home and forget about him. She would wonder if she'd imagined him, a trick of the light, or if in fact a man – the living spit of Richard Blair – had actually walked casually up the main street of the village and waved to her – one sunny evening that could have been any other sunny evening over the last sixty-odd years.

With a niggling chest pain, Miranda turned her car, a nifty three-point manoeuvre that she managed while keeping her tongue firmly in her jaw and her arm angled on the back of the passenger seat like a long-distance lorry driver with a habit born too long ago to change. She pulled in opposite the supermarket, not really needing anything, but with change in her purse, enough to buy a decent bottle of wine, some local cheese and perhaps a nice freshly baked soda bread.

'Hello, Mrs Corrigan, it is a lovely evening for out and about.' Mr Singh looked up from sweeping the shiny new tiles that had been part of his shop refit at the same time as he'd got a new sign over his front door. At this hour of the evening, the disinfectant pine smell was welcome to cover over the aroma of day-old sausage rolls in the small deli counter at the back of the shop.

She stood there, for a moment; the pain in her chest had abated into something like a dull ache now. It was something better than the menacing rhythm that had throbbed through her, as she'd considered the terrible things that might have befallen Ada only a short while earlier, when Anthony had rung in a panic because his wife had not arrived home from the mills at her usual time.

She didn't need anything in the supermarket, not really. She waited for a moment, enjoying the warmth of the evening sun through the plate glass window. Outside, the burnt glow picked out summer foliage so you knew the summer was settling in for more than just a careless visit. Mr Singh lived in what Miranda assumed was a large flat with his wife over their supermarket. The shop had started out as the front room of one of the town's main street houses, which were generous in proportion. Mostly, they were built for wealthy families a century earlier.

As time passed, the shop had gradually extended. When Mr Singh arrived in Ballycove a decade earlier, he opened up the side of his premises to car parking and constructed a long extension to the original shop so now it was a full-size supermarket. He was perfectly placed to hear everything that was going on in the village, but his gentle manner was not predisposed to gossip, so he shared information as a village service rather than a tattletale.

'You should be out there enjoying it, Mr Singh.' Miranda smiled at him and glanced about the shop, unsure what to purchase exactly. She moved across to the small selection of wines, chose the best red he had and placed it on the counter top.

'Oh, I will close up soon, but with tourists about you never know who will need something at a late hour. I hate to think of people having to drive to the next town, especially if they've just been customers next door.' He smiled as his head nodded towards the pub next to his supermarket.

'Well, that's very thoughtful of you,' Miranda said gently.

'Oh no, I'm not just thinking of the tourists, but I am thinking of my family and neighbours too. Who wants to meet a drunk driver on roads that he doesn't know?'

'True, very true,' Miranda murmured. She took out her

purse and handed over the price of the bottle of wine. 'Speaking of strangers, Mr Singh, I was passing by earlier when I noticed a young man coming in here.' She looked at her watch. 'About six-foot, sandy hair, blue eyes...'

'Ah, yes.' Mr Singh smiled as though the memory of the man was a happy one. 'He is staying in the lodge; it is in the grounds of Blair Hall. He only arrived here this week, but already he seems to have settled in very well.' He shook his head.

'Is he... one of the Blairs?'

'I believe he is related to the original owners, yes.' Mr Singh picked out a paper bag to wrap the bottle, normally Miranda would decline, not wanting to put him to any bother, but this time, to keep him talking she nodded for him to carry on. 'Yes, he's here for a while. I am not sure if it is a permanent move, but certainly, he will be here for the rest of the year.'

'And, he's on his own. There's no...'

'Well, I can't say if he's married. You should ask Kate that. She notices every eligible man who comes through the door. Sometimes I think she only works here to find a decent husband.' Mr Singh laughed. Perhaps it was in relief that he had no daughters to worry about, just two sons, safely tucked into medical school.

'No, I was actually wondering if any of his family were with him, you know, people my age – father, mother, perhaps? The Blairs were well known in these parts. It would be nice to know if they were back in the village.' Miranda smiled at him.

'That would be nice,' Mr Singh agreed, then tilted his

head to the side a little. 'Welcome them back with a nice bottle of wine?'

'Maybe,' Miranda said.

'Well, as far as I know, he seems to be shopping for one person only, but I'm sure Miss Mooney could probably tell you more than I could.' He smiled now, folding over the wrapping across the top of the bottle. 'She arrived earlier when he was here and they had a long chat, just over the bread counter.'

'Ah, it makes no odds. I'm not sure I'm that interested, just keeping a friendly eye out, that's really all.' Miranda picked up her bottle of wine and headed out into the evening air.

It had been a most unusual day, she thought to herself when she sat in the car. So unusual that she didn't think twice of driving up to the old Blair place to drop off the bottle of wine that she'd just bought as a welcome gift. The lodge was probably the only habitable part of the estate now. Even though, in the distance, she could see the imposing chimneys of the Hall still stood tall, it had been decades since anyone had stayed there. That notion filled her with a kind of nostalgic grief, which she knew wasn't for the loss of anyone in particular, but had more to do with the notion of time passing by. Even the lodge would not provide accommodation for the faint-hearted, but it was encouraging to see a drift of blue smoke coming from the stout chimney stack.

Miranda pushed open the old-fashioned little gate and strolled up the narrowing garden path. She remembered the old gamekeeper who had lived in this cottage in her youth, of course; even then, he'd done very little gamekeeping. She suspected that he had difficulty keeping the rabbits from his own vegetable patch, arthritis having bent him over long before she'd ever known him. He and all of his generation were dead many years ago, but still, it did no harm to remember. She tapped the peeling door gently, deciding she would just leave the bottle and welcome him quickly before setting back for home.

'Ah, hello, I'm just...' She held out the bottle, but really, it was hard to think what to say to the man who opened the door. She was, for a moment, almost speechless; then, she smiled at his expression of amusement and held out her hand. 'You must be Richard's son... David?'

'I am,' he said, holding back the door to invite her in.

'No, no, I mustn't intrude, I just... well I heard that you were in the village and I thought I'd drop over, just to welcome you... I've come bearing gifts.' She made a little show of presenting him the bottle.

'That's really very kind of you, please, do come in... It's all rather modest, but...'

'Oh, I'm sorry, I'm Miranda, Miranda Corrigan. I knew your father very well...' She was following him through a narrow hallway and into a cosy, if shabby living room that contained kitchen, pantry, dining and sitting area in one high-ceilinged generous square.

'Of course, you are Miranda Corrigan.' He said the words and then stood back and looked at her for a long moment, as if comparing her to some mental image he'd had of her. 'My father told me about you...'

'Only good I hope...'

'Well, he did mention that I should ask you for any tips on the best place to catch a decent salmon...' They both laughed at that and Miranda felt herself warming to this young man as easily as she had to his father all those years earlier.

'My salmon-fishing days are well behind me now, I'm a little sorry to report.'

'House-warming drink?' he asked taking out a huge duty-free bottle of whiskey and two delicate glasses from the old dresser.

'Why not?' she said and she took the small old-fashioned glass from him. 'How is your father?' She had to ask.

'Oh, he's good, actually. Retired now, of course…'

'Of course,' Miranda echoed. Wasn't everyone these days? 'Still in London?'

'Only when he has to be. He's bought a little house in the country, so he has time to fish and tramp about the fields all day long.' He laughed at that. 'And you? You're retired now?'

'No, although I probably should be.' Somehow, it felt okay to admit this to David Blair. Why was that, when it rattled her nerves to admit it to her own family? 'Actually, it's impending; I'm just sort of dodging the bullet.'

'Can't say I blame you. You need to be ready to make those big changes. No point doing it for the sake of it, not if you don't have to,' he said, smiling easily and sitting at the narrow kitchen table that took up the centre of the room.

'I must say,' Miranda said, dropping in to the chair opposite him, 'this cottage is much cosier than I'd have expected.'

'Yes, I was surprised too. It's taken a week to get it like this though. There's a huge bonfire waiting in the yard if anyone fancies celebrating Guy Fawkes this year.' He nodded towards a small window above the sink, which faced the back of the property. Miranda saw beds and mattresses, moth-eaten and damp-marked.

'Just you, so?'

'Yes, just me.' He sipped his drink thoughtfully. 'Actually, it's part of the reason I'm here.' He smiled, a lopsided movement of his lips that made her catch her breath with its resemblance to his father. 'I'm meant to be getting over my divorce.'

'Oh, I'm so sorry,' Miranda said and she reached her hand towards his arm. It was instinctive and although they had only just met, it felt right.

'These things happen. We were out of love for much longer than we were in love. In the end, it was inevitable, but still... well, it's the finish of something I once thought would last forever.'

'Ballycove is a good place to heal,' Miranda whispered.

'That's what my father said.'

'He was always going to be a wise man.' She smiled, her mind drifting back to years ago. 'It is nice to have a Blair back in Ballycove again. I hope you're going to stay for much longer than it takes to mend your broken heart.'

'That very much depends on if I can find something to occupy my days with. I'd like to bring the Hall back to life, but... well; I would need to find some kind of work to do as well.'

'Oh, and what is it that you do?' Miranda couldn't see too many openings for merchant bankers if he'd followed in his father's footsteps. 'Not a banker, I presume?'

'No, heaven forbid. My father encouraged me to see beyond the family business so... I've travelled;

project-managed mainly, everything from portfolio work to garden centres.'

'That's interesting,' she said thinking of a little project that was on the horizon at the mills. 'Would you be interested in project-managing a little party for me?' she asked eyeing him squarely.

'A birthday party?' He looked at her now quizzically.

'Sort of, the mills will be a hundred and fifty years old next year and I wanted to do something rather special…'

'I see,' David Blair said softly. 'Well, I'd be very interested in helping out, as it happens.' When they shook hands, Miranda had a feeling that this was a business relationship that could grow into a solid friendship.

'Great, pop into the mills when you get a chance and we'll firm things up.' Then she raised her glass to him and they toasted the mills, and new and old friends.

An hour later, Miranda turned over the engine after leaving David at the lodge. The pain in her chest had subsided now and the realisation brought with it a feeling of tranquillity. She would go home, listen to the radio and tuck herself into bed at a reasonable hour, and then she chuckled to herself. What was she like? Calling in on young men she didn't know out of the blue? Really, she would lose the run of herself one of these days if she wasn't careful.

The cottage was warm when Miranda let herself in that evening. Sun streaming in during the day had picked out her flagstone floor to rest upon and so even beneath her shoes, it felt as though the warmth still lingered. She never felt alone here. The children might as easily be in the next room, pottering away at a job she'd given them earlier or niggling each other in the way that only siblings can.

It was funny, but once Ada, Simon and Callie had left, she never felt any great loneliness in their absence. She had expected to feel a little lost, here with just her memories. Empty nest syndrome and all of that, but it seemed to Miranda, there was never time to be lonely. Instead, her time was filled with the mills, her garden and an array of friends who descended upon her often when she least expected them. Bridgestock Cottage had always, from the first day she'd opened it up, been a place to entertain and Miranda loved to have her kitchen filled with people. There was always enough in the larder to feed one more guest. Miranda could happily sit and while away the hours while watching the birds play in the garden or the flames licking up the chimney, depending on the time of the year.

Perhaps it was why, on evenings like this, when she possibly should have been driven to some sense of loss or loneliness, all she felt was an odd sense of expectation, as though something surprising was about to happen. Miranda sighed, but it was a contented sound. In the larder, she had some cold chicken left from the previous day. She would pick some fresh lettuce, rocket and tomatoes and sit outside watching the swallows play between their nests.

Yes, it was this kind of simple evening that she could share with Callie and they would contentedly potter about together. What a shame Ada couldn't find that same joy in these everyday things also.

9

The Past

The burdened silence that fell about the cottage had more to do with everyone holding their breath than it had with excitement or dread. Miranda knew this, but she also knew that keeping quiet, making herself as small as possible so she didn't intrude on her father's thoughts was vital this morning. Today was his first day at the mills. No-one had said it exactly. The job had been offered weeks earlier, but this was the day Harry Reilly had geared himself up enough to put on a shirt and tie. Miranda couldn't imagine why anyone sweeping a yard would need to wear a tie, but she knew enough not to say anything that might faze her father at this critical stage.

They sat, all three of them, at the breakfast table. Only the sound of eating broke up the noiseless morning. A pot, blackened with age, stood in the centre of the little scrubbed table. Her mother had made porridge and for a treat emptied in a handful of early blackberries that Miranda had brought home a few days earlier. A grunt that was almost animalistic signalled something that might have been approval or that her father was ready for more.

Her mother answered by spooning out the remaining porridge into his bowl and he quickly scraped this away before pushing back his chair and walking to the mirror. He flattened down his wiry hair as much as it was possible after years of being neglected. Miranda watched her mother as she wet the old comb and moved it gently through. The action seemed to both calm her father and make him look quite presentable.

When he turned around to face Miranda, he looked quite dashing, apart from his darting eyes, which still signalled the unrest in his personality. She could see he must have been a handsome man once. Her mother beamed with pride even if there was no hiding it was patching over her worry. She parcelled up a thick heel of bread and a cut of fatty bacon from the day before, wrapped them carefully in an old handkerchief that she'd laundered until its white had faded evenly to cream.

'So, you have everything?' she said needlessly as he reached for his jacket by the door.

'I...' He looked down into Annie's eyes and Miranda could see that for all his gruffness, for his enormous blackening presence in their little home, in that moment, he was little more than a frightened boy being sent to school for the first day. Perhaps on every level, he wanted to go to the mills, but on the actual day he'd managed to build himself up to make his way there, his reserve was already crumbling before he left the house.

'It's going to be fine... you're going to be fine; this is just a step on the start of your new life; our new life together as a family. There are lots of other men there, men you knew before the…' Annie hated the war, fought hard to keep it from her lips. She raised a hand and laid it on his arm. It was a delicate movement and something caught in Miranda's chest when she saw it, as though it confirmed that this stranger really was her father. He truly was the man her mother had spoken about for all those years. Even if he seemed to be just a shell of a man, beneath that shell lay someone they should both love very much.

With that, Annie opened the front door to the streaming morning sun. It flooded through the doorway, so Miranda could not see her father's face as he set off for the mills that day, but when he pulled the door behind him, it felt as if they both let out a long exhalation of relief.

Annie Reilly turned to her daughter now and tried to smile, but it was more a setting of her features into something that might disarray her worried expression. Neither of them fully expected that Harry would be fit to do any job properly, even sweeping; when the smallest things could rattle him so he lashed out his fists at whatever object happened to be closest. At least he had not hit Miranda or Annie, but seeing him make smithereens of her grandmother's oil lamp had been enough to push Miranda well away from him when they were in the cottage together.

Miranda didn't really believe her father was fit for work. In truth, she wasn't sure he was fit for life in Ballycove at all. Perhaps he just wasn't fully ready to leave the hospital when he did and she felt a little guilty sometimes for wishing him home so earnestly over the years. Maybe, if he'd stayed in the convalescent home a little longer, they might have cured him

'I'm sure he'll be fine,' Miranda said bravely to her mother.

'Of course, he'll be grand; it's just first-day nerves,' her mother said brightly, but they both expected him to get no further than the corner of the road on that fateful day.

Miranda knew the heaviness she felt in her heart this morning had as much to do with Richard returning to London as with her father's dark departure for the mills. Until yesterday, she could almost convince herself that those deliciously long summer days, Richard Blair and his little boat would be around forever. All three had combined to mark the days out delightfully; at least she could escape the burdening silence that seemed to follow her about.

'Why don't you make your way up to old Mrs Bridgestock good and early this morning, pick some more blackberries for her and take along the washing I've folded up and ironed for her,' her mother said after a moment and the words brought something close to relief into the little cottage, as if things were back to normal, to how things were before Harry returned.

'Okay,' Miranda said easily. There would be no going out on the boat today. Richard's parents were expected to arrive early and from the sound of things, he would be whisked off to London before he had time for breakfast. 'I'll take the long way around and perhaps I might pick up some plums as well,' she said then, because, down along the riverbank, some plum trees overhung the walk and it wasn't unusual to see the ripest fruit lying prone on the ground as you passed by. Miranda smiled at her mother; they both knew that Bridgestock Cottage was probably the only place that could help her feel a little less bereft today.

★

It was with a heavy heart that Miranda set off for Bridgestock Cottage. There was no casting off the reality that Richard Blair would probably be already making his journey back to London. She was surprised by the stabbing loneliness this produced within her; of course, she reasoned, it also signalled the petering out of the summer holidays and the approach of autumn and with it darker days ahead. Still, Miranda loved the sprawling cottage, hiding at the end of a long country lane. It was a rambling stone building with one room leading into another, an Aladdin's cave of never-ending doors and fireplaces filled with pictures and ornaments, many of them much older than Mrs Bridgestock.

'If you were my daughter, I couldn't ask for any greater kindness,' the old woman said when Miranda arrived with the freshly picked fruit. She smiled and handed Miranda a boiled sweet before sinking back into the chair she spent most of her days in, looking out her window at the cottage garden beyond.

'Richard Blair is heading back to London today,' Miranda said easily when Mrs Bridgestock had finished explaining why her husband had seen fit to sell off most of the land, he'd farmed for years, so they could live out a gentle retirement together.

'Well, Miranda, I know you will miss him, but it's probably as well. No matter how much he wanted to stay here in Ballycove, it wouldn't have been right.'

'Why do you think that, Mrs Bridgestock?' Miranda asked, moving forward in her chair, because she had spent many afternoons listening to Richard reasoning out why it would be a very good idea indeed.

'His life is in London; it was always going to be. When Edwin Blair left Ballycove everyone knew he'd never want to come back here again. And without his parents, what would Richard be doing here, up at that hall? It's no place for a child, not really. Old Lord Blair is as odd as a hen in a hairdresser's. The grandmother seems to keep the show on the road and they had all that money and nothing to show for it. Sure, the duck and her mother know, it's a miracle the mills are still running; they've lost that much money over the years.'

'Well, that hardly seems…'

'Oh, no? It's not natural, for an only son of them lot to take off like that, unless of course he's running away from a sinking ship – well Edwin Blair married well enough to be sure he'd never have to bother with the mills again.' She shook her head and then looked across at Miranda. 'You mark my words, that lad will have had his future mapped out for him long before you ever met him, whether he knows it or not – the day's not that far off when Ballycove would only slow him down.'

'Ah well, it's a good job I was only going fishing with him so.' Miranda smiled and shook her head. Really, what did the old woman think? That she was going to marry Richard Blair? They were friends. He was the best friend she had in the village. They had the most wonderful summer and Richard had every intention of coming back again next year. She walked back down the lane again with Mrs Bridgestock's words ringing in her ears. Wasn't it what the whole village was saying about her own father – that he was as mad as a bag of crabs? In some ways, the sentiments fostered even greater warmth for Richard Blair.

Miranda knew what it was to be tarred with a brush you inherited as opposed to one you fashioned for yourself. She skipped along jauntily, deciding to shrug off the cares that normally gnawed at her. Instead, she took the river path that ran away from the village. She let herself out through a narrow wooden gate, which harked back to a time when Mr Bridgestock worked this land and took precautions to keep his cattle from straying too close to the river's edge. Closing it firmly, she looked up towards the blackened chimneys spitting out fumy smoke into the sunny blue skies.

Through the woody hedges, Miranda saw windows high up in the old factory – she wondered if people sat behind those on days like this, wishing they could walk along the river path just as she was doing now. More likely, she figured they were just in place to let in daylight for as many hours as they could. Perhaps they overlooked huge machines far below that paid no mind to day or night, but trundled on loudly spewing out milky yarn regardless.

Miranda stood for a moment, straining her sight to see through the thick shrubbery to the mills – they were such a vital vein to their little town. Almost every family was dependent on their survival one way or another. The mills were the only source of employment really, if you didn't have a plot of land. Even if you did, most of the wives about the village knitted with the yarn and sold their work on for pin money. This provided the little extras that made life slightly sweeter.

It seemed like the mills themselves had been on the brink of bankruptcy for as long as anyone could remember and even Miranda was not immune to the overhanging expectation that one day they would close. Miranda didn't rightly know what would happen then, how they would all get by, but she knew for certain that it was something that haunted the village, like a ghoul that would surely arrive sooner or later to suck the lifeblood from the village veins.

Richard spotted his father's cab snaking along the driveway. Everything was ready, his trunk packed. His grandmother had set a hearty breakfast before him first thing, as if he could be spirited away at any moment on the long journey back to London. Surely, twenty minutes wouldn't put them up or down either way. He almost knocked down his grandfather on the stairs. The old man stood back, a little perplexed, but then smiled when he looked down at his grandson.

'You've heard their car then – they're here,' he said a little sadly, as if he felt the loss of Richard already from the estate. 'Ah, can't wait to be getting away I suppose.' The old man rubbed the side of his head.

'Oh, Grandfather, if I could stay here forever I would…' Richard said hopping past him on the step. 'I'm going to nip down to the river, one last time. You won't tell them that you've seen me now, will you?' He was almost at the bottom of the stairs.

'Go out through the kitchen, down by the pantry…Your parents never use that door.' The old man's eyes danced with an unfamiliar emotion and Richard wished for once, he had more time to stay and get to know both his grandparents even better.

'You're a sport – thanks, Grandfather,' Richard said, before nipping into the dark kitchen and unlatching the door to lead him out into the yard, which would bring him quickly out of sight.

'Take it easy.' His grandfather was at his back. 'Anyone would think you'd never see the girl again.' He laughed gently then, but it made up Richard's mind in an instant as if he knew, with some foreboding accuracy, he had to race to the riverbank as quickly as his feet would carry him.

10

Callie

Callie was at work the following day when the call came through from Dennis's PA cancelling their usual dinner on Tuesday evening. This came with the territory with a married man. It was one she'd consigned herself to long ago, so Callie thought little of it and decided she could stay a little longer in the office instead. She shook off the notion that he could cancel their long-standing arrangements without so much as an excuse and with the ease of asking his secretary to clear his evening for something more important.

It wasn't that he'd ever been in the habit of making excuses, nor she to him. That was one of the clearest tenets of their relationship – they were both important people. Fitting each other in was an indulgence, not a right. Callie had known from the outset that as soon as Dennis felt as if she needed him, he would no longer want her. The position of wife was already taken in his life, so Callie instead had firmed out space as the uncomplicated woman he wanted, rather than one he answered to.

In the back of her mind, she believed he respected her far more for it, although occasionally she would hear Ada's voice creep into her heart telling her that she was expendable to him. Her sister, no doubt, would have demanded a wedding ring and served him with an ultimatum years ago. Callie had never wanted a husband for the sake of one. While she wasn't afraid of commitment, she chose love, all-consuming passion over a legal promise. And she had fallen madly and deeply in love with Dennis all those years ago, so much so that she never thought about an alternative to their relationship now.

She put down the receiver automatically, examined her lovely manicure before her eyes cast about the tastefully decorated office that Theme had featured on their website, a black and white photo of their star designer at work. These last few months – well since her mother's heart attack – something had stirred in Callie. It was as if an uncertainty had been opened up in her and it made her question little things in her life.

It felt now, as she looked across the foggy city, as if it was all rather empty. Her life, her success, all the things she'd been striving for had opened up before her, led her on this glittering road to a full stop and perhaps it was time to seek out new experiences that were not on this chosen path. This room, this building, the company, it was soulless. Out there, in the foggy, murky streets, people were cruising along with real life. Over in Ireland, where her mother and sister were rubbing off each other, there was life. There was something worth holding onto.

For the first time in a long while, Callie sat back and assessed where she was in life. She considered not just her successful career or her beautiful home; true she had the smartest friends, a wardrobe to covet and an art collection that was enviable, but what had she really, that was lasting? Her designer shoes made poor bedfellows. It struck her then, as she cast her eyes across the city, this was not her home; perhaps she had just outstayed her welcome. Like a guest at a party whose taxi never arrives, it was all wonderful for a while, but the time had come to go home.

Callie wasn't sure she knew what that meant exactly. She'd never imagined herself living in Ballycove again. She needed a holiday, quite simply – that was all that was wrong with her. She needed to breathe in the fresh air of Ballycove and sit at her mother's table with the warmth of Bridgestock Cottage filling her up so her reserves were replenished again.

Callie realised she was spinning the large rose gold ring around tightly on her finger. It was a nervous reaction to stress. She stopped abruptly when the phone rang.

'Callie,' the clipped tone was unmistakable, although Callie could count between her two hands the number of times she'd had a direct phone call from the Managing Director.

'Yes, Veronica,' Callie said keeping her voice steady. 'What can I do for you?' She tried to sound professional and laid-back, the antithesis of one who's had her heart broken and feels not a jot of guilt for sleeping with her boss's husband.

'It's more like what I can do for you, actually. Are you free for lunch today?' Veronica never asked employees out for lunch and Callie felt her heart lurch with impending doom at the very notion of it.

'Of course, I can move things around here to suit you,' Callie said coolly.

'Say one o'clock, my driver will pick you up at the door.'

She'd hardly completed the sentence when the phone clicked dead and for a few moments Callie thought time may have stood still. Certainly, as she looked out across the London rooftops, it seemed an eerie silence had settled on her world and she wondered what on earth could be coming her way next.

Callie couldn't imagine Veronica having lunch anywhere other than Claridge's. According to Dennis, his wife never let her hair down, but Callie wasn't always sure what to believe from Dennis when it came to his domestic arrangements. His wife was an elusive woman. Callie watched her as she walked ahead into the restaurant. A typical English rose, fair-skinned, delicate, a slight blush to her cheek and perfectly groomed. She walked with the confidence that comes with a lifetime of privilege. Her clothes were impeccable, her suit fitted to perfection, her jewels expensive but understated, her shoes, high-heeled, looked as though they'd just left the shop, encasing her dainty foot like a glove.

Veronica was a doll of a woman, but her green eyes were steely and her mouth ran in a thin and cruel line, covering teeth that were just a little too small for a genuine smile. Callie, hardly a huge woman by comparison, felt ungainly in her presence, as though she was somehow uncouth, awkward and under par. She suspected that had more to do with her own feelings of guilt and inadequacy than it had with any real differences between them.

'Thank you for coming,' Veronica said as she glanced at the menu placed before her. She ordered quickly: salad, water, no wine, no thank you.

'Well, it's not every day I get invited to lunch in the Foyer,'

Callie said smiling, but never taking her eyes off the woman opposite.

'There's always a first, I suppose.' She smiled, well, the corners of her mouth raised and she nodded at the table opposite. 'Have you been here before?' She looked disdainfully about her. 'Of course you have what a silly thing to ask.'

'I don't usually come here for lunch, so this is a bit different.' Callie wouldn't go so far as to say it was a treat, at least not until she learned why she was here.

'We can make small talk, if you like, but I have a feeling that we are similar, you and I? I think that perhaps you would prefer to cut to the chase?'

'Always,' Callie said sitting back. If she was going to be admonished for some mistake she'd made at Theme, she'd much prefer to eat her lunch alone with a decent bottle of wine all to herself.

'I hope you know that I'm not a stupid woman?' She didn't wait for an answer. 'It may seem as if I don't know what my husband gets up to, but in fact I know very well what Dennis is like. The truth is, I probably knew before you did that he would try to begin an affair with you. If anything, I can only wonder why it took so long.' She fingered a cigarette case that she had placed on the table. 'Damn Europeans, best to be shot of them I think; there was a time when you could light up a cigarette where you wanted and when you pleased,' she said then, perhaps needing a cigarette even more than Callie felt she needed a drink. 'Anyway, what's done is done and now he's moved on to you.'

'You knew?' Callie whispered. She had to let the shock

behind the words wash over her. It was enough to deal with that in her own time; for now, she needed to concentrate on the woman in front of her.

'About Dennis's philandering ways or about you in particular?'

'Well, both, I suppose…' Callie felt herself blush.

'Of course I knew. As I said, I'm not a stupid woman.'

'But why…' Of course what Callie meant to say, although she didn't have the meanness of spirit to say it, was: *What now? What should we do about this man that clearly neither of us wants to give up?*

'Oh, why do you think?' She raised heavily lashed eyes to heaven. 'Money.'

'I don't understand,' Callie said reaching forward to sip her water; it felt as if her soul was on fire. 'Money?'

'Yes, money. I have it and he doesn't. You do realise that Daddy left this company to me? If I divorce Dennis, he'll have a chunk of mine and because he's always floated about Theme, he will take a slice of that also and I don't want to share with him – and regardless of what you've done for my business, I have no intention of sharing with you either.' She smiled and Callie sensed that she wouldn't be good at sharing anything. 'No siblings you see.' She put her hands up as though to confess that Callie's assumption was correct. 'Spoiled rotten by Daddy and what can I say?' She giggled then, but still Callie couldn't warm to her.

'So, what happens now?' Callie asked, but her throat was dry, because it seemed that there was probably only one way this conversation was going to go.

'Well, that's why we're here, isn't it?' She moved her cigarette case aside while a waiter brought over a carafe and refilled two glasses of still water for them. 'To consider our options.'

It seemed to Callie that the seconds dragged on for hours and all the while the two women never took their eyes off each other.

'Do you have a proposal for me?' Callie said when the waiter left.

'Do you think I should have?'

'Well, whatever you think about my personal life, you can't argue but I've made your business a great success. My designs have put Theme on the front page of every fashion magazine worth mentioning. I have steered the company into huge profits from where it was when I began.'

'This could be true, of course, but with fashion, well, who's to say? Every dog has its day, after all, and what's considered out of date yesterday could be having a "moment" tomorrow. That's the nature of it; call it fickle, if you will.' She sneered at Callie.

'You can call it whatever you like, but spreadsheets don't lie.'

'Hmm.' Veronica raised the corners of her lips in a movement that was meant to be a smile and glanced at her watch. 'And so, here we are. You and I, the wife and the mistress, the employer and the employee. What would you do?'

'Honestly, I'd divorce him, take the hit and make sure my business thrived without him,' Callie said flatly. 'But then, I'm not you.'

'No.' Veronica sighed. 'You are not.'

'Has he said something?' It was dawning on her; this was not just about the having of an affair. Callie cast her mind back to that phone call from his secretary earlier, cancelling their meeting this week. Perhaps he had promised his wife he would not see Callie again. It could, Callie knew, be awkward between them at work if they weren't both grown-up about things. Is that what he thought? That she couldn't take the rejection without making a scene?

'What my husband says or doesn't say is of little consequence; in my experience his words are rarely honest.' There was something in her voice, something that didn't quite sit with all she'd said so far, something pitiful. For once, Callie could see the heartache she and Dennis had caused with their heedless falling in love.

'So?' Callie narrowed her eyes now, assessing this woman she felt she knew so much about, when in fact it was perfectly obvious, she hadn't the slightest measure of her.

'I can't sack you because my husband has had an affair with you.' She smiled satisfactorily. 'However, I can offer you a severance package…' Her eyes darted to Callie's and then away again.

'You're cutting me out?' Callie wasn't sure if she was speaking or not; she was far too hurt and simply too stunned to make any better answer. 'But you can't, I've already begun to design next year's collection. You can't just…'

'Oh, but I think you'll find I can. If you look at your contract carefully, everything I'm going to do in the next few weeks is perfectly legal and within my rights as an employer.' She slipped a folder from her bag across the table between them for Callie to examine. She looked about the restaurant, an expression of extreme satisfaction in her features, as if she was a proud cat stretching out, having trapped some negligible mouse. 'As you'll see, it's a more than generous severance package but...' She stopped, sat forward in her chair until Callie raised her eyes from the proposal before her. 'There is a caveat. I want you out of London; otherwise, the suggested amounts are off the table and we'll cast you off without so much as a penny.'

Fashion was fashion, but at this level, it was all about profit and loss. Veronica wanted to secure the future of Theme, and that was all she cared about. Callie couldn't think straight now. It was enough to try and get her head around Dennis's wife knowing about their affair; this was just too much on top of that, but she knew, she had to be clear about her options.

'I have spoken to my financial people about a generous package, and of course in situations of severance at this level it's not unusual to attach conditions.' She pushed the salad away. It seemed neither of them had much of an appetite today. 'We can offer you bonuses at your current level for the next three years, based on the profits we've made to date with you at the helm.'

'So, I would retain my current bonus package?' Callie kept her voice even, but she knew, under the circumstances, it really was a very generous send-off.

'Yes, I have never been an unfair employer. You would have to agree that I've always made sure people were generously rewarded if they bring in the results.'

'Of course.' That was true. Callie knew she had hammered out a lucrative contract with Theme, but it had not been difficult, and they had been happy to meet her demands in the past.

'My legal team will set out the conditions clearly for you and you would sign an agreement. It will prevent you, for an agreed number of years, from taking up employment with any of our direct competitors, nor would you in any way endeavour to damage the company by your actions or words by association. Really, after that, it would just be about all the normal confidentiality agreements that you would expect.'

'You hardly think I'm likely to go off and blab to the nearest red top, do you?' Callie hated that her voice sounded bitter, but suddenly, this conversation made her feel as though she was on the outside. Was this how it would be, when she left? Probably, but she knew there was no point fighting it. Callie, at forty years of age, had been, through her own stupidity, relegated to the status of a has-been. 'This isn't something I can decide on immediately; I will need time to think.' She kept her voice clear and even. There was a resolve in it that she didn't really feel. The truth was she didn't feel anything at all now.

'Dennis can't help you with this,' Veronica said softly and Callie couldn't detect any undercurrent in her eyes. 'There really is no alternative. Any of our competitors may welcome you with open arms, but you know how it will be: you'll be the outsider, brought into someone else's team. London may not close its doors to you, but its heart has shut tight on you already.'

'Still, I think everyone deserves a little time to let the dust settle,' Callie said tightly. The truth was, at this moment, she couldn't even hear her own thoughts. All she knew, as she left the restaurant, was that she was Callie Corrigan, sacked from her high-powered job. The sun cut brightly through a cold afternoon breeze. She turned towards the Thames. She would amble back to the office, sit for the afternoon taking in the London skyline. She had to clear her head so she could think.

11

Simon

Half past ten in the morning felt like an eminently respectable time to contact an investor. Simon smiled as he punched in the number. It was also the perfect hour to organise a lunch meeting. The fact was, he had only just rolled out of bed, but he'd planned this call the evening before. It would set off the tone of his business relationship with Gabby.

'Oh, Simon?' It was a question more than a greeting. Gabby had not expected him to call so soon, if at all. 'Lunch, how lovely,' she said then when he suggested it. It was not that he'd bottled out of putting the proposal directly to her, but rather that he sensed his chances of winning her over would be far greater if they were tête-à-tête. 'The Sea Pear – what a treat, yes, of course, I'll meet you at one.' She had hung up on their call, but there was an unmistakable girlish sound to her voice, hardly recognisable from the woman he'd known married to John all those years.

So, he'd showered and shaved, put on his best shirt and

the tweed jacket that was his standby uniform for when he needed to look great but as if he hadn't tried at all. Then he'd withdrawn a sizeable portion of his dividends, folded the bills neatly in his wallet and made his way to the Sea Pear, a little restaurant that had been the toast of Dublin for the last decade. Gabby was already there, sitting at a table in the window, checking through her phone, perhaps reading the daily paper; but she put down whatever she was browsing when he arrived.

'I'm sorry, I thought I would be here first,' he said apologetically and he checked his watch; he was running five minutes early.

'No, no, I was over this side of the city anyway and I decided to just amble in when I was finished with the accountants.'

'Oh?'

'Yes, all rather boring stuff, but taking apart a marriage is a lot less simple than John seems to think. We were married for long enough so our financial arrangements have been tangled up together. It's not as easy to untangle them as I'd hoped.'

'I'm sure you'll get there – hopefully sooner rather than later,' Simon said softly, because even though he'd never been married or even come close to having that kind of emotional attachment, he understood that she must be in considerable pain. 'Anyway, let's talk of more cheerful things than this…' he said, ordering the finest wine he could see on the menu while cringing ever so slightly at the price tag. Instead, he told her of his recent jaunt in the Caribbean on a yacht owned by a friend of a friend. He regaled her with funny stories from nights out and people they once had in common. By dessert, he was fairly sure that thoughts of John and the messy divorce that lay ahead were forgotten for at least an hour.

He drained the last of the wine between them and recognised that glassy look about her eyes that betrayed the fact that she did not have hollow legs and it had been too long since she had just let herself go and whiled away an afternoon on nothing more than idleness.

'So,' she asked eventually, 'you said you wanted to see me. I presume, there was a reason.' She was smiling, a little coquettishly, and he had to admit, it rather suited her.

'Well, I wanted to see you, because I thought on the one hand, we might have some fun...'

'And we have,' she said sipping the last of her wine.

'And there's also the question of...' He steadied his features into what he hoped appeared to be a fine balance of kindness, generosity and loyalty. 'I mentioned to you before that John wanted to join me on a new venture?' He stopped for a moment. 'It's an opportunity to get in on the ground with a company that are going to rocket. At the moment, I'm in a position to invest, but if we really want to expand, there's room for a further investment of five hundred thousand...'

'For shares?' Gabby asked, suddenly sobering up.

'Yes, shares. It's a clean investment opportunity, an injection of cash to propel the company into the global market,' he said easily, because he had learned everything there was to do with EasyTech Limited.

'I've never invested in shares before, Simon. My father was always against the idea. He called it little more than upper-crust gambling.'

'True enough, they're not for everyone and that's fine if you don't think they're for you. I just wanted to give you the opportunity before I went back to John.'

'John, my John, you mean – my ex?'

'Well yes, he's rung me again about investing and I just thought, well, having bumped into you last week, I'd rather—' he lowered his voice, smiled seductively '—well who wouldn't prefer to jump into bed with you rather than John, even if it is only in a business capacity.' He smiled then and watched Gabby blush deep purple down into her neck, but she smiled at his naughty innuendo all the same.

'And you say John actually thinks he can invest all that in...'

'EasyTech – they're a digital company. You'll see them everywhere soon. This is going to be bigger than Google.' He smiled knowingly. 'Say what you will about John, he's got his finger on the pulse this time...'

'I see,' Gabby said and sat back, thinking of the possibilities. They both knew that half a million was easily affordable to her. Gabby was sitting on four generations of shopkeepers' money and a sizeable chunk of Dublin property in some of the best locations. 'And if I take a look at this?'

'I'm here to offer you first refusal. After this I have to offer the opportunity to John – he's being rather insistent.' The words came off as apologetic, which was exactly what Simon had been hoping for. 'The thing is, I'm closing the deal at the end of this week, so I'm a little pushed on deadline.'

'Okay, well, as you know how I'm fixed, it's not going to be difficult to release that kind of money. I would wonder where John thinks he's going to lay his hands on it.'

'I think...' Simon made a show of examining his wine glass as if to cover his discomfort. 'That is, I understand he's going to borrow against an expected windfall from his divorce.'

'Is he now?' Gabby managed archly. 'In that case, I'm going to make you an offer that might be considered unfettered lunacy, but here we go. You can count me in. I'll have a half a million transferred to your account by Thursday and then you can tell John that you have a new investor.' Gabby stuck her hand out across the table; although she didn't look happy about their deal, she did have an expression of satisfaction.

'He who laughs last,' Simon murmured.

'Well, if the returns are as good on this as both you and John seem to think, I do hope we'll be laughing long past the divorce settlement,' she said, managing a contented smile. Then she raised her glass to clink on their future business partnership, but seeing it empty called across to the waitress. 'Champagne, please.' She smiled at Simon and he just hoped he had enough cash in his wallet to cover the meal, but any anxiety was tempered with the ecstasy of knowing his ship had finally come in.

12

Callie

Callie woke to the silence of Chester Square on a Saturday morning. She felt sick, as if her whole body was selling her out. It was a strange feeling, one she couldn't quite remember ever having before, and then she groaned. Her meeting with Veronica. She had tried to contact Dennis the previous day but he either did not see her messages or he had already begun the process of distancing himself from her. It seemed she was alone. She had played it over in her mind ever since and this morning she decided that she would not think of it for this whole day if she could help it.

Instead, she closed her eyes and emptied her mind before opening them once more. There was something oddly timeless about sleeping with her window open, the heavy net billowing slightly in a draught between the open bedroom door and window. She lay for almost twenty minutes, luxuriating in the liberty of ignoring her alarm clock as it ticked a gentle reminder of each passing second.

Normally, it was set to go off at six thirty. It took at least an hour to get herself ready for the day ahead. Not that she spent an hour on her appearance, but before she left the house, Callie had always caught the morning news, drank at least two cups of Barry's tea and watched the garden birds eat from the little feeders hanging from the poplar tree that dipped across the border wall from her neighbours.

Today she might take a stroll into the nearby craft market and see if there were any interesting stalls. Perhaps she'd visit an art gallery or sit in the park watching London pass her by.

Yes, she decided as she lay for one final delicious moment in her cool cotton sheets. She would have a day off, a real day off, a day of pottering about and then a jaunt about the little streets surrounding Chester Square. She would start with a lovely luxuriating bath and then have a leisurely breakfast. She would watch the robins feeding and the swallows darting in and out of the little timber gardening shed. The shed was home only to the bicycle she never used and a trunk of wool and fabric that she could neither bear to part with nor put to any use. A man named Pedro mowed and hoed the garden while Callie worked at Theme; but it was still the gardening shed as far as she was concerned.

It was the afternoon before Callie emerged onto Chester Square. Warmer now than it had been all week, she guessed it must be at least twenty-five degrees, so she'd taken down a large fedora and wore her coolest linens and darkest sunglasses. The air before her steamed so hot, it felt like all the beautiful flowers of the previous evening had been dried out of their scents. She imagined the paths beneath her feet heating up her espadrilles, so her heels itched with scratchy heat.

The craft market was a welcome oasis from the burning sun and it took some time after Callie took off her shades to adjust to the dim, cool light. Even so, the stalls were packed with ordinary wares, nothing to excite, or make her stop for more than just a glance. Sometimes she wondered, as she wandered about these places, if she wasn't trying to recapture the magic that Jack had found when he stumbled upon her homemade little stall all those years ago. It seemed like she was a different person then, the whole world opening up to her.

These last few years she had become hemmed in, even if she'd never realised it; but today, as she ambled from one stall to the next, she could sense the free spirit lingering close by that had almost slipped away. In the end, there was nothing else for it – she'd wasted almost an hour, but it felt like bubble gum to her brain, so she made her way back out to the sun once more. She turned left, up Brighton Street, and was heading home when she noticed the gallery. It was the same one where Dennis had picked up that divine painting for her – had it been a farewell present?

She cut around the jammed traffic and marched along the path. Across the road she spotted an Italian restaurant, Luigi's. God, but after yesterday, she'd be so tempted to treat herself to a plate of pasta. Perhaps in her depleted state, a large portion of carbs might be like a tonic to her empty soul. At the gallery, she pushed the glass door in and then noticed the closed sign that swung across. Inside, the lights were gently dimming. Perhaps, Callie thought, she could come back another day.

On the street, it felt as though the temperature might have dropped. For all her mooching about, she hadn't actually organised anything for an evening meal. She debated for a moment, it seemed like such a cop-out, but suddenly, she decided to give in to her yearning for carbohydrates – just about the worst sin in the world of fashion. The thought drove her across the quiet road even faster.

She pushed open the restaurant door to the strong aromas of fresh basil, garlic and pizza dough. The owner welcomed her with the genuine warmth of a neighbour who hadn't set eyes on her in weeks. She sat at a window table and placed her order while chatting to him, until a couple arrived, hot and bothered and in search of a cool corner table and a bottle of his most expensive champagne.

The owner winked at her; perhaps he knew that tonight the man planned to propose to the diminutive blonde who seemed to hang upon his every word. Callie smiled. She really had to stop deciding that she knew exactly how things were for random strangers. To take her mind off the couple, she gazed out the window.

Across the road, in the little gallery, a gorgeous young woman had emerged and was closing up for the evening. Callie watched as she carefully moved the prints back further from the window, and then pulled down a metal shutter so it dropped to her shoulder height. The place was in darkness now but from the corner of her eye, Callie caught a familiar shape approaching. Then, he was upon the girl, wrapping his hands about her eyes from behind. The girl turned and held his face within her porcelain-coloured hands before she kissed him long and hard on his mouth.

Callie felt her chest contract; there must be some mistake. It was Dennis, standing, just yards away, his body leaning in close to the girl from the gallery. It was Dennis, kissing a strange young girl full and passionately on her lips. It was *her* Dennis, wandering about the London streets with some young woman when he could have returned Callie's call and supported her in her darkest hour.

'Ah, and here we are…' A waiter stood before her, placing her main course on the table with a flourish. Callie found herself laughing. What was happening to her? It was unreal, to be sitting here on her own, watching her lover with his arms around someone else. Why was that? 'Are you all right, madam?' She had to pull herself together.

'I'm fine, it's okay.' She watched as Dennis's hands worked their way up and down the young woman's back, her face nuzzling into his neck. Then she pulled away, and Callie could see. It was painfully clear, Dennis wanted her all the more, because she pulled away and she realised, this was real. She was sitting in an Italian restaurant, a mistress watching her lover with the younger model who would soon replace her.

And then, like a coin falling down through a series of complex slots, she realised the reality of her situation. Veronica assumed that this new affair Dennis was having was with her. Somehow, she had missed a step – they all had – and Dennis was playing four miles ahead of each of them easily. *Oh, my God.* So many different thoughts and emotions flooded through her in an instant, but the most important she knew was this: she had to get out of London and she had to get out sooner rather than later. She took a deep breath. 'Perhaps it's the sun, would you mind if I had a glass of water?' Callie kept her eyes on the couple opposite and by the time she sipped the water they had wandered off into the evening.

That evening, Callie walked slowly back to Chester Square, each step measured out so she remembered to put one foot before the other. Her heart was breaking, her life falling apart, because suddenly she realised that everything she had become, her whole life, was all connected to Dennis Wade and everything she thought it to be had been thrown up in the air and it felt as if it was falling down about her ears in a million jagged pieces.

13

The Past

A low sobbing sound deep in the foliage dragged Miranda's attention away from the high chimneys overhead. Miranda was not sure at first if she had heard properly. Thinking of badgers and river rats she stepped back, carefully. At the same time her curiosity was too much for her and so she trained her eyes along the length of scrub. Buried deep, just a little to her left, she could just make out a jittering, humping darkness. She knew immediately it was human. This was no badger about to break her leg like Billy Bonner. She peered a little closer, trying hard to train her eyes so her sight could navigate from the brightness of the day, right through the darkened shadows of the undergrowth.

It took a moment and then she saw it, the flash of a familiar silver pin. She strained her eyes just a little more, almost feeling pain behind them, such was her concentration. It was her father, that hunched and broken sobbing mass – it was her father huddled into a ball and sobbing like an inconsolable infant. The silver veteran pin he always wore so proudly on his lapel catching the light occasionally as his body heaved in the otherwise gloomy darkness. Miranda stood for a moment watching him, rolling on the balls of her feet, unsure whether she should let him know she was there and perhaps offer some kind of consolation.

What could she do, she wondered – tell him everything would turn out for the best in the end, just as her mother did with her? Her mother would put her arms around Miranda if she was upset. She would draw her close and reassure her that all would be well. But the truth was, Miranda did not believe that all would be well for her father.

For a start, she had heard it whispered too often that her father was not 'right', would never be 'right' and that men like him needed to be 'watched'. There was no telling what a man with shell shock could do next; that was what Mrs Bridgestock said when they heard he would be coming back.

On the other hand, Miranda knew she could not just leave him there. She could not head off into the bright day, knowing that her father was curled up in a ball, sobbing his heart out as though for all the world his happiness was at an end.

'Father,' she whispered towards the hedge. 'Father, it's me, Miranda – come out, Father, I'll take you home.' She whispered the last part more urgently. After all, the last thing any of them would want would be to alert people that her father was even stranger than they already believed. Miranda moved a little closer to the hedge. He was within reaching distance now and she placed her hand gingerly on his bunched-up shoulder. 'Daddy, it's me, it's Miranda, come home with me now, you're not feeling well.'

Her words were soft so as not to frighten him. Sometimes, Miranda thought it was strange, but her big, strong father looked like the most frightened person in the whole world.

'Come on, Daddy, I'll take you home. Mammy will make you a lovely cup of tea and you'll feel much better in yourself.' She felt his shoulder tense beneath her hand and then, suddenly, the sobbing stopped and it seemed as if the silence was almost worse than the heart-wrenching sobs. 'It's okay, Daddy, I'll take care of you,' she was saying, hunkering closer to him, fear filling her even deeper with every moment of silence that passed from him.

And then, she felt herself flung back, away from him, so she scratched through the woody branches. She was flying through the air, the thorns and hardened ends of summer pulling at her hair and skin cattily. Miranda, while she was being propelled backwards, was not sure what was happening; then she landed on the path with a resounding, painful thud. Dazed for a moment, she sat an inelegant bundle of brown limbs stretching at odds from her cotton summer dress. Her sandal, she noticed with some remote part of her perception, had landed on the far side of the path.

Then, the hedge began to shake, as though a huge wild animal was erupting angrily within it. Far down the path behind her, Miranda thought she heard approaching footsteps, then her father emerged from the hedge, his face a distorted angry travesty of the man she believed he truly was. Suddenly, she was aware, he was charging at her, and she realised that he did not see her any more; instead, the spittle that formed about his mouth, the anger raging in his eyes, were meant for someone else. His eyes saw only some long-feared enemy on the battlefield who had reared up in his mind to be defeated once again.

Before she could move, he had swiped his large hand across her. He knocked her back onto the path and for a dazed moment, she was not sure what had happened.

'Miranda, are you all right?' Richard was running along the path towards her, bending down, trying to lift her to her feet, while her father stood, watching them with an odd mixture of calculation and fear in his eyes.

'I'm...' She had hardly stood when Richard had been pulled away from her. Her father was standing over him, his hands fixed about Richard's throat, tightening hard, holding down the breath he needed so badly to release. He was shaking him viciously, over and back, throttling the life from him as fast as he could. Still his eyes were unseeing. They only focussed on some far-off point that he had so long since extinguished it was only real in his own twisted imagination.

Miranda tried to shout, tried to plead with his now bulging eyes, but panic prevented anything more than the raging of fear and terror in the very depth of her soul. Each time she tried to put herself between them, he pushed her back. She watched, horror-filled as her father held him tighter, shaking him from side to side as though he was little more than an old rag doll. Miranda closed her eyes, tears stinging in them. There was no escaping what lay ahead, and she knew that Richard was as good as dead already and probably she after him.

Then, she felt as though she was falling, falling far down until she arrived with a painful thud. Someone had lifted her away from them, placed her on the grassy bank. Paddy

Corrigan was wrestling with her father now, his young thin arms no match for the great big man her father had become. Somehow, she would never know how, his words, soothing above the panic, seemed to reach her father. And almost as if his fingers had been eased with oil, his grip loosened on Richard, letting the boy fall like treacle to the path.

With the heavy thud of his body, it was as if whatever manic spell had overtaken them was ended. Her father pitched as if his feet would never find purchase on the earth again, then he knelt for a moment and began to sob, before stumbling away down the path towards the village.

When she opened her eyes again Paddy Corrigan was looking down on her. He had knelt down, his legs beneath her shoulders, her head cradled in his arms. He was whispering in her ear: '*Please wake up, please, please, please, wake up.*'

'It's okay, I'm all right,' she wheezed moving her hands up to her head. She could feel blood, warm and sticky in her hair from when she had hit the ground. 'I'm fine.' She looked around. 'Where's Richard?' she said now, feeling panic rise up within her.

'Oh, thank God,' he breathed. 'I really thought you were a goner.' He shook his head, only half smiling at her. He still held her head in his forearms and began to lay her gently on the grass, perhaps a little embarrassed at the proximity of her. 'He could have killed you,' Paddy said. His colour had drained to an alabaster white that Miranda supposed was corpselike. 'He's a bloody madman.' He shivered now the drama of what had just unfolded began to hit home. 'We will have to report this to the police… A man like that shouldn't be just roaming about the place, a bloody…' He stopped abruptly when he caught her eye. 'What? What is it? You're okay, aren't you?'

'Yes, I'm fine really, fine.' Miranda pulled herself up. 'Richard?' She looked across the pathway. His jacket seemed to sprawl across to cover far too much of him. It might have been just a rolled-up old piece of clothing left in the rushes and reeds. The brown tweed jacket that he was probably meant to wear on his journey back to London, lay motionless, a curled-up ball; the life shaken from it.

A dry emptiness filled her brain as though there was no room for thought or fear or conjecture. Instead she threw herself upon the jacket, except it wasn't just a jacket, it was Richard. Her lovely friend, left lying on the riverbank, his body curled up to protect himself, a useless stupid thing to do beneath the wrath of her father. For a moment, she thought they were too late.

'You saved our lives,' Richard hoarsely murmured to Paddy. It was a simple sentence, but it sent a shiver through Miranda because somehow, she had a feeling that this terrible experience had bonded all three of them, sending ripples across their futures that they couldn't begin to understand.

14

Simon

'What do you mean the company has ceased operating?' It was Simon's first phone call of the day, but he had a feeling there would be many more. EasyTech had made the financial papers this morning, but for all the wrong reasons. He was reeling. 'You can't just shut down the company...' His voice drifted across the line. They had only floated a week earlier. He had just been coming to terms with the notion of real success. He had started to swagger again, had tasted the delicious flavour of Dublin's welcoming business fraternity. The company had floated above the expected price and, overnight, he had netted a million euro. Well, he had netted a fraction of Gabby's million euros, but still it was success on the kind of scale he'd always hoped for.

'Of course we can. Don't you get it? The whole premise of EasyTech was that it would be a site where people could get all those things they couldn't get elsewhere...' Tim Salworth sighed on the other end of the line. This was his reputation too – it was his idea after all and somewhere, or somehow, it had been corrupted. 'It was naïve of us; perhaps, to think that…Anyway, the police have been very clear. We are not allowed to start up any of the systems until they give us the say-so. They believe we've been used for scamming innocent shoppers and they can't see that it's just about buying and selling.'

'Yes, and it's been doing a bomb,' Simon said, and then bit his tongue, because of course that was half the problem. 'You said… you said that it would be a superhighway where people could purchase sought-after items they couldn't just go out and buy.'

'And that's what it is; it's what it was always meant to be but…'

'Go back over it all and tell me exactly what happened.' Simon caught sight of himself in the window. He was standing, in his boxers, looking out at the street below. At eight o'clock in the morning, it was far too early for him to even think, never mind reason. He didn't normally get out of bed for another hour at least. The call when it came had woken him from a dream where he had returned to Ballycove in the most vulgarly expensive car he could get his hands on – it was one of the more delicious dreams he indulged in these days.

'Well, we weren't here at the time, but a security guard in the reception of the main building answered the door to half a dozen policemen in the middle of the night. Apparently, they had a warrant and they've just cleaned us out.'

'Can they do that?' Simon searched for the remote control to the huge flat-screen TV he'd just recently had installed on one wall of his flat. 'Really, just swoop in without a word to any of us and make off with our business…' He was talking to himself, rather than expecting any real answer from the other end of the line. The lads in EasyTech were basically a bunch of nerdy kids. They lived their whole lives before computer screens. What did they know of the real world?

He flicked on the news channel and there, in terrible Technicolor, were images that made the blood drain from his whole body. Uniformed policemen carrying out an early morning raid on a Dublin tech firm. They had little information for the general public, other than accounts being frozen and after further investigation the possibility of legal proceedings against certain unnamed criminals already known to the fraud squad. 'I will have to talk to a solicitor,' he said curtly before hanging up.

'It could be a million times worse…' Finn Delaney said. They were old friends, met on the rugby field and while Finn practised law at the bar, he was always happy to give a little free advice to his teammates. 'They could have locked you up for as long as they're going to lock up all that gear.'

'Christ, don't say that, it's bad enough,' Simon said. He'd managed to catch Finn between cases, rattling about the Four Courts; perhaps Finn was relieved to leave the place for half an hour and sit in a cosy coffee shop mulling over a dilemma that didn't directly affect him. 'I'm ruined.'

'Well, technically you're out of business, but I think it'll be a straightforward enough legal argument. If they call you, you're going to have to tell them that you're just the money man. You put your faith in the geeks and it was unfounded.' Finn shook his head at the stupidity of his friend. 'Did it not strike you as odd? The whole premise of the thing? It's like they thought they'd get away with reinventing their own Silk Road in full sight of everyone.'

'Dear God, every single penny has gone into...'

'Don't think about it. Just break the news to whatever investors you had, make a voluntary statement to the police and get out of this city as quick as you can. That's the best advice I can give you, except...'

'What? Tell me something that'll give me some hope, because at this point...' Simon felt as if he'd never been so low before in his whole life. Every single hope and dream, every single thing he owned, it was all gone. He had the clothes he was standing in, the car that was about to fall apart beneath him and a bad debt large enough to topple a Third World country hanging about his neck.

'My only other bit of advice to you is, to go and get a regular job, Simon. You've tried so many things, maybe it's time to just settle for a happy, normal life,' Finn said sadly shaking his head before making his way back to the Four Courts and Simon had a feeling of being lost forever to the world he knew. None of his friends would want to be seen with him for a very long time after this debacle.

15

Callie

'I was thinking of coming home, Mamma,' Callie explained when she rang Ballycove the following day. She had come to an agreement with Veronica: two weeks to cement things in place with a contract that suited them and not a word to be made public until at least six weeks were up. Callie had no intention of hanging about London for any longer than she needed to. Clearing out her office and a few calls to people who counted for something would take an afternoon, and then she would close the door on her time with Theme and start to focus on what might come next.

Dennis had taken off for a few days in New York. Apparently, there were buyers to schmooze and he didn't have time to do much more than ring Callie before he left. It suited Callie perfectly; obviously Veronica hadn't said a word to him and Callie certainly didn't feel she owed him anything, not even an explanation. She still wasn't ready to face him. After all, the writing was on the wall. Regardless of whether she wanted to continue their affair or not, she knew he had moved on.

And then there was Veronica; their meeting had changed things. It had given Callie a new perspective, not just on Dennis, but also on the women around him, and she realised that for too long she'd been blinded by his charm and charisma and now her blinkers were removed.

'Oh, darling, I'd love to have you here.' Miranda's voice was warm. It felt like the hug Callie so badly needed was reaching out across the Irish Sea. 'Are you sure everything is all right though?' Miranda was perceptive as always.

'Of course, everything is great. I've just got some time to take and I could do with a bit of a break from London – it's all been so hectic here of late.' Callie could hear the forced cheerfulness in her own voice, but she hoped that the miles might mask it from her mother. She'd felt sick to her bones since that meeting with Veronica, actually sick as if she might be coming down with some terrible bug – she needed fresh air, she needed home, but the last thing she wanted was to be a burden. Really it would be too much if she worried Miranda about this crossroads she was facing, especially when she knew it was all her doing that caused it.

'And you know Simon is on his way here too. It'll be marvellous to have you both here together; I'll have to get rooms aired.' Callie imagined her, ticking things off her to-do list. Miranda loved a full house; she adored it when people came to stay and was never more in her element than when she was entertaining people at her big kitchen table. It was another thing that marked mother and daughter out as being so different to Ada.

'Well, don't be going to any bother now, Mamma, I'm

well able to make my own bed up and so is Simon when it comes to it.' She tried not to sound cross, but really, she knew what her mother was like when it came to Simon: she still spoiled him like a little boy.

'No, don't worry. I'll ask Mrs Price to come up from the village. This whole house could do with a good going-over.' Miranda's voice sounded as if she was looking around her now and quite looking forward to getting to grips with a thorough spring clean.

'Don't be daft; it's only us, Mamma,' Callie said softly, but of course, she liked the idea of Mrs Price going up to Bridgestock Cottage. She had always encouraged it, especially since her mother had that turn a while back. At least with Mrs Price dropping in occasionally, the heavy work was being done without her mother feeling she had to do it. Jeanne Price cleaned for some of the other big houses in Ballycove, but Callie had a feeling that her favourite stop on her rounds was with Miranda. Often, she'd bring her son along and while Mrs Price set about cleaning the tops of kitchen presses or hoovering under the beds, her son would gather fallen leaves from the paths or fill the inglenook with logs so Miranda would not have to bring them from the shed herself.

Then they'd sit and drink tea with apple cake and talk about whatever village gossip was currently doing the rounds. It was funny, she rarely drank coffee in Ballycove; now even the smell of the stuff was making her stomach churn as if she'd become intolerant of its very aroma, never mind actually drinking it. Yes, Mrs Price was a very good idea. 'Has Simon said how long he's staying?' she asked softly. She wondered just how much he had shared with his mother about what had happened with EasyTech. Callie was only relieved she had shied away from any investment in the thing.

'Well, it's hard to say, I have a feeling he's looking for a little retreat – Dublin has been cruel; he's been through a trying time of it recently, you know.'

'Oh, yes, I know.' Callie tried not to sound weary of it, but Simon had camped on the phone for a night wheezing about how awfully things had turned out for his investor.

'There's just one small thing, Callie.' Her mother broke into her thoughts. 'Have you mentioned to Ada that you're coming to stay for a while?'

'Well, no. I only really decided today, so you're the first one I mentioned it to.' Callie closed her eyes for a moment, the reality of how her life was changing hitting her once more in a cold sweat of anxious realisation.

'It's just, I wouldn't want her to feel as though she was being hijacked, so to speak.' Miranda sighed. 'You see, I'm afraid I've upset her already...'

'Oh?' Callie might have guessed. 'What is it this time? Have you offered Anthony a job again?'

'No. No, nothing like that – it all started when we had the painters in at the mills...' Miranda began. 'I'm afraid she pushed me into voicing my concerns about the future of the mills.'

'But I thought profits were healthy last year.' Callie was bewildered.

'Oh, they were and they will be again this year. We're doing really well.'

'Then, I don't understand.'

'She wants me to step down, or at least to step aside so

she can assume the role of general manager and I told her that I'm just not ready to go yet.'

'Now I see,' Callie said and of course she did. They'd all known it for a long time. Ada had her heart set on running the mills, but anyone who knew Ada, knew she was the least suited to the role. 'You know, Mamma, no matter who takes up after you, it will be impossible to fill your boots. As they say in show business, you're a hard act to follow.'

'Ah, go on with you. We both know that there are a number of people who could do what I do and maybe better, given half a chance, but they aren't interested in coming back to the mills.' Miranda was laughing, but there was honesty to her words and Callie had a feeling that she'd spent a lot of time agonising over making a good decision on this.

'Well, let's not worry about it yet. We'll talk about it all when I get home – is that okay?' Callie said, thinking that it would provide a bit of respite from thinking of Dennis Wade and Theme and the complete mess she was leaving behind her in London. 'I'll ring Ada, let her know that I'm just coming back for a holiday, not to make a takeover bid on the mills.' The very idea, but they both knew, it was what Ada would fear.

'There's something else, she'll probably mention it to you…' Miranda's voice held a note of excitement. 'Well, it's not a big deal, really, but you know Ada.'

'Go on.' Callie was intrigued.

'I've hired someone new.'

'Well, that's hardly news.' Callie laughed. As far as she knew, Miranda had always taken on new staff without consulting anyone. Why should this be any different?

'Well, it is news, actually. It's David Blair.'

'David Blair? Why is that name so familiar?' It rattled around in the silence between them for a while.

'The Blairs owned the mills; they signed it over to your father years ago. It was a… gentleman's agreement, if you like. The Blair family left Ballycove and we haven't seen hide nor hair of them for decades.'

'Oh, well, that's nice. It's come full circle so. There's a Blair back in the mills.' Callie liked the idea of closure, as though something had been completed. It actually felt now, when she thought about it, as though some incomplete part of a puzzle had just clicked into place.

'The thing is, he's a bit of a whizz,' Miranda said softly. 'I've asked him to take on the celebrations for next year – he's a project manager, so it's probably a little basic for him but…'

'But, that's a splendid idea, isn't it?'

'Well, yes, I thought so. He hasn't actually started yet, but you know what Ada is like.' Miranda sighed now.

'I'm sorry, Mamma. It should be a relief, handing over something that would have been extra on top of everything else; really, sometimes Ada is just too much.' Callie wanted to knock some sense into her silly sister this minute.

'Well, it's still a relief. I mean, I know how Ada thinks and she'll get over David. Whether she wants to admit it or not, she's never going to make a career in party planning. She'll just have to put up with it, but for now, well she's a bit…'

'Sensitive?'

'I've never seen her as bad. Even Anthony is like a cat on hot bricks around her. He's checked in with me a few times these last few days. It's as though he suddenly realises they are married and he's actually worried about her.'

'Well, there you go, there's always an upside,' Callie said and they both giggled at that.

'You know now, anyway, if she's a bit off, or if she says something to make you feel you're not wanted…'

'Don't worry, Mamma, I'll ring her now and tread lightly with her.'

16

Miranda

Miranda felt every one of her seven decades as she got ready for work on Monday morning. Her head was spinning slightly with dizziness that could be attributed to the want of a good night's sleep more than anything else, she suspected. It seemed to Miranda that sleep was the one thing she missed from her youth. There was a time when she could fall asleep soundly and wake when she needed to. These days, she often lay awake until the early hours of the morning before her eyes drifted off into a broken, discontented slumber, and then wakening before the alarm clock had a chance to sound. It wasn't as if she spent her days lazing about either – God knows, she'd wondered often how her son-in-law was ever tired enough to go to bed.

It seemed to Miranda that Anthony had spent a lifetime sitting before the television. She had to pull herself up often, because she knew the truth of it was that Anthony had been in his way, a silent stalwart behind his wife's seeming pristine perfection. It was also Anthony who worried about and cared for her daughter Ada most. She could see that clearly from the number of calls he'd made to Miranda over the last few days.

Anyway, it was the start of a new week. She drained the last of her cup of tea before grabbing her keys and pulling the door tight behind her. Not that it was a particularly tough week ahead, but the notion of having to rub along with Ada was hardly alluring. Of course, as to the future, she would have to make some kind of decision. This had rattled about her all weekend. The truth was, she was not ready to retire, even if Ada was working herself up into a sweat about taking over. Quite simply, Miranda was not ready to let go.

'Good morning, Miranda,' Darina welcomed her with a half glance to the coffee shop when she arrived at the mills. 'You have a visitor,' she whispered, nodding over at a familiar-looking young man who was concentrating on his newspaper, demi café at his elbow.

'Oh.' It was all Miranda could manage, because it felt as though she had just glided across the decades and she was faced with Richard from all those years ago. 'Of course, David, he's here to see me?' she checked with Darina again.

'Yes, he says he can wait, but he'd like to talk to you this morning if you're free.'

'Well, of course I'm free.' Miranda smiled at her assistant, who managed her diary so there was always room to fit in something extra. 'I'll just take off my coat…' She dropped her bag and coat in her office and made her way across to the coffee shop.

'Hello,' she said taking the chair opposite him. 'You're all settled in and ready to come to work so?' She was smiling, transported by those familiar eyes to many decades earlier.

'Yes, that's right. I'm getting fed up of my own company knocking about the estate now. It's time to put my mind to something different, so I'm reporting for duty, if you'll still have me?' He shook her hand warmly.

'Of course we'll have you.' Miranda smiled. 'I've mentioned you to my daughter, but I'm afraid I'm woefully underprepared for your arrival. Perhaps we can have a chat here and in the next few days I'll get a little space cleared for you in the offices. We'll settle you in properly then.'

'Really, there's no need to go to any great bother for me. I'm used to working at a coffee shop table if I need to.' He looked about him. 'It's really very nice here, not at all what I expected.'

'Yes, I suppose it has changed a lot from the way your father might remember it. We've had to move with the times to survive, but the changes have always been sympathetic. I've tried to keep the stuff of the place the same as when your great-grandparents were here.'

'My father has talked so much about Ballycove over the years, but he said very little of the mills, so I'm afraid much of the history will be lost on me. Still, you're exactly as he described you, so it feels as if I'm returning to a place I might belong.'

'Well, that's so nice to hear,' Miranda murmured. 'Actually, it's lovely to feel that we have a Blair back in the mills again. I'm sure your father is tickled to think that you're going to organise our anniversary celebrations.'

'He was really fond of this place and of you, I think. Sometimes, when he talks about it, it's as if his heart is still here.' David shook his head and laughed – a gentle, easy sound.

'I was fond of him too,' Miranda said a little wistfully, but it was all such a long time ago now. 'Anyway, enough of the past – tell me about your plans for the Hall?' She looked at him now; it really was like looking at Richard. He had that same friendly warmth; he was a people person, used to dealing with others.

'Well, actually, I'm just going to try and secure it first. Make sure that it can be made safe and then, depending on the cost, I'll begin to renovate – no great master plan, just a dream of making things right with it.' For the first time since she'd sat opposite him, Miranda saw a little of his father's shyness.

'I see,' she said and it seemed to her that perhaps there was more that he wanted to say; after all, young men don't just get up and leave their lives behind for a nostalgic old wreck, do they? 'You're looking for an escape, I think?'

'Perhaps.' Then his face creased into an easy smile. 'My father said Ballycove would do me good, a therapy of sorts. After my marriage ended… I drifted a bit. I suppose… he was worried about me. He pulled me up in some ways, gave me a reason to stop and reassess, if you like.'

'Well, your father was right. Ballycove is the perfect place to stop and take stock. I only hope that you find everything you need here and with a little luck, you'll get to stay forever,' she said, reaching out and placing a hand on his arm warmly; then she straightened herself up a little, cleared her throat with a low cough. 'You know we can't compete with the kind of money you were earning in London?'

'I know that.' He smiled at her and she had a feeling that

they wouldn't be able to offer him a fraction of it. 'I don't need to earn so much now; my living costs are small. It's really to keep my hand in and keep my overheads covered as much as anything else,' he said.

'I can offer you a contract, to take on this project and if at the end of it you wish to remain, who knows…' Miranda had a feeling that they might share the same areas of expertise, certainly around sales and marketing, and if she was to cut back a little on the time spent at the mills, then perhaps…

'Let's see how the celebrations go first, shall we? It's a big deal and I'm very honoured to be given the opportunity to organise them. It's special too, what with my family connection to the mills.'

'Yes, it certainly is and I'd like to concentrate on marketing it well. I'd like to…' What was it she'd like to do? Go out with a bang? Finish up on a high note? Was she really thinking like this? Thinking of packing in a lifetime's worth of work at the mills, when the very idea kept her awake all weekend? But Richard Blair had retired, so maybe it was time for her to think of doing the same. Then again, Richard had a wife to spend his days with. He had a society wife called Constance. Funny how some names stick in your memory.

She smiled at how her mind wandered these days. Maybe that would have made a difference, if she still had Paddy here to pass the time with. She had a feeling that they would get along just perfectly.

'I'd be delighted to start as soon as it suits you.' He thrust his hand across the table at her and as they shook firmly, Miranda knew that she had made the right decision.

★

It was as Miranda was doing her morning walkabout on the shop floor that she noticed Ada had not turned in for work. Miranda loved this hour. It gave her a chance to chat with staff and customers alike and normally she ambled about with no particular agenda, other than to look about the mill and catch up with everyone. Normally, Ada was second to arrive, just after Miranda. Of course, Miranda herself was late this morning, so perhaps the same sense of lethargy had descended upon Ada. Miranda had a feeling her own had as much to do with their disagreement the previous week as it had to do with any sleepless nights she may wish to blame. She would ring Ada as soon as she returned to the quiet of her own office.

Ada. She would not be happy with the news that David Blair would be joining them to take on duties, but it was not to affect Ada's job, so she would just have to put up with it.

'Yes, Mother,' Ada answered, as usual on the second ring.

'Hello, Ada, I just thought I'd give you a buzz to check everything is okay,' Miranda said, keeping her voice as light as possible.

'Of course, everything is fine…'

'Oh good, I worried when you didn't come into work that maybe you weren't feeling well, but that's good. So, you're taking a little time off, are you?'

'Mother, I spoke to Darina earlier and told her that I would be late today…'

'And everything is okay?' Miranda asked.

'As I told you last week, everything is fine; I'm just out of sorts, probably coming down with something.'

'Not sleeping?'

'Among other things.' Ada sounded as though her patience was at an end, as though she was speaking to someone too tiresome for words. 'I told you about the headaches; honestly I've been chewing painkillers like they're sweeties. Don't you remember?'

'Oh, yes. Yes, of course, well take care of yourself; don't come in unless you're up to it.'

'I'll be there shortly,' Ada snapped.

Menopause, Miranda thought as she put down the phone softly. Of course, Ada was in complete denial and Miranda knew enough to realise that pointing this out would be akin to declaring World War Three. They would have to tread carefully around Ada while she was like this. Miranda remembered only too well the maelstrom of emotions she bottled up when she was at that same stage – Ada with her steely reserve would have nowhere to put all of that, so there was a very good chance she could explode if prodded at the wrong time.

Miranda chuckled; she wouldn't fancy being the doctor who told Ada to take up yoga in an attempt to deal with her hormones. Still, the conversation threw her a bit out of gear so, for the remainder of the day, it felt as though she was off balance with everything around her. In the end, just after lunch, she called through to Darina to see if there was any way she could move around a meeting she was due to have with the restaurant manager to agree menu changes. After that, there was nothing on her desk that couldn't wait until the following day, so she picked up her coat and bag and headed home.

She had a feeling that an hour or two spent in the garden

might be just enough to clear her foggy brain. She changed into old gardening trousers, pulled on an ancient gilet and set to on clearing out the weeds and tidying up the narrow pathway that snaked from the door of the cottage to the original walk-through gate. It was physical work, the kind that made her bend and stretch and warmed her up. It made her stop thinking of the mills, the anniversary, of Ada and maybe most importantly a member of the Blair family returning after all these years to Ballycove and all the memories that stirred in her.

It had thrown her, more than she cared to admit, the effect that David Blair had on her. It was, for all the world as though she was looking into his father's eyes and while that was lovely to remember, it was also unsettling. After all, Richard Blair was in the past; it was all such a long time ago. It was before she married Paddy, before she had a family of her own and of course, before she'd ever set foot in the mills. As she worked, she began to wonder if there might just be more to everyone coming home to Ballycove than a simple visit.

17

The Past

The time after that terrible day fell into a sort of melancholic haze for Miranda. Later she would realise that, as traumatic as the riverbank had been, what came next was far worse than any nightmare she had ever dreamed. They must have returned home to the cottage that night; although she couldn't remember if they'd walked back through the town, or if someone had taken them in a car. She did not remember if her mother pushed open the front door of their little cottage, or if she squirreled deep within her purse to find a key that they hardly ever used. But what came next was something she could never forget.

A small light flickered wanly from the old Sacred Heart picture above the stove, throwing a narrow hazy red about the black of the kitchen. Miranda had almost walked past the strange sight of her father's feet dangling from the attic, so deeply was she buried in what had gone before. It was her mother's screams, shrill and hysterical, that stopped her in her tracks. Miranda strained her eyes to penetrate the black to pick out his discombobulated features, grotesquely set at an odd angle against the rope. His mouth sneered down at her but his eyes were filled with pathetic vulnerability that, even then, she knew would always elicit pity in her when she remembered him long into the future.

Miranda wasn't sure what happened next, but she felt herself hauled mulishly from her frozen spot and at some point she remembered sipping sweet black tea in old Mrs Bridgestock's cottage. There was no telling if that was days later or indeed if she'd just conjured up the safest place in her imagination to hide from what life had opened up before her.

Eventually, they had gone back to the cottage and it was as if her father had been completely erased from its walls. After that day, she never came across so much as a sock belonging to him; her mother had expunged him from their lives.

People came, the tea was made and she and her mother probably went to bed. But really, it was as if they were moving through a foggy nightmare and melancholy mists shrouded them from the mundane reality of normality. They couldn't have a funeral – not a proper one at any rate. The bishop himself couldn't fix it so Harry Reilly hadn't committed the greatest mortal sin available to him. The priest was good enough to say a few words; they were not kind and they were not warm, but still his presence seemed to give her mother some consolation and perhaps it was as much as they could hope for.

She turned up for the little service, sat beside her mother in the front row, hazily aware that the wooden box before them held what remained of her stony father. Still, it wasn't real – it wasn't that she didn't understand that their lives had somehow fallen off a precipice and things would never be the same again. Their house felt as though the air had been sucked from it. Whatever constrained happiness they'd had since her father had returned had finally been quenched and even that measure could not be reignited.

Later, Miranda would hardly remember any of it, apart from being next to her mother. She would remember never letting Annie out of her sight, the hushed whispers that didn't quite make it to her ears and the endless cups of tea that seemed to be passed from one neighbour to another as though the drinking of it would somehow make things better.

At some point, Richard's parents had whisked him back to London. Even though Lady Blair tried to convince Annie and Miranda that they did not blame Harry for what had happened, there was a reticence in her manner when Miranda asked for him. It was one afternoon, when she had come to drop off a huge apple pie that she proudly said she'd made herself, that she yielded to Miranda's questions and admitted she wasn't sure if Richard would ever be back.

'My son was… understandably, shocked…' Lady Blair said.

'I'm so, so sorry,' Annie said for the umpteenth time.

'Really, Annie, I understand. There wasn't a thing any of us could have done. I know well enough; remember, I nursed men like Harry after the Great War. I knew it then, the poor man, he couldn't have helped himself if he tried. It's a measure of him, that he came back here and…'

'Some might say it was the coward's way out,' Annie said hoarsely.

'But you don't believe that, do you?' Lady Blair smiled kindly.

'No. I know well enough the man he truly was and I know that the man they sent back to me was only a shell of the one we let them have...' Annie shook her head, as if playing the whole thing over once more and still none of it made any sense.

'So, Richard may not be back next year,' Miranda echoed softly, because really, it was the only the thing that buoyed her up on those dark days: the notion that perhaps the sun would shine next year and perhaps good times were possible once more.

'I'm not sure they'll ever let him come back to Ballycove again...' Lady Blair said and there was no missing the sadness that filled those words.

And so it felt as if Miranda was mourning two deaths. The one for Richard, who would never return to Ballycove and this, once she realised the truth of it, caused her almost as much grief as mourning her father's passing. No-one mentioned her father as he had been in the end. When they spoke of him, it was as if he'd always been that young man who went to war, cheerful and responsible, and Miranda somehow never thought of him in any other way in the days that followed. She was grateful that as they sipped their tea, they all agreed that he was a good man.

Of course, they all knew, even then, he'd been broken by the war. Her mother may have remembered a good, strong man – a man worth waiting for or at least that was how it seemed. But in the end, the man who'd lashed out so violently at Richard Blair was a jaded, rootless soul with a simmering violence that stole away her only, lovely friend.

Beyond their front door was even worse, because at least at home she could be left alone to mourn and miss and mope miserably. The village felt it too. It sat on the air, like a stench of overhanging calamity, stubborn and unmovable. When they saw her coming, invariably she'd see them fix their smiles and check each sentence so as to veer on the right side of forced cheerfulness. Miranda couldn't stand it – their false optimism, the utter fruitlessness of everything about her and so she chose to withdraw from all of it.

Each night, she dreaded closing her eyes when her mother pulled closed her bedroom door. It was the same dream, over and over, walking along the sunny path, not a care in the world, except the looming hidden knowledge that everything was about to pull away from her. He would rustle in the hedge, a sleeping bear awoken from his eternal hibernation and her legs would not carry her.

In the background, far, far away, she heard Richard scream from fear-filled lungs. His words were indistinct, she saw him move about, try to get away. But the bear had tightened about his neck, a growling, sweating thing, with eyes empty to the soul. Somewhere, far off across the water, she felt she was being moved far away so all she could do was cry out helplessly and it was loud enough to wake her mother every night.

'Aye, it surely is a tragedy,' old Mrs Bridgestock said for the umpteenth time when she visited her with eggs and ham from Cleary's shop. Annie had insisted Miranda still had to visit the old lady, just to get her out of the cottage for a short time. 'But you have a duty to your mother – she's lost too much to cope with you falling down on her too. You have to pin a smile to your face when you can and let her see there's something worth going on for.'

'It's hard,' Miranda said softly.

'I imagine it's the hardest thing anyone will ever ask of you now, but…' Mrs Bridgestock's large brown eyes were full of kindness. She would not say that her mother had begun to fade away before their very eyes. She would not say that it seemed like overnight her hair had turned a grey the colour of a gun barrel. What had once fallen black and silky about her face was dried out and rigid about her head. It was not her hair or even the fact that her bones protruded through her skin in a way that reminded Miranda of the sad eyed babies on the Africa calendar; rather it was her mother's eyes that haunted her the most. Sometimes, Miranda caught her staring off into the distance and she wondered if she'd ever come back to her again.

'You need to get out and show her that life is worth living. Make up with the other girls about the village and show her that you have the capacity to be happy, even now.' She smiled then, an uncertain upturn of her lips, as though she might convince them both.' You know, if you pretend long enough, you might just fool your heart into being happy once again.'

It seemed that autumn stretched into the longest season Miranda had ever known. She settled back into school again, one eye constantly on the window, balancing her grief with memories of Richard Blair and the summer they had spent out on the boat. She wondered about him constantly. Did he think of her as often as she thought of him? Did that kiss mean anything at all, or had she just built it up into something more than it had ever been? It had been little more than a peck on the cheek, no matter how much she wanted to build it up in her imagination.

'Penny for them,' her mother said as she popped down a fat envelope from Postie Kavanagh before her one October morning. Miranda took it in her hand for just a moment; there was no mistaking the postmark. It was clear and black with the imprint of the King of England across the stamp. Her name, written with boyish neatness across the front lifted her spirits immediately. 'Richard!' she screamed with excitement before ripping open the heavy blue vellum envelope.

Inside, matching blue notepaper, three sheets in all, were folded tightly. At the top of the first one, the Blair name and address so Miranda could write back in return. Such was her excitement that she read down through the letter twice before she really understood its importance. In the end, to stop her mother asking her, she held it out and her mother read it slowly and evenly while they sat in the silence of their little cottage.

London,
4th October 1949.

Dear Miranda,

You will have to forgive me for my letter writing skills. I have only really learned to write very formal notes, thank yous and invitations, so I may wander off in my words, because there is so much to tell you and so much I want to know about.

First of all, of course, I must say how very sorry I was to hear about your father. My grandmother is awfully upset about it all. I'm sure you already know she holds herself in part responsible for the whole sorry affair. She told my father that if she hadn't insisted he come and work in the mills, well then perhaps things may not have unfolded as they did.

Now, as to my father, I'm sure Grandmother has told you what a spin he went into after it all. I've never seen him so wound up and I'm not even sure it was connected to your father's passing or my injuries. He got it into his head that I should never return to Ballycove, but of course, we both know wild horses couldn't keep me away next summer.

In the end, he has relented just a little, although he made me promise that if I was allowed to return during summer holidays, there would be no more talk of me running the mills one day or settling down in Ballycove. (As if Grandmother would trust the mills to me! I'm sure she knows all too well that I'd be far more interested in spending my days out on the boat, fishing rod in hand!)

So there it is. I'm committed to a future in a dreary bank once I've managed to get in and out of Cambridge, but that's a million years away yet and so, for now, I'm looking forward to next year and out-besting your record salmon catch this year. I warn you; I've been reading up extensively while I've been recuperating and I have every intention of purchasing some very clever bait to catch the fattest fish you've ever seen!

Well, I'd better sign off now, just to add, in case you've been at all worried about me – which of course, I wouldn't believe for a moment – I'm up and about now. Really, after all that fuss my father made, there was little more than bruises and two broken bones to contend with. Worst luck, I'm enrolled in the horrid boarding school my mother was so keen on. Between ourselves, the broken bones were far more fun!

I look forward to receiving your letters with lots of news from Ballycove and all the adventures you manage to get into while I'm not there to keep an eye on you.

Your Friend,

Richard.

Her mother finished off the letter with a smile. 'Oh dear, Lady Blair really is the kindest woman. Imagine, after all this, her feeling guilty about what happened that day...' she said sadly, then she looked down at the letter in her hand once more and brightened. 'You'll see him before you know it.'

'Well... it's a whole year away, but at least he's well enough to be back at school and he's allowed to come back to Ballycove.' Talk of the factory and taking it over, that was all just too far into the future to mean anything really. Miranda was just glad to have heard from Richard. 'I will write to him this evening, after school.'

'There's only one thing, Miranda.' Her mother had a look of devilment in her eyes that Miranda hadn't seen for far too long.

'What's that?'

'Well, you'll want to have some adventures to tell him about, won't you? You're going to have to get out there and start making them...' Her mother was nothing if not pragmatic.

18

Ada

It sounded like it might be the worst storm in years. How had she not realised that this was going to blow in across the sea? Ada pulled her scarf up closer about her neck, dug her chin into her chest and walked with even greater determination back towards her parked car. She'd been here for over two hours, walked to the end of the beach and sat looking out into the darkening sky. It was ages since she'd done that, just sat on the headland alone, watching the sea crash against the rocks below. It was funny, but sitting there, time had ebbed from her like the waves rushing from the shore. She knew that it was a slowing down; the reality was that time was slipping from her. Like the tide turning she was entering the second half of her life and all this time she had expected things to be different by now.

What had she expected? That she would be like Miranda? Well, she certainly thought she'd be running the mills. Remaining second-in-command all these years, she felt like an understudy, left too long waiting to step into the main part. Her world was turning, not just lapping in and out, but a sea change was occurring in her life and the conversation with Miranda about the future, was better than any dark cloud to alert her to the dangers of possible storms ahead at the mills. The return of Callie was just one thing too much to think about, and so, she found herself pushing her sister's impending arrival to the back of her thoughts with each considered step.

Ada felt empty, somehow, drained of fight and yet filled with emotion. That emptiness was a vulnerability that might allow the raging storms to cast her aside, blow her along the beach like tumble weed. She dug her heels in the wet ground, even harder; the wind was pushing her backwards now as she set on with even more determination. She knew she had to make it back to her car. She was beginning to descend the headland. At least on the narrow paths there was some shelter and she could move quickly between the walls of scotch grass. It would give her a chance to wipe the rain from her eyes and catch her breath before the final trek to her car across the beach.

The tide was rolling in faster than she'd ever seen it before; it roared and crashed against the jagged rocks beyond. She could hear the knocking movement of the rocks, as though they had been battered, loosening them out for the next round. It was hardly two years since a woman lost her life here. Like Ada, she had come along the beach for an afternoon stroll, perhaps lost track of time and then the weather and a quickening tide made partners to overwhelm her with a shattering wave and drag her out to sea. It took weeks to find her body.

Ada shivered at the memory of the local fishing boats,

circling the coastline for weeks on end. This beach was so pretty in summer, but locals knew too well the dangers of winter swells and stormy weather. Ada hunched for a moment at the neck of the path, a few more steps and she was down on the shingle. She took a deep breath. Perhaps this was real fear – she had a feeling that it was made worse by the anxiety that had been sitting in her stomach these past few days. She would walk quickly, with purpose, keep close to the overhanging cliffs along the way. Further down the beach, just a little way, she thought she saw the shape of someone walking. It gave her a little courage. She was not alone.

She set off on a half jog – she was no runner. Ada didn't see the point in doing any exercise beyond walking in her mid-heel pumps and taking care of her diet. It was years since she'd actually run anywhere; but today, her fear dictated her pace far more than her notions of decorum. Soon, it seemed she was catching up with the figure before her on the beach. It was a man, and Ada thought he was walking dangerously close to the waves. She assumed he was not local. She would have to warn him, she decided. The last thing she wanted was to have him on her conscience.

'Hey…' Her voice hardly penetrated the din of the storm. 'Hello, you…' she shrieked then, but he didn't turn towards her. It seemed he was ambling along, watching the waves thump ever nearer with each new swell. She would have to walk over to him. Damn it. 'Hello,' she said as she made her way across the shingle, down towards the water's edge. 'Hello…'

'Oh, hello.' He turned bright blue eyes at her and a warm smile that knew nothing of danger.

'You're not local,' she heard herself say a little stupidly.

'No. Well spotted.' He laughed now and it seemed that this place, the ruggedness and wildness of it, suited him. It tossed his dirty blonde hair about his head and scratched a healthy colour into his pale complexion. 'But I hope to be, one day,' he said then, perhaps to fill the silence between them.

'Right,' Ada said, shaking herself out, 'well, if you were, you'd know that this beach is really dangerous during a storm.' She looked out towards the waves. In the distance, she could see the lighthouses begin to fire up, their beams searching out the coastline for stray boatmen. 'Freak waves, they can drag you out. The tide comes right in.' She pointed behind her. 'You could be completely cut off in a matter of minutes.'

'So, you might have saved my life?' He was mocking her, but it was a friendly gesture.

'You could say that.' Ada wasn't great at making small talk. 'Anyway, if you have an iota of sense, you'll make your way back to where you came from and do it as far from the shoreline as you can manage it.' She began to turn, picking her way back along the shingle to the safety of the grassy ridge beneath the cliffs.

'Hang on,' he was calling after her. 'Wait for me.' Then he was beside her, matching her step for step, but she had a feeling he was much fitter than she was and could easily make it back to the road before her. 'So, you *are* local?'

'Me? Yes, born, bread and buttered here, all my life, really,' Ada said, keeping her eyes on the ground before her feet. 'My family have the mills.' She nodded towards the headland; even now, the towers shadowed against the darkening sky.

'Oh, you're one of the Corrigans,' he said as though he knew her family well. 'I met your mother today; we had coffee together. You're… Ada?'

'That's right,' she said, thinking of her mother's ability to mix and mingle as though every day was a social opportunity. 'And tell me, do you have a name?'

'Oh, sorry, yes, of course, I'm David Blair.' He stood and stuck out his hand to introduce himself. 'We're going to be working together, I think,' he said then with a friendly smile that reached to his eyes.

Ada wasn't sure if it was this news or some other communication that passed between them but it unsettled her, it distracted her so she missed her footing and tumbled when her foot became wedged between two rocks.

'Steady,' he said grabbing her before she fell. She almost keeled into him, not quite, but close enough to feel the warmth of him. It lingered just long enough to flick some primal switch within her, as if that fleeting moment might stay with her long after they had left this beach. 'Not the best walking shoes for the beach,' he joked straightening her up.

'No, well, I don't usually come here, just today, I…' She looked at him, doing her best to examine him among the swell of emotions that was battering her from the inside out. 'Well, I had a lot to think about, so…' She looked down now; she was wearing her work clothes. She did look like an oddity. She must seem like a slightly bonkers woman, out walking in her tweed suit and loafers. At least, she'd had the loafers in her car and she had discarded her dainty pumps.

'Here,' he said, 'take this.' He took his heavy wax jacket

and put it around her shoulders. It felt warm and smelled of that same musky maleness that had captivated her a moment before, even here where the sea whipped away any warmth or scent and rolled it up in salt, sand and breezy air.

'I can't take your jacket,' she began, but he patted her away, pointed to the heavy sweater he was wearing underneath.

'It's only to the end of the beach,' he said. 'Was that your car, the Mercedes?'

'Yes.' She nodded. It wasn't far away now. Then, she remembered the words that almost sent her flying. 'You said we'd be working together?' Ada stood, stock-still. For just a moment, it seemed like the storm had paused and all she could hear was the blood rushing from her head. 'Working together?'

'Yes, haven't you been talking to your mother?' he said laughing and enjoying her discomfort, it seemed. 'I'm going to be project-managing the celebrations next year to mark the anniversary of the mills.'

'Oh.' It was all Ada could manage and she didn't think she'd ever felt more relieved than when they got to the end of the beach and she could get into her car and drive away from David Blair. She flung the car into drive, jammed on the accelerator, skidding as she turned out of the little parking area. Miranda had brought the Blairs back to the mills and all Ada could think of was their conversation only a few days earlier, when she'd shrugged off Ada's offer to do that very job. It was hardly a saving bringing in some new project manager.

Of course, the thing that rattled her most was the one thing she had walked so hard along the beach to block out.

Now, the arrival of Callie seemed almost inconsequential compared to David Blair and she wasn't so sure which was worse. The notion of him taking up employment at the mills, or the electrifying effect he had on her from the moment they met. Ada had never experienced anything like it: a surge within her of giddy discomfort. He threw everything she thought she knew sideways, with his easy manner and cool blue eyes. It was only as she parked in her own driveway that she realised she was still wearing his coat.

19

The Past

And so it was, the years passed into each other and Miranda looked forward to summer eagerly when Richard Blair was sent back from London to stay with his grandparents in Blair Hall. By the time Miranda was seventeen, the young Princess Elizabeth was about to become Queen of England. Eisenhower was the president of America and every little girl wanted to be Cyd Charisse or Doris Day. It seemed like the summer would never end and Miranda spent every spare moment of it with Richard Blair. It was a summer of brown limbs and long days, of walking along the shoreline with the waves cool and soothing against her feet. Most evenings all of the other youngsters in the village arrived, hot and sticky, both restless and weary. They stretched out on the warm rocks overhanging the river, refreshed by the cooling evening air and lolling the hours away, chatting about everything and nothing, sitting on the cusp of futures that for most were mapped out years earlier.

Miranda knew she was probably luckier than many. There was no preordained plan for her. She was not expected to take over her father's fishing boat, or work in her mother's bakery or help out on a farm until some local boy proposed to her and she could then live the same life her mother lived before her. In many ways, Richard was in the same boat as the others here – he would be a banker, even if as time went on he dreamed of running the estate like his grandparents.

She looked at him now, lying out on the rock across from her, his eyes shaded from the orange evening sun. He was off to university in a few weeks' time. Miranda felt what was becoming a familiar rumble of fear within her. Ballycove was not his future. Perhaps his grandmother believed that after a successful career in London, one day he would return to take over Blair Hall and bring it back to what it once was. Perhaps she thought he would save the family's dwindling fortune, but if she did, there was no pressure put on Richard.

Of course, Richard's father was set against any talk of Ballycove. Miranda had seen him, only once over the last few years, a haughty broader version of his son. There was no missing that he disliked Ballycove intensely and perhaps Miranda even more. It was hard to reconcile father and son and Miranda, for one, was glad he didn't spend too much time about the place. Every time she remembered the way he'd greeted her last time sent a shiver through her. 'Don't take it personally, it's just his way,' Richard had said, but Miranda wondered at the kind of sentiment that could drive a man so he would deny his own son what he wanted most.

Richard looked at Miranda then, bringing her back to

the present, aware that she'd been watching him. He smiled that lazy smile that made her insides lurch. This was love, she knew it, and maybe the fact that everything had been so easy these last summers was as much as they would ever have.

'It's going to be fine,' Richard reassured her later when he walked her home. 'It's no different to me heading off to boarding school. I'll write to you every week and I'll be back again next year; that's what's going to keep me going for the next few months.' Except they both knew lots would have changed. For one thing, school was somewhere he detested, full of horrible boys and boring lessons. University was in Cambridge – a place that sounded full of possibility and adventure to Miranda. Since the war, there had been women students admitted, even if their numbers were restricted. She could already feel that he was entering into a new world that was far beyond what she was ever likely to experience.

'I know that. I'm not worried, not really. I'm happy that you're getting to do what you want. That's the main thing, isn't it?' She looked at him now, keeping her smile fixed in place to hide the apprehension. She would not be a drip, droning on about how much she was going to miss him. No, she had decided, she would write to him, as she always had, with news of home and funny stories and wait to hear all about this new world opening up for him.

'Good, because there is nothing to worry about.' He spun her round declaring, 'And before you know it, I'll be back for holidays.' He laughed then, spinning her back into his arms, and kissing her forehead before spinning her out again.

'You're crazy.' She laughed at him. 'And you can't dance, even if you think you can – you're no Fred Astaire.'

'Who wants to be Fred Astaire, when I've got my very own Margot Fonteyn right here in my arms?'

'Seriously, I hope Cambridge knocks some sense into that daft head of yours.' She giggled.

'I think that's the general idea.'

'You know what I mean,' she said, snuggling into his shirt. They spent most days and every evening they could on the riverbank. The only other pull on their attention was chores that invariably were rushed to make more time for each other. Even then, Miranda had helped out with the fencing at the Hall and more often than not, Richard ambled the scenic walk with her to Mrs Bridgestock's cottage each morning.

'I'm going to really miss you,' he said pulling her close so she could smell the heady mixture of their days together, a combination of the salty sea, soap and that special scent of him that intoxicated Miranda even more with every passing day.

'I think we both know that I'll miss you more,' she said a little sadly, because her life would change very little in the next few weeks, but his was opening up in a way she could hardly imagine.

'You could move to Cambridge. I'm sure there are jobs, things you could do. We could organise lodgings for you…' His voice trailed off, because they both knew that leaving Ballycove was as impossible for her as staying here was for him at the moment.

'Maybe, some day.' She smiled wryly, but she knew in her heart that she couldn't just up and leave her mother – there might not be much for her here, but for her mother there would be nothing at all, if she left.

'I'm going to hold you to that, unless of course I make enough money in my first year banking to give up entirely and move back to the Hall with my grandparents.' He laughed then, but she knew it was what they both wished for more than anything – they'd talked about it often enough over the years.

'Enough of this talk of leaving and what if...' She pushed him away so he stumbled and almost fell on the ground. 'Come on, if you catch me before I make it to the fence, I'll kiss you again,' she said racing off across the field with Richard at her heels. They stopped, breathless and giggling when he caught her up and kissed her.

Later, she would think it was probably the best summer ever, but it came to an end all too soon, with Richard heading off to university, and they made plans for the holidays.

Miranda jumped at the opportunity of a job in the mills when Paddy Corrigan called to her house one evening. Jobs were scare in the village – certainly, jobs for young women – and although her mother was delighted to have the extra help at home, they both knew that a few shillings extra each week would not go astray. Most of the other girls from her class had been pitched off to relatives in the north of England and one across to New York – it all sounded very exciting, but Miranda had a feeling that those girls weren't in for as much glamour as they may expect. The mills meant she could be close to her mother and even if Richard was in London, she knew that there was no place for her there. If anything, the place for both of them was here, in Ballycove, even if Edwin Blair disagreed entirely.

'You're early.' Paddy was waiting at the narrow door that led into the floor of the mills, on her first morning.

'Just trying to make a good impression,' Miranda joked but they'd known each other for years and perhaps he knew how much it meant to her to have a job in the village. She stood for a minute looking around her. This place was much bigger than she'd expected and for a moment, it almost felt as if she'd left Ballycove entirely. The mills bustled with hectic activity. Miranda had no idea what each machine did, but as she stood there that morning alongside Paddy Corrigan, taking in enormous washing vats that cast a miasma of fug about the whole building, she knew she'd never been more eager to learn about every corner of the place.

The hesitant aroma of washing wool was overtaken only by the throttle and crash of the huge looms. Finally, at the furthest end, a number of women stood measuring and cutting across a table lined with measures and nicked with false starts by huge scissors that glinted in the morning sunlight from the high windows above. Immediately, Miranda could understand how her father would have been startled here and perhaps she should have resented this place, because it could be blamed for his downfall. She sighed now, breathing in everything about the place. She was wise enough to know that the war was the only factor at fault for how things had turned out for her father.

'Come on, we'll start you over here.' Paddy looked at her now. 'Can you sew?'

'Yes, not professionally.' She shrugged her shoulders. 'But I'll give it a go.'

'Good,' he said and he led the way along by a huge loom that smelled of diesel, wax and maybe the hint of fabric burn. They rounded off, passing various familiar faces from about the village, all older men; perhaps many of them had been here on that terrible day too. Still the welcome was warm for her and it added to her feeling that she was a lucky girl to have been picked to join the workforce here. 'For today, we'll see how you go here.' He patted the back of an empty chair that had been pulled in close to a seamstress table.

'Ladies.' He smiled at Imelda Mooney and a few more girls who had been ahead of Miranda at school. 'It's Miranda's first day. Will you set her up and we'll see how she does here?' And then he was gone, back to a group of men who were huddled at the end of a machine that was halted and obviously causing them some irritation.

'Lucky you.' One of the girls leaned over. 'I'd say Paddy has his eye on you.' She smiled then and the line of girls giggled as if they'd been on markers so every movement was timed together.

'Oh, stop it. I'm sure Paddy Corrigan has eyes for nothing more than that broken machine over there,' Imelda said, but she blushed as she mentioned his name.

'I think you're right, Imelda.' Miranda slipped into her seat. 'Now, who's going to help me set up and show me what to do?'

That first day at the mills just seemed to fly by. Miranda had never known time to disappear so quickly, because it felt as if she'd only just taken her coat off when a loud siren wailed that it was time for lunch. Soon, each day was falling into the last like this and before she knew it Christmas was upon them and, even if Miranda was missing Richard, she was certainly fulfilled at work. She was fast becoming the best seamstress in the mills. Her work was neat and efficient and even if the other girls teased her about Paddy, still, the growing friendship between them all gave her an added reason for loving working in the mills.

They were having breakfast, Miranda and her mother, when she heard the post box rattle in the hall. She was first to skip out to collect whatever letters might be delivered; although, over the weeks her enthusiasm was fading with no letter from Richard in some time.

'Oh, dear,' she sighed one morning when the postman dropped only a bill through the letter box.

'No word?' her mother asked.

'No,' Miranda said and, truthfully, the fact that Richard had not written a letter in weeks was the only dark cloud on her horizon. 'Of course, I'm sure life in Cambridge must be far more exciting than here in Ballycove,' she said as she dropped into the chair at the kitchen table.

'Well, whatever about that, I'm sure he's going to be very busy.'

'No-one is that busy, Mammy.' She didn't mean to be so short with her mother, but it was what she had been thinking these last few weeks.

'Look, Miranda, you don't just go to Cambridge and expect to get by on your father's money. He'll be working hard, trying to get through examinations. He won't want to let anyone down.'

'Hmm.' Maybe her mother was right, but playing at the back of her mind was that promise Edwin Blair had extracted from his son all those years ago. She had kept that letter, had read it again, only last night. Richard's time in Ballycove would be at an end once he went to university. His father had been very clear about it. It had dawned on her a few weeks earlier: if Richard's future was being mapped out in London, perhaps it was kinder to let him go. After all, what was to be gained from writing to someone who didn't or couldn't write back? Maybe, in his own way, Richard was letting her down gently; although she couldn't believe that. Surely he felt as strongly as she did that their connection was special.

'Of course he is, he's probably up to ninety now with preparations for Christmas.' Her mother lowered her voice. 'It's a different world. I'm not sure it's one we'd ever fit into.' She squeezed her daughter's shoulder as she placed a fresh pot of tea on the table before her.

'It's probably time for me to let him go, isn't it?'

'I don't know.' Her mother sat down opposite her. 'Why not send him a Christmas card, and then if he doesn't send one back, let that be that?'

'Good idea,' Miranda said, but she didn't feel half as brave as she managed to sound and, instead, she swallowed down the immense loneliness she felt at letting Richard go, once and for all.

20

Simon

Clearly, Ada was upset when she phoned Simon that evening.

'It's as if she's in complete denial. All she can think of is the anniversary and now with hiring a project manager just to oversee it all… I'm not sure what to think.'

'Oh?' Simon's ears pricked up immediately. He was sitting in a little coffee shop, just off Grafton Street. To be honest, he'd have preferred to be drowning his sorrows in the pub, but there was no telling where that could end up. Ada was just lucky to catch him sober. It made a change from every other day since his investment shares had sunk without a trace. He'd spent too many days blind drunk, trying to forget about the mess he'd made of things. He figured at this point, he couldn't pick an area of life where he'd actually managed to make a stab at something and see it come to any kind of decent fruition.

At some point, he'd recognised that life was trickling away from him and that this latest debacle might have been his final chance for success at something worth having – even if he wasn't entirely sure what that was. He knew this much: it was the first time he'd ever felt really badly about the effect his actions had on anyone else – and that surprised him. He actually regretted getting Gabby involved and that was as big a shock as anything Ada might be able to tell him.

Simon realised he could no longer hide from the notion that he would have to actually do something about his current financial woes. To agitate him all the more, there was a niggling pain that throbbed about his temple and he had a morbid feeling that it was more than just a hangover this time. 'How's that?'

'Well, it wasn't so much in what she said as… well, actually, she did say that Callie and I would make an excellent team here… I mean, has she completely lost it? The very last person on earth I'd want to work with is Callie.' Ada sounded as though she was completely at sea, searching for something, anything to catch hold of. He could imagine her, sitting primly in her drab office, her beady eyes jumping fast from one corner to the next, catching pieces of dust and mentally ticking off the cleaners for their sloppy efforts. 'It's as if she's changed. I could hear it in her voice, see it in her eyes – she's not the same woman that we've known all our lives.'

'Perhaps she's taking stock? A heart attack, or whatever she wants to call it, well, it makes your situation all the more real – she's not a young woman, maybe she's just realising that.'

'Exactly,' Ada said tartly. 'She doesn't have forever, but now… well she won't retire and still, she seems to be running at a million miles an hour, cooking up plans behind my back and making little comments about Callie and now…'

'She can't go on forever…' Simon said gently because he knew that, as the only son, it was expected that he should be just a little more sensitive to his mother's needs. 'It's like any big life change – she's having to come to terms with things before she lets go, that's all it is… I really think you're getting worked up about nothing,' he said and instantly regretted it. They all knew that Ada hated to be reminded that she could get worked up. No-one ever referred to her big meltdown just as she was meant to be finishing college. It was years and years ago now, but at times like this, Simon couldn't help the niggling feeling that perhaps she was putting herself under too much pressure, worrying about what would happen – after all, what had she to worry about? He could put her situation in perspective in a short time, if she knew exactly what his own was like now.

'Oh, Simon. Don't be so bloody obtuse. You know well that the point here is not how long she can go on for. This isn't about mortality and you know it. It's about the mills and what her intention is after she's gone.'

'Well, surely that's up to her?' He was enjoying this, just a little; it made a pleasant change from worrying about himself. In the hierarchy of their little family, he'd always been able to prod annoyingly at his older prissy sister and that had not changed over the years – neither had his ability to take some juvenile satisfaction in it.

'Really? So it's *you too, Brutus*, is it?' Her voice was beginning to crack and it sounded as though tears were very close, which was not at all like Ada. 'Let's call it as it is, shall we?' she said, taking a deep breath. 'For all we know, our mother is on the verge of handing over the mills to God alone knows who. At least, and you mightn't be awfully keen on this, but at least if I took over, you would have your income, you might even have an increase, but with someone from outside the family…'

'You're jumping the gun by a mile, don't you think?'

'Am I? Am I really?' she shot back at him. 'Simon, you're being paid dividends to what amounts to a decent salary from the mills and your input for that is absolutely zero. Do you really think that if some hard-nosed administrator or, worse, a flashy CEO is appointed that they'll continue to let you bleed the place like that?' Then she lowered her voice so it almost contained venom. 'Do you think Callie would have the same bleeding heart that our mother has with you?'

'Well, that's all well and good, but it seems to me that crossing that bridge is a long way off yet,' Simon said a lot more confidently than he felt. If he was honest, this had always been a worry for him, nagging at the back of his mind. Usually he numbed it out with much more pleasant thoughts. But just now, his future financial survival was uppermost in his mind in ways it had never been before. 'And anyway, even if Mother did appoint some hotshot, you seem to be forgetting, we have shares in the mills. We are hardly without a voice.'

'Yes, and you seem to be forgetting that between us we hardly have forty percent. They are worthless against Callie and whoever manages to get their hands on the remainder.

'You're over-thinking things,' Simon said smoothly. His mother would never just hand over the mills to a stranger. Still, he shut his eyes tight, trying to block out the image of Callie. Callie, his clever and successful sister – the notion of her taking over the mills was unthinkable and thankfully, because of her glittering London career, it was also unlikely. Callie could see right through him, always could. The notion of her controlling the mills made his forehead throb even more. 'And anyway, it could be worse.' He almost managed cheerfulness.

'Really? I don't see how it could be any worse for me – or for you, for that matter.'

'Oh, Ada. You're blowing a tiny conversation out of all proportion. You've worked all your life in the mills, been Mother's right hand for over twenty years. Do you really think she'll forget that now? And who else is there anyway? Callie isn't going to give up her career in London and last time I was home any of the young guns in the mills hardly had a word of English for me and the old ones are almost as old as Mother.'

'Simon, you're not really that naïve, are you? All Mother has ever wanted is to keep the mills going. She never gave a damn if they were Corrigan or Blair mills – she's kept the place running out of duty for Ballycove and some long-ago promise made to our father or maybe to God himself, who knows?' Ada ended the sentence almost shouting and he heard her exhale loudly to calm herself before she went on softly. 'You need to come home, Simon.'

'Oh, really?' Simon leaned back in his chair. They'd been here before, Ada feeling just a little pushed out because Mother had a new teacher's pet. 'Well, I'm sure that if she has hired someone with the intention of giving them a senior job one day, they'll be competent at whatever job they're hired for and that will be that.'

'She's hired David Blair,' Ada said flatly and Simon felt cold sweat rivulet down his now throbbing forehead.

21

Miranda

A great storm loomed far off across the fields. Miranda knew it was futile to rake the fallen leaves as there would be a new carpet in place tomorrow to replace them, but still, there was something soothing about the growing wind in the trees. It was Miranda's mobile phone, shrilling loud and tinny in the garden room, which pulled her from thoughts of her family and the feeling that they were on the cusp of some great change. She left aside her rake, pulled off her gardening gloves as she moved and just made it before the final ring to pick up the call.

'Mum.' Simon's voice sounded frail compared to his usual carefree self.

'Simon, how lovely to hear from you – how are you?' Simon wasn't a regular caller. He could ring every other day, and then sometimes not for two or three weeks at a time. He never rang during working hours and so Miranda guessed it must be much later than she'd assumed when she heard his voice.

'Oh, I'm fine, you know. I was ringing to see how you were, actually.'

'Me? Same as always, doing a little gardening, making the most of a dry day here…' He had been due to stay with her a week ago, but somehow, days had fallen between then and now and although his room was made up, he still had not managed to make it west. There was trouble of some sort. Miranda had not asked. There was nothing new in her son's financial woes and asking was tantamount to offering to bail him out, and she had made a vow not to do that again.

'Bit early for gardening, isn't it?' She could hear the hint of laughter in his voice. 'I didn't think you normally finished in the mills for another hour or two.'

'Is it?' She pulled up her sleeve, hated in that moment that her voice sounded as though she wasn't quite sure – she sounded old, frail and uncertain of anything and maybe everything. 'Silly me, I thought it was later. You don't normally ring so early in the day either.'

'No, well…'

'Are you coming this week, then?' There was something up; she knew it as thoroughly as if he was standing before her hedging about the truth of things.

'Well, as you ask, yes, I'm hoping to leave Dublin soon and… Mother, things are not good here.' Simon's tone was a slightly nervous murmur across the miles.

'And you're coming here to lick your wounds?' Miranda did not want to sound callous, but the truth was, she didn't believe in running away from things.

'No, Mother, I'm certainly not licking wounds or anything like it. I've had a stroke of bad luck with some shares, that's all.' But there was a strain in his voice that went just a little beyond anything that could be caused by a financial loss.

'Are you sure that's all?' she asked gently. Simon had never, so far as she'd known, managed to dig a financial hole deep enough to get in trouble with the law, but now, something in his voice sent a shiver through her. There wasn't much she could do to help him, so she pushed aside that niggling fear and decided it was best to give him the benefit of the doubt.

'Yes. It's not a big deal; not really, I think I'm a bit jaded. Perhaps life in Dublin is just moving a little fast for me at the moment.'

'That's understandable, even if I never thought I'd hear you say you'd tired of the city.' Miranda laughed at this. 'It'll be nice to have you here; you know Callie is staying as well?'

'Is she really? Well, that will be cosy. It seems like a long time since we've been all under the same roof together, doesn't it?'

'Far too long,' Miranda said, trying to remember the last time.

'I'll be home on Friday night, so I should be back in Ballycove for dinner.' It would be good to have him here, Miranda thought as he hung up and suddenly, she felt her mood lift as if the clouds had been pushed back over Bridgestock Cottage.

Maybe a visit from Simon was just what she needed to take her mind off Ada – Miranda wasn't entirely sure at this stage if she was worried about her daughter or just irritated by her. Normally, when Simon arrived, they went out for lunch and generally gadded about the place as though they were both on holidays. Each of her children was so different.

God, Ada. Perhaps she should call her again, just to see how she was. Miranda stood for a moment, the phone in her hand. There would definitely be rain. She should really gather up her gardening gear before the downpour and put everything away.

As it turned out, the rain held off. Miranda rushed about storing her rake and wheelbarrow and securing the shed for a storm that might never come. She had a feeling, as she pulled the latch across on the old-fashioned gate, that her locking up was more psychological than it was anything else. She was expecting storms but they weren't of the meteorological variety.

After dinner, Miranda poured herself a small glass of sherry and took up her mobile once more, but a niggling pain in her back and down her arm was enough to alert her to the fact that the last thing she needed was adding any stress to her day from Ada. She found herself shivering and looked to the window. It was open, just a crack. She fastened it and picked up a rug to put about her shoulders. She decided she would make herself comfortable, perhaps lose herself for a short while in a book, or maybe the television. Far off, in the distance, the storm was beginning to drift in across the waves and Miranda fancied she could smell the sea air as the winds began to rattle occasionally in her chimney.

The knock on her front door startled Miranda from her thoughts. She looked at the clock that sat above the old stove in the kitchen as she made her way along the narrow hall.

'David,' she exclaimed, surprised, but delighted to see him.

'I thought I'd return the compliment,' he said holding out a bottle of port. 'Hope I'm not intruding.'

'Of course not, come in, please.' She stood back and closed the door firmly against the stormy night outside before leading him through her warm kitchen and towards the small glass and brick room that was sitting, living, dining and potting room all in one. 'This is lovely.' She looked at the bottle.

'My father likes port. He says his grandmother used to call it Irish port – with lemon, sugar and hot water.'

'Ah, yes, I'm not sure we can take credit for that, but it's certainly my favourite way to drink it too.' She held the bottle for a moment. 'I was having a sherry, but I have...' She stood back from the open cupboard and took down a bottle of Irish whiskey, which she poured into a glass for him that sat upturned on the draining board.

'Don't mind if I do, but only a very small one, because even if I'm not over the limit to drive, I don't fancy my chances in that storm.' He smiled at her as a huge roll of thunder bellowed overhead.

'You'll think I'm mad, but I was sitting out here, waiting for the storm.' They had taken an armchair each in the little living room. Miranda loved it like this, with the elements shut outside and only flickering candles to distract her from watching the lightning flash across the land ahead.

'Not at all, I'd say it's the perfect spot for a night like this.'

'Your cottage must be nice and cosy too, I'm sure, far cosier than Blair Hall ever was, well in my memory at least.' That was the truth. Even when Richard's grandparents had lived there it seemed to be a cold and unforgiving building – hardly a home at all.

'My father remembers the Hall fondly, but I must say, I really like the gate lodge.'

'Yes, well your father is looking back with the rose-tinted glasses of youth. When we were young, we didn't notice draughts or leaks or rising damp.' Miranda smiled.

'He remembers quite a lot,' David murmured. 'Sometimes, I think all his memories are from those summers he spent here in Ballycove.'

'They were happy times.'

'I've often wondered why he didn't move back here, but...'

'Oh.' Miranda shook her head a little sadly. 'Those were different times. Richard's father – your grandfather – had very fixed ideas about him working in the bank. In fairness, looking at things now, he was probably right. Any of those old houses, well, all they've done is break families. Big estates like Blair Hall, once the land was taken away, there was nothing to keep them running. Your father needed to make his way in the world and there just wasn't a living to be made at the Hall.'

'But the mills, surely he could have...' He shook his head. 'Sorry, I don't mean...'

'Nothing to be sorry for.' Miranda smiled at him. 'The mills were losing money hand over fist when your great-grandmother handed them over to Paddy. They hadn't made a profit in years, if the truth were told. Your family only kept them open to keep families in three square meals a day in Ballycove.'

'But you managed to make a go of them?'

'We did, after a lot of hard work and coming close to losing the lot at the start. We had a little luck and a lot of good will and...'

'I think you're massively underplaying your own hand in them.' He sipped his drink thoughtfully. 'People here in the village say you were the saviour of the mills and by extension the saving of Ballycove.'

'Shh, they don't really mean that.' Miranda laughed. 'You're in Ireland now; people don't generally talk such sentimental nonsense until the person is dead and buried.' They both laughed at that.

'Anyway, nothing was ever made great by one person alone. I had plenty of help.'

'You're being very modest, but since you've given me a job, I'm hardly in a position to argue with you.' He clinked her glass.

'I'm delighted to have you at the mills,' Miranda said softly. 'It's as if some crucial part of the place has finally come together.' For a moment Miranda thought she heard the thunder rumble quietly somewhere in the distance. 'It's funny, it wasn't something I ever realised was missing, but now that you're here… well, I'm glad.'

'Yes, me too,' David said softly, 'me too.' They sat in companionable silence for some time, watching the giant silver moon emerge and dip through heavy black clouds. It was a night to take stock, maybe a night to catch breath. A streak of lightning, dazzling across the land, illuminating all in its path, jolted them from their peaceful reverie.

'I think I could be really happy here,' David said once they were sitting in almost darkness again. 'You know, that's no mean feat, after the last year.'

'It's a good place to soothe the soul,' Miranda said and she knew it was the truth. There was nothing more healing than walking the land with the Atlantic Ocean blowing away your worries.

'It's funny, but I never understood the notion of *coming home* before I came here. Doesn't that sound a bit crazy, considering my life has been spent just about everywhere else?'

'Not one bit crazy at all,' Miranda said gently and she smiled when he reached out and squeezed her hand to let her know that there was some connection building between them that would go much deeper than just a professional one.

The following morning, Miranda woke with a slight headache – probably from the sherry and a gnawing pain travelling determinedly from around her ribcage from her back to her chest. It was a twinge, that was all – her body telling her she was not as young as she tried to convince herself. Miranda prided herself on her good constitution; keeping a clear head had not let her down before. Somewhere, over the last few days, she'd obviously had too much on and not taken enough time to look after herself properly.

She settled into her favourite chair, decided against the book or the television; instead, she watched as the storm rain from the previous evening washed over the land and swept down in gushing new drains towards the sea. She would spend time just looking out her window, as the morning grew bright and the winds and rain settled in around the village and back up the hills to gnarl about her cottage.

Perhaps it was more than just Ada who had upset her? It was David Blair too. She could own up to that here, in the silence of Bridgestock Cottage; not that she wasn't delighted to have him at the mills. She liked him enormously, even more than she had expected. She was truly happy about that, even if it was going to ruffle Ada's feathers even further. No, it was more the idea that she had spent an hour in the company of Richard Blair's son and it was as if she had been transported back to a different time.

Of course, it was utter madness, this harbouring of emotion for all these years. But that was what it was; she'd never truly let Richard go. She had loved Paddy – she wouldn't have married him if she hadn't felt a great deal for him – and they'd had a family together after all. They had been happy, in their way. It was a contented, settled sort of happiness, which didn't turn her head or upset her. It was peaceful and easy and had Paddy lived, Miranda was quite sure they'd have ambled along the path until the present moment.

She still missed him, sometimes. Admittedly, not as much now as she once had, but she missed his easy company and having someone there she could rely on. She had liked being married, knowing that there was always someone to turn to. She could depend on Paddy Corrigan; he was just that sort of man.

And what of Richard Blair? Well, those feelings were slightly different. Miranda was old enough and wise enough to know that there is a huge difference between first love and everlasting love. There's a gulf between infatuation and commitment. She had hardly spent a lifetime looking over her shoulder, wondering about Richard, but she would be lying to herself if she didn't admit she'd never forgotten him. She had wondered, over the years, how he had fared.

She had wondered too, if they would ever meet again and sometimes, when she allowed herself to, she played out in her imagination just what would happen if they had grasped what might have been an opportunity that day he'd returned to the mills after his grandmother's burial.

This week, looking across the table in the mill restaurant at David had somehow cast Miranda back in time. She might have been sitting opposite his father once more. There was an uncanny resemblance, even down to how he spoke and how he listened to her. It was everything from his dirty blonde hair and blue eyes to how he held his hands, like a pyramid, as he explained the finer details of his plans.

Of course, she had to offer him a place in the mills. How could she not? Even if he didn't have a set of skills that she could use, she was only too aware that the mills belonged to the Blairs once and only their generosity and honour had permitted the Corrigans to take ownership. These thoughts might have filled Miranda with regret, but she was too old now to dwell on such empty emotions. What bothered her more was the feeling of guilt that had manifested itself when she looked at him. It had been easier to cover it over when the Blairs were not around. Richard throwing her over for some society belle made it easy to forget what perhaps should have been.

Of course, the truth of Paddy's dying words still haunted her when she let her mind wander across how things might have turned out. Miranda sighed; it was all too much to think about now. The one thing she was sure about was this: she was much too old to be feeling disappointment any more.

22

Ada

Ada marched into Miranda's office the following morning. There was no point putting it off, or waiting for the right moment. She would catch her before she set off to mingle with the staff and customers. Ada had never seen the point of her mother's walkabouts. After all, the employees were doing simple jobs, most of them for many years; surely they could do what needed to be done with their eyes shut at this stage. Her mother, however, couldn't be told and Ada believed that she got a lot more out of her walk around the mills than any of the people she stood and spoke to each day.

'When were you going to tell me?' Ada closed the door behind her, to block her anger from Darina outside.

'Excuse me?' Miranda looked up from the colour charts she was studying. She looked tired, as though she hadn't slept; perhaps the storm had kept her awake too.

'Oh, don't play so innocent with me, Mother, you've hired David Blair to start here in a week's time and you didn't even think to consult me on it.'

'Actually, I rang you yesterday…' Miranda removed her glasses, folded them slowly then looked up, considering her daughter. 'You told me that you weren't feeling well enough for work so I really didn't think it was the time to go into mill business. And anyway, I have hired people before; it's never been something that I've run past you, nor…'

'This is different – you know it is.' Ada cut her off before she finished. 'This *role* that you've *created*, it's hardly like hiring serving staff or delivery boys.'

'There is no difference at all, as far as I am concerned. All of the people who work here are of equal importance to me,' Miranda said evenly.

'You know very well what I mean. The celebrations and organising them were going to be part of your role. Even I offered to help out, but no, now he will be taking over where it seemed only a few days ago the only one you considered fit for the job was Callie.'

'Yes, well, perhaps my role has to be looked at; I'm wearing far too many hats at one time. This means I can take things a little easier.'

'But that's what I've been saying all along.'

'Is it?' Miranda looked suddenly bright-eyed.

'Well yes, of course it is. I'm tired of telling you that it's time to slow down. Other people your age have retired; they are living the good life.' Ada felt herself relaxing a little; perhaps her mother was finally seeing sense.

'The good life?'

'Yes, you know, going out for day trips, tending to the garden and… taking things a little easier, smelling the roses!' Ada wasn't exactly sure what people did when they retired, but she assumed it was just more of what they already did when they weren't working.

'But I do all those things already.' Miranda sat back, assessing her now. 'And then some – I'm already living the good life.'

'Well…' Ada could feel her temper bristle again; perhaps she really was stressed, just like Tony had said this morning. 'Let's say you could do more of it, at your own pace.'

'Exactly,' Miranda had said, as though she'd just had a moment of eureka.

'Exactly,' Ada said and she tried to keep the smugness from her voice.

'That's what I thought when I hired David.' Miranda was smiling now, as though she'd trapped a fly in her web.

'But…' Ada began, 'I meant…' She was silenced.

'I know perfectly well what you meant, darling. You want me to take some of the pressure off, and I know that you'd be happy to help me out, but you have enough on your plate. David Blair could be the answer to all our prayers, don't you see?'

'No, Mother, not really,' Ada said a little flatly. Really there wasn't much point arguing with her when she was like this.

'Well, he can take on some of my work now and even when I do retire, who knows, he might be the person to take on the sales and marketing brief. Then the general manager's job will be half the size it currently is, much more doable for…' She clapped her hands as though it was all decided. Perhaps, Miranda had made up her mind when she met David Blair. There was no point arguing it. Miranda had always maintained control of all of the staffing issues in the mills. That wasn't going to change anytime soon and it certainly wasn't going to change now she'd set her heart on having David Blair here. Like it or lump it, they were stuck with him.

'So,' Ada said, dropping neatly into a chair opposite Miranda. 'He is joining us on a permanent basis?'

'I've offered him a contract; he really isn't sure what the future holds and it seemed the most sensible arrangement on both sides. I like him enormously, but who knows what the next year will hold. There isn't enough work to support him being here full-time, unless of course I decided to cut back, as you've suggested.' Miranda smiled.

'You know, Mother…' Ada heard the words before she'd even planned to say them. 'I can take on some of that brief.'

'I know you're always at hand if I need to ask and you're so good, Ada; but really, you have enough pressure as things are.'

'But that's just it, Mother – you seem to think that I'll…' Ada wasn't sure she could bring herself to say the words, but they both knew what this was about. Miranda still saw her as weak – not quite up to the job. 'It's not fair, Mother, you're judging me on what happened over twenty years ago and I'm a different person now.'

'I know that, and thank goodness you're well and healthy now; but, as I've said, I'm conscious that the financial brief is a large one and it has enough responsibility attached to it.' And there it was, Ada knew. Over twenty-five years ago, she'd fallen apart. Her final exams and it felt as if her whole world had fallen in on top of her. Tony had been there, to pull her out, but there was no denying the weeks of heavy medication, counsellors and psychiatrists it had taken to get her back to herself again.

Except of course, she wasn't. She'd never been the same girl again. Aside from a daily medication routine, her mother had been reluctant to let her off into the big bad world immediately and yes, perhaps it had been a cop-out. Ada had been grateful to return home and life had sort of rolled into something tolerable after a while. Tony, the mills, her mother, and a finely tuned cocktail of stimulants and antidepressants had all been part of the deal – a year later, by the time she'd completed her finals, it seemed the bright lights had dimmed and she'd already settled into a life that suited everyone. Ada sighed. There was no point thinking back to that time now. She'd learned the hard way that the only way to survive was to do so with efficiency and as much emotional mastery as she could muster.

'Dear God, Mother, have you not been listening to me at all?' Ada felt her blood pressure rise. 'Next you're going to be telling me that Callie is coming in to do part-time hours to help out with next year's designs.'

'I wish,' Miranda breathed. 'No, dear, I can't see Callie settling back here, can you? I think her little break here is more restorative than anything else, but...'

'I'm almost afraid to ask what you're thinking now,' Ada said flatly.

'Well, wouldn't it be the dream team to take over here, when I've retired. You and Callie, if only you could get on with her.'

'Oh, Mother, really, you seem to think I'm incapable of running the mills; you seem to constantly forget I've spent a lifetime here,' Ada said, but her mother's attention had already drifted down to the desk before her.

'Just, while you're here, I'm letting David have the old pattern room as an office for now.'

'But that's huge; it's twice the size of my cubbyhole. It'll cost a fortune to paint it and varnish those old floors. Can't he just make do with a corner in the admin office?' Ada stopped, knew she sounded as though she was just whinging and jealous.

'Ah, no. I don't think he can really work surrounded by the cackle of admiring females. He'll be in and out a bit and when he's here, he'll be making calls, drawing up plans, all of that.'

'Well, I think it's far too big for one person, especially someone who only just arrived with half a brief.'

'Yes, I know, we could probably double you both up in there if we needed...' Miranda was smiling at her now.

'You are joking, I hope,' Ada said although she wasn't much in the mood for laughing.

'Of course I am...' Miranda pushed her chair back a little from her desk, leant forward. 'So how are you? You never called me back yesterday to let me know you were feeling any better.'

'Oh, that.' It was harder to lie to her mother when she was right in front of her. 'I probably just needed to feel the wind in my hair – migraine almost certainly, nothing to worry about...'

'But you were gone all day.' Miranda's voice was clipped, a worried tone that only her daughter would recognise. 'Tony said you hadn't arrived back when I rang last night...'

'Yes, well, I fancied taking a little time to myself. It's hardly a crime. I walked along the beach.'

'In the storm?' Miranda said and, strangely enough, the one truth was the hardest to swallow.

'The storm settled in just as I was returning from the cliffs.' Ada shook her head. 'I got soaked through,' she sighed. 'That's when I ran into David Blair.'

'Ah, of course. Well, what did you think of him?'

'How do you mean?' Ada knew her mother had never particularly cared about Ada's people-judging skills. Miranda went on her own gut instinct when it came to hiring people and no-one could ever tell her that she'd got it wrong.

'Did you like him?'

'He's, well… I don't know, I suppose he's all right,' Ada said a little guiltily, because after all, he did give her his jacket while he went without and then, there was that unsettling effect he stirred up within her.

'All right?' Miranda repeated.

'Why?' Ada checked. She'd never felt so conflicted about anyone in her life. On the one hand, his effect on her was disquieting, in a pleasant if disturbing way; on the other, the last thing she wanted was for her mother to be handing any more responsibility over to a complete stranger – regardless of how attractive he may be.

'Ah no, I just wondered, that's all. I think we'll all get along famously; he could be the breath of fresh air that gives us our second wind.' Miranda was smiling at her joke, and Ada knew there was no going back now; David Blair was joining the mills and there wasn't a thing to be done about it.

Ada walked back to her office. She had taken the heavy wax jacket to work with her. Anthony had been a bit strange about it, actually. Again, today, he'd been up and cooking breakfast before she left. Something had got into him; perhaps he was watching too much *Dr Phil*. This morning he had presented her with a boiled egg and soldiers, instant coffee, and he'd sat opposite her making what she supposed was his attempt at light morning banter.

Funny, but a couple of months ago, when she'd been climbing the walls with boredom and feeling unappreciated, she'd probably have been just thrilled to have Tony fussing about her. She'd tried to prod him into being more attentive, but at the time it had completely fallen on deaf ears. That was what made his efforts now seem so pathetic; he'd finally *got* it – but perhaps it was just too late.

All those months ago, she'd made some small efforts and then given up, because really, she decided, her focus was the mills. She convinced herself that her marriage was no better or worse than any other in the village. After all, her husband was at home, not spending his days and nights in the local pub, or having affairs or giving her black eyes to hide behind oversized sunglasses. No, Tony was not a bad man, he was a good man – and she was a good woman – wasn't she? It was just that somewhere along the way their connection had frayed; perhaps the tethering rope was never a very strong one to begin. At this stage, Ada knew, it was up to her to pick up her end, because Tony was doing his best to pick up his – the question was, could she be bothered? Or was it too late to save the dying embers between them?

Ada passed by the old pattern room, her mind drifting to

David Blair, and somehow his tenancy in the office next to her faded any ambition to put things right with Anthony at this point.

Some of the storeroom men, accustomed to heavy dirty work, had taken on the job of clearing out the pattern room. Ada could hear them occasionally. Although the walls were thick between her office and the room next door, the doors were glass and the profanities that accompanied heavy lifting and dragging of old storage units were hard to miss. By the end of the first day, she felt as though she'd heard every curse under the sun. When she heard them finish up for the evening, she was relieved and decided to go and grab a cup of celebratory coffee. On her way past, she couldn't resist poking her head through the door to take a peek.

The men had worked hard; they had cleared out all the old remnants from the pattern room. Years of old cut-offs and leftovers that had been stored for no particular reason, other than there was nowhere else to put them, had been moved with only a small old-fashioned bureau left against one wall. Ada had never seen that desk before. It was miniature by today's standards, a dark heavy wood; its lid rolled down to conceal the flat writing area and no doubt pigeonhole shelving within. She ran her hand across its side, noticing a small brass plaque, almost level with the surface. The name on it was very faint, but it was there: Paddy Corrigan. This had been her father's desk, at one time. Perhaps her mother had forgotten it was here.

She opened the roller door gingerly. Ada could remember her father, quite vividly, a tall, hardworking, dark-haired man. He might have been tanned if he ever managed to get time to spend outside. Sometimes, Ada thought she could hear his voice, or at least, how she imagined he must have sounded when she was a child. Of course, he died so long ago that it was hard to pick apart the real memories from the imagined ones now.

Inside, the desk was neat and tidy. Perhaps she took after her father in some ways. An old-fashioned nib pen sat in its groove and to the left two bottles of ink and blue blotting paper. There were papers, all dated just before he died, closed up here because perhaps no-one had had the heart to look at them for so long. Ada had a feeling that her mother, in those first years after his death, was filled with a mixture of fear and grief. She had worked as hard as three or four men, rarely taking time to stop, never making time to properly grieve. No doubt, this was put aside, something she would look through, some day – when she had time.

At the top, at eye level to the writer, was a line of cubbyholes, neatly filled with the basic necessities of office work. To the left, three drawers; she opened the first two, one containing envelopes, the second headed note sheets, smaller in size than the A4 typing sheets they currently used. These were, she decided, probably just for his personal notes to send a thank you or a well wish. How quaint, she thought, holding a sheet to the light to admire the watermark. She wasn't normally a sentimental person, but there was something about this desk.

She tried the third drawer, but it was stuck or locked, she couldn't decide which. She dropped down before it now, determined to see what it contained. She tried forcing it, but Ada was not a strong woman. She had a girlish shape and strength to match. Outside, in the hallway, she heard footsteps come towards the open door. Perhaps the men would help her open it. It was only old Bert, the janitor who was hardly any stronger than herself.

'Oh, Bert,' she called after him. 'Come here – do you know if there is a key to this desk?'

'Why, that's…' he stroked his chin '…that's your father's desk. I had forgotten it was ever here.' He shook his head now. Bert and her father would have been of similar age. Bert had been here as long as Miranda and was even more reluctant to leave.

'Yes. Yes, it is. I think we all forgot it was here.' She looked at it now, felt an overwhelming sense of ownership of it. 'I think, if you can organise it tomorrow when the men return, I would like it moved to my office and a key organised for the locked drawers.'

'Well, if it's…' He pulled his eyes away from the desk, meeting hers and thinking for a moment. Perhaps he knew Miranda had not wanted it. It had been left here for almost forty years, forgotten about.

'Surely it is better in my office than to be hidden away for another decade, Bert.'

'Of course,' he said, clearing his throat. 'I'll ask the men to move it over first thing.' He bent down now, looked at the locked drawer. I don't remember ever seeing a key that might fit that. I can have a mooch about, but…' He shook his head. 'It could take a few weeks to get a new key made, and they have to be sent over from the factory in England.'

'That's fine,' Ada said nodding at him that he could go on his way. She stood for another moment in the room that was to become David Blair's office. There was no doubting it was going to be a huge space, with the right colours and some office furniture it would be fit for a CEO, never mind a glorified party planner. That thought sent a shiver through Ada and she closed the door with a slightly louder bang than needed.

23

The Past

At Christmas, with the paths icy and her breath a foggy blast on the rigid cold air, Miranda was making her way back from early mass when she heard the news. Her mother was walking along beside her, gingerly clinging to the railings for fear she'd slip on the treacherous frosty ground. The Blairs were in mourning with Richard's grandfather, on his mother's side, having passed away the night before. It came just a week after the passing of dear old Mrs Bridgestock, who to Miranda had been as good if not better than any grandparent.

'I suppose the mills will close for a day extra now,' her mother said solemnly when Mrs Ryan had carried on to the next people she could pass the news along to.

'I don't know – I suppose that'll be down to Paddy Corrigan and even more down to the Blairs if he can track them down now.'

'Ah, you know, I still miss Lady Blair,' her mother said wistfully. The Blairs had moved to England a year earlier, closing up the Hall and leaving the mills in Paddy Corrigan's hands to keep the cogs turning and perhaps make a profit if he could. Annie often talked about the family and the kindness they had shown, even if it had turned to tragedy in the end. The Christmas card that arrived that year with an English stamp took pride of place on the mantel and Miranda supposed that if she didn't take it down herself at the end of the Christmas holidays it might still be sitting there the following year. 'And young Richard of course…' She let the words drift. Annie mentioned him less often these days. There was no point in asking if she had any news, because they both knew that no letters had arrived in ages.

'Well, I suspect he's not missing me very much,' Miranda said far more lightly than she felt.

'He might think the same of you…' her mother said. Miranda knew that Richard had graduated just a few months earlier. Really there was nothing to keep him from coming back to Ballycove now – nothing except perhaps the fabulous life he was probably living in London or Cambridge. 'Come on.' They had reached the end of their row of cottages. 'I'm looking forward to breakfast…' She smiled then. They had been fasting since the night before and they were both famished.

Inside the little cottage the aroma of a hefty chicken was hanging on the air while they settled at the kitchen table. Miranda placed the teapot and a quarter of brown soda bread she'd made the previous day on a gaily patterned plate, while her mother busied herself checking the oven on the old stove and rubbing condensation from the frozen windows. Just as they were about to pour the tea a knock on the door broke into their relaxed breakfast.

'Not to worry, I'll answer it,' Miranda said getting up from the table. It was a day too early for the wren boys. As likely as not, it was one of the youngsters down the road arriving to show off the contents of a Christmas stocking too splendid not to share. 'Oh, it's you...' Miranda said when she saw Paddy standing on the doorstep.

'Don't look too pleased, will you,' he joked.

'Who is it?' Annie called out from the kitchen.

'It's Paddy – Paddy Corrigan,' Miranda replied.

'Well, bring the lad in – he's just in time for a cup of tea,' Annie said warmly.

'Don't mind if I do.' Paddy edged past the suspicious Miranda. After all, he had a bit of cheek showing up here on her day off, on Christmas Day too – which seemed even more of a nerve. 'Thanks very much, Mrs Reilly,' he said seating himself in Miranda's chair and holding out her mug before Annie filled it for him. Miranda took down a fresh mug and plopped into the chair at the end of the little table that had only ever been her father's.

'Well, what has you out and about on Christmas morning? Not looking for my Miranda to go into work on the holiest day of the year, I hope.' Her mother eyed him over the spectacles she always wore these days.

'Oh, no. Far from it, Mrs Reilly.' He buttered a slab of the brown soda and sunk his teeth into it happily. 'No, the only reason I came knocking on your door today was because I thought it might be urgent.'

'Well, it's always nice to see you, Paddy, whatever about the urgency,' her mother said, looking pointedly at Miranda. It was no secret in this house that Annie thought Miranda could do a lot worse than end up with Paddy Corrigan now that Richard had slipped off the horizon. She was convinced Paddy had an eye on her daughter and as far as she was concerned there wasn't a man in the village to touch him for a mile when it came to making a go of things.

'That's very nice of you to say so.' He held out the slice of brown bread in his hand, inspecting it as if it was a rare treat. 'I think this has to be the best bread west of the River Shannon,' he said appreciatively before popping the final corner of it in his mouth with gusto.

'Well there's plenty in it – help yourself.' Miranda got up and walked to the little larder, taking out the remainder of the loaf and putting it down in front of him.

'She makes it herself,' Annie said as though it was some great secret.

'You don't? Do you?' Paddy looked at Miranda with a new-found keen interest. 'Well, it's prize winning, that's what it is, prize winning.'

'So, what brings you to visit us on this Christmas morning?' Miranda asked, silently cursing the light blush that had risen to her cheeks.

'Ah.' Paddy reached inside his heavy overcoat and pulled out a long slim envelope. 'This morning Mrs Cullen arrived at my door with an urgent telegram that arrived early in the day. No doubt ye've heard all about the passing of Master Edwin's father-in-law in London.'

'Yes, of course, we heard it on our way from mass – poor Lady Blair, such a lot of tragedy.'

'From what I could gather, the old man was well into his nineties, so hardly unexpected...' Paddy said gently, 'but...'

'There wasn't post today, surely?' Miranda leaned forward; any mention of the Blairs always held her attention.

'No, but when Mrs Cullen was coming out of the side door of the post office, she saw this envelope. She said she was very sorry, but it must have slipped out of the postman's bag a while ago.' He held the envelope forward for Mrs Reilly to inspect.

'Ah, it's for me.' Annie Reilly held the envelope as if it was a prize possession, stared at it for a long while before looking across at Paddy for some further explanation. Then she looked towards the mantel. 'Well, it can't be a Christmas card, because that's arrived already.' But sure enough, at the back of the envelope the return address had been embossed in the Blair coat of arms. She ripped it open with an excited jerk. There had never been bad news from the Blairs – no reason to think there might be now. Unfolding the letter, she pushed her spectacles just a little higher on her nose. 'Oh…' was the only sound to leave her lips then she folded up the letter reverently, placing it on the table before her. When she looked up there were two sets of enquiring eyes watching her. 'It's… well, it's nothing to concern ourselves with today…' She managed a watery smile and reached for her mug of tea.

'You can't just say that, Mother.' Miranda was gagging with curiosity but her mother's glance told her to stop before she went on.

'It's just really a letter from woman to woman telling me about her life with his Lordship now… nothing of any great note,' she murmured and took the letter from the table, folding it safely away in the pocket of her cardigan. They sat for a short time longer, making awkward small talk before Annie said she might just go for a lie-down. 'Why don't you two go out for a bit of a walk together – it might be nice on Christmas morning, Miranda, and you know I have no intention of leaving the house for the rest of the day on those icy paths.'

'Right,' Paddy said, buttoning up his coat ready to escort Miranda on a walk about the village.

'Ah, no, sure I've the dinner to see to and all of that here…' Miranda said uncertainly, but the truth was, there was a change in her mother and she had no intention of going out the door and leaving her here on her own.

'Well, perhaps another time,' Paddy said. 'They'll be expecting me back too. My father's not as young as he used to be and I promised I'd clear away the paths around the house for him before the dinner.' He smiled then at Annie. 'You have me well set up for that with your strong tea and Miranda's lovely brown bread.'

Miranda walked him to the door and stood for a moment before she let him out. 'Thanks for bringing over that letter, Paddy; even if it is a bit of a mystery, it was kind of you to make the journey especially.'

'Sure, Miranda, that was no hardship. I was only delighted to see you and your mother for the minute. She's a lovely woman, your mother, generous to a fault,' he said then before skipping off down the street – no fear of Paddy Corrigan slipping on the ice, he moved much too fast for that. When Miranda arrived back into the kitchen her mother stood at the fireplace, the letter lying open on the table.

'He's gone, is he?' Annie said, but her voice sounded like an echo, far off and strangling in her throat. 'You'd better read that letter, child. It's not good news, but you're better to know, especially as its old news from the date on that postmark.'

Miranda took the letter in her hand and let herself gently into her mother's comfortable chair as she read.

> *The Long Acres,*
> *Cotswolds.*
> *November 1954.*

Dearest Mrs Reilly,

My apologies in advance for this note – it is with a heavy heart that I have to tell you this news. I know that you and I had harboured hopes of some future union between my grandson Richard and your lovely daughter Miranda.

Today, Edwin shared with me some news, which I suppose I should greet with enthusiasm at the very least, and perhaps, when time allows us the comfort of hindsight possibly, we'll both be happy with this turn of events.

Richard has met a girl. It sounds as if they are considering becoming engaged this Christmas. Certainly, my understanding is that promises have been made and I'm quite certain that this information has not been shared with Miranda. I thought it kinder if it came from you, rather than have her hopes dashed in some public and humiliating fashion. The girl is much too good for that.

I don't suppose there is much use in supplying you with more information, even if I had it to share, but there is one message I would like passed along. Whatever or whoever has turned Richard's head in Cambridge, there is no doubt in my mind that he truly loved Miranda.

I wish you both well and hope that this news comes at a time when Miranda has met someone who will make her every bit as happy as she so wholly deserves.
Yours Truly,
Esme Blair.

The disappointment grew to despondency, a heaviness that weighed her down and was made worse because there had never been a final word. It felt as though someone had thumped her in the chest, knocked the air from her lungs. She managed, although there were a million more questions she wanted to ask, like who or how and maybe, most unreasonably, why? There had been no explanation, not even a good luck in your future letter to finish things between them properly.

Miranda was heartbroken; there was no easy way around it and so when Paddy Corrigan asked if she'd like to go here or there with him, she turned him down every time. The seasons seemed to run into each other and Miranda slipped into working in the mills and not much more could take her from the house apart from mass, even dear old Mrs Bridgestock was no longer alive to pull her from her melancholy.

After a time, the mills began to take her mind off Richard and how their lives had spun away from each other. Before too long, she had fallen in with a gang of girls who cajoled her out to dances and made her laugh once more. When they offered her a place in the flat they shared attached to the mill, she was happy to move in with them. It seemed as if she was finally growing up and having fun again. On the evening that she moved in, she swore that would be the last of pining for Richard Blair. Flora and Imelda worked either side of her on a long machine that some of the stronger lads fed with coarse wool on one end and more unloaded it as a fine fabric on the other.

'I'm telling you; Paddy has his eye on you,' Imelda Mooney whispered to her one day.

'He has not,' Miranda said defensively, but she knew only too well he had. Hardly a day passed by that he didn't make it his business to stand next to her and make some attempt at small talk. Once he asked her to the pictures, but she had been able to cry off with the excuse of bringing her mother to the vigil mass.

'He has too,' Flora said then. 'You could do worse, you know. My father says, Paddy could be Ballycove's first millionaire, yet.'

'He probably could be,' Miranda agreed, keeping her eyes on her work. 'If he's that much of a catch, you'd better get in there quick the pair of you.' She laughed then, but the truth was, Miranda had believed for a quite some time that the only boy for her was Richard. Anyone else seemed to be unthinkable to her, even if clearly she would not be Lady Blair one day.

'Come on, there's a gang of us heading into Dublin on Saturday – say you'll come. We've got tickets to the boxing match. What are you going to be doing here when everyone is out having fun?' There was great excitement in the factory. Somehow, Paddy managed to get a dozen tickets to see a big boxing match in the city.

'I've never watched a fight in my life.' Miranda laughed, but Flora nudged her. The girls were dying to get to Dublin for the night. 'Okay, so, sure, it might be fun,' she said although she had a feeling she wouldn't enjoy it.

'Right, we'll take the van from the mills and leave here in the morning. That'll give us time for a look around the city and then get to the fight,' Paddy said, and there was something about him in that moment. Miranda could see why all the other girls fancied him, even if he still couldn't hold a candle to Richard Blair for her.

'You have to forget about Richard,' Flora said to her later. 'Paddy Corrigan is mad about you and you don't want to let him slip through your fingers. You can't spend your life thinking of Richard Blair – he's engaged or maybe even married at this stage, for all you know.' It was true. They were working in the Blair family mills, but it was as though Paddy owned them. There was never any sign of the family about. Blair Hall was abandoned and they hadn't been seen about the village for years. 'It's time to start living, properly.'

'I know, but…' Miranda looked away. This was breaking her heart, but Flora was her best friend and she knew how to keep a secret. 'I love Richard, have done for years – it's not that easy, just to let him go.'

'Maybe that's all you can do, Miranda. He's not coming back to you. I'm sorry, but I care about you and I want you to have a good life and from where I'm standing, Paddy Corrigan can give you the best life around this village.'

'Maybe you're right.' Miranda smiled, but it was half-hearted. It was funny though, as the weeks marched on and Paddy organised more outings for what was becoming a gang of friends, Miranda grew fonder of him almost in spite of herself. She could see he had a generous heart. He was funny and he was attractive, better looking than any other boy in the village. A sprinkling of power and persuasion all helped him too. Once she agreed to forget about Richard and let him go, it was as though her heart was finally letting in someone else and accepting that there may just be another man out there for her.

'I was thinking,' he said to her one night as they watched the moon roll in and out of smoky clouds. A group of them had decided to walk along the riverbank after they left the local pub. 'Would you come to the Christmas Hunt Ball with me?' He didn't meet her eyes, perhaps afraid that once more she'd knock him back.

'I didn't know you hunted?' She rounded on him. Paddy had really lost the run of himself if he was knocking about with the country set.

'Don't be daft, of course I don't hunt. I've been invited to come along because of the mills. Mrs Blair always puts a few pounds the way of the Hunt, just to pay for drinks and whatever, so this year they asked if I'd…'

'Oh?' Miranda said. It was funny, but she never really considered the fact that Paddy was almost like the last relic of the Blairs in Ballycove.

'Don't look so surprised, I'm not a complete yokel. I can hold my own with any of the horsey set.' He looked out across the river, perhaps aware that her hesitation had as much to do with Richard and his family as it had any real interest in him. He lowered his voice then, but it still held that familiar note of kindness. 'You know…' He stopped, looked into her eyes for a moment, and she could see that he was filled with mixed emotions, torn between wanting her and maybe something else that she couldn't put her finger on. 'You know that Richard has a new girl over in London.' He said the words slowly, gently; perhaps aware of how much they might really hurt.

'Yes,' she said and she thought the sound echoed off the sea. 'Yes, I did know.'

'She's called Constance – sounds posh, doesn't it? Her father owns the firm Richard worked in for the summer. It's a different world to Ballycove, Miranda.'

'I see,' Miranda said, although, with the rising lump in her throat and scorching sensation of tears behind her eyes, she could hardly see in front of her, never mind take in this shattering additional news. 'Oh well, it wasn't as though there were any promises between Richard and me,' she managed after a minute.

'I'm glad. So, it doesn't upset you too much?' He was watching her now in the darkness and she could feel something solicitous in his eyes. He didn't want her to be hurt, perhaps that was why he was telling her here, in the shadows with the others far enough away not to hear his words.

'Oh, it's hardly a surprise,' Miranda said with more bravado than she felt. 'I haven't exactly been staying at home waiting for him either, have I?' she said in a voice that didn't sound much like her own.

'No?' It was a question more than any kind of agreement.

'Well, I'm out here walking along the river in the moonlight with you tonight, amn't I?' she said gently.

'That's true,' Paddy said and they walked on in silence for a while. 'You know, I'd love to take you out on your own, some night...' He let the words slip between them.

Perhaps the hunt ball wasn't as important as just spending time with her.

'Well, maybe, in a few weeks, when things aren't so busy…' Miranda said; of course, what she meant was, when her heart stopped feeling as though it had been broken in half.

It took months for Paddy Corrigan to convince Miranda to go to a dance with him. In the end, she went as much out of exhaustion at turning him down as because she could no longer find a good enough reason for not going. Soon enough, they were walking out together and within the year, they were, as far as most of Ballycove was concerned, going steady.

'So, then, tell me, where are you bringing me?' she asked him as they bumped along the dark country roads south of Ballycove. She had come to look forward to these adventures with him. They could end up anywhere from a picnic on the river bank to delivering an order that had been forgotten and stopping off in a quiet pub along the way.

'Well, let's just say it's a surprise,' Paddy said and he smiled at her. It was a dark November night and Miranda had dressed to go dancing, with her heaviest coat around her shoulders to keep the frosty night cold from biting into her. They pulled up to a little closed-up railway station where the wind howled along the tracks, and cut icy into Miranda's legs when she stood on the platform.

'You're bringing me for a train ride?' she said a little nervously, because she really didn't know what to expect next.

'No.' Paddy turned to face her. 'No, but I wanted to take you here to talk to you. Miranda, I know your heart was broken.' He smiled his most endearing smile to stop her denying it. 'I know you loved Richard and that you can't see

how you'll make room for me in your heart.' He held up his
hands to stop her protests. 'But the truth is, you know, I've
always been very fond of you. I wouldn't want to see you
hurt and that's what would have happened if you'd ended
up with Richard.'

'Oh, Paddy, come on, we're meant to be having fun,' she
said, trying to lighten his mood.

'And we will, don't you fret, but I wanted to bring you
here because I wanted you to know that a couple of years
ago, when you hardly knew I was alive, I came here with
my bags and all the money I had to my name. I was going
to catch a train and take myself far away from here. I had
it all planned out. I would go, make a packet of money and
become a very rich man. Maybe, one day, I'd come back
and buy up the Blair place and the mills too. I hoped...' He
stopped a moment, picking his words. 'I hoped then, that
maybe you'd notice me.'

'Oh, Paddy.' Miranda was touched, as much by the
hoarse honesty in his voice as by the notion that anyone
could like her so much and she hadn't even realised. 'Well, if
it's any consolation, the women would be lining up for you
now...' she said laughing.

'Maybe, but that's because they think I'm going to be
someone, a big shot. Whereas you...' He scratched his head,
as though he was trying to figure something out. 'I have a
feeling that all the money in the world isn't going to sway
you, Miranda.'

'I'm afraid you're right,' she said softly.

'But, if you could feel for me, even half of what I feel for
you, I think that I could be the richest man in Ballycove,
even if I never had a penny.'

'Oh, Paddy, that's such a thing to say.' She shook her head and felt her heart soften even more towards this lovely young man.

'The thing is…' He dropped to an old wooden bench and pulled her down opposite him, taking her hands in his. 'The thing is…' He cleared his throat and looked down along the railway tracks. 'I'm very glad I didn't get on that train. I'm glad because here we are together, you and I.'

'I'm hardly the reason you've made the leaps you have though, Paddy.' Miranda knew he had come from so little, but now, he walked about Ballycove and he was a success by anyone's measure in the little village.

'No, but the truth is, Miranda, I'm on the cusp of something much bigger and I want you with me for it.'

'I…'

'No, don't say anything until you've heard what I have to say.' He let her hands go, took his scarf from about his neck and tucked her hands inside to keep her warm. 'The Blairs have offered me a share in the mills. I can run it as I see fit. I'll be my own boss, with no-one to answer to and a good share of the profits for my wages.' He exhaled and it was a sound of relief mixed with bridled joy.

'They're just giving them to you, just like that?'

'Well, no, not exactly. You see, over the years, we've come to an understanding. I've kept the mills ticking over, kept the family going with a small income, but things are changing for them now. Lord Blair is getting older. The health problems he had when he was here have only got worse and he will never improve, and I think they want to set things straight in some way.'

'Oh?' Miranda acknowledged, although she wasn't exactly sure what that meant.

'The mills are just about breaking even. They're giving a small income, but most importantly they're giving work to half the village. Lady Blair very much wants that to continue, but she and her husband are in financial dire straits and they seem to think the only way out of them is to get out of Ballycove as quickly as they can.' Paddy looked into Miranda's eyes. 'I could buy the mills from them, but I'd never raise the finance to meet the market value, so they've offered me a share if I continue to pay them a portion of the profits each year.'

'And she chose you?'

'Yes.'

'Of course she would, I mean if anyone can make a go of them…'

'There's that, but I think Lady Blair has always felt that there was an outstanding debt, since that day on the riverbank when…'

'You saved Richard's life?' Mostly, Miranda tried not to think of that terrible day, but there was no getting away from the fact that if Paddy had not arrived when he did, there was every chance her father might have killed Richard before her very eyes.

'I wouldn't go that far, but… well, she was very grateful.'

'That sounds very generous and I think they are making a wise choice, whatever her reasons.' Miranda heard her own voice drift away from her now, but there were so many other realities beginning to fall down around her. The Blairs were leaving Ballycove for good. Richard had moved on – perhaps he was already married? Certainly, from the sound of things, he would not be returning to Ballycove anytime soon, not for Blair Hall and not for Miranda.

'Well, yes, I suppose it is. To be honest it probably has something to do with the Blair lands and the tax man as much as it does with any deep relationship I've established with them. They are just glad, I think, to be able to walk away and see the place remain open and giving employment to the locals. Whatever income I can generate is only a mild possibility as far as they are concerned now.' He smiled then, a thoughtful look in his eyes. 'The thing is, Miranda, I think I can really make a go of it.'

'So, it's good news for everyone, really,' Miranda said. She hoped she didn't sound resigned, because it really was good news. 'I'm happy for you, Paddy. You have worked hard and I know it's well deserved. So, you think you will be able to make it more profitable than it has been?' It seemed a bit of an uphill battle if they hadn't turned over a profit in decades.

'Of course, I can make it profitable,' he said laughing now. 'The thing is.' He dropped down on bended knee, pulled a small heart-shaped box from his coat pocket. 'The thing is, I'd like you to be by my side when I'm doing it...' He opened the box and inside sat the daintiest diamond cluster ring Miranda had ever seen.

'Oh,' Miranda exclaimed. 'Oh, Paddy, I'm not sure I... that is, I never expected it, it's very...' Soon, she was about to say. It was very soon, but the truth was, they'd been walking out together for a full year and even if she hadn't expected it, she knew most of the village did.

'I know. It's a bit of a surprise, but I thought, with everything else that's going to happen and now, well, there's no reason to hold back.' His eyes were full of hope, but there was no mistaking that for anything near surety. He really did not know if she would say yes, or if she would turn him down. 'Here, try it on, at least,' he said and he took the ring from its box and placed it on her finger. 'I spoke to your mother earlier this week, Miranda. She'd be so happy if we made a go of things.' He was smiling, a little more nervously now.

'I…' Miranda admired the ring on her finger. *Really,* she thought, *really, what am I waiting for? Richard Blair has gone off and forgotten about me. He has probably already married his Constance.* And for all she knew he could have started a family too. There was no-one else in the village she could imagine marrying and she did love Paddy, differently to the way she'd fallen for Richard, but he had qualities she hugely admired. He spoiled her, treated her, he was kind and he made her laugh – most important, she knew where she was with him and he made her feel like the world was a safe place whenever he was near.

24

Simon

Dublin had descended into days of squally showers and Simon rather liked the idea that the city was depressed alongside him. It almost felt as if even the weather understood there was no point putting out anything better than its worst. The forecast was for light wind and warm sunshine in the west, so it seemed to his downcast mind that he didn't belong there just yet. Really, he knew that leaving the city was a much bigger step than sitting in his old banger and driving west. It was this understanding that fed his reluctance to just pack up and go.

He had asked everyone he could think of to see if he could perhaps get a tenant for his flat. At least that would free up a little pin money. Rents in Dublin were astronomical at this stage and he'd been lucky with this place, picking it up for a song from one of his friends who wanted to offload quickly before heading to start a new life in San Francisco. It was a tiny flat, but in a substantial old building and the postcode was the very best in the city centre. He counted as his neighbours a senator, a rock star and more international businessmen than he could possibly number. Of course, they owned complete five-storey grand residences, while Simon lived in a cramped coach house that emptied him into a back lane, rather than onto the pristine Georgian square of his more distinguished neighbours.

The flat looked rather sad now, since he'd boxed up almost everything worth selling and let it go to one of the nearby charity shops. All he would take were his clothes, and anything else he wanted to keep safe he stored in the low attic over the main living area of the little flat. Soon it would be time to let the new tenant take possession and Simon, while he'd spent most of his time here yearning for something better, something bigger, something more ostentatious, felt a nostalgic melancholy at the notion of leaving his little corner of Dublin behind.

'Come on, old boy, it can be your farewell.' Hughie, one of his oldest friends was throwing a dinner party. 'You can't just slink away to the country for who knows how long and not have a little bash before you go.'

'Hughie, I've never been less in the humour to party,' Simon said sadly. He'd already asked Hughie for a sum to ease the burden of the loss, but Hughie's money was all tied up in his father's estate. There would be no more cash until the old man was gone and then Hughie had every intention of spending like a diva.

'Well, okay, so, Thursday night, some friends of Mia's are coming over – it's just dinner, nothing too crazy, but at least it'll give us a chance to see you before you go,' Hughie said gently. They were worried about him; Simon could see that and it was rather touching. Even Mia, who'd done her best to come between Hughie and all his friends, had a bit of a soft spot for Simon. Well, he was rather charming to her once he realised that she was going to become a permanent feature in Hughie's life.

Hughie lived in a very trendy penthouse that overlooked the city rooftops, but gave views right out to the Wicklow Mountains and across Dublin Bay. Everything about their home had Mia's stamp on it. Simon had to admit, it was tasteful and managed to be both demure and bold at the same time. He supposed it was what you got if you threw enough money and good taste at the right designer.

He brought along two bottles of the most expensive plonk he had left in his kitchen. There was no point bringing them home to Miranda – she would be as happy with something from the local supermarket and a bunch of handpicked flowers to match. It would be a brave man who'd try and pass off a bunch of dog daisies to Mia. He handed Hughie the bottles of wine and kissed Mia on each cheek, taking in the expensive perfume that she always wore.

'It's lovely to have you,' she said and he had a feeling she meant it. Mia was a decade younger than either Hughie or Simon and with her thick dark hair and blunt-cut fringe she looked more like someone who'd stepped out of London fashion week than the usual girls they'd made a habit of hanging about with. Mia was a self-made woman, who worked hard and paid the bills and somehow or other, she saw something in Hughie that Simon was still trying to figure out.

'Tragic bores,' Hughie whispered when they were out of earshot of their dinner companions. 'Mia has to entertain them this evening, so she really is glad of your company to liven things up.' He snorted and handed Simon a stiff drink. 'Come on through...' Hughie led the way into the large central living area of the apartment. It was a pristine white and grey runway, with the long dining table pulled out so it ran alongside the floor-to-ceiling windows that walled two sides of the apartment. They would be dining with the sun glinting from the west, out across the Wicklow Mountains and picking up the last of the day's rain in its setting.

'This is our friend, Simon Corrigan. He's dining with us tonight before he leaves Dublin, which is going to be very soon, next few days in fact,' Hughie said. 'Simon, this is Günter and Sally Muller. They're over here on business and Mia is helping them with some of the details.'

'Hello.' Simon shook their hands, each of them had good strong handshakes and he wondered for a moment if they were husband and wife or father and daughter, until up close, he spotted the tell-tale signs of Botox and fillers that had been applied a little too generously to Mrs Mullers face.

'You're leaving Dublin?' Günter asked then. He was a small fat man, probably in his fifties, but he looked more. Eating well and exercising little had taken a toll on more than his waistline.

'Yes, I'm... going to help out at home, in the family business,' Simon supplied quickly. It was the excuse he'd been giving since he'd realised that he could no longer afford to live here. It was certainly much better than the truth, which was he'd failed and he was running home to the safety of his mother and hoping that if worked it out, he might just talk her into making some kind increase in his annual dividends from the mills.

'Corrigan...' Sally said in a Scottish accent. She tilted

her birdlike head to one side, her small eyes regarding him carefully. 'No relation of the famous Corrigan Mills, I suppose?' She was smiling now, looking at Mia as if there was something unsaid passing between them.

'Yes, that's us. You've heard of the mills?' he said lightly, because of course, his mother worked hard to make sure that they had hit the lucrative British and German markets for years.

'Heard of them? You're joking, right...' Sally laughed. 'We love them. We're doing our best to buy a mill property similar here in County Dublin, but we'll have a lot of work to do to bring it anywhere close to where your mills are.'

'Well, they're not actually...' Simon stopped himself; of course, they weren't actually his mills, but he was a director in the company. 'So, you'd be interested in buying the mills, if they were for sale?'

'In an ideal world, we'd have gone straight for the Corrigan Mills, but when we visited there last year, we spoke to an old lady...'

'That would be my mother, Miranda.'

'Yes, what a lovely lady... but she assured us at the time she wouldn't consider selling up...Has that changed at all?' Sally asked, sitting forward a little further on her chair.

'Well, that would depend... on many things.' Simon laughed.

'Simon's mother had a heart attack a few months ago and well, that changes things, doesn't it?' Mia said evenly. She was standing over the table, making a show of checking that everything was just right. From the kitchen, Simon caught mouth-watering aromas and knew that there would be a band of caterers working hard to meet Mia's exacting standards. Mia, for all her success, couldn't boil an egg without having the fire brigade on standby.

'Yes, well, you've met her?' Simon looked at the couple before him. They were nodding enthusiastically, proof that they had been welcomed to the mills like thousands of tourists before and after them and treated to his mother's warm reception. 'She has poured her life into the mills, but each of us… I have two sisters, and, well, we have our own careers. My sister Callie is a very successful designer.'

'Callie Corrigan, she is *the* Callie Corrigan of Theme knitwear,' Mia supplied.

'Oh, I didn't realise there was a connection,' Sally said and managed to close her mouth again.

'Yes, and of course, I'm here in Dublin. I have many interests and I really can't see myself going back to Ballycove to take up the mills at this stage.'

'And you have another sister?' Günter asked.

'Yes – Ada, she's the financial controller in the mills. She knows the place inside out, but I don't think she's going to take over as general manager. She's more a numbers girl, always was.'

'So, if there is no-one to take over…' Günter was leaning forward now. He angled his head back towards Mia. 'Do you think we could make an offer?'

'Well, you might want to think about it first, I mean, there are the Boyne Mills here and…' Mia was saying, but she was smiling; perhaps she sensed there would be a bigger commission.

'What if I put it to my mother… get the lie of the land, so to speak? I'd need to have some idea of a ballpark figure… you know, can't sell a pig in a bag to my mother.' Simon laughed then, but it was a nervous high-pitched sound, as if the answer to his prayers was so close that he was afraid to take a chance that anything might blow it out of his reach once more.

'Well, as you know, it's a very different prospect to the Boyne Mills you've been looking at, considerably more expensive,' Mia said to Günter who obviously held the purse strings. 'Corrigan Mills have a worldwide reputation. For the brand alone you're talking about a significant investment.'

'Of course, of course,' Günter said and his eyes had narrowed, as if he was calculating the figures in his head. Sally watched him, a greedy look in her eyes; she wanted those mills more than anything.

'Think of it, Günter, you and I, we could live there, in the west of Ireland, let your sons take on the running of operations in Germany and Scotland. This could be a whole new beginning for us,' Sally was saying, low and steady. Her voice was slightly pleading.

'Yes, I think we will offer two million. See if that entices Miranda Corrigan to sell?' he said then, smiling, a movement that pulled back his thin lips, but didn't reach his eyes, so he looked as if he might be about to pounce on a nearby innocent prey.

25

Miranda

The knock on Miranda's door gave her a start. Stephen Leather had been her friend for almost as long as she had been in the mills. The years had taken inches from his height and added it to his waistband; his hair had greyed into the kind of silky thickness most women of his age would trade their best shoes for. Now he walked slowly, stooped always, but his eyes held onto the sincerity that he couldn't conceal, even if he wanted to. He'd stepped into his father's legal business and took up the reins of the mills and Paddy's affairs five decades ago as their solicitor. He made sure that everything was above board. He'd drawn up all the documents, to ensure that a lifetime's work could not be brought to nothing. Later, when Miranda might have found it hard to explain to someone else, she talked easily to Stephen about her fears for the future.

Stephen's sons were the same age as her children. They had grown up together, gone to school, fought and played together and they knew as much about each other's children as they did about their own. Stephen understood her worries about Ada taking over the running of the mills. He understood too that Ada was blind to the vital ingredients that she was missing if she wanted to take on the role.

'Miranda,' he said gently, breaking into her thoughts of fishing boats and long walks through the boggy wetlands in wintertime all those years ago. 'Is everything all right?'

'Oh, Stephen, is that the time?' She hated that she sounded melancholy. Her voice, sometimes, when she was caught unawares, had taken on a wistful quality as though it had drifted into old age without her. 'Of course, everything is fine.' She nodded towards the door behind him and he closed it with a gentle click. 'It's been... a funny couple of weeks, that's all, and I suppose I just started thinking, it's time to go over my will again...'

'You want to make changes?' He sat down before her, dropped his briefcase to the floor by his feet, his full attention on her. 'I haven't brought a copy with me. If I had known...'

'No, don't worry. I have a copy here and I'm not even sure that I want to make changes, but I needed to sit with you and go over it all again, to be sure.' She smiled at him now. 'There may be some alterations, but I need advice...' Her voice trailed off.

'Legal advice?' He took his reading glasses from his breast pocket.

'Perhaps, but more... a friendly ear and maybe the voice of reason.' She laughed at that, because she really felt as though she didn't have time to think these days, let alone feel as if she was reasonable any more. 'Maybe it's my little scare a few months ago and I'm just being a silly old bird, but I feel it's time to set out how things are going to be and I'm not sure what to do for the best any more.'

If Miranda was predisposed to having favourites, well surely, she always reasoned, Callie deserved to be the one.

She had been looking forward to Callie's return home from the moment her daughter had mentioned it. Not that she was lonely, or that she needed someone in Bridgestock Cottage, but it seemed to her that her home was at its loveliest when there were people to share it with.

Callie for her part returned like a giant sigh of relief and when Miranda looked into her daughter's eyes, she could see she needed to be here more than anything else in the world. She looked ragged, worn from the inside out, as if London had shaken the vitality out of her and left only a vague shell of the original. An emotional drought had filled up her eyes, so they were sunken and dark-ringed and it seemed like their dark colour had faded into a watery reflection of grief.

Miranda knew that this was not just a career break. Callie, for all her glamour and striking physical presence, was here because she could not be anywhere else. When they settled in the little sun room with two large glasses of brandy, Miranda decided she would not ask her daughter any questions. Instead, she would fill her with information about Ballycove and the mills. Soon Simon would be here and Miranda knew he would be good for Callie too. You couldn't help being cheered up by Simon.

'Is Simon being a total pain?' There was no beating about the bush with Callie. 'I bumped into Charlie Warde and he didn't say exactly, but I have a feeling that Simon has just been badly burned in some new scheme. I hope he's not pestering you for more money.'

'Ah, well, that's certainly filling in a few blanks for me.' Miranda laughed. 'He's coming to visit, but I'm quite sure he's going to be only too well aware that I have no intention of rescuing any more dead ducks.'

'Yes, well it will be nice to have him here; he certainly knows how to liven things up.' Of course, livening things up would be good for her, even if Callie sounded as enthusiastic as a child going to the dentist.

'There's nothing quite like having a younger generation about the place to make me feel much better in myself,' Miranda murmured.

'Simon and I are hardly youngsters.' Callie laughed.

'Perhaps, but to me, well, it's like filling this cottage up with new life. It's rather lovely.'

'You're priceless, Mother; do you know how many women your age would much prefer to be left in peace?' Callie shook her head. 'You know we're both coming back to lick our wounds.' Her eyes drifted towards the window, catching on the old chimes that hung from the huge willow at the end of the garden.

'Perhaps, but...' Miranda let her words trail. She had not asked Callie why she needed to leave London so badly. Her daughter would tell her in her own good time. For now, she would just be happy that she'd chosen to come here; after all, she could as easily have decided to lose herself on some warm Mediterranean island for a few weeks. 'When I was young, this cottage and old Mrs Bridgestock were like a refuge for me. I've always wanted it to be a tradition I carried on. It's meant to be a place you can turn to when you there's nowhere else. I think old Mrs Bridgestock would be delighted with that,' Miranda said softly, her mind drifting back to long ago, when she'd sat here as a girl listening to stories and hiding from the father she could not understand.

'How on earth did you manage to get a Blair working at the mills again? Is he that same clan – who started it off back when St Patrick was a lad?' Callie broke into her thoughts.

'Yes, he's old Lord Blair's great-grandson. His father stayed in Ballycove as a child, but we haven't had sight nor light of any of them in decades.' There was a melancholy in Miranda's voice that she couldn't throw off when she mentioned the Blairs. Maybe, some small part of her hoped she could help to swing fortune in his favour, somehow, in some small way. 'He just arrived, turned up in the village one day and once I'd met him, I knew he was perfect to take on the project of the anniversary celebrations.'

'And you gave him a job, just like that?'

'Well, yes,' Miranda said lightly, then went on, 'I should probably mention he's got a great track record in sales and marketing and...'

'And?' Callie believed her mother to be the last of the bleeding heart brigade, but Miranda knew, that just wasn't true and especially in this case.

'All right, all right,' Miranda said eventually to stop the banter from the other side of the line. 'The Blairs were very good to your father. There's a connection between our families that I'm not even sure I can begin to explain, but when a Blair needs something, I'm going to give it freely if it's in my power to do so.'

'Go on, try me,' Callie said softly.

'Excuse me?' But Miranda knew exactly what she was asking.

'Tell me what the great connection is between the Corrigans and Blairs.'

'Oh, really, Callie, I wouldn't know where to start,' she said. The truth was she wasn't sure what she could tell, because much of what she knew was based on that terrible day, so long ago when Paddy had saved Richard's life; but of course, it had all ended in tragedy for her father anyway. It was funny, but after all these years, that day had been the one thing she'd never wanted to share with anyone. Even now, it was too painful to linger on. She settled on: 'You do know they just handed over the mills to your father in a will, don't you?'

'Yes, of course, but even that in itself is a bit...'

'A bit what?'

'I don't know, unusual – overly generous? It's an act that speaks of overcompensation, don't you think?' Callie was trying to draw her out.

'I'm not sure what I *think*,' Miranda said.

Miranda wasn't sure why, but the conversation unsettled her. Perhaps because she had assumed Callie would be happy with whatever she chose to do with the mills provided it was in the best interests of everyone concerned. She'd never really thought of Callie having a vested interest. In fact, Callie was the one person she imagined wouldn't give a damn what happened with the mills because she had, so far as Miranda had ever been aware, no personal ambitions connected to them.

Now, Miranda was not so sure. Callie was successful in her own right, but her interest had never been the money.

It wasn't the plaudits or the approval either; rather, Callie had an ambition that stemmed from deep within her, and Miranda suspected it had as much to do with stepping out of the shadows of the mills as it had to do with anything else.

Miranda hadn't considered David Blair as someone who might be in the running to take on the mills, even in a temporary capacity, but the conversation with Callie prompted something in her. It was just a thought, but as the days wore on, it rattled into an idea. A mad, unexpected idea, but one that seemed to make greater sense the more it settled on her. It seemed that perhaps rather than having no options at all, she was now faced with one too many.

Callie was right about one thing at least, to make a decision about the future of the mills Miranda should, if she wanted to be fair, at least make the decision somewhat consultative. If Ada and Simon did have conversations about it behind her back, then it was surely time to have it all out in the open. Perhaps she couldn't do a lot about that today. It was a Friday after all and most everyone had left the mills for the evening, but she would call a meeting of the board; that meant putting a deadline on her thoughts. It was a welcome deadline.

Miranda looked out her office window at the rushing water beyond. She was getting tired and even if she'd never imagined a year ago that she'd feel like this, she knew it was time to stand down. The lethargy she felt most evenings now was beyond tiredness, she knew. It wasn't caused by her day's work, which wasn't all that arduous at this point. Rather, it was a combination of her years of work and the breathless, racy way her body seemed to hijack her more often these days. It seemed she was being worn out from within and even if she didn't like it, she was glad to be in a position to think and plan for everyone's future.

'You're working late.' David Blair smiled as he held the mill door open for her.

'When you're my age, you hardly notice the time when you're lost in thought,' she said waiting while he pulled the door tight behind them.

'It's funny, but that's what my father says.' He shook his head and changed over the bag he carried from one hand to the other.

'It's such lovely weather; surely you should be taking out your father's boat or picnicking along the riverbank with some nice girl?'

'Oh, don't worry, I'll make time for a spot of fishing.' He laughed gently. 'No, it looks like I'm going to be spending a few hours putting together a proposal for you, for next week.' He looked a little embarrassed then.

'David, we're a small firm. If you want to run something by me, just take me for coffee some morning.'

'Well.' He looked down at the case in his hand, moved gently from one foot to the other in an action that reminded her so much of his father. 'What about dinner?'

'Dinner?'

'Well, yes, we both have to eat and unless you have other plans, I'm bored with my own company.' He laughed then. 'My treat, of course,' he said quickly.

'Tonight, now?' Miranda looked at her watch, but she didn't really take in the time, because truly, there was nowhere she had to be. 'Okay, that would be lovely.' And the aches and tiredness seemed to waft from her body because there was something nicer to focus on. They set off for the village and pulled into the local pub where the food was a mix of wholesome dinners and light lunches, but it was well cooked, the décor was homely and the service was friendly.

'Well,' Miranda said after they'd both ordered the stroganoff. 'What's this big proposal you have for me?' She smiled at him then, much preferring this atmosphere to a stuffy meeting room. She sat back and sipped from her glass of wine.

David Blair. She was not sure why he came here, but Miranda realised, as she sat listening to his proposal to break further into the knitwear scene, that she very much liked having him here. It was not just that he was so much like his father. The resemblance was striking: sandy blonde hair, his eyes blue and sparkling. He had the broad shoulders, the quick-wittedness and still a kindness that lurked in his every word and action that marked him out as Richard Blair's son. It was more than that. David Blair had a presence all of his own and it filled up every space around him, so when Miranda spent time with him, everything else faded into a sort of background noise that she knew would be there long after he had left.

'I've been scouting about, looking at our sales figures, thinking of new territories...' he said reaching into his bag.

'No, don't bother with the numbers.' She put out her hand and smiled. 'I know most of them anyway.' She shook her head. 'It's what comes of living alone; you spend too much time in the office.'

'Ah, there are worse things I'm sure,' he said gently. 'So, then, as you know, the Corrigan brand is fairly well established in the main European and US markets, but...'

he leaned in a little closer '...you've barely scratched the surface in Australia.'

'Not a place I imagined would be big on woollen goods.' Miranda laughed and heard a tinkle in the sound that had been missing for too long.

'Well, that's what most people *would* think. After all, just next door they have more sheep than most of Europe and their climate isn't exactly cool, but...'

'But?'

'It's a wealthy country; in fact, it's a whole continent. It ranges from very warm top temperatures to decidedly cool ones, which lends itself to cosy jackets and occasional cool nights at the barbecue – then of course, there's a whole market for beach rugs.'

'Beach rugs?' Miranda let the term sit on her lips for a moment, thinking back to when her children were small and the biggest, most awkward thing she carried to the beach was a blanket so they could sit on it for a picnic. It was the one thing she would not think of leaving behind, preferring instead to sacrifice buckets, shovels and even sun cream back in the day, in favour of her large chequered blanket.

'I have good contacts there and with a little thought I think we could make our way into some of the more expensive stores. Just to test things, at first, but... worth a shot, I think.'

'It's somewhere I'd never thought of...' Miranda said softly, but then if she was honest, breaking into the lucrative European market had been as much by accident as by any deliberate planning on her behalf. 'Gosh, you've got me all fired up now,' she said laughing and it was true. The last few days, she'd thought a lot about the future of the mills, but not once about their expansion and it had left her feeling deflated and empty; but now, here with David, she could taste that familiar sweetness of ambition. It would do no harm to look at the figures. He'd gone to so much trouble and, after all, this wasn't even part of his brief – how could she not?

'With the right designs, I don't see why we can't make a good fist of the Australian market,' he was saying to her now. 'The thing is, no matter what corner of the world you live in, people are looking for something different. Australian fashion was never stronger, but the average woman wants to make her mark with something unique to her.'

He smiled easily and Miranda figured it was what would make him into such a good salesman.

'We could float a number of pieces this year, a limited collection, see how that goes and then hone it down to what sells best.' He spoke with the passion of someone truly committed to the idea of making this work. 'We haven't much time, just two months,' he said, reaching into his bag. He took out a couple of photographs he'd taken with him from the storerooms. 'I know, this is old stock, but I'm thinking along these lines, with a colour refresh – taking this season's tints.' He held up a picture of a coat that Callie had designed almost two decades earlier. 'The cut is classic and the fabric…it's very luxurious; it falls like water. I've never seen anything like it.' He slipped it across the table to her, perhaps hoping that she would see it with fresh eyes. 'The wool is so light, it might be silk, and the design is…' he stopped for a moment, settling on: 'exquisite.'

'It's a merino blend. I've been in negotiations to order

more of it. It's been hard to track down, but I've found something very similar, perhaps even a better quality from a supplier in France.' Miranda smiled, remembering her last trip and the wily old sheep farmer who plied her with local French wine in the hope of getting a better price. 'Then, we blend it with a silk thread, so it retains its strength, but still has this lovely softness to it at the same time.'

'It's really, very elegant,' David agreed. 'And the design is…' He shook his head. 'Well, the cut and quality, it's a luxury product, just waiting to be branded.'

'The design is by my daughter,' Miranda said shyly. She was actually very proud of Callie and her achievements, but everyone already knew about her success. Years of playing things down for Ada had made her feel self-conscious in case it might sound as though she was bragging.

'Ada?' He looked surprised.

'No – Callie.' She smiled at him.

'Ah, I've heard of Callie – she's *The* Callie Corrigan.' He smiled at her now. 'Well, looking at this, she deserves to be successful; I shouldn't be surprised, really.' He held the image out to look at it anew. 'Would she mind us using the design again?'

'Callie? God no. She'd be delighted.' She shook her head, thinking of her unaffected daughter. 'I'll mention it to her. She'll be thrilled, I'd say.' It could only be a good thing to keep Callie involved and interested in something new rather than the other company business that threatened to dominate their family for the near future.

'And we could have a range of samples run off for the trade show in Melbourne?'

'We'll see,' Miranda said. 'If we go ahead, maybe Callie

will come in and take a look at mixing the colours with us.'
It would do her good, Miranda thought.

'She's here, in Ballycove?' David asked.

'Yes, she's here for a little visit.'

'Well that's nice, gives you a bit of a chance to catch up,
I suppose,' he said softly.

'Yes, I suppose it does,' Miranda said. 'What about you?
Do you get to see your family often?'

'Actually,' he said, breaking into a smile, 'I have family
coming over at the end of the month, so…'

'Ah, that's nice.' Miranda smiled at him now. 'Give *you* a
chance to catch up too…' They both laughed.

'It's my dad. He's been itching to get over here for ages
and I promised him, as soon as I got the cottage into some
kind of shape…'

'Ah,' Miranda said softly and realised that not so long
ago, she'd have looked forward to seeing him again, but
now it seemed like just a distraction to the settling up
she had to do in the rest of her life. She had enough to
contend with between Ada and her current strop and Callie
becoming suddenly opinionated about the mills. Then there
was Simon; well, he was just being Simon. That probably
annoyed her more than anything else – the niggling worry
that he was bringing home with him again. It really was time
for him to grow up. She knew him well enough to know his
finances were too limited for his lifestyle. He would have
to settle into something new, although, with his work-shy
ways, she had no idea what that might be.

'Perhaps you'll get a chance to meet up with him, but
of course, I'll have to get him settled in first,' David said
and Miranda found herself nodding at him automatically,

as though she was one of those silly toys that people have on the dash of their cars. 'You know, since I came back here, he speaks about you quite often.'

'Oh, yes. I was very fond of him, once,' Miranda said wistfully.

'He thinks nobody will remember him when he comes over,' David said, 'but he talks about Ballycove with the kind of affection that suggests it means more to him than I'd realised before. I think if things had been different...' He nodded towards the window. 'But I suppose that was all a lifetime ago.' He smiled then and began to gather up the samples and projections he'd prepared as their meals were placed before them. 'Well, let's tuck in. I'm famished.' And with that, they began to eat and Miranda was left remembering times that she'd long since forgotten.

It was the most pleasant evening Miranda had spent in some time. After the few hours with David Blair, it felt as though she was normal again, as though she might even be well. Her aches and pains disappeared and she slept soundly that night with neither dream nor sound to wake her from her deep sleep.

The following morning, she woke with something close to a spring in her step. She had not made up her mind what she would do next, but she was certain that very soon, she would know exactly what she should do. For now, she had a feeling that the coming week could test her reserves, so she decided she would take the weekend to do as little as possible and she set off for an amble along Briar's Way and hoped she didn't meet anyone at all.

26

Miranda

The following week, Miranda didn't have time for daydreaming or for living in the past. Instead, she had a diary packed with meetings and a million things to do in between. Her eyes drifted towards the on-line schedule Darina kept updated. She had two hours to sit and put together some ideas for next year's lines. The mills ran a season behind the big fashion houses, so it gave her time to plan and take inspiration for colour trends from the international collections. This year, it was the turn of jewel colours – ruby, sapphire and emerald would dominate the magazine spreads.

Miranda planned to provide a line of accessories that would complement or supplant those colours in the shopper's wardrobe. The secret to the success of the mills was very simple. Their customers were looking for a slice of Ireland and that small sliver, served up with thoughtful design and genuine Irish warmth, had kept the mills in the black. The magic ingredient that bobbed them to the top of their game was Miranda's keen eye to provide a product that was covetable, not just traditional, and so the planning of the lines each year was something she put much time and effort into.

The two hours flew by, as she knew they would. This was one of her favourite parts of her job; another was the buying and selling of product. She loved meeting people, bargaining with them and getting the best price, no matter what side of the transaction she was on. And then, of course, there were the mills themselves. Her heart was stuck here now; perhaps it had always been. Certainly, she had invested a lifetime in saving them and making them what they were.

Miranda felt that tight knot once more in her stomach. She had decisions to make and clearly she would have to make them based on what was best for everyone and more than what sentimentality seemed to be demanding.

There was no doubt that Ada had invested a lifetime in the mills, but it was a duty, not a love that kept her eldest daughter here. Miranda still worried that her daughter had run away from living before she really had a chance to start a new life. At that terrible time, when Ada had crumbled beneath the pressure of exams and her own exacting standards, Miranda had provided a security that was meant to get her through, not serve as a direction for her future. A job was carved out for Ada and, God knows, if Tony had wanted, one might have been made for him also. It was a blessing that he didn't want to work in the mills, even if it wasn't so much a blessing that he hadn't wanted to work anywhere else either.

Miranda put down the colour swatches that she had been studying on her desk and sighed. Ada. What was she to do about Ada? It was a simple question – her daughter had indeed devoted her career to the mills and she was in every way more entitled than any of her children to take over the running of them when Miranda stood down. There was no question of that, but… Miranda couldn't quell the fear that while Ada was capable and loyal, she was not fit for the pressures the general manager's job would settle upon her shoulders.

The problem was, she'd never be brave enough to say that to Ada. She could tell herself that her fears were all about her daughter's unsuitability to the role, but deep down she knew too well – she couldn't be the cause of Ada having another breakdown. Instead, she talked about the mills being about so much more than just the Corrigan name on a label. They were about community, tradition and pride. Was it so wrong to be proud of her own achievements here? It was a lifetime's work that had not only saved the mills, but it had fed families, kept people in this little town when otherwise they might have had to take a boat to England or America. Corrigan Mills and Miranda's acumen had put Ballycove on the map; without it, they wouldn't see a tourist from one end of the year to the next.

Even now, Miranda knew, the mills were full of European tourists, enveloped in a warm Irish welcome and enjoying the hospitality of the mills. In an hour's time, that same welcome would be extended to a tour bus of Americans, just arrived from Pennsylvania to experience what it is to be in Ireland.

Miranda would make her way down to the mill floor and do her best to meet and greet every single person today, if she could. Over the years she'd seen the youngsters learn, before her eyes, what it was to extend a genuine *Ceád Míle Failte* to everyone who walked into the place. In all the years Ada had been here, she still had not managed to learn what it was to extend that genuine warmth to people and that was what made Miranda falter now that she had to figure out what would happen when she stepped down.

Miranda picked up the colour swatches again. The card in her hand held a spectrum of plums and wines, all the way through to a dark bloody red – there was not a ruby among them. 'It's no good,' she murmured finally to herself, 'this won't do at all.'

Simon offered to pick her up at the mills; *for once*, he wheedled, she could surely finish a little early.

'Go on, be a devil,' he'd goaded her adorably. He made it absolutely impossible to be cross with him. 'Let's get out of Ballycove, find somewhere along the coast that does a decent sea bass and a good bottle of white.'

'You're a terrible influence, you do know that?' Miranda laughed into the phone.

'I may as well be good for something,' he said drily. He was downstairs, knocking about the shop floor. She imagined him, in her mind's eye, picking up various objects, examining them and then putting them back again. He was too urbane for the traditional bent of the mills to suit his tastes. The funny thing was, though, that any of their scarves or blazers would have really suited him, but Miranda supposed it was that thing of familiarity breeding contempt. Simon had never liked the mills – oh, he enjoyed the annual stipend that came from being a shareholder, but he'd never felt any emotional attachment to the place, and refreshingly, nor did he pretend to have any.

'I won't be long, just a little while will clear up all I have to do here,' she said as she closed her diary for the day. In less than five minutes she was watching her son as he browsed through men's woollen suits. He was a handsome man. She had often wondered, over the years, if his good looks had been more of a curse than a blessing. For sure, there had never been a babysitter or teacher who complained about him, not like they did about Ada, who had been such a serious child by comparison. Miranda watched him now as he spoke to one of the young assistants. Even she, a fairly reserved Czech girl, was smiling and twirling her rather drab hair coquettishly as she listened to him.

'Mother.' He whirled about as if he'd felt her eyes on him all along. 'How lovely you look today,' he said, but something in his eyes gave away the fact that it was an empty compliment.

'Oh, Simon, I look worn out – don't try to flatter me,' she said laughing, because he had always had the same effect on her that he had on every other woman he turned his charm on. It was his greatest redeeming feature and his only deadly weapon.

'Well, let's get going then, before I'm tempted to go trying on this suit.' He looked at the finely made Donegal Tweed. 'I must be getting old. Who'd have thought I'd pine after a tweed blazer?' He laughed then and linked her arm, tipping his smile towards the girl who had only just realised he was the boss's son. 'What about that little restaurant in Ballylahan? I've never been, but I hear it's awfully good; apparently you haven't lived until you've tasted their shark steaks?'

'Good choice – I've been there, of course, but to be honest,

I've never been brave enough to have shark.' Miranda found she was buoyed up by his easy charm. It felt good to forget about Ada and the mills, and what the doctor said and even better to forget about what the consultant didn't say. 'But, maybe if it's on the menu tonight... well who knows?' Simon offered to drive them over to Ballylahan. It was a lovely balmy evening, with the sun shimmering round and orange across the fields. Miranda sat back enjoying the scenery while Simon talked of the last time he'd eaten shark.

The restaurant, a small Italian-owned place, with check tablecloths and shrunken waxy candles slipping down the sides of wine bottles, was surprisingly busy for a weeknight. Of course, this was peak season, so Miranda remembered. She shouldn't be surprised; however, she hadn't bargained on having to wait for a table to be freed.

'Ah, Mrs Corrigan, how lovely to see you again – you come back for more of my gelato, no?'

'No, well, maybe yes; it is very good. But my son is taking me out tonight, so I'll have to be much better behaved.' She smiled at the old Italian, who winked at her playfully.

The last time she'd come here, she'd been part of the local bridge club and some of the ladies insisted on making their own tea – since they were convinced that no foreigner could possibly make it right. Miranda had a feeling that most of them were too tight to pay for a decent cup and so she'd asked the owner to make them all espressos with a double shot of liquor. That had loosened out even the stuffiest of them and the evening had turned into a great success. By the end of the night, the club president was playing old Gilbert and Sullivan numbers on the battered piano and she was being joyfully, if somewhat tunelessly, aided by some of the older, usually fustier members.

'Oh, I do hope you won't be too well behaved. I must say, I really enjoyed your last visit.' He laughed with a bellow that shook his whole body. 'Here, you come this way – you have no reservation?' He checked with a young girl who was frantically trying to free up tables for the next group of diners. They followed him to the back of the restaurant, where he put them sitting at a small booth for two, which if it lacked a view of the sea, made up for that with privacy and probably the most comfortable chairs in the house.

'So,' Simon said as they finished off their desserts. He was sitting back, looking about the restaurant with an expression Miranda had never really understood, but she always felt it was somewhere between being above all he surveyed and still wanting to possess all of it.

'So…' she said laying her napkin on the table. 'Should we ask for coffee, or perhaps we should just go back home and let Giuseppe have the table for the next lucky diners,' she said nodding her approval at their host.

'If you'd like, but I'm sure your friend wouldn't mind if you had a quick cup of coffee before we left.'

'Oh, he might. The last time I was here, coffees took longer than the meal.' Miranda smiled now at the recollection.

'Well, I'd like one and there's something that I wanted to talk to you about. It's a bit… delicate.' Simon lowered his voice.

'So, maybe it's better to talk about it back at the cottage?'

'Maybe, but it's not anything bad or terrible, just an idea,' he said nodding to Giuseppe and ordering two coffees and the bill.

'Well, fire away,' Miranda said, but she had a feeling that this is what this whole evening was about, a last supper before he asked for what he needed.

'No, don't look so worried, no one is dying, but...' Simon leant forward, placed his hands over hers, holding on to them. 'I don't want to upset you, but I've been thinking about you a lot lately, about how things are changing and...'

'And...'

'And, well you were right.' He inclined his head a little, making him look like some kind of devilishly handsome, sympathetic cleric. 'Back there, at the mills, when you said I lied.' He shook his head, a curl of a smile uplifting those lips that were so like his father's. 'You don't look well. You look tired, really drained and I just think... well, I've thought it for a long time, actually, but I've never been brave enough to say it...'

'So you've plied me with dinner and good company to break it to me gently?' She smiled at him. Simon was being unusually forthright; normally he liked to skirt around unpleasantries, which only made her wonder if perhaps she looked every bit as tired as she felt sometimes.

'Maybe,' he said emphatically. 'I hope you don't mind me saying it, but I just think you need to take care of yourself a little more. You're not old and certainly I know you're as sharp as any of us, but... well, why would you be working so hard when you could simply be taking it easy? You have the whole backdrop for a great retirement: friends, hobbies, a love of entertaining and a good brain so you can still enjoy all those things at your own leisure.'

'So, I'm no longer fit to work in the mills though?' she said softly, swallowing the edge that sat just beyond her voice. She wasn't sure if she was upset, hurt, touched or just enraged, but she certainly wasn't happy.

'It's not about being fit enough, Mother. It's about taking care of yourself when you need to and you're quite simply, not,' he said flatly. She pulled her hands from beneath his. 'All I'm saying is I want you to stick around for many years to come and to enjoy life a bit. You've worked so hard; now it's time to slow down.'

'Oh, Simon, Simon.' She shook her head sadly.

'What? I'm only saying it for your own good. After all, you're the one who's had the heart attack.'

'But don't you see, Simon, quality of life is different for each of us.' It was the best she could manage. There was no point making recriminations now. After all, when she'd been hospitalised for almost a week, there'd been no sign of Simon. He said that he couldn't bear hospitals or to see his mother so unwell. She had a feeling it had more to do with a certain distillery heiress that he had notions of marrying until her father made it plain that he would not be funding Simon's lifestyle as well as his daughter's. 'Perhaps I'd prefer to work in the mills than spend each day trying desperately to fill it with leisure activities. How do you know, I might be dead of boredom in a week if I give it up at this stage? Some might say it's what's keeping me going…' she said finally.

'Really, Mother, even you don't believe that. You don't have to agree with me now, but just think about it – you could walk away from the mills. There are plenty of hands waiting to take it on. Plenty of good people who'd only love a chance to bring it to its next phase.'

'Oh, are there? Who?' Miranda feared now that if he was about to promote himself as some kind of white knight ready to come home and save the day she might just keel over on the spot.

'Well, there's Ada, for one.'

'Ah, so Ada has been having words with you, has she?' Now this was all beginning to make some kind of disorganised sense. Perhaps Ada was paying for this dinner, because some small part of Miranda couldn't imagine Simon going out of his way on her behalf otherwise.

'Well, she did ring, yes, but I think she's worried about you too,' he said as their coffees were placed on the table before them. 'She seems to think that you are unsure about the future of the mills, that there might be some question over what will happen to them when you're...'

'Dead?' Miranda said the word plainly.

'When you decide to hand over the reins.' He made a bit of a play of dropping sugar lumps in his coffee then stirred it thoughtfully with the delicate spoon that tinged like a high-pitched tuning fork, a solitary sound as it hit the cup's sides. 'And I suppose I always thought that Ada would take over one day too...'

'So?' Because she had a feeling that Simon was about to reach the crux of his reason for bringing her here.

'Well, if Ada is not going to automatically succeed you, I wondered if you'd like to hear my thoughts on what might be the best long-term solution for keeping the mills up and running and everything as tickety-boo as it can be, if you're not actually there yourself.'

'Well, of course, I'd be very interested to hear your thoughts, Simon.' She had to say that and, to be fair, she was very interested to hear, not that she expected to pay a blind bit of notice to any of his suggestions. After all, there was no losing sight of the fact that he'd hardly done a hand's turn in his life. Added to which, any of the schemes he'd dreamed up had all fallen in ashes either through poor management or lack of application within a short time of getting off the ground.

'Really?' he said, a little taken aback, since he'd probably expected her to cut him off instantly.

'Absolutely, tell me what you think is best...' She was actually enjoying his surprise now.

'Well, I met a man named Günter Muller and his wife Sally, at a dinner party a week ago. Never laid eyes on him before, hadn't a clue who on earth he was, not really one of our gang, to be honest, but you know you meet all sorts of people on these evenings.'

'Günter Muller?' Miranda repeated the name thoughtfully.

'Don't worry, it's not about Günter; well, it is in a way, but... We started talking, as you do, and when he heard that I was the same Corrigan of the woollen mills, well it was as though he thought I was royalty. They had visited last year, apparently, met you and went home with a truckload of woollens for every one of their relations. The thing about the Mullers is that they own lots of mills, all across Scotland, Germany and the North of England.'

'Ah, darling, I meet so many people; honestly, it's hard to remember after a while.'

'Yes, well you obviously made a huge impression. Anyway, they went home to Germany with a yearning for Corrigan Mills and the surety it would never be theirs.'

'Well, that would be right.' Miranda laughed.

'The thing is...' Simon leant closer over the table to her, dropped his voice and turned the full-volume charm of his eyes on her. 'The thing is, Günter says that all of the mills they own are being preserved. They mill like you do, with passion and heart, not just with a calculator. They aren't in it for the money, but just like you, they've managed to make each of their outfits really profitable, but still kept their identity separate.'

'So, Corrigan Mills would always be Corrigan Mills?' Miranda supplied.

'Effectively, yes. The people who have always worked there would still have their jobs and...' he pinned his most winning smile in place now '...it would free up a substantial lump sum for you to retire; well, for all of us, really.'

'Ah,' Miranda said gently, because now they were at the root of what Simon wanted from her. 'So, I would sell the mills for a good price and you'd all get a share of the sale?'

'Well, we do all own twenty percent, Mother, and I can't see Ada not wanting her share.'

'No,' Miranda said thoughtfully, nor could she see Simon not wanting his.

'So, you'll think about it?'

'Yes, Simon, I'll definitely think about it,' Miranda said and, unexpectedly, she found herself wondering if perhaps she could meet with Mr Muller, just to see what he had to say for himself at least.

27

The Past

It seemed change was in the air in Ballycove and if it moved gently, it also did so swiftly and stealthily. On a dry September morning, with the wind whipping up autumn leaves, Miranda made her way from her mother's little cottage to start on a new journey. She was watched by most of the village and all of the staff at the factory as she made her way to the small church for a simple ceremony to marry Paddy Corrigan. She'd had her dark hair done by Mrs Mooney, piled high on top of her head, with fat curls falling about her face. Her lips, full and sensual, were painted a pale pink and one of the girls she worked with had teased her eyelashes so they curled upwards, making her feel like she'd just stepped off an album cover for some English rock band.

Her mother had helped her pick a dress, a simple white, to the knees with a tiny feathered hat perched on her head. On her feet, she managed to borrow a pair of white sandals that she had just about made scuff-free with a lot of shining and a dab of white fabric dye from the mill store. They pinched her toes, but it didn't matter; it was not a long walk to the top of the church and it was worth it for such lovely shoes.

'I didn't think I'd be so nervous,' she whispered to her mother when they stood outside the church, listening for the opening bars of the wedding march.

'Ah, go on with you, what have you got to be nervous about? Paddy isn't going to back out now.' Annie laughed. She was kidding her, of course. Paddy backing out was the one thing Miranda was sure would not happen.

'But what if...' Miranda felt that knot tighten in her stomach. She was thinking about Richard Blair, not that she expected him to turn up at this late stage. The truth was that even if he did, she wasn't sure what difference it would make. When all was said and done, she loved Paddy – of course she did. She wouldn't have agreed to marry him otherwise. But with Richard – well, it felt as though they had unfinished business. Not that she wanted to throw herself at him, or imagined him flinging his arms around her; no, rather it was that there had been no ending. There had been no explanation, not even a word.

Miranda shook herself out. She would stop thinking of him now. This was her wedding day and Richard Blair was just a girlhood crush – not real, grown-up love, not like things were with Paddy.

'Are you sure you're all right?' Annie touched her arm lightly. 'It's just nerves. Everyone has them, don't worry.' She smiled at her then.

'Of course, I'm really happy Ma,' Miranda said and she truly was. One of the ushers opened the heavy church door for them, and Miranda felt time stand still. She heard the organ bellow out the notes above her head, watched as the sun's rays picked out shafts of dusty light across the aisle. Family and friends were waiting for her, filling seats from one end of the church to the other.

At the top of the aisle, Paddy stood, tall and strong, his dark hair pushed back neater than she'd ever seen it before. There was no doubt, he was an attractive, broad-shouldered man and she was lucky to have a future to look forward to with him. She decided there and then, there would be no more looking back. She caught Paddy's eye and she knew that she was doing the right thing.

It turned out to be even better than she hoped. Paddy Corrigan wanted the same things as her in life. They shared a love of Ballycove, its history and old stories, the people who lived in it and the people who worked in the mill. They were both hard workers and determined to make a go of anything they took on.

Paddy had his heart set on Blair Hall, once he made a go of the mills, but even though the Blairs had gone and it seemed they would not be coming back, they both knew they were nowhere near able to afford the grandness of the Hall. Instead, they settled into working hard in the mills and getting into a stronger position to buy it out one day.

Still, they needed a home. They were a young couple, healthy and vital, and although there was no family yet, they hoped one day to fill a house with the happy laughter of children. When old Mrs Bridgestock had passed away, no-one paid very much heed to her neglected cottage. For one thing, it was too far out of town to be noticed very often and for another, the trend these days was to build something modern and streamlined. Bridgestock Cottage was anything but streamlined; in fact, it was hardly even a cottage, more a higgledy-piggledy assortment of rooms thrown together over two floors and disparate ends that veered off in two arms of a U.

Miranda had always loved it – to her, it was so much more than an uneven and sprawling cottage – it was a refuge and it was filled with happy memories from times when they'd been too precious not to cherish. The cottage itself rambled along in corners and curves, a never-ending volley of rooms leading into one another. When you actually looked at it, it was hard to tell where the house began and ended and where the outbuildings took their start. It didn't dawn on her for quite a while that it might suit them perfectly, until one day, her mother sent her up to make sure that the place was not being bothered or broken into since it was so far off the beaten track. Miranda ran back to the factory, full of enthusiasm.

'You have to come and look at it,' she begged Paddy, who couldn't refuse her even if he tried. He dropped the logbook he'd been studying and threw his jacket across his shoulder. They walked and half ran their way out to the cottage, full of the giddy excitement of youth and love and hopefulness.

'Now,' she said, covering his eyes. 'You have to think of what it could be like, not what you see today.' She dropped her hands and stood beside him, hoping he could see what they might make it rather than what it had become. With dispassionate eyes, Miranda could see, it was cold stone, rotting windows and gardens that threatened to overtake it before too many years were out. Still, in her imagination, she could conjure so much more of what it could become.

'Well.' He paced the length of the garden, taking in everything about the cottage from the roof, right down to the roots of the wisteria that was fading fast as its season came to an end. 'We would have our work cut out for us.' He shook his head, but Miranda knew him well enough to know that didn't mean he wouldn't say yes. 'I'll wager there's no electric or gas or even a shred of carpet we might make our own.' He squinted as he looked towards treacherous slates that seemed to hang against the laws of gravity. 'And, it'll surely need a new roof...' They walked nearer the cottage, right up to search the darkness behind neglected windows. 'Does it even have running water, indoor plumbing?' He shook his head when he saw her smile, then he put his arms about her waist. 'I can see what you mean all right; certainly, there are the makings of a lovely home for us here...'

'Oh, Paddy, I think I would love it far more than stuffy old Blair Hall.' Miranda felt, deep down, she'd never been meant for Blair Hall and now, with Paddy, she knew she could be happy here for the rest of her days.

'Well, now...' He smiled at her. 'It would be a step in the right direction. If we put our mark on it, we certainly couldn't lose out.' He let her go again, paced back to the furthest end of the garden. 'Yes, I think a lot of this work – well, I'm sure there are plenty in the village who'll help us out...' He was smiling at her now. Miranda knew he was right. Paddy had been kind and generous to people all his life. There were plenty about the place who'd be only too happy to help them put the place to rights. 'And you have your heart set on it?'

'I have my heart set on it.' She folded her arms, smiled, and knew that it was the right place for them to settle. Mrs Bridgestock had been happy here and Miranda had a feeling if she lived to the same age as the old lady, she would be happy here too. 'And, it's a lovely place for children, safe and plenty of gardens to run off any excess energy...' she said smiling. She knew that would be the clincher.

'Grand, well, if you're happy—' Paddy put his arm around her shoulder '—I'll go and find out if we can buy it.'

Paddy was right of course, the buying of Bridgestock Cottage was the easy part of getting it back on its feet, but they were young and energetic and if Paddy worked hard at the mills, Miranda worked every bit as hard as him at the cottage when her day's work was done. There was clearing and cleaning and no end of patching up, it seemed. Of course, quite a lot of the work she couldn't do, but Paddy always seemed to know someone who owed him a favour and so Miranda rubbed along with an assortment of handymen who all dug in happily alongside her.

When they married, Paddy had managed to secure a little caravan for them. Miranda had never stayed in one before, and it all became such an adventure. They parked it at the side of Bridgestock Cottage and filled each day with making up their new home. It was a bright and breezy April morning when Miranda woke up in their temporary home and realised she felt differently. It wasn't a pain or an ache, nor was it just an attitude, it was something she couldn't put her finger on, but at the same time, she knew that something had changed.

The doctor confirmed it; their first baby was on the way. They would be a proper family by Christmas. It meant so much to both of them, since it seemed they had in common families that were somehow touched by loss along the way. Paddy had been raised by his father and grandfather, a kindly old man who worked all his life in the mills.

'Well, that puts the tin hat on it,' Paddy said, his arms around her and his eyes filled with love. 'That roof is just going to have to be on before we have a little one here.' They had run out of money, so now they had a rambling cottage, almost renovated, but with a roof that still leaked and rotted beneath the grey slates, more with every passing day. 'Maybe…' He smiled at her then and headed off to the mills with an idea.

By the end of the week, they had settled on a thatch roof and payment would be the caravan they'd spent the beginning of their married life in. They would be living in Bridgestock Cottage well before the baby arrived and Miranda felt she had not been happier in all her life.

It seemed to Miranda that in those early days Paddy could do no wrong. Everything he touched turned to something better. The mills were an example of it, but in some smaller way, she saw it each time they walked along the street in Ballycove. His friendly words to people, his genuine interest in their welfare worked like an enchanting balm, creating a wafting sense of delight about him.

And the mills were flourishing. 'We will have to run extra shifts if it keeps up like this,' he told her one evening.

'The Blairs must be very pleased.' She smiled at him. She rarely thought of Richard now. Her days were too full to let her mind meander to the past for very long.

'You could say that.' He smiled at her devilishly.

'What is it? Something has happened – what?' she said, but of course, he couldn't keep a secret from her even if he wanted to.

'You're not going to believe it,' he said putting his arms around her waist. They were standing in the kitchen on a warm summer's evening. Outside a gentle breeze brushed against the long grass that still had to be tamed. For now, Miranda enjoyed watching birds and butterflies dip in and out of it, as though they were playing on green ocean waves. 'Only Mrs Blair herself rang me today and...' he made a funny face, as though he might explode with excitement '... Lady Blair has signed off on her will and...'

'Don't tell me, they're going to sell the mills to us,' she joked, because she knew that finishing the house had cleared them out financially for now.

'Even better,' he said, releasing her immediately, his face loosening into a kind of excited relief.

'Come on, what did she really say? Is she giving you a raise?' Miranda looked into his eyes but she couldn't quite make sense of what he was thinking. She pulled him close. 'Seriously, did she offer you a pay rise? After all, that big order with the hospital board, getting that alone has secured the mills for the foreseeable. Every other mill in the country wanted it.' That was true. Paddy had pitched against the biggest mills in the country and he'd managed to swipe an order from under their noses to replace every worn-out blanket across the province. It was why they were so busy; it was also why he spent every waking hour in the mills, but they both knew it was only for now, until he got things up and running.

'No.' He held her at arm's length, searching her eyes for that connection that told him she believed in him. 'No, Miranda, she is giving me the mills.' He said the words slowly and emphatically.

'But... why?' It was bewildering, but she had a feeling he might just have an answer.

'She wants us to have them, you and me. She feels it's the best thing for the mills and maybe the best thing for her family and Ballycove too. Richard is never going to come back here now and his father, Edwin, never wanted to.'

'So there is no-one else?'

'If she leaves them to her son, he will sell them on, piecemeal if it's the most profitable way. She doesn't want to think that they might end up little more than a shell and a vague memory about Ballycove.' A flicker of something else passed across his eyes now. 'She mentioned you, Miranda.'

'Me?'

'Yes, that day with Richard on the riverbank. She still feels as if she was in some way responsible for making your father... well, for what happened.'

'But she was only being kind – trying to help us out by offering him a job when no-one else would.'

'I know, but she won't be talked out of it. She feels guilt as if it's a physical weight, particularly with what it led to.' They never mentioned her father's suicide, but she knew that was what Paddy was alluding to.

'None of it was her fault.'

'I told her that, but still she wanted you to know, that she hasn't forgotten and the mills will be made out to both our names.' He sighed. 'She still credits me with saving Richard's life.' He shook his head modestly.

'But you did. You know that if you hadn't come along, well... there's no telling that we wouldn't both have been dead on the towpath.' She reached out and touched his arm, her brave and clever husband, and Miranda knew, in that moment, that she loved him as much as it was possible to love any man. He pulled her close then and whispered in her ear.

'Whatever the rights and wrongs of it all now, the fact is that from Monday morning, we'll be going to work in Corrigan Mills.' His words were filled with a mixture of joy and pride and it seemed the future stretched out long and happily before them.

It was grey and gloomy, a fitting day to bury Lady Blair; or at least that was what Paddy Corrigan thought as he sat staring out the kitchen window. He had freshened up and taken down his best suit. At least he would look respectable – although he felt it was hard to balance his emotions now. The least he could do was turn up and do the Blairs proud.

Opposite him, Ada, his eldest child, was happily stacking up her crayons. She counted them over and back, checking that she got the same number each time. She was such a neat and tidy child and Paddy felt that tremor of sadness looking at her. Like a little doll, petite compared to the other ten-year-olds in her class at school, she went about her play without as much as a flicker of attention his way.

So very different to her brother who had no interest in anything that was not fun. The only thing Simon was likely to be counting were the days to the summer holidays. He spent half his time cajoling treats from his grandmother and what remained of it skiving off in case Miranda might give him a rake or hoe to straighten out the garden that had become his wife's passion.

'You'll need to be getting a move on,' Miranda broke gently into his thoughts.

'It's such a shame you can't come; having you by my side would make this whole thing so much easier.' Paddy looked across at his darling wife. Miranda was almost ready to give birth to their third child and apart from her obvious discomfort, to add to her woes, she had been experiencing moments of dizziness that would surely land her in hospital if she were not taking care of herself at home.

'I'm sorry too, my darling, but really, I'm not even sure the little Presbyterian church has pews big enough to hold me now.' She was making fun of herself, trying to jolly him along. 'Now, speaking of which, if you don't get going you'll end up having to pay your respects from the church grounds.' She nodded towards the old clock above the mantel that had been in this cottage far longer than either of them.

Miranda had been right, of course, St Andrews was a tiny church, much smaller than the large Catholic church that dominated the skyline of Ballycove. Paddy, for his part, had never stood in the Protestant church before – but he had to admit, he liked the fact that it felt a lot more homely than the larger church he spent every Sunday morning sitting in.

Paddy managed to squeeze into the end of a pew at the rear of the church alongside some of the older tenants who still lived on the estate. These days, their lands were no longer in the hands of the Blairs. There was among them a palpable sadness at the loss of a woman they considered one of their own. And, alongside this, many unanswered questions hung over the village as to the future of the Hall and the mills, because until now, Paddy hadn't made anyone wiser about the way the cards would fall.

The minister who spoke was young and enthusiastic and it was obvious, to Paddy at least, that he'd never met the Blairs, although he made a decent fist of giving her as good a send-off as he could. At the end of the service, it was Richard rather than Edwin who stood to share his thoughts of his grandmother. With his soft and genuine words, he painted a picture of a once vital woman who had met her end stoically, but she had never lost her love of Ballycove. Paddy watched Richard, the man who once had sole possession of Miranda's heart, and his mind wandered across how things might have turned out, making him very thankful indeed for the life he and Miranda had made together.

The Blair family crypt was an impressive sandstone structure, raised over the other modest graves in Ballycove. It held the remains of Blair ancestors going back over two hundred years. After a short ceremony in the blazing sun, Paddy made his way around the mourners. Edwin ignored his outstretched hand, but Richard moved between them, quickly and stalwartly.

'Thank you for coming,' he said in his clipped English

tone. 'I know it would mean a lot to my grandmother,' he said, shaking his hand warmly, his eyes meeting Paddy's with a ferocious openness that Paddy understood meant so much more than perhaps either of them could put into words.

'Of course, everyone in the village wanted to turn out today to show their respects. Your family has been a part of this village for as long as anyone can remember. Miranda and I have only the warmest of thoughts for all of you at this sad time.'

'And where is Miranda? Has she come along with you also?' There was no escaping the interest in his eyes. Richard Blair looked about the crowded churchyard hopefully.

'I'm afraid she had to stay at home this time. We're expecting our third child and... Well, she's in a rather delicate state, so it would have been too much for her...'

'Ah, well, you must send her my regards...' he said a little wistfully.

'Miranda will be delighted to hear that, and of course, congratulations are in order. We heard you're about to become a father too?' Paddy said quickly.

'Ah, yes, well...' Richard Blair's eyes clouded over, a darkening of his features, and then he smiled a little awkwardly. 'Of course, I'm a little behind you and Miranda, but then... I married Constance the year after you married Miranda. It seemed... like the right thing to do...'

'But you were engaged for quite the time beforehand. Miranda had known, long before we ever...'

'No...' He looked sadly at Paddy and suddenly, it felt as though a penny dropped through the slot of recognition between them. 'Is that what you heard? Miranda believed

I was engaged? That I had forgotten about her?' Richard's voice petered off. 'But my letters? I wrote to her every week? Didn't she get those?'

'There were no letters,' Paddy said solemnly and then, on the far side of the little churchyard he caught Edwin Blair's eye. 'Perhaps they were intercepted?' he said carefully.

'Dear God.' The anguish that filled those two words seemed too huge to fit into the space between them. 'So... everything might have turned out differently, if only...' Richard said, following Paddy's gaze across at Edwin. 'Oh, I don't think I can bear to think of it...'

'Listen to me.' Paddy gripped his arm. 'This is all water under the bridge. We've all moved on. I'm telling you now, thinking of this, mulling it over – it's enough to drive a man insane. You have to put this from your mind. What's done is done – Miranda is happy with her life now. We have a good life together, a family, and we're running the mills...She's... if she means anything to you, really... you must keep this a secret.'

'I can't... think,' Richard said, stumbling backwards as if the very breath had been knocked from his body. 'How did this happen?' His eyes began to well up with enormous tears. 'How could this have happened?'

'We both know the answer to that, don't we?' Paddy said evenly, but although his voice was steady his heart was beating in his chest so wildly, he thought it might explode. He couldn't imagine the pain Richard Blair was feeling at this realisation. 'Look, there's no turning the clock back now. Everyone has moved on – you will have a child of your own soon and... Well, who's to say what might have happened between you both anyway?' Paddy said a little sharply.

'We would have been happy. I wanted to marry her. I wanted her to be Lady Blair one day… to live with me in the Hall and…' He wiped his eyes harshly with the back of his hand. 'We would have been happy… I know that for a fact,' he finished with conviction.

'I won't argue with you. What do I know of things? But I will ask you this one thing – please, put this from your mind, say nothing. Miranda is the most precious thing I have in the world and if anything should happen between us…' He was aware that people were watching them now. He would have to move along soon or the village gossips would be discussing this moment for the next decade.

'Exactly,' Richard said solemnly, 'you know exactly how I feel about her too.'

It was with an even heavier heart that Paddy made his way back to Bridgestock Cottage after the funeral. He had been planning on dropping into the mills, but it was closed as a mark of respect to Lady Blair and, Paddy knew, he had to go home immediately and stay with Miranda. He managed somehow to pass off meeting Richard and the rest of the Blair family beneath a breezy cloak encompassing good wishes, condolences and mourning in one swoop.

In the following days and weeks, life trundled on, and somehow the worry that had closed around Paddy's heart that day loosened its grip after Miranda gave birth to a darling little girl they called Callie. The child was different again to either Ada or Simon and there was no denying this child was the living spit of Miranda. She was a long angular baby, with gypsy dark eyes and hair that already promised to be as dark and strong as her mother's.

In fact, life became so busy that Paddy almost didn't notice when the threat he'd felt so vehemently that day came to call. It arrived, innocuously enough, a heavy vellum envelope that had the Blair crest embossed on the seal. He was about to pop it on the table for his wife when he turned it round and felt the blood race from his head to his feet. Of course, it was from Richard Blair – who else? He stuffed the letter into his jacket pocket and with it the seeds of guilty compliance that he had never been built to carry.

28

Ada

At least Simon understood, which was a bit of a surprise to Ada. After all, they'd hardly been the closest of siblings over the years. Now, it seemed that he had grown up; perhaps the disappointments of the last few years had done him the world of good.

'Oh, don't worry, Ada. Of course Mother will leave the mills to you. Who else is there? Callie and I have our own jobs and lives – can you see either of us returning to Ballycove now?'

'No, I suppose not,' Ada said and when she thought about it, that was the truth. Callie and Simon had glamorous, elegant lives – far removed from a backwater place like Ballycove. The mills or moving back would be so far off either of their plans. 'I suppose that should make me happy,' she said then. 'Still, I can't help but worry, Simon…' Ada sighed. There was no shaking this heavy feeling that Miranda was not going to relinquish the mills to her. 'I suppose,' she said, 'that it's about timing. Perhaps she's not ready yet. Maybe she just wants to be able to steer the place past the celebrations?' It was a question, as much as anything else; she needed someone to tell her she had nothing to worry about.

'I'm sure that's all it is,' Simon said smoothly. He was sitting in her kitchen, which in itself was unusual. Ada wondered if Tony had invited him over – to take her out of herself, as he put it. He really was acting very strangely lately, making dinner for them, opening a bottle of burgundy for her and handing her the glass as soon as she came through the door from work. It was almost laughable. She felt as if they'd fallen into some kind of warped 1950s television advert, but things had screwed up badly. Surely, it was she who should be handing him his slippers and pipe after his long day in the office?

'And then, there's David Blair,' she said softly, pouring them both some freshly brewed coffee. David – she thought about him far too much and it was with a mixture of emotions she wasn't brave enough to put a name on. On the one hand, he was quixotic, mesmerising in the way he moved and spoke and held her eye for longer than anyone else. On the other, she did not trust the way he and Miranda just seemed to click. Having almost every lunch break together and cosy chats that seemed to have developed into their own private shorthand – it was almost galling, as if he'd managed to sidestep them all with a shared history that he hadn't even been a part of.

Not that her mother would just hand over the mills to an outsider – because that was what he was, a wild card, blown in to Ballycove with no clear future and a past, which even if it was woven in some way into the mills, still remained mysterious to Ada.

'Ah, yes, David Blair,' Simon said unevenly. 'Mother has mentioned him. He seems to have really charmed her.'

'Hmm, well you know Mother,' she said and then turned, feeling Simon's eyes on her.

'What's he like then? Really, like, I mean this David Blair?' Simon's voice was light, but Ada had a feeling that he was really, genuinely interested, perhaps even a little perturbed.

'Oh, I don't know, he's a bit…' She searched for the words. Truly, she didn't want to like him, but he gave her no reason not to. 'I suppose he *is* charming. They go walking, well, ambling at any rate, together, along the tow path, most lunchtimes.' Ada thought when she spotted them returning to the factory, like mother and son, a sort of intimacy between them that she couldn't name, but all the same, she recognised at once that same connection her mother shared with Callie. 'He seems to be good at his job. You heard about the big Australian buyers that he's planning to bring on board?'

'He's really just a glorified salesman so.' Simon exhaled.

'Well, yes.' When Simon said it like that, Ada felt a little silly for being so put out about David taking over a role that they all knew would only exist until the anniversary of the mills was past. 'Charming goes with the territory, I suppose.'

'As long as he hasn't got his eyes on the general manager's job, Ada; that's what you want to be watching out for there. Mother does seem to be very smitten.' Simon said the words lightly, but Ada knew the comment was loaded with so much more than just a mild caution.

'You can't be serious?' She tried to laugh it off, pretend

that the notion of an outsider whipping her job from under her had never occurred to her. 'Mother would never hand the mills over to some… some stranger.'

'Ada, he's hardly a stranger to the mills. His family built the mills – we both know that if it wasn't for a lot of work by Stephen Leather, the ownership of them would still be a legal quagmire that could drag out through the courts longer than a session in *Bleak House*.'

'Yes, but he's not family. Mother's first loyalty has always been to family.'

'Are you sure?' He picked up the milk jug, poured just a tint to colour his coffee slightly. 'That might have been the case years ago – when we were kids, starting out – but we're all settled, as far as Mother is concerned. Her big commitment now is to the continuation of the mills – that's why she's still there, Ada. She's going to do what she thinks is best for the mills and if David Blair can convince her he's the best man for the job, she'll put him in place before you have time to save a spreadsheet.'

'She wouldn't…' Ada felt the blood in her veins grow cold with a mixture of fear and jealousy. There was no denying that Miranda had moved swiftly and stealthily to install him in the mills to start. Ada still wasn't sure how it all came about.

'Oh, listen to me – I'm sure she wouldn't. And anyway, we all have our company shares; together we could oust an unfavourable decision once Mother has retired.'

'You really think she could just offer the job to David Blair?'

'Or Callie? Have either of you thought about the fact that she's come home with no great hurry to return to

London?' Tony said as he came into the kitchen and flicked on the kettle absently. He was a tea man, a dozen cups a day, loaded with sugar, and strong enough for a donkey to trot across the top.

'Callie?' Ada heard her sister's name high-pitched on her voice. 'Callie would never be interested in it.' She shook her head. There was no way Callie would leave Theme to return to Ballycove and the mills, would she? 'Tony, I think that's the most unlikely scenario I've ever heard.' She tried to laugh, but it sounded false, cutting through the lemony fragranced air between them. That was unthinkable, unimaginable. 'Simon, he really is a wag – you almost had me convinced there, for a second. Even Simon agrees there's nothing less likely than Callie giving up her job in London to come back here and run the mills. She'd die of boredom within a month.'

'Well, to be fair, she doesn't look very bored to me at the moment,' Simon said softly. 'She's been looking over some of her old designs for Mother, just in case they go ahead with this Australian idea. I might as well not be there at all, now they're comparing colour swatches and stitching details.' Then he laughed. 'Anyway, it's good for me, because Callie is a fabulous cook and she's got full access to Mother's garden so I'm eating like a lord every evening.' He patted his slightly flabby stomach.

'I didn't think she was staying long enough to put designs together.'

'Gardening leave? Hasn't she mentioned that?' he said lightly.

'And you know what that's all about, don't you?' Tony said knowledgeably.

'No, tell me.' A trickle of sweat ran down Ada's back. She

had assumed that her sister had returned home to assess exactly how their mother was. After all, it was only a short time ago that Ada had tried to press on her the notion that Miranda might not be able to manage on her own any longer – at the mills. The last thing she'd intended was for her to up sticks and come back here for an extended period.

'Well, it's a euphemism, isn't it? She's over here thinking about making some kind of major career move and I'd put money that she's thinking about leaving London far behind her. The question is, will she settle here or will she high tail it off to New York or Paris or some other far-flung spot?'

'Actually, Ada, when you think about it, between Callie and David, we'd be almost better off if Mother sold the mills altogether,' Simon said softly.

'How can you even say something like that?'

'Think about it, Ada. If Mother sold the mills to someone outside the family, you could still hold onto your shares. If you wanted you could buy mine and Callie's too probably, then you would be general manager and there'd be no way either Callie or David would be in the running.'

'Callie is in a much better position to buy the mills outright than I am to buy even part of it…' Ada said without even trying to hide the note of dejection in her voice.

'Seriously?' Simon shook his head as if he didn't believe a word of it. 'Ada, if you really think about it, between all those pensions you've been paying into for years and selling this place, I'm sure you could borrow the rest and then you'd be queen of your own castle. You could probably buy the place outright. It's not as if it's not a sound investment in the right hands. Imagine never having to look over your shoulder again…'

Simon didn't stay for very long after he drank his coffee and Ada was relieved. The whole conversation had thrown her off keel. Later when she thought about it, she wondered if Miranda had given some thought to selling. With the way she'd been behaving lately, nothing would surprise Ada. Perhaps Miranda was playing games around her. Perhaps the idea of hanging on for the anniversary celebrations had as much to do with whittling down options, far bigger than just contenders for the job that was rightfully Ada's, as it had with anything else.

After Simon left, Ada could not settle; instead she hummed about the house like a bee unable to find its way back to the hive. It was as though she was carrying too much energy to just sit. Tony offered to make more coffee, then tea. He even offered to go for a walk with her and his solicitude only made her more unsettled.

'Since when do we go for walks together?' she bit at him.

'I just thought, you seemed to be very...'

'Very what exactly?'

'Well, it's not good to get so caught up in yourself Ada. It's not like you. I'm worried about you,' he said gently and of course, they both knew, he'd been the one person who'd seen her descend slowly all those years ago into meltdown. As she'd become more anxious about her final exams, Tony had been the one who had called in to her flat each day and made sure she ate something. In the end, he'd been the one to call Miranda when he knew that she needed a lot more help than he could give with beans on toast and scrambled eggs.

'I'm not caught up in myself, Tony,' she said. 'If you'd ever had anything that meant as much to you as the mills do to me, you'd understand – this isn't a game. It's my whole life – I've invested the last twenty-five years in this and now I have this terrible feeling that it's going to be taken from me.'

'To be fair to your mother, she never made any promises.' Tony's words withered with a glare from Ada. He sighed. 'All I'm saying is, when she divided the company up into shares, she said it then – it was for the future of the company, to set things out as they were going to be.'

'She never said that.' Ada rounded on him, her face filled with fury, her voice holding that pathetic note of fear.

'Ada, she didn't say it in those words, but we were all there when the shares were given out. She was very clear – we all had a stake in the mills, we were happy with the arrangement at the time.'

'Well, that was then,' she said. 'God, Tony, in the real world, nothing stays the same. Don't you understand that yet?' She looked at the huge television screen. It was muted, for a change, but still, there was no getting away from the fact that her husband spent most of his life living vicariously through the cheap shows he watched while everyone else around him worked for a living.

'Some things are meant to stay the same forever,' he said a little sadly. 'Promises are made to be kept, Ada.' She could see in his eyes that this conversation had turned to something that didn't include the mills.

'Yes, Tony, because this is all about us, isn't that right?'

'I'm just saying that you are more important to me than any mills and I had hoped that you would feel the same.'

He shook his head sadly. In that moment, Ada felt such a mixture of emotion for this man who had always stood by her, but who had turned into someone she hardly saw any more. He blended with the furniture of her life, so much so that she couldn't imagine what she'd do without him, but on the other hand his presence was as banal as a kitchen appliance, useful but hardly stirring. They'd become boring, predictable – dead. 'We should do something together, make a plan.' His words were uncertain but pleading, as if he'd rehearsed them after watching a marathon session of *Oprah*. 'Date night? Isn't that what you suggested before?'

'Dear Lord.' Ada shook her head before taking her porcelain mug and rinsing it in the sink. 'I'm going upstairs to lie down, Tony,' she said wearily. 'I'm much too tired for this.' She closed the door with a soft, thoughtful click, imagined him sitting there, looking out at the neat garden, trying to figure out if she was about to have another breakdown. And then she wondered if he had some inkling of her feelings for David. Of course, attraction on that scale was so far off Tony's range of emotions, he'd never have the imagination to see it. Still, there was something off kilter about this new, interested side to him. It was something she'd have given anything to see only a few months ago. Too late now, she thought, just too late now.

She drifted off into a half sleep; her head bursting with the possibilities Simon had laid out before her earlier. She could buy the mills; he was right. She'd religiously invested in a number of high-yielding funds that could be turned quickly into cash. She knew exactly how much they were worth. There was enough to buy the mills and then some. The only thing that niggled her about the conversation was the idea that perhaps Simon might have suggested the same thing to Callie, because the one thing she was fairly certain of was this – Simon would want to sell his share. Regardless of whatever else was happening with the mills, Simon would be more than happy to sell his share if the price was the best he could get.

That thought made her smile, so she drifted off into a sleep far more contented than she'd expected. Soon she was dreaming, not of the mills or her future as general manager – but of David, bending to kiss her as they walked along the towpath by the river. The dream was so vivid she thought she could hear the summer flies buzz lazily above the water. His very nearness made her quiver, so it sent rivulets of desire through her sleeping body, waking her in an unfulfilled, empty frenzy, with only one thought. She was in love with David Blair – and she would sacrifice whatever half-life she had with Tony for half a shot at something with David.

As she pulled herself up from the bed, she made up her mind. There was chemistry between them – she could feel it as surely as she was breathing. She thought of Callie and her go-getting attitude to everything in life and Ada knew there was only one thing for it: she had to make sure Callie did not manage to snap David from under her nose. With David Blair, for once, Ada was going to be the winner.

29

Callie

If Callie prided herself on one thing, more than talent or savvy or even good luck, it was her optimism. Even now, spending time here, when life as she knew it in London was crashing down about her, she felt a sort of grounded hopefulness. It was a combination of things of course; it was walking along the riverbank or through the rocky fields and hills that circled Ballycove protectively. It was her mother's generosity and appetite for life. Callie knew that no matter what should come or go, she would always be her mother's daughter and they would always share a bond that went beyond any measure. It was keeping busy with things that were grounding, like gardening and baking, cooking and spending time in Bridgestock Cottage. Miranda had been shrewd enough to invite her to look over some designs. They both knew it was an exercise in diversion and it had worked. When Callie was immersed in work all her worries faded into the background.

The exit agreement with Theme weighed heavily on

her mind as she tramped about the countryside or pulled weeds from her mother's garden. She could not design in London. That was the central tenet of Veronica's agreement. Callie figured that stipulation was not just because she was afraid of the professional competition, rather Dennis's wife wanted her out of London and away from her husband.

Callie wanted to laugh out loud when she thought about it. Veronica was one mistress too late. Had Dennis let their affair slip in order to keep her off track on his current love life? Did it really matter now anyway? The reality was that Callie had seen Dennis for what he was and while he had hurt her very badly, she couldn't sit and mope about it without realising that the cards had fallen for her rather lucratively and she was quite sure that, at least, wasn't Dennis's plan. The notion that when he found out Callie had left Theme and London with several million in her pocket thanks to his wife's misunderstanding would surely leave him reeling – it made Callie smile.

She pulled the gate behind her, listened to it click heavily on its old hinges. She was setting off with no particular destination in mind, but looking at the clouds overhead, she would need to be heading home again in the next twenty minutes. Any longer than that, she had a feeling that the rain would be too heavy to make it enjoyable. Not that she minded rain, no; Callie had never particularly cared whether there was sun or showers, because as far as she was concerned there was beauty to be appreciated in either. It seemed to her that the greens were never richer than when they were saturated with a light mist. The greys of the sky above the village always heightened her sense of nostalgia and there was no joy to compare with the gentle formation of a rainbow over the far-off hills.

Her legs were bringing her back along the river, away from its mouth and inland, but still on its path. It was a lovely walk, the grass rich and swaying in a whisper of afternoon breeze; the river still, save for an occasional splash where greedy salmon broke through hoping to catch flies or just a glimpse of the world above. She could walk along here for miles quite happily.

She considered that this was a good place to try and set her thoughts straight. A month ago, she couldn't have imagined working anywhere but Theme – now there was no going back there. What she wasn't sure of was whether she wanted to start up on her own. She'd never seen herself as a business owner; it just hadn't been on her agenda. Sure, she'd gone out and sold her designs, but that was just getting-by money. She didn't want to be in that lonely, cut-off place where every decision came down to her and the livelihoods of others depended on her making all the right moves. When she'd said this to her mother, Miranda had laughed.

'You know, you are exactly the type of person who should be running your own business.'

'Oh, Mamma, it's easy for you to say, you've been doing it all your life. I…'

'I didn't have a choice; it was either step into your father's shoes or see the lot go down the drain.' Miranda shook her head sadly. She had saved the mills; they all knew that, even if she wouldn't talk of it. Stephen Leather had told Callie the story many years before and even now, Callie wondered at her mother's resourcefulness and energy in what must have been the darkest of days. 'Anyway, you know, we'll all be there for you. We'll all do what we can to help.' Her mother smiled knowingly. She wanted her to strike out on her own. She lowered her voice then. 'It wouldn't have to be in London, you know.'

'You mean, set up here, in Ballycove?' Callie almost laughed; it was as if her mother knew so much more than she possibly could. 'Oh, Mamma, I don't know.'

'Well, think about it, you'd have no overheads, you could sell your house in London, or keep it, to visit when you feel you need to shake the cobwebs of Ballycove from your hair. You'd be welcome to live here for as long as you want and you know there's plenty of space at the mills to set up a design room and work area.'

'I could see Ada loving that.' Callie laughed then.

'Oh, Ada, honestly, we all pussyfoot about her and maybe it'd do her good to have you here.' She was thinking then, looking out towards the garden. 'Anyway, it would be completely separate; if you wanted to pay your way, you could contribute a nominal rent to the mills or offer to put your name on an accessory line, or something small.'

'Really, Mamma, you're incorrigible.' Callie smiled. Scarves and hats with the Callie Corrigan logo would sell for ten times anything currently stocked in the mills.

'I know, it's why I'm still running the mills.' Miranda sighed. 'Perhaps I should just be less so.' She shook her head and there was a weariness in the movement that caught Callie unexpectedly, so much so, that the seed of worry it caused remained, even while she walked along the little towpath far beyond the mills the following day.

This walk led nowhere, really, but the path swept along

the lazy part of the river and on, and on, until the rushing falls crashed loudly on jagged rocks. In summertime, the banks lined up with old men and fishing rods, their lunches packed in the early morning to make the most of the day ahead. Callie cut through land that had once belonged to the Blair family and when she thought of it, probably still did. She wondered about how a family could disappear so thoroughly from the landscape of a place. She had a feeling that her mother liked having David back here, and that it had more to do with that notion of setting things straight than it had with the obvious fondness she felt for him in the short time he'd been here.

The towpath meandered gently past the mills and finished up about half a mile to the south. Now Callie felt a chill pass over her as the darkest of clouds rumbled in front of the sun. The weather forecasters had promised thundery showers today. Callie liked the rain, but thunder was something she'd prefer to be indoors for. She cast her eyes off towards the grazing land that ran, hilly and rocky, as a backdrop to the mills. The cottage was only a fifteen-minute walk across country if she set through, but the fields were muddy and she would surely end up in a worse state if she took them instead of the road.

Doubling back, she increased her speed, keeping her eyes for once on the far-off distance, her attention dragged from the riverbank or the deep hedgerows that rustled constantly with the birds and wildlife that hid within. She would short-cut past the village, through the industrial estate – a couple of old warehouses, built by an optimistic government thirty years ago and sporadically home to various fledgling businesses.

Now, as she cut through the Ballycove Enterprise centre, she noticed that one of the five units had been taken over by an auction house and another by some kind of gym or social hall. Her mother had mentioned that at some point. Ballycove was turning into one of those satellite towns, with a growing population settling into some of the new estates that had mushroomed in fields that had never seemed big enough to accommodate anything more than dairy herds or winter grazing for old ponies set on long retirement.

In the furthest corner, the smallest unit stood forlornly. The last time she'd been here there was only one unit open. Today, cars parked outside all of the factories apart from the empty grey one on the end. It was flanked on one side by a factory churning out ready meals – Nuts and Bolts, which seemed to be some kind of healthy eating, food company. On the other, a one-stop computer repair and website design business. They both housed much larger units than the one Callie's eyes rested on now. She walked towards it. The estate was quiet enough, no-one much about but herself and empty parked cars; she doubted it was ever really busy.

She peered in through one of the lower windows on the premises that had once been home to what she presumed was a wholesaler. Outdoor Pursuits had left some shelving behind and a sign above the door that said they had once stocked all you needed from walking to skiing gear and everything in between.

Callie stood for a few minutes, listening to the sound of the wind, slowly whipping its way up through the estate. It was a grey place, with torn-up tarmac, weeds and a scattering of cars that told a story of owners who were not making as much money as they would like. For all of that,

Callie liked it. It was low-key, probably cheap to rent and she had a feeling that if she put a little energy in to involving the other tenants, this whole estate could be transformed. Suddenly, something felt lighter in her. She could sense her optimism rising. This may not be the place for her, but surely, she would settle into something that would kick-start her enthusiasm again.

She backed away from the empty warehouse, and then headed home towards the cottage, a new hopefulness in her step. She was in many ways no nearer to making her mind up about what the future held, but she realised there were possibilities, even here in Ballycove, that she hadn't seen before and, of course, that meant there would be many more beyond this place.

Callie loved the aroma of the mills; it was something that took her back to her childhood. It was not the greeting of scented candles or rich coffee or even fresh paint. Rather, it was an altogether older, far less glamorous smell. It hit her when she stepped behind the façade of the shop and the restaurant, once she slipped through the door that read staff only and was key-pad-locked with the year of the mills' opening. It filled the narrow-vaulted tunnels that masqueraded as corridors to the older production areas within the mills' building. Of course, the smell of old machines, diesel and hot-pressed and cut fabric reminded her not only of the work she loved so much, but also of her childhood.

More than either of her siblings, Callie had spent all her spare time in the mills. She loved everything about the place, so when it came to deciding on her own career, it had always been in her head that she would work with knitwear. She may not be spinning yarns, or personally dyeing her own colours or shaping up the finished product, but she was working with wool, seeing it change from something natural into, if she was lucky, something of great beauty.

Now, she stopped to admire batches of brightly coloured rugs, folded and awaiting packaging, no doubt ready to be shipped off to various corners of the world. Callie ran her hand along the soft fabric. Really, when she stood here, listening to the cranking along of this wonderful old building, it hit her how very proud she was of everything her mother had achieved. Overhead, thick old beams stretched across the vast roof of the building. This corridor and all of the rooms were just partitioned off, albeit long enough ago to make the partitions feel solid, stable and permanent, but it gave the mills a hidden warren-like character that she had always loved as a child.

'Hello.' David Blair was standing at the end of the hallway, smiling at her, suddenly pulling her from the thoughts of childhood that had flooded her over. 'Sorry, did I startle you?'

'No, no, not really,' she said walking towards him, relieved perhaps to be pulled back to the present moment. 'I was just admiring the stock.' She smiled at him.

'Well, no harm in that,' he said. 'I suppose, it's quite the compliment, coming from *Callie Corrigan*.' He emphasised the last words, made a face to let her share the joke. 'David Blair,' he held out his hand to introduce himself and bowed slightly, as if meeting royalty which made them both giggle.

'Yes, well, don't lose the run of yourselves, I have very high standards.' She laughed, he was exactly as her mother had described him, affable, which made a much bigger impression than his good looks.

'Are you here for Miranda? I saw her leave just half an hour ago.' He nodded back towards a long window that threw the low light of winter into his office.

'Ah, no,' Callie said.

'Did she know you were coming?'

'No, I just called on the off chance that she might like to take a break and have a coffee with me.' Callie smiled now. It didn't matter; it was good that her mother was busy. 'Never mind, we can have coffee anytime.'

'Well, I'm free, if you fancy having one now,' he said, pulling the door of his office behind him. 'My treat.' He smiled.

'If you're offering to pay, I can hardly refuse.' Callie laughed again.

They settled into a tight table for two in a corner of the restaurant, a pot of tea and a window view of the river beyond.

'I'm still pinching myself, you know,' he said as he shook out two sugars into his cup. 'This place, it's just everything I need at the moment.'

'Ballycove or the mills?' she asked sipping her tea. It was hot and black and the tangy taste lingered on her lips pleasingly. She couldn't remember the last time she'd drunk coffee now and that thought struck her as odd, because, in a way, she'd gone off coffee just as she'd begun to feel this niggling sense of unease in herself. She put the thought that was rising in her mind firmly to the side. She couldn't be… She had to focus to listen to David once this thought settled on her.

'Well, both I suppose. Ballycove first though, the mills – working here with your mother and surrounded by all the history both our families share in this place, well it's like the icing on the cake for me.'

'It's funny,' Callie said. 'We forget that the Blair family history is as much tangled up in this place as the Corrigan ties. I suppose it's always been the Corrigan Mills for as long as I've known it.'

'Well, it is the Corrigan Mills – if it had been left to my family, I'm not sure it would have survived. Your father pulled this place back from the brink and Miranda has done a commendable job of making it into something very special.'

'Yes, Mamma certainly has the magic touch.' Callie smiled.

'And, she seems to have passed it on to you,' David said, watching her.

'Oh, I don't know about that. With me, it's all design. She has the magic ingredients that set her apart from any of us.'

'Why is that do you think?'

'Oh, I don't know that I'm the right one to answer that. If I was to take a guess, I'd say it's a mixture of passion and charm. Mamma loves the mills – Ada thinks she loves them more than her own family, but I don't think that's true.'

'And even if it was?'

'I'm not sure I'd blame her, most of the time. But then, I'm probably just as guilty when it comes to work.'

'Oh?'

'Yes, well, it consumes me, or it has.' She stopped, looked around for safer ground. 'I've never married, having a family of my own has sort of slipped me by; my career has been my whole life.' Callie felt there was hollowness in the words, but even if her heart was breaking for Theme and all the work she'd put in over the years, she'd realised since she came back it was not breaking for Dennis. 'I was never one of those girls who craved a big marshmallow white dress or walking down the aisle.' Still, there was no escaping the fact that her time to have a child was running out.

'So, you've never been in love.' His eyes were sad. 'I'm not sure if you're lucky or just sad that you've missed out.'

'I didn't say that…' She smiled. 'You're very easy to talk to.'

'I think you might be guilty of that too,' he said laughing, perhaps because, essentially, they were strangers, bordering on a conversation that was delicate. Their humour managed somehow to cover over any embarrassment. 'I think we could be great friends, if time allowed.'

'You know, I think you might be right,' she said now, thinking of all those other friends flung to the four corners of the world. 'Will you go back to London one day or is this home now?'

'That's the big question – I'm not sure I have an answer for that yet.' He smiled sadly. 'How about you? Your mother says you're on gardening leave.'

'I'm not sure.' She felt better for saying it; the only other person she'd been so candid with was Miranda.

'I see,' he said.

'No, I don't expect you do, not really.' She leant in, a little, over the table. 'You see, I haven't said anything to Ada or to Simon, but I'm taking time out – to consider…' She smiled then. 'I think maybe I'm finished with London.'

'But you're…'

'I know.' She could feel a weight lifting from her. 'I know, I'm Callie Corrigan, *the* Callie Corrigan and I seem to have it all, but...' She was poking fun at herself, but perhaps, it was the first time she had actually seen it all for what it was – empty. 'And maybe,' she said now really enjoying the honesty of her words, 'maybe, London is finished with me.'

'Well, I don't believe that, not for one moment,' he said, sipping his coffee and laying the cup down again. 'You know, sometimes, all we need is a break, to get a little perspective, just to catch up with ourselves.'

'No, it's more than that.' Now she felt the knot tighten in her stomach again. 'I messed up—' she put her hands out '—really, messed up.' She wasn't sure she could tell David Blair about the affair or even half of what might be ahead if she went back, but it was her mistake, her own doing that she'd ended up here and she was damned if she'd shirk responsibility for it.

'Whatever it is, it can't be that bad. Seriously, unless you murdered someone how bad could it be?'

'It's really bad and taking the time out has shown me that I have a choice. I don't have to live that life any more.' Everything about her life in London was so different to here. Even her lovely house in the right part of the city – it was all so far away from the life she'd come from and where she suspected now, she might belong.

'In that case, perhaps you're lucky.' He smiled, a lazy movement of his lips.

'How do you figure that?'

'Well, you've got the choice and more importantly you've seen it's a choice you need to make. You're right, of course, the fame and the money, the bright lights; it's all empty if you don't have genuine happiness.'

'I'm just learning that now,' she said softly.

'At least you are.' He looked out the window towards the river. 'It took me a long time to see it and I left it too late.'

'You were married?' Callie nodded towards the white band on his ring finger, where a wedding ring had obviously sat until recently.

'I still am, technically.'

'I bet you were good husband material.' She smiled.

'You'd think so, but not quite good enough, it seems. My wife, Alison, didn't agree; in fact, she figured she could probably meet a better one and apparently, she did.'

'I'm sorry.'

'Don't be, I've done quite enough of feeling sorry for myself at this stage. It's been over a year now and I only took off my wedding ring when I got to Ballycove.'

'Why did you take it off here?' She looked into his eyes.

'Too many questions – I figured it would be easier to start fresh. Pretend to everyone else that it had never happened, but I'm still carrying it about with me, so it turns out that pretending doesn't work so well.'

'But you're happy here?'

'I am. I've surprised myself by finding a different kind of happiness. My father suggested the move – there was talk of relocation at my last job so I walked instead and they were kind enough to pat me on the back with enough guilt money to set me up for a few months.' He smiled now. 'But then, I came to the mills one afternoon, sat over there—' he nodded towards a table in the centre of the restaurant '—and it just felt like I was exactly where I was meant to be.'

He smiled again. 'It sounds ridiculous, I know, but I went home and thought about the reasons for staying here or returning to London and there didn't seem to be any real contest.'

'Mamma is delighted you joined the mills,' Callie said softly.

'She's great – I love working with her, but I'm not so sure that Ada's exactly thrilled.'

'No, well, don't worry, that's just Ada. There's more to her manner than meets the eye. She'll thaw, given time.'

'She reminds me of my ex.' His eyes crinkled in the kind of amused smile that was neither happy nor judgemental.

'Is that a compliment?'

'In some ways, I suppose it is, but I'm not sure Ada would see it like that. I'm hoping she's only got the good stuff going on and she mellows with me sooner rather than later.'

'Oh, I'm sure she will, don't worry.' Callie saw Ada out of the corner of her eye, watching them from the shop floor, then she turned on her heels and Callie could have sworn that the look on her face spelled jealousy, far more than it did dislike.

30

Simon

Simon was woken, cruelly and unforgivably, by his mother's alarm clock. He groaned; it was years since he'd got out of bed at such an unearthly hour – it wasn't even seven thirty for God's sake. He dived further beneath the bed covers, intent on getting at least another three hours of sleep, but then he heard Callie's eternally cheerful voice chattering away to his mother and he knew it would be better for him if he made an appearance. He could always slink back to bed later – when his mother had left for the mills.

'Simon, there you are, I didn't expect you to waken for hours yet. Have you plans for today?' his mother asked brightly, placing a gaily patterned mug of piping hot tea before him.

'No, no, nothing especially, I have a few calls to make, but apart from that, I'm free as a bird. I might pop into the village later; grab a pub lunch, just to see what the locals have been up to.' Simon had all but lost touch with any of the kids he'd been in school with, except for Tim Leather. They'd kept in contact because they moved in similar circles for a few years and also because Simon always felt it was handy to keep close to the Leathers. Tim's father Stephen was probably his mother's closest advisor when it came to the mills. 'I might call into Tim; see how the good life is treating him.' He popped a slice of buttered toast in his mouth from Callie's plate. It seemed she'd gone right off her food these days. She was sitting with a cup of hot water and looking as peaky as he'd ever seen her. 'You all right, Callie?' he asked then, because his sister was probably the healthiest, most robust person he knew, apart from his mother – whose rude health had always been legendary until her fall a year earlier.

'Yeah, I'm fine, it's probably some kind of bug doing the rounds.'

'Maybe you should take it easy today, darling.' Miranda sat beside her daughter, but Callie moved her cup of tea further away as if even the smell of it might make her retch again. 'Oh, dear.' She patted Callie's shoulder and moved to the far end of the table, eyeing her with concern. Neither of them liked to be fussed over, totally opposite to Simon, who would have been milking a tummy bug for all it was worth.

'No pub lunch for you today, I'm afraid.'

'Urggh,' Callie said before disappearing back upstairs again.

'Never mind, I have a feeling it's not life-threatening,' Simon said commandeering the remainder of Callie's toast in her absence. 'Waste not want not.' He smiled at his mother but she did not smile back; instead her features were knitted into the kind of thoughtfulness that had cut her off from whatever he had said.

Stephen Leather and Sons operated the only legal practice in Ballycove. According to the sign over the door it was established long before Stephen had even been born by Charles Leather – probably Tim's great-grandfather. The practice had written every will, codicil and land agreement for the people of Ballycove for almost a hundred years now. The building, a newly modernised tall Georgian at the better end of Ballycove, had been in the family as long as the law had run through their veins, according to Tim.

Simon arrived just in time for lunch and hoped it wasn't a court day when Tim was likely to be taken up with all manner of unpleasantness.

'Lunch is on me,' he said slapping Tim on his back as they made their way into the local pub. Tim Leather had not aged well. Unlike Simon, he did not colour his hair, nor did he spend time on a skin regime of even the most basic measure. He had sunk into a provincial practice, marriage, fatherhood and a love of good food with the predictability of an only son who had been raised only for this end in mind. Still, Simon knew, he was a good egg, and if anyone could explain how he might sell on the mills to Günter Muller – it was Tim.

'So, you see, it would be the answer to all my mother's problems,' Simon said as they finished up dessert. 'She can't appoint Callie, and she's not keen to hand everything over to Ada and, of course, I've never had any interest in anything to do with the mills.'

'And these Mullers – they're looking to buy a mill in Ireland anyway?'

'Yes, they were looking on the east coast, but of course, we both know that the Corrigan Mills are the most prestigious around; so, if they had a shot at buying them, I think they'd offer well above the market value.' It wasn't strictly true. Simon had a feeling that the softest part of Herr Muller was his teeth, but that was beside the point. Tim wasn't an auctioneer; his area of expertise lay in a different field and one that might be far more relevant if Ada or Callie decided to put a spanner in the works.

'Well, that sounds very exciting. All the same, I'm sure that there'll be a lot of people in Ballycove worried about the future of the mills, but once you settle that, then…'

'The thing is…' Simon leaned a little closer to Tim and lowered his voice further. 'Well, you know what my family is like, between Ada and Callie and my mother – it's never easy to get agreement. Sometimes, I swear it's like brokering agreements in the United Nations, apart from the fact that we all speak the same language.' Simon laughed at this, hoping that it would make his motivation for bringing Tim to lunch appear less underhand. 'I suppose we're all at different stages in life. Both Callie and Ada are sitting on tidy retirement packages already, even though neither of them has any intention of retiring anytime soon, whereas I need to free up some capital…'

'Whoa there for a minute.' Tim held up his hands. 'If this lunch is about an investment in one of your business ventures we can stop right here, Simon. I never mix business with old friends. It's a recipe for disaster.'

'Tim, come on, I'm up to my eyes in investors. Really, that's not what I asked you here for at all.' The smooth lies really did slip from the lips down here in Ballycove – if only he could work the same magic back in Dublin. 'Actually, what I wanted was to ask you a few questions about how I could go about selling my share of the mills if Callie and Ada refuse to sell theirs.'

'Ah, right,' Tim said, taking up an after-dinner mint from the small saucer that had arrived with their bill. He chewed on it thoughtfully, then looked at Simon. 'I'm not sure that you can. It depends on how the articles of agreement were drawn up when your mother made the mills over into a company with you all as shareholders. You'd have to check that out.'

'Can't you?' Simon asked.

'I don't think that I can do that. It wouldn't be exactly ethical to advise you on something like this. We act on behalf of your mother and in the interests of the mill – that means in the interests of all the directors. This couldn't be said to be in the interests of all of them, could it? I mean, if Ada isn't keen to sell, it's unlikely she's going to want a new set of investors in the mills taking up the space that is currently owned by you.'

'So, you won't tell me?' Simon tried not to sound petulant, but it was not easy.

'I will tell you that in the company documents, which should be kept safe somewhere in the mills, you will find the answer to your question, but off the top of my head, I couldn't tell you if I wanted to. I simply don't know the ins and outs of your company agreement. My father drew up all of those documents as you probably remember.'

Well, Simon thought as he made his way back to Bridgestock Cottage for an afternoon nap, it wasn't the worst news he could have got. There was no doubt in his mind, having broached the notion of selling the mills to the Mullers with both his mother and Ada, that neither of them would be in agreement. Not that he'd really expected them to be, but there was more than one way to skin a cat. He hadn't even tried Callie yet, but he knew her well enough to know that it was all about timing. He couldn't just barge in to a conversation about it. It would have to be brought up at the most opportune moment and no doubt that would yet present itself.

For now, he had only two things to do. First, find that document that set out the terms and rules for the ownership or more importantly the transfer of ownership of the mills. He'd looked up recent sales of mills and the last one listed had been the Muller acquisition in Scotland – they'd paid six point two million for a wreck of a place that seemed to offer little more in the way of international product than fishing caps and gilets. The Corrigan Mills were in a completely different league.

By the time Simon reached the cottage, he'd put the price at a generous twelve million and he'd already spent most of his share in his imagination on a villa in Monte Carlo and a very nice sports car to replace his old banger. He'd shake the dust of this place off his shoes quicker than it would take him to say adieus to everything about it that, to his mind at least, had always held him back.

Now all he needed was to get into the mills on a day when there was no-one else about and have a good root about his mother's office where she kept a huge safe locked with a combination that included all of their birthdays and her own anniversary date.

First though, before he even went inside the cottage,

he decided to call Günter – just to keep the lines of communication open. He needed to make sure the German wasn't tempted to make an offer on anything else. Simon was laying the ground so he could extract a really hefty price for the mills and if not, then perhaps float the possibility of selling the mills off one lovely expensive slice at a time.

31

Ada

It was always the same, as far as Ada was concerned. Her mother and Callie – they had frozen her out. In their way, it was not a nasty or mean thing, but rather it seemed that they had their own shorthand language so, when she was with them, they finished each other's sentences and then laughed as if it was something new. Worse, it felt as though she was missing out on something in the conversation. She put it down to the fact that they were just different people. Callie was so much more like their mother than she, with her analytical brain and need for complete order. Still, the conversation with Simon unsettled her enough to rouse her from her normal routine to drive up to Bridgestock Cottage and call on them.

'Well, this is a lovely surprise.' Her mother embraced her and Ada had a feeling that she meant it. 'What brings you up here?' They were in the garden, a perfect rural idyll – the last place Ada would have chosen to spend a Saturday afternoon. 'Here, come sit with me.' Her mother had set herself up on the old swing, a large soft pillow at her back; she patted the seat beside her. Callie was sweeping leaves from the paths that meandered too close to the trees to be a sensible idea.

'I'll get us all some tea in a minute,' Callie said, standing up for a moment and arching her back, a movement that at once displayed her svelte shape and also suggested that she'd put in quite a bit of back-breaking work in the garden.

'You've been busy,' Ada lied, because honestly, she wouldn't be able to tell what was done in the garden since she'd been here last. Simon had mentioned that when Callie and their mother weren't cooking up secret plans between them, she spent the rest of her time divided between the garden and the kitchen.

'Maybe you can talk some sense into her,' her mother said in a lilting happy voice that Ada hadn't heard in some time. 'She's killing herself out here and really, all of this work, I can just get Bert's son up and he'll take care of the lot for me.' She shook her head good-naturedly. 'She's trimmed the beech hedging back for autumn already today.'

'Really?' Ada looked along the apparently infinite hedging. It certainly explained the leaves.

'Oh, Mamma, I'm enjoying it. When do I get the chance to do this in London?' She pulled off the heavy-duty gardening gloves and popped them, with her rake, into the barrow already filled to overflowing with leaves. She ran her hand through her hair, pulling it back from her face, and looked towards the sun – they really were, Ada thought, so very different. 'You're in luck, Ada. I've been baking.'

'I didn't know you baked.' Ada wasn't sure if it was a

good or a bad thing, her sister taking so enthusiastically to country life.

'Well, I don't really, but there seemed to be so many ingredients between the garden and the store presses and I found a recipe book that belonged to our grandmother – so you're sampling my best offering so far.'

'You're in for a treat – jam and coconut buns. I haven't had anything like them in years. Actually, I'm sure most young people have never tasted them. I think I'll bring the recipe down to the mills, see if we can't add them onto the early morning baking now and again.' Miranda had her eyes closed, reclining in the old swing. She looked younger and happier than she had in years.

'Well, I'll try them, but you know I don't usually eat between meals so...' Ada said and thought how much nicer it would be to be sitting inside today. It was actually a little chilly here in the garden. 'It's not too cold for you here, Mother?'

'Oh, Ada, don't be such a fusspot. I've enough clothes on me to keep me warm at the top of Mount Everest; really, you're such an old biddy sometimes.'

'Here, take this and it'll warm you up while I organise the tea for us.' Callie took the rake from the barrow and placed it in Ada's unwelcoming hands.

'Right so, I will,' Ada said with an edge to her voice that made Callie and Miranda exchange a glance that she knew meant more than she'd ever fathom. She started to gather up the leaves and branches into neat piles along the grass. It was the kind of work that she detested, but somehow, she felt that by doing it, she might just manage to curry favour in some small way with her mother.

'It's nice, having you both here, for a change,' Miranda said sleepily, her eyes still firmly shut against the sun, but her face set in a serene smile. She seemed to be in that lovely relaxed place, not asleep, but drifting on the edge of a contented nap. Ada continued to rake the leaves away from the grass to small piles along the path.

'No Simon today then?' Ada asked, as much out of something to say as any real curiosity. It was the weekend. No doubt her brother would travel to the bright lights to stay with some old school chum and carouse the pubs, clubs and parties until the early hours.

'No, he's gone into the mills. He'll be back later.'

'The mills – what's he doing there at the weekend?' Ada actually thought to herself: *What's he doing there at all?*

'Oh, didn't I mention it to you? Oh, dear.' Her mother shook her head, but they both knew, Miranda never forgot anything, regardless of what Ada might have insinuated about her being ready for the scrap heap. 'He's all fired up about David's idea for a fair in Australia. He suggested putting together a men's collection. Just a couple of pieces from the older designs, a sort of vintage man range. He's really enthusiastic about it. He rushed off first thing this morning while the mills are closed.'

'I suspect he has his eye on that pretty cashier as well, Mother.' Callie laughed as she set down a tray with three steaming mugs and scones for each of them. 'You know Simon, never a man to give without getting something back for himself.' She shook her head and handed a mug to Miranda.

'No, I think it's more about making the mills seem more multinational, believe it or not,' Miranda murmured.

'Well, he never mentioned that to me.' Ada bristled at the thought of his impromptu visit to her house to when he talked about everything but being *fired up*. 'He did mention that you were running up some designs for us though.' She looked across at Callie now, eyeballing her so there was no room to fudge.

'He exaggerated, I'm afraid.' Callie smiled easily, in that way she had of making everyone think she had nothing to hide, when for years, Ada had a feeling she was hiding a lot more than any of them would ever know about. 'No, David has pulled out some of my old designs and they're just being reworked, with new material, buttons – detail work.'

'I see,' Ada said, although she hadn't the foggiest what the difference was between designing something and reworking it.

'Callie won't be putting her name to the pieces she's doing, Ada; they are strictly a favour to me.' Miranda had opened her eyes now and was watching her daughters intently as though measuring them up against each other.

'Yes, didn't you hear? I'm on gardening leave. No work for me – well, not the designing kind at least.' Callie laughed at that, sharing a joke with Miranda that was probably meant for all of them, but Ada couldn't see where the humour was in it.

'Really?' The least Ada could do was seem surprised; after all, they needn't know that she had any inkling of what they might be up to. 'I just thought you'd come home to check up on Mother – after her little scare a few months ago, that you were just here to...' Her words drifted off, partly because she felt Miranda's eyes boring into her and partly because she didn't need to say any more to get her point across.

'Well, if I was coming home to see how she was, it would have been a bit of a wasted trip, wouldn't it?' Callie stared pointedly at Ada and they both knew that the conversation about their mother's health was at an end.

'Well, I must say, I'm a little chuffed that everyone is so worried about me,' Miranda said acidly. They all knew Miranda never wanted anyone making plans for her or deciding that they knew what was best for her. 'Lucky I still have the wherewithal to look after myself then, isn't it?' And with that, the atmosphere that had been in the garden soured as tangibly as if someone had drawn a dark cloud over the three of them.

Ada, being Ada, was probably the least affected by the change in mood. All the same, she sipped her tea slowly and crossed her arms when she left it down on the ground at her feet. The silence seemed to stretch on for an age and then, in the end, it was Callie who broke it.

'Mamma, you know that Ada has been worried about you since you had that turn.'

'There's really no need to be worried.'

'I know, but you gave her a terrible fright and…' Callie turned that high-watt smile now towards their mother. 'And you know, Ada, I couldn't come over any sooner, but I'm here now and I have to say, I've never seen Mamma looking so well or fit or healthy. She's taking care of herself and there's no need to worry.'

'Humph.' Their mother said and Ada had a feeling that she was biting down a remark that might make them all feel uncomfortable with how close to the truth it could be.

'Look,' Callie said squishing in between them on the

swing. 'Why don't I cook dinner for all of us? Next week, some night, just the family – what do you say, Ada? You and Anthony, Mamma, Simon and me – it would be a lovely way for us all to catch up and spend some time together.' Her mother smiled at this idea; of course, she'd always had a full kitchen at every opportunity.

'I'll have to ask Tony if he's available…' Ada said and then stopped, because they all knew that Tony was always available; it was more a question of whether he could be bothered to pull himself away from the television for a few hours.

'He'd love it,' Miranda said firmly. 'Actually, just the other day, when we were talking on the phone, he asked me for ideas to get you both out of the house a bit more.' She closed her eyes once more against the sun.

'Really?' Ada asked. It seemed to her that Tony was acting more strangely with every passing day. Still, there was a desperation to it that didn't exactly fuel any attraction in her for him. Compared to what she considered David's sophistication, it made poor Tony seem rather pathetic, she thought sadly.

'Really,' her mother confirmed before her face returned to that serene expression that had been there previously. Ada sipped her tea quietly, her thoughts a maelstrom of questions thundering through her brain so fast that she wasn't sure which one needed answering first.

'Friday, so?' Callie said to no-one in particular and both of them at the same time.

'Friday,' they murmured in a disjointed chorus.

*

Ada wasn't sure what was wrong with her. Regardless of what Tony thought, she didn't feel down in the dumps so much as a sense of foreboding that she just couldn't shake off. It was to do mostly with the mills, perhaps the notion of things dying between herself and Tony too, but then, sometimes, she'd feel this uncontrollable dizziness, perhaps at the notion of the huge changes she was hoping for herself. In the coming week she would look into the ins and outs of buying out Simon's share of the mills. There was so much to do, from freeing up equity to actually putting a value on the share. Then, when she was quite sure it was the right thing to do, she would ring up Stephen Leather to find out if it was even possible to buy her brother's shares, or if indeed her mother had managed to block this also.

'Go for a walk,' Anthony encouraged her, as though it had worked for him at some point.

'Maybe,' she said, but the truth was, a combination of lethargy and the fear of running into David Blair and her mother together, prevented her from leaving her office most days and by the time she arrived home in the evenings, she was simply too tired to move much more than to top up her glass of wine.

Why was she afraid of bumping into David Blair anyway? She had vowed that she would in some way move their relationship nearer to where she wanted it to be – where did she want it to be? Ada wasn't sure she could answer this honestly, even to herself, if she tried. His effect on her was something she'd never experienced before. She wanted to dislike him intensely. It would be so much easier if she could point out his many faults, but the truth was she'd only spoken to him on a few occasions – that first when she met him on the beach, the second when she returned his jacket and then occasionally bumping into him at the mills and hardly passing the time of the day because she seemed to redden at the very sight of him.

The jacket – now that may be partly to blame for how she felt. Guilt? It could be. She had put it in her car the following day, with every intention of just handing it over. But it was the waxy, leathery maleness of it – it filled her car with something too masculine but at the same time, too familiar to ignore. So, she had pulled in to the hard shoulder, taken it in her hands and breathed in the scent of him. Had it been some sort of animalistic thing – an imprinting of his scent on her senses?

She had checked the pockets too – their contents told her very little, aside from a penchant for mints and a note with a phone number scrawled across it in undeniably girlish writing. There was a loop to the numbers, as though the person had taken time to get them right, to impress him. Ada found herself wondering at odd moments about the girl who wrote those numbers. Was she just some passing stranger hoping to see him again? Or was she someone vital to him, whose life would map up against his and take him from Ballycove just as quickly as he'd arrived? Was it better that he leave Ballycove with some stranger that she didn't know or with Callie? Oh, she'd seen them together, in the mills; there was no missing the connection between them.

The notion of David and Callie together made Ada feel as if she might be physically ill – she didn't dare admit that what she felt was that old familiar feeling Callie always brought up in her – envy. And still, she was adamant; she could not be falling in love with him. That would be quite ridiculous and completely beyond her range of experience. She wasn't even sure she'd fallen in love with Anthony. No, the connection she felt with David Blair went much deeper than mere attraction and that affected her in a way that was very worrying.

Yes, perhaps he'd leave just as easily as he'd appeared to throw her world upon this unfamiliar axis.

That thought made her feel conflicted, because it would be a good thing, wouldn't it? If he left? After all, Ada did not want her mother handing over the mills that were rightfully hers to David. On the other hand, the notion of not seeing him ever again – well, that was one that she just didn't want to think about.

These last few days, she caught herself stealing surreptitious glances across at Tony, comparing him in some childish way to David. Poor Tony, with his lifestyle of armchair sports, high carbohydrate diet and love of beer did not fare well in the comparison. There probably wasn't very much between the two men in years, but lifestyle had left its mark on both of them and it was very apparent that David had the better lifestyle of the two, by a mile.

What was she like? It was just a phase, that was it, she told herself. Her hormones, the menopause? Working too hard – she needed to take a break, that was all. Perhaps she would shake herself out of it and put David Blair from her mind; although, if she was honest with herself, she knew it was the last thing she wanted or intended.

★

And so it was that Ada walked with both mission and purpose. The mills, while being a huge building, was a small place and the following day, Ada nearly jumped out of her skin when she looked up to see him standing at the door to her office.

'Hey, neighbour,' he said, tapping lightly on her door. He could have been standing there for God alone knew how long.

'Oh, yes? Hello,' she said, hoping she sounded professional and businesslike.

'We're officially neighbours on this corridor – I thought I should come in and let you know I'll be moving in tomorrow.' He smiled at her now, a playful pull on one corner of his lips. His dipped his voice. 'Probably won't be having a moving-in party, but I'll make sure there's a bottle in the drawer if you ever feel like you need a little fortifying.' He laughed at this, apparently oblivious to her deep embarrassment. Damn hot flushes, she was burning up from within like Vesuvius with nowhere to go. Then he moved closer to the desk, looked into her eyes for just a moment, and she thought she might drown in their depths. 'You okay? I do hope I didn't scare you?'

'No, no. Well, you did make me jump, a little.' She felt a smile creeping over her own features now. 'Just arriving there, but no harm. It was a pleasant surprise, so I'll get over it.' She could hear her voice, but it didn't sound anything like it usually did to her. It was more playful, girlish, and she knew, without a doubt, there wasn't a solitary thing she could do about it. 'I checked on it, a couple of days ago – it's going to be very swish.' She half nodded to the wall that separated the two offices.

'I don't know about that, but I have a feeling I'll be happy here.' He smiled at her now, and stood grinning for a moment, as though there was something else he needed to say to finish the sentence. Then he looked around her office, his eyes settling on the old desk that had once been her father's. 'Hello, that looks pretty ancient.' He walked over towards it, stroked the top of it with his palm. 'It's very… unusual.' He looked about him as though taking in everything about her office and then settled his eyes on her, for what seemed like an eternity.

'It was… my father's; it's been stored next door for years. I asked the men to move it in here, for now. My mother doesn't know… I mean, she's probably forgotten it was even still in the mills. I didn't tell her about it, you see. I wouldn't want to upset her.' It was partly true, but the real reason she hadn't said anything yet was that locked bureau drawer.

'Of course.' He put a finger to his lips. 'Your secret is safe with me. I know what it's like to want to forget about the past. Your mother might be better off.' He smiled sadly then and Ada felt like there was so much more she wanted to learn about him, but she knew she'd never ask. 'Well, pop over when I've settled in. We can have a little moving-in drink to christen the place.' He winked then and was gone before she had a chance to say anything more, but she had every intention of accepting his invitation.

32

They had ten wonderful Christmases in Bridgestock Cottage and Miranda was happier than she could have ever wished. Their baby, a little girl they called Callie after old Mrs Bridgestock, arrived promptly on her due date. Everyone said she was the picture of Miranda and something inside her felt that there was some little extra connection with this tiny girl. She became a contented, composed child, who seemed to have the ability to make the cottage even happier when she smiled.

Of course, each of their children was developing into the person they would one day become. Ada grew into a delicate child without being spoiled; the oldest of the family. She took on the responsibility for the others, like a second-in-command, as if she was born to it. Simon became a fair-haired, reedy boy, dodging duty with an easy charm and a winning smile. And it seemed, before long, Bridgestock Cottage had become a home and they had three healthy, vibrant children– each as different to each other as it was possible to imagine.

Miranda made the cottage into a home filled with family and welcoming to all, especially any who had nowhere else to call a home for Christmas dinner. Miranda loved Christmas.

'A toast.' Paddy held up his glass one Christmas Day. 'To my lovely wife, who's made me the happiest man in Ballycove.' He smiled at Miranda and she knew they were very lucky. They had a happy home and the mills were making enough money to enable them to see their way to almost fully repaying the overhanging debts that had built up over the years. She looked down the table at Paddy and held his eye for just a moment; yes, they were lucky, she knew that.

Later that night, when everyone had left and the children were tucked up in bed, they sat looking out at a clear night sky, the frost settling on the land outside their window. 'It's going to be a good year for us,' Paddy said to her, pulling her close within the circle of his arm.

'I couldn't ask for any more than this,' Miranda said honestly.

'Well, you're going to have a lot more,' he said laughing now.

'What, you've got something to tell me?'

'I wasn't going to tell you until it was all done, but in the New Year, I have an appointment with some of the bigwigs in the Irish Army. I'm hoping that they'll make a huge order. It could run for the next five years with a bit of luck.'

'Can we cope with that size of order?' The mills were working flat out, as things were.

'Oh, yes, it's the only way to grow. I will look at taking on more workers and we may have to work into the night, create shifts that go right round the clock, but Miranda, it could...'

'Well, I'll leave all that to you.' She smiled at him.

The New Year started with a blizzard. Miranda and the children didn't leave the cottage for three days apart from to play in the garden and when they did eventually venture past the front gate, it was to walk slowly to the village only to burn off the children's excitement.

'You can't go driving off to Dublin in this weather; surely, they'll make a different date to meet,' she said to Paddy as the snow seemed to be starting up again.

'I'm afraid I'll have to. The last thing I want is one of the other mills getting in there before me and at least the roads will be empty.' He rubbed his back thoughtfully; it was a habit he had developed only in the last few weeks.

'Are you all right?' She nodded towards his back. 'You're not in pain?' He worked too hard, never gave a thought to looking after himself. If he wasn't bent over mending a machine he was out hauling in wool or dragging the mower across the uneven gardens they were still trying to tame.

'Ah no, it's just the way I slept, I expect, a niggling that's just not moving.' He smiled at her then. 'Nothing that a good night's sleep wouldn't sort out.' He was on his way then, off to sell more blankets and Miranda didn't think of it again, because that evening they had too much to celebrate and within a week the factory was working as it never had before. They were producing hundreds of mossy green woollen blankets for the Irish Army, with strict delivery deadlines.

'But when do we get paid?' Miranda asked him months later. She wanted to know, because it seemed like the cheque was never going to arrive.

'All in good time,' Paddy said and, in the meantime, the bank was happy to step in. Except, all in good time seemed to take an awfully long time. Winter moved into spring, blankets were produced and invoices sent; orders were increased and so too was the overdraft. Paddy became greyer of face and the niggling pain in his back became worse. Miranda wondered if it might not be stress and then came the terrible news that the army contract had fallen through. It turned out that payments had been made, only not to the mills. Thousands of pounds had gone astray. It would take investigations, inquiries and court cases to put it all to rights. Unfortunately for the Corrigans the banks were not prepared to wait.

'What can we do?' Miranda asked Paddy one evening, as they sat sharing a bottle of stout in the garden. The children played among the trees that bordered the vegetable garden and a little stream which ran just thick enough in summer for slim brown trout to make their way along through jagged rocks beneath.

'I don't know,' he breathed and it seemed for the first time she noticed just how gaunt he had become. His normally healthy skin had faded to grey and his eyes seemed to have sunken into sockets bony and black. 'Don't worry your head about it now,' he said and she figured he was worrying enough for both of them.

'To be honest, Paddy, I'm far more worried about you than I am about the mills. We'll be all right. The mills, somehow we'll pull them back, but you're not taking care of yourself; that back isn't getting any better.' It was true, she heard him moan softly in the night as he twisted to find some comfort. 'Will you go to the doctor's again, tell him that it's hanging on too long and your wife is nagging you about it?' She smiled at him now.

'Ah, Miranda, no doctor is going to believe you'd even know how to nag me...' He laughed.

'Please, Paddy, for me.' She tied her arms about his shoulders. He had lost weight. She could feel his chest, bony and sinewy compared to the big barrel of a man she'd married a few short years earlier.

'Fine, if it makes you happy, I'll make an appointment, but it's nothing more than a touch of backache. It's the same as my grandfather had and probably his father before him.' He shook his head and went back to thinking of ways he might save the mills.

It turned out not to be a simple case of backache. Miranda blamed herself later. She should have noticed something, perhaps pushed him into more tests or taking things easy or... Well, by the time it was confirmed, they knew it was all they could do to take away the pain. Within two weeks of collapsing on the factory floor, Paddy was sent home with the doctor, a grey-haired morose chain smoker, telling them he was 'riddled with the cancer,' and 'he should make the best of what he had left.'

'Come on, Miranda,' Paddy tried to cajole her. 'Sure, what do they know?' But he had wasted away to half the man she'd married.

'Oh, Paddy.' Miranda didn't want him to have to be

strong for her. She wanted to be strong for him. She wanted to tell him that it would be all right, that they would be grand again. She wanted him to know that somehow, she would manage on her own. She would rear three children to make him proud. She would manage to keep the roof over their heads and food on the table.

'The mills…' he breathed, because even thinking about the mess that had grown from the army contract, drained them both now. 'The mills could be the saving of you,' he whispered.

'We'll be fine, Paddy, just wait and see.' Within a week, she had managed to plaster a smile on her lips that she hoped could fool the world that all was well. She hoped it would help Paddy, because God knows, there wasn't much else she could do to help him now.

'Maybe…' He was looking out the window to where the children were playing in the garden. 'Maybe if I contacted the Blairs…'

'No.' She rounded on him. 'No, Paddy, let me see what I can do first.' The last thing she needed now was any contact with Richard or his family. Then she continued more gently, 'if they think that we can't manage, that I can't manage, well, they might decide to take some action and…'

'Miranda, you're worrying too much. The mills are ours now. You remember Richard Blair; he would only help.'

'I don't want his help,' she whispered as she leaned her head beside him and she realised that now all she wanted was to have Paddy well and fit again.

And so, the Blairs remained unaware that Paddy Corrigan, was dying and with his passing, the slip of a girl that once went fishing with their son was about to step into his shoes.

★

The end, when it came, came quickly. Miranda spent four days at Paddy's bedside. The local doctor organised for the strongest painkiller he could manage and Paddy, even if he wasn't always in his right mind, at least did not suffer as much as he might have. The priest tried to set up camp too, but Paddy sent him packing.

'You'll get your chance,' he breathed. 'I need to talk to Miranda.'

'Paddy, you don't need to tell me anything,' Miranda said gripping his hand as though it might somehow hold him in her world for just a little longer.

'But, I do, my love.' A tear slipped from his eye.

'I've known all I need to know, darling. I know that I've been loved as few women are ever lucky enough to be loved. I know that no matter what parts us, the time we've spent together is worth more than any years I have to stay here without you.' She tried not to cry, but it was impossible to keep the reality of this moment from her eyes.

'No, Miranda. You need to listen to me. The Blairs... the mills...'

'Oh, Paddy. Don't be talking about the mills now... You mustn't worry yourself with them.'

'But, Miranda, I want to tell you.' He coughed then; it was a painful, rattling, bony sound as if all that was left of him were nuts and bolts and nothing to cushion them any more. 'The mills are your best chance at a future for you and the children. If you can save them, they could be our legacy, well yours... to our family, to Ballycove...' He took a long pacey breath. 'We owe it to everyone who works there, to make the most of it… There's a way, to save it. I just know there is and if this bloody disease hadn't set it, I would have figured it, Miranda, you know that.'

'Oh, Paddy, I've known that all along.' She hated this disease. Cancer, it started in his spine and wasn't going to stop until it took him from her. 'I…' She didn't know what to say. He wanted her to promise him that she would save the mills, but that was something neither of them could guarantee.

'Whatever you do, I'll be near you, all the time, Miranda. I won't leave you on your own, I promise, just…'

'Oh, Paddy, you know if there was anything I could do for you.' Suddenly, the enormity of what he was asking hit her. He wanted her to carry on the work he'd started. He wanted her to save the mills from certain closure; perhaps even from a worse state than when he'd taken over. 'I'd do anything for you; you know that, but the mills? We have three small kids, three…' She shook her head. It was impossible. At last count, they owed the banks tens of thousands of pounds; it would take decades to pay it all back at the rate they were currently making profits.

'Exactly, Miranda. We have three children; you are going to need the mills even more when I'm not here – and what about all those other families also?' He looked away for a moment. 'There's no-one else, and you know that as well as I do.'

'Of course there is, there's…' Miranda exhaled, because there was no-one else. There was nobody in the village who could do what Paddy had done. He had turned the mills around from losing money to making a healthy profit and he would have done more, if it wasn't for bad luck and

a rogue accountant somewhere in the Irish Army. 'I'll...'
There was no choice; she had to agree, if only to give him
some peace. 'I'll do my best for you, Paddy. I'll work as hard
as I can, but you know how things are...'

'I know how things are, but...' His breath heaved, as
though his chest might finally give in. 'If anyone can bring
them to rights, you can, Miranda. I'll be right beside you, all
the way, if I can figure a way to make it easier, I promise, I'll
let you know.' He smiled at her then, that familiar crinkling
of his eyes that had always made her feel like she was the
only person in the world for him.

'Oh, Paddy, I don't want to let you down.' She rested her
head on his chest, couldn't take seeing the hope in his eyes
any longer. She knew there wasn't much time left, maybe he
did too. 'I love you so much.'

'I know, darling, you never could let me down, not if
you tried,' he said gently then and his breathing evened
out so she knew he was slipping into the light sleep that
punctuated his waking hours. She rested her head against
him for some time, waiting until he opened his eyes again.
'There's only one more thing...'

'Yes.' She raised her head.

'Richard Blair?'

'Oh, don't let's talk about the past now, Paddy. We're
here and now. This is what matters... you and me. I will try
to save the mills, but I don't want to involve Richard Blair
or his money.'

'It's not that, Miranda, you don't understand. He loved
you, he really loved you and I should have told you but...
I was afraid.' Paddy wheezed a shallow, rattling breath. 'At
the funeral... we spoke about... that time.'

'Oh, Paddy, it's all so long ago now.' Miranda shook her head. She didn't care about Richard Blair at this moment; all she cared about was Paddy.

'No, no, you have to listen. There was a mix-up, some kind of stupid mix-up. He didn't stop loving you; not for one second. I'll bet he never has...'

'But the letter, his grandmother herself wrote to say he was engaged...' Miranda smiled at him, assuming the morphine was playing tricks on his memory.

'I know all of that, but... I think he was telling me the truth. He only got engaged to Constance because he heard we had married. It was all some misunderstanding, or at least that's what we should suppose; although I'd have my doubts that Edwin didn't...' He sighed. 'Anyway, I had to tell you...' He smiled at her now and it was such a heartbreakingly grainy flicker, but it caught in his eyes that gentle generosity that she loved so much. 'You should find him, after all of this; tell him what you know. He will help you.'

'Oh, Paddy, none of this is of any consequence now, don't you see – my life was here with you, and it's where I was always meant to be.' She bent down on his chest, knowing in some deep part of her that her darling Paddy had carried this as a guilty secret and it had weighed on him far too heavily when he was already carrying enough in life. She listened to his measured and weakened heartbeat beneath her ear, so precious now that its beat was slowing to a stop. He fell into a kind of easy stupor these last few days, between his words, and then could wake with a breath and take up his sentence as though he'd just left off.

'There was a letter...'

'I thought you were asleep.' She smiled at him, remembering that letter he'd delivered long ago from Lady Blair. 'It's long gone now, Paddy, please don't be worrying yourself. You were only the messenger delivering it. Everything was as it was meant to be.'

'Not yet, my love...' he whispered. 'Richard Blair...'

'Oh, don't be worrying about the Blairs or the mills now. Let's just enjoy this time together.' It was all too much; this was just detail from the past. It was worthless, superficial stuff now in the face of her dying husband, her children playing in the garden and her future thrown up in the air. Why was he worrying about this now? Surely he knew that it didn't matter? 'This is all in the past, Paddy, it makes no difference to us now.' She heard herself say the words and they sounded as though they'd been dried across desert sands.

'It was, but I wanted to tell you, I just...' He sighed. 'Well, there just never seemed to be the right time and...' He pulled his breath in raggedly. 'Maybe, I was afraid to tell you. I was afraid that if you knew, you'd hightail it off to England and that would be the last I'd see of you...' He smiled now; it was a poignant shadow of the smile she'd grown to love.

'Well, all's well that ends well.' Miranda wasn't going to be thinking of things now that couldn't be changed. Her husband was dying – that was all that mattered to her.

'I've kept that to myself all these years...' He closed his eyes.

'You daft old thing.' She laughed at him now. She didn't think about Richard Blair any more, not like that. She'd made her bed and she was more than happy with it. The only time she thought of Richard was if she passed by the bridge and those happy childhood days popped into her brain. Perhaps now, with the work ahead of her at the mills, she would think of him more often, but she didn't expect it to be with any notions of far-off fields being greener. 'Lucky me that you didn't tell me – what if I did leave? We wouldn't have our lovely children, or this home or—' she bent down now and kissed him lingeringly on his forehead '—I wouldn't have had the happy years we've shared and, Paddy, I'm going to treasure these times for as long as I live. You had nothing to worry about; I ended up exactly where I belonged.'

'Thank you,' he said on a shallow breath. 'I can go in peace now.' He closed his eyes and fell into a soft and contented sleep. Miranda thought her heart would break, but she rested her head beside him on the bed and waited for the children to come in and wish their father goodnight. Outside, she heard her mother, calling them in for their supper; the light was fading fast off behind Briar Hill in the west.

The room, their bedroom, with its little window and old-fashioned fireplace was silent, bar the tick tock of an old carriage clock that was another remnant from when Mrs Bridgestock lived here. Miranda closed her eyes and slept for the last time alongside her husband. When she woke, the children were standing over her and Paddy had eased out of her world as gently as if he'd tiptoed through the door and let himself out into the darkening garden beyond.

33

Callie

By her own calculations, Callie figured she was roughly ten weeks pregnant. It made sense of how she'd been feeling for the last few weeks and maybe how she'd been acting. She'd never felt happier, playing housewife while her mother went out to the mills each day. The pregnancy test had inked out a clear blue line and as she held it in her hand, Callie felt her whole world had slid into a sort of parallel place – a place she'd thought she'd never have access to. She'd kept it to herself, these past few weeks, knowing only too well that her mother would worry and Ada would ask questions Callie was not prepared to answer. She needed time to think and wasn't that what coming home to Ballycove had been all about?

Callie had left her phone in the cottage and was greeted by its ring when she arrived back. She had successfully detoxed from the constant stream of calls and emails since she'd come back here – none of it mattered any more, now she was no longer at Theme. She picked her phone up from the kitchen table. Her breath caught in her chest when she saw the caller's name. Dennis. She dithered for a moment, which was most unlike her, and then the call died in her hand taking the decision from her for now.

Dennis was ringing her, trying to contact her and she supposed she should be happy about that; after all, he was the father of her unborn child. She'd have to tell him sooner or later, but for now, she knew the truth was she had a sense that talking to him would not make her feel any better.

Truly, she had nothing to say to him. Of course, she could cry and scream at the unfairness of it all, but she knew she had no right. She had been his mistress, no more and no less. When it came to having privileges around honesty or loyalty the ground beneath her feet was shaky at best. The funny thing was she didn't feel as if her heart might break for him now. Here, in her mother's homely cottage, she could see through Dennis and all they'd had together. If anything, she might have regretted the years and energy she'd wasted on him, but Callie had never been one to linger in regret and anyway, her baby would make up for all of that.

So instead, she decided to put it down to experience. She had learned the hard way, it seemed. She had fallen, blindly and stupidly, for the man she thought he was and now, well, she could see that he could have been so much more. Yes, when it rang again she was ready to answer it.

'Hey, babe.' Dennis's voice was smooth on the other end of the line and, vaguely, she pictured him, sitting behind his sparse desk looking across the London skyline.

'Hello, Dennis,' she said curtly. 'What can I do for you?'

'Well, that's not very friendly,' he said, but there was

caginess to his voice and she wondered how much he knew at this point.

'I'm on leave, haven't you heard? On holiday means I'm not really expecting calls from work.'

'So, that's how you're playing it...' His voice dipped to something she'd heard only used on other people. 'There's a rumour doing the rounds here that you've left... resigned from the company...'

'Oh?' Callie was enjoying this now. She had agreed on her exit package that no formal statement would be made for at least six weeks. For her it was about making sure that her financial arrangements were in place and since the agreed amount had been deposited in her bank account a few days earlier, she didn't mind Dennis knowing now. 'Well yes, but you'd really need to ask your wife about when that's going to be made public.'

'Veronica?' he said.

'Yes, Dennis, I believe that's her name.'

'But I don't understand...'

'Don't you? Really?' Callie laughed and even if he did break her heart, she knew that she didn't love him any more. Perhaps she hadn't loved him in a while and this moment was one that she was going to enjoy. 'We met, that last week I was in London, had a lovely lunch and a little chat about how the land lies. She was quite happy to agree a favourable exit package; of course, she doesn't know about your little friend in the gallery, but she was happy enough to think that I was leaving you behind.'

'You've already agreed a severance package... and...'

'Yes, Dennis. I've resigned and your wife has been kind

enough to open the door widely for me with a very, very generous golden handshake.'

'But you're... we were together, you and I...' Dennis wasn't sure what to say and Callie could hear so many different questions he wanted to ask, but shock prevented him from getting them out in time.

'I did think so, until I saw you and your little friend from the gallery.' She heard him gasp on the other end of the line. He had, for once, no smooth answer to cover his guilt. 'Dennis, just so you know, I intend to tell Veronica that our affair has ended and you're now seeing someone else, so probably best if you tell her before I do.' The silence that yawned across the phone was filled now with shock. Callie knew that if she'd been in London, Dennis might have been vindictive, but of course, he couldn't touch her now. 'I'll be ringing her next Monday morning, so...' It was the least she owed Veronica: let Dennis do the honourable thing, even if only because he was afraid she might spill the beans first.

'You selfish cow,' he muttered before slamming down the receiver.

'Goodbye, Dennis,' she said to the empty line.

She was standing at the kitchen table, contemplating the next time she would contact Dennis – probably after her baby was born – when she heard Simon in the room behind her.

'Hey, what are you up to?' Simon asked.

'Oh, nothing, just back from a little walk, catching up on calls,' she said lightly.

'So I hear. It's been ringing all afternoon.' He smiled at

her. 'Dennis.' He put his hands up. 'I didn't answer it, but it must be pretty urgent, when they're looking for you here, perhaps it's a yarn emergency.'

'Perhaps.' Callie smiled wondering how much he'd heard. At least, Simon still made her smile and that was good.

'So, that's it?' He was leaning laconically against the sink, a large mug in his hand. He sipped from it as he watched her. 'Callie Corrigan and Theme are parting ways?'

'Yes, that's it. Everything has its time and it was time for me to move on.' She placed the phone in her pocket, not entirely satisfied that if Simon figured out her password, he might decide to check through her messages.

'And pigs might fly! Come on, they've given you a decent goodbye gift, I'll bet.' He drained his cup, his mouth still drawn up in a smile. 'The great Callie Corrigan – you don't just walk away; they can't go down to the job centre and replace you tomorrow morning,' he said dropping the mug into the sink.

'What are you getting at?' Callie had no intention of telling Simon about Dennis or Veronica or the total mess she'd left behind her in Theme.

'Well, first of all, Ada is as jumpy as a kitten after a ball of wool that she's just never going to catch. Mother is being cagey about what her plans are for the mills and here you turn up and settle into Bridgestock Cottage as though you might never leave.'

'Ah, Simon, you're reading too much into things; perhaps you're listening to Ada – you know she's always been very protective of her role in the mills.'

'It's the future of the mills, Callie. We all have a stake in it.' He almost sounded aggrieved.

'Yes, indeed we do, but none more so than Mamma and she will decide what's best to do for them when the time comes,' she said pulling off her coat and scarf. She hung them purposefully on the back of the door.

'Here's the thing though, Callie: it's our business too. We all have shares in the mills and as Mother has always pointed out, the mills are part of our family heritage. We need to make sure that things are done right,' he said evenly.

'Right?' She smiled at his choice of words. 'Oh, Simon, you know Mamma is fair and wise. Her choices will be made for the best, even if Ada is trying to convince you otherwise.'

'Really? You seem very sure.' He ran the cold tap over his mug, flicked on the kettle for a fresh brew. 'Ada thinks…' He paused, perhaps considering his next words. 'Well, she thinks that Mother might be planning on handing the whole lot over to David Blair – is that what you mean by doing the wise and fair thing?'

'Excuse me?' Now, when she looked into his eyes, Callie recognised he was genuinely worried. 'Mamma would never do that,' she said quickly. 'You're mad – there's not a chance Mamma would leave it to anyone outside of the family. Hah, David Blair, indeed.' Callie shook her head. 'Simon, listen to yourself. Do you not remember how long it took for Stephen Leather to get the deeds of the mills sorted? Can't you remember back to how determined Mamma was to have everything in the Corrigan name? I think the last thing she'd do is make any decisions that would undo all that work now, don't you?'

'Are you sure? After all, it looks as though she has no

intention of leaving it to Ada and we all know that she wouldn't leave it to me if I was the last Corrigan on the planet,' he said bitterly.

'For a start, that's not true, Simon. You never wanted it; you said it often enough over the years. I'm not having this conversation with you. The fact is that if Mamma wants to hand the mills over to the next stranger who knocks on the door, she's perfectly entitled to. You left here, just the same as I did. You couldn't wait to shake the dust of the place off your shoes and just because things have gone belly-up in Dublin does not give you some kind of automatic right to come back here and throw your weight about.'

'That's not what I'm doing. All I'm saying is, the mills are part of our heritage. They need to be protected. I for one have enough loyalty in me not to want to see them being just handed over to David Blair or anyone else who isn't going to be committed to running them in the same way that our mother has all these years.'

'So you'd prefer to sell them onto a wealthy investor who'll pay lip service to keeping everyone in their jobs, until one day they decide to downsize in a global plan to make every mill they own look the same? So our mills would be just another part of their happy meal?'

'Actually, the Mullers, who are interested in the mills, have already acquired other mills and they've never changed anything in them. You can check it out if you want.'

'I'm sure that there is a noble sentiment in there somewhere, but Simon, it's not for us to decide – it's up to Mamma and we have to respect whatever she thinks is best for the mills.' Callie sighed; she was sick of this conversation. The future of the mills was not something she wanted to be drawn into at this stage; after all, she had enough to try and figure out without worrying about something that really didn't affect her directly. 'Still, it's nice to think you're taking an interest in them – my, how we've all changed,' Callie said absently.

'Well, things have changed, haven't they?' he said quietly. 'Who's to say that if Mother doesn't sell the mills, I might offer to work there myself?'

'Please, don't tell me you've had a conversion on the road to Damascus moment!' She laughed, but even to herself, she knew it sounded a little hysterical. *Simon wanting to work at the mills?* Well it was just so far off the realms of anything she'd ever expected for her brother. 'Simon, we both know you'd be bored out of your tree in a week. Once you'd chased down every bit of skirt in the town, you'd wither up with boredom.' She shook her head, waved him away when he held up a teabag for her, offering to make two cups instead of just one.

'It's not off the scale of possibility that I might actually be capable of managing the place, you know.'

'I'm not saying you couldn't, we all know you have a good brain, but running the mills isn't just about being a great designer or a savvy networker. What Mamma wants is someone who's passionate about the mills and all they mean to her. I'm not sure any of us has that love for the place. You've never shown any interest before...' She didn't finish off the sentence, but it was clear the mills, as far as Simon was concerned, would be a consolation prize and they both knew that Miranda wanted them to be so much more than that. 'I'll wager that if I offered to buy your share this minute, you'd sell in a heartbeat,' she said softly.

'How much?' he said flatly.

'What do you mean, how much?'

'It's simple, how much would you offer me for my shares?'

'Are you serious?' Callie looked at him now. His eyes were bright, his face alert and interested. Gone was that familiar lazy swagger.

'Absolutely. Wouldn't it be the answer to at least one of Mother's problems? You buy me out, leaving you and Ada to choose from. That should make it at least a little easier for her.' He spat out the words, but managed to smile at the same time, even if there was no warmth in his eyes.

'I haven't even thought about it. I've only just walked out of Theme. I've been looking at...' But she stopped. There was no point telling Simon about the little unit in the industrial estate. She'd made no plans, not really, no promises – there was nothing to tie her to anything at the moment. 'I'll tell you what, let me think about it.'

'Sure, but be quick, because you mightn't be the only one looking to buy my share,' he said before dropping a teabag in his cup and dousing it with boiling water.

'Fine, I'm going to get dinner started so unless you want to help me by peeling some vegetables I suggest that you drink your tea and leave me to think in peace, or you will get the sharp end of Mamma's tongue if she hears that you've been stirring things up with Ada.'

Callie was grateful that Simon took his fresh mug of tea up to his room. Later, just as dinner was almost ready to serve, he arrived downstairs, sweetness and charm flowing from him. When Miranda came back from the mills, Callie thought it was as though he'd had a complete personality change, but still their conversation unsettled her. Suddenly, she could see the predicament Miranda was in. It was as if she had glimpsed, for a moment, what it must be like to have the future of other people weigh so heavily upon her shoulders. Not that there was anything much Callie could do to help; rather she had a feeling that any overtures in either direction could make things a hundred times worse.

She would think about buying Simon out. She had the cash and perhaps he was right: it was the best they could hope for at this stage. The idea of owning a larger share of the mills filled her with a kind of warm, unexpected exhilaration, but for now, she would put it to the back of her mind, with any notions of setting up on her own. Instead, she served up dinner and made sure that their evening was as pleasant as any spent at Bridgestock Cottage.

34

Simon

As Simon saw it now, he had two options. He could sell his share of the mills to one of his sisters. This idea really tickled him; well it would have if Callie wasn't so bloody chilled out. There was a time when he could have played them off each other – knowing that if Callie made an offer on his share, Ada would have sold her soul to place a higher bid. Of course, it wouldn't work now. Callie was the one with the big wad of hard cash – Ada for all her investing and squirrelling away couldn't compete.

There was another approach. He could goad them into giving him money – it would be easier with Ada. He could see his big sister had developed a crush on David Blair. It was laughable really. It only heightened how truly pathetic she was. The problem was, he couldn't hold it over her as he might have when they were kids – he'd managed to get months out of a crush she'd had on the sacristan's son. God, he'd had every penny of pocket money off her for over a month when he came across her trying to post a letter through the kid's door.

Now Callie, that was a different score. He couldn't imagine holding anything over Callie. Holding anything over? He was talking about blackmail, pure and simple, and he was fairly certain that Callie was keeping secrets – certainly there was more to her gardening leave than met the eye. Still, he had no chance of ever getting to the bottom of that, not when the London fashion gossips had managed to keep their lips sealed. Simon knew he was an amateur by comparison.

Was he really thinking of blackmailing his own family? Yes, yes, he was – it was a measure of his desperation at this point. His internal monologue started up again: his share in the mills was no good to him as things stood. With the cash value in his hand, he could make a real stab at something on his own – he just knew he would. Selling his share was the only real way of raising any cash at this point; it was as simple as that.

Perhaps he could try again to convince his mother that selling to the Mullers was in the best possible interests of everyone. Frankly, he didn't much fancy his chances on that either, but if pushed, he reckoned there was more chance of getting Miranda to sell than there was of seeing the Pope wearing a bikini for Easter ceremonies.

His search in the mills had been fruitful, in some ways. He'd located the articles of association quickly, as he knew he would. His mother was methodical and very little changed in the mills over the years. That went for everything from the herbaceous border that ran along the gravel entrance to the passcodes on the safe in his mother's office.

Making sense of the document took far longer than finding it. In the end, he'd made a copy and placed it carefully, rolled up under the driver's seat in his car. He'd been at the mills, ostensibly to pick out a few pieces for David to showcase to the Australian market. That had taken all of ten minutes; it was just a matter of looking at the back stock and picking out a couple of ensembles that were timeless and pairing them with an unexpected shirt or tie.

The result of all this cloak and dagger activity: there was no selling his shares without the express permission and agreement of the other members of the board. His mother had locked down the transfer of shares with more clauses than a billionaire's pre-nup. The only loophole seemed to be a transfer of shares between directors still standing. That meant, without Ada, Callie and his mother, he was stuck with the shares and no way of raising finance from them. Even if Callie decided to buy his shares, which frankly he thought was unlikely, she'd never offer a fraction of what the Mullers might have been prepared to pay.

'Perhaps it would be worth letting the Mullers approach the board,' Mia said when he rang to sound her out about other buyers.

'I'm not sure,' Simon said; after all, the whole idea was that he would bring the deal to the table and maybe, if things swung his way, earn some of that generous commission that Mia planned to make off his back.

'Look, Simon, they are intent on buying here, sooner rather than later. There are other businesses, in much worse shape than yours, and Günter is happy to hand over a very generous asking price. Think what he'd be prepared to pay out for Corrigan Mills. It could cover all of your bad debts and help you start over with a clean slate somewhere completely new.'

'Fine, I'll talk to Mother again.' Simon knew his voice sounded sullen, but he couldn't help it. There was a tonne of unopened messages on his phone from people who seemed to think he owed them money. How on earth could he be responsible for rent on the EasyTech premises or a leasing agreement on equipment that ran into the price of the national debt? Normally, Simon could close his eyes to the idea of a failed business, but this was different. This time, knowing that if those debtors didn't manage to extract their dues from him, they may just figure out Gabby had invested and for the first time in his life, he actually felt badly about how it might affect someone else.

He shoved his phone into the inside pocket of his sports jacket. His mother intended to go for a walk. He would join her, see if perhaps she might just meet with Günter and Sally Muller. Miranda walked more slowly these days, although Simon had a feeling that this was not age-related, but rather the fact that when she got out of breath, it seemed to cause her pain across her back and chest.

'Are you sure you're okay, Mother?'

'Of course, I can't let life pass me by just because of a few little niggling pains, and anyway, the doctor said it's important to be active.' Still, she seemed quite happy to sit on one of the brightly painted benches that lined the riverbank. It was a lovely day to walk here, the river lapping playfully against the bank, the sun shining a soft yellow ribbon each time the clouds parted to let it cut through to the water. It was warm, but a light breeze made it just comfortable for walking.

'So, there's something you want to say to me?'

'No flies on you, Mother.'

'No,' Miranda said softly.

'You know, I've hit a spot of bother, with a company I invested in.'

'You invested in?' Miranda looked at him now, because they both knew that he didn't have a red cent to invest in anything.

'Well, I was organising the funding for it. I was the front man and I managed to get decent investment and everything was going so well.'

'And then, it wasn't?' Miranda shook her head. It was old ground, too familiar; she didn't want to walk over it again.

'So, I've been thinking, my position and yours...' He broke off because the silence between them seemed to grow even heavier.

'My position?'

'Oh, Mother, please. Let's call a spade a spade. You've got some big decisions to make and you don't seem to be able to make them.'

'The Mullers?' she said cutting to the heart of what he wanted to say.

'Yes. They'd like to meet with you. They'd like to come down here and sit with all of us and put a proposition together for us so we can consider it in a way that's fair to everyone.'

'As you know, Simon...' Miranda lowered her voice as if what she was about to say next were the last words she wanted to utter. 'I own forty percent of the mills. I won't give you the whole lecture of a lifetime's work, of your father's input or the fact that we have a responsibility not just to that legacy, but also to all of the people who are employed in the mills. What I will say is this – if you and your sisters decide to sell the mills, as far as I'm aware there's probably very little I can do about it. But...' She sighed now, a deep and weary sound that made her chest rattle in a way that reminded Simon how frail she was becoming whether she would admit it or not. 'I have a feeling that neither Ada nor Callie will want to sell their shares to the Mullers – it would be up to you to convince them and because we're having this conversation, I have a feeling that you haven't managed that yet.'

'No,' he said softly.

'No. Because they don't want to sell. The fact is that Ada wants the mills for herself and Callie wants to keep them in the family – she may not want to own them any more than she does now or work in them, but she recognises the responsibility we hold over their future.' Miranda sighed, watched as a cormorant flew low over the water, scanning perhaps for the possibility of his next meal. 'I'm sorry, Simon, but I'm not going to call a meeting with the Mullers. It's not what I want and I don't think anyone else wants it either.'

'I see,' Simon managed eventually, because of course he did. He was trapped here, with a share in the mills that was of no real use to him and no way of getting his hands on a penny unless one of his sisters decided to buy his share and that was as likely as hell freezing over, it seemed to him now. It was not like when they were children and he could get between his two sisters. Callie didn't play those games any more and while he might be able wind Ada up, there was no way Tony would stand by and watch his wife hand over a fortune she probably didn't have without testing the ground with Callie and Miranda first.

It was bloody hopeless and Simon knew that no matter how much he might dream of selling the Mullers his share, Günter Muller was nobody's fool. He would not hand over any money without being quite sure he was getting exactly what he paid for.

On the journey back to Bridgestock Cottage, Simon made up his mind to call Mia and tell her that there was no chance of Corrigan Mills being sold on to the Mullers. He would have to find some other way of raising some cash, except Simon knew only too well, every single bridge he'd ever had was now well and truly burned.

35

Ada

It was the champagne. Ada could blame it on the three glasses of champagne she'd had at lunchtime to celebrate a huge order from customers Miranda had been working on for almost eighteen months. They had opened four bottles, enough for staff and customers if the mills had been busy. The order meant production would be running at full tilt and more for the next two years at least. It was a coup and even Miranda acknowledged that she was just a little carried away with having won it for the mills.

Ada didn't feel drunk exactly, but she felt giddy. A sort of childish exuberance created a heady cocktail mixed with her already raging hormones. She sat at her desk, listening to David's cool voice talk to contacts on the phone next door. He was drumming up interest on the Australian front. Ada imagined his hands, with long slender fingers holding his pen, doodling idly while he spoke. In her mind's eye, she saw his striking eyes, his strong jaw and broad shoulders stretch across his white shirt. She imagined his thigh, tight and muscular in his expensive trousers. He was everything a woman could want and more. She wondered if he'd had lots of lovers over the years.

She smiled then, thinking of Tony and their solid, repeatable lovemaking that never varied – well, that was when it used to occur. Of course, that was quite some time ago now. When David's voice descended into throaty laughter, she thought she might explode with longing for him. She pulled the tiny compact out of her bag, patted fresh powder on her face, applied some lipstick and opened the top button of her blouse before she made her way towards the office next door. She took a deep breath and knocked lightly on the glass.

'Hey,' she said as silkily as she could manage. 'Busy?'

'Ah, er, no, no, not really,' he stammered. 'Erm, what can I do for you, Ada?'

'I thought maybe we'd have that little house-warming party you promised me before.' She laughed then, remembering that Callie smiled always and laughed often. It was outside her usual range of communication components, but she decided to try it anyway.

'Right, well, I've only got whiskey, no champagne here, I'm afraid.' He looked at her for a moment, as if trying to make his mind up about something, then smiled a little sadly and reached towards a cupboard at his back. He pulled out a drawer and placed a new bottle on the desk, cracking the seal. He pulled out two glasses and filled them a finger each.

'Am I your first guest?' Ada asked in what she hoped was a rather coquettish voice.

'As a matter of fact, you are.' He handed her a glass and they toasted. 'To business…' he said softly.

'And pleasure.' She smiled, finishing off his words as if they were meant to be, just like her mother and Callie. She sipped the whiskey, enjoying its fire racing through her body. 'So, David, what *do* you do for pleasure?' she asked rather pointedly. At his back, she watched as the other staff left the mills, one by one, some in groups. From up here, they were just small inconsequential people in the car park.

'Oh, not much, at the moment. I'm basically trying to get a handle on the briars that are growing all round the Hall.' He laughed then, that impossibly perfect sound that turned Ada's legs to jelly and made her unsure if she wanted him to sweep her away and make love to her or if she should run away and hide from the torrent of emotion he welled up inside her.

'So, you're planning on resurrecting the old place,' she said, suddenly interested because she'd always dreamed of living the life of lady of the manor – when she was a small girl she often wondered at what cruel twist of fate had seen her born into a cottage rather than a castle.

'I don't know about resurrecting it. That might be a bit ambitious, but for now, I'm finding the whole place very therapeutic. It's like I've come to live in one long holiday and even here is like stepping into a world I'd only ever heard of – I'm not sure I ever really believed I could actually be part of it all.' He smiled then, a lopsided, happy dog sort of grin that was probably meant to be friendly, but it shook up Ada's hormones to a fever pitch of desire and longing.

'Oh, David, you are funny,' she managed, but she only said the words for something to say and to cover the tell-tale hot flush that was taking over her whole body. She managed to paste over the fact that he actually enjoyed being outside, gardening, clearing away – that in some way, it made him the polar opposite of how she liked to spend her time.

'And what about you, Ada? What do you do when you're not here?'

'Oh, I'm happy to potter about mostly, although I do like a glass of wine, but of course, with this place and my mother to keep an eye on, well, there isn't much time for a whole lot else at the moment.' Ada no more kept an eye on her mother than she did on Tony, but she was hardly likely to admit that to this Adonis. The last thing she wanted was for him to actually know she was about as interesting as a cabbage.

All of this chit-chat was making her nervous and she only realised she was idly fiddling with her wedding ring when it fell from her finger and rolled under David's desk and across the floor. Ada dived for it immediately, forgetting all decorum. She crashed with David in a sort of complicated rugby scrum as she rescued it before it rolled down into the grated heated system that ran around the perimeter of the building. They both reached it at the same moment, their hands touching and she knew, she just knew... this was it.

She turned her head to look at him, but unlike her imagination, he was not looking into her eyes. He was looking out towards the car park where Callie was just striding towards her mother's car. Ada wanted to be cross – that her moment, her one chance had been hijacked by her sister, but something, perhaps the alcohol, her menopause, or her sheer bloody-minded jealousy decided on the instant that she was not letting this moment slip past her. In a move she thought was classy, she reached out and turned David's face towards her, so for a moment they were eye to eye and then she reached in and kissed him, full and hard on his lips.

For a brief second everything seemed to be just perfect. She was kissing David Blair. He was kissing her, well, their lips were together and there was considerable action going on between them. Then she felt her balance pull beneath her hunkered legs, as if she was swaying jerkily from side to side, a rocking vessel on an uneven sea. She felt his hands on her shoulder, steadying her up – or so she thought, and she groaned her pleasure. He wanted this as much as she did. And then, as he pushed her back, gently so he managed to hold her from falling while still coming up for air, it became obvious, in one awful grotesque moment. Ada realised she had been doing the kissing; he'd been doing his best to manoeuvre himself away from her.

'Oh, God,' she said, suddenly mortified. 'What have I done?'

'It's okay, Ada, it's okay. It was a mistake, too much alcohol in one day. We shouldn't have opened the whiskey. It's really bad to mix spirits and...' His voice trailed off, but there was no denying the change in his posture. It was embarrassing, uncomfortable and it was all too painfully obvious that if she hadn't tried to force herself upon him, he'd never have chosen to kiss her.

'I'm sorry. I'm so embarrassed,' and on cue, she felt that awful, tell-tale heat rise within her again, except this time, David Blair realising that she was going through the menopause was the very least of her worries. This time, she had so much more to be embarrassed about and the menopause didn't even come close.

'Really, there's no need. It's just one of those things,' he said, standing opposite her now, she noticed he had put more space between them. He placed her wedding ring on the desk between them. She picked it up wordlessly. It only served to heighten her mortification. How could she have been so stupid? How could she have let herself down like this? 'Actually, I'm quite flattered,' he said then. 'You're a very attractive woman, Ada. I'm just not...'

'Not interested,' she said, knowing only too well how to finish off that sentence. It was amazing how some things can be so crystal clear.

'I'm not interested in anyone at the moment, if you want the truth of it. I'm just getting over my divorce. It's the reason I'm here.' He shook his head then and the sound that emanated from him was not laughter, but it was self-deprecating. 'I'm running away from it, you might say, but there it is.'

'I'm sorry, I don't know what came over me.' Ada flopped uncharacteristically into the chair behind her. 'I've never done anything like that in my life, you have to believe me,' she said then and she knew, when she looked at him, he registered the complete shock that haunted her hollow eyes.

'Don't worry about it, we all do things, crazy things sometimes. Really, it's forgotten about already,' he said softly. Ada couldn't look at him; instead she gathered herself up silently and made her way back to her own office to sob her heart out where she could not be seen by anyone now that the mills were empty. Twenty minutes later she heard the soft click of David's door as he made his way home for the evening. She'd made such a complete mess of everything, of absolutely everything.

Ada felt as if her body might be on fire. She welcomed the cool film of sweat as it seeped out into her blouse. Funny, but now she didn't care if people saw damp patches on her linen shirt. A few short months ago she'd have preferred to die of sunstroke than take off her jacket and admit in some silent way to experiencing hot flushes.

Of course, it was a symptom of how she felt about almost everything in her life these days. The familiar points of axis in her world had shifted and she knew exactly when the catalyst had occurred. David Blair was ten years younger than her, she'd guess, but as the days had passed and she'd watched him in the mills, she knew what it was to want someone with every fibre of her being. It was foolishness, the kind of crush teenage girls experience for celebrities, but there it was and even though she wouldn't admit it, the desire was driven even harder by jealousy for the obvious connection he was building with Callie. Bloody, perfect Callie seemed to have him eating out of her hand and there wasn't a damn thing Ada could do about it.

She sat now in her soft-grey-coloured office; she hated that damn colour. In the end, Miranda had told the painters to slap it up, since Ada had dug her heels in; clinging onto the pale mushroom walls that had been there since last time round. It was madness now, when she thought about it. She actually resented the thousands of euro she'd saved for the mills over the years with her careful penny chasing. Her father's ornate desk caught her eye again.

She'd managed to studiously ignore it, mostly.

Her father's desk. She went to it now, clung to it as if it might be her only life raft on an unforgiving ocean. She wondered then, if her father had lived, would things have turned out very differently for all of them? He had loved her, she was sure of that. He had seen in her that same ordered brain that he had passed along the Corrigan line. A wave of grief for her long-dead father washed over her. Perhaps sorrow was better than despair, a sort of self-preservation – to save her from curling up further with the embarrassment of what had happened with David.

No key had been found. The maintenance men had looked in every pot of keys they had and still, nothing had turned up that might possibly have fitted the antique lock.

It was not a small keyhole, not at all the kind of delicate lock you'd expect in an old roll-top desk. Rather, her father, or someone else before him, had seen fit to attach a somewhat ugly-looking cast-iron cumbersome thing. She got up from her chair; it wasn't as if she'd done a rap of work all week anyway. She walked over to the offending desk and bent to her knees to examine the lock once more. Dropping her glasses down before it, she squinted; half whispered the words...*F. Whitfield &Co's Lever Lock*. Ada looked up at the clock behind her desk. It was just after seven. Everyone had surely left the offices now.

'Christ,' she muttered, as she pulled a steel ruler from her desk. She levered it in against the tiny gap where the door closed around the ancient clasp. It creaked, a lonesome almost warning sound and then splintered before the top parted and one dry wooden crack emanated from it. Ada fell to her knees, sneezed at the escaping pungent smell of damp papers and slowly rotting timber. Then she smiled. It was open and whatever secrets the old desk had hidden were hers now and she couldn't wait to see what had lain here all these years.

First up, disappointingly for some, were ledgers filled with old orders that her father had been checking off against the great progress he had made since taking over the mills. Ada put them aside. She would enjoy going through those at another time. There were some legal documents too, a right of way that was all but forgotten now and pages laying out a dispute about poachers on the stretch of river outside the factory boundary.

At the back, standing proud, Ada picked up a familiar photograph of her mother on her wedding day. She'd grown up with a similar image for many years in their home. However, this one was slightly different to the one that sat next to her mother's bed. In this photograph, her mother stood alone; she was a beautiful young bride staring somewhat wistfully down the church avenue, almost as if she was waiting for someone that she knew would never come.

Ada held the photograph, faded and old in her hand for a long time, taking in her mother's face, and it stirred something in her. For a brief moment, she was aware that once, a long time ago, her mother had been just like her, with dreams and fears and yes, maybe even regrets and each and every one of them filled in the corners of her eyes so they didn't carry up the smile her lips would have you believe was real.

There were treasures too, her father's cigarette case and a lighter. There was a fountain pen, dry now of ink, but when Ada held it in her hand, it felt as if she might be reaching out to him by some long-forgotten route. The thought pushed her emotions to the topmost of her chest, and soon she felt the tears rush from her eyes, but she was not sad. Rather, it felt like a release, as if the crying that she should have done many years before was finally being let go.

After her tears had passed, she wiped her eyes roughly and reached into a slim drawer that almost blended invisibly with the wood around it. Here, she took out a letter, addressed to her mother, well, her mother before she became Miranda Corrigan. The writing stretched across the page, as though it might run on forever. The paper, faded and put away hurriedly, was creased in places that told her it had been taken from its envelope many times long ago.

'Miss Ada, you're still here.' Old Bert put his head around the door. His eyes rested for a moment on the damaged desk. 'Oh, I see you got the better of it in the end...' He stood for a moment, lingering softly; perhaps hoping to share in the secrets her father had locked away so long ago.

'I'm afraid, after all that, it's full of ledgers and statement books, Bert.' She found lightness to her voice that she didn't really feel. 'But his cigarette case was here too, so it's nice to have come across that.' She wiped her eyes again, hoped he'd leave her to it.

'Ah, well, sure it's lovely to have a keepsake.' Bert shook his head thoughtfully. 'Now, don't you go staying here for half the night poring over them ledgers, Miss Ada. We all know what you're like with accounting books.' He smiled kindly at her and for the first moment in her life, Ada felt some compassion towards this old man who'd dedicated his life's work to keeping the mills in top condition.

'I won't, Bert,' she said gently, wanting to add something more, but instead she settled on: 'Goodnight.' She listened as he shuffled along the corridor and rattled each door on his way, turning keys to lock the offices so if they did have a break-in the insurance company would be satisfied at any rate. When she was sure he'd made his way through the door that led into the stairwell, and so to his final round of the shop floor, she opened the letter her father had squirreled away all these years.

'Dear God,' she murmured, because now she realised what a weight of secrets this desk had hidden for so long. Suddenly, all thought of the future of the mills or how she would manage to wrangle what was rightfully hers didn't seem to matter any more. Even making a fool of herself for David meant nothing compared to this. The woollen mills had belonged to her father and, surely, this was enough to prove that neither David nor Callie had any place in them.

36

The Past

There was nothing for it. Miranda had gone through the books again. It was simple. Without payment for the stock they had already delivered to the army, there was not enough money to pay the wages that they owed the mill workers. Miranda sat at Paddy's desk. She wasn't ready for this, and she felt that in her bones. Even sitting here in Paddy's chair, surrounded by the notes and trinkets that filled his desk, it was too emotional. She couldn't think. One day, she knew, she'd have to sift through all of his letters and daily notes that took up his life here; but for now, her most pressing obligation to him was to save the mills.

She closed down the desk, turned over the little key within its lock and slipped it onto a tray that stood on top, empty apart from the heavy set of factory keys that Paddy had brought everywhere with him. She got up from the desk and moved across the floor, stood beside the window for a moment. Along the walkway there was another room. It was where the bookkeeper worked. Miranda decided that for now, she would set herself up in there; it would be less distracting than this lonesome spot.

Miranda couldn't remember a time when she'd felt so tired. She was spending every waking moment trying to secure payment for the army work. It was either that or sit by while the mills were bled of money and they all faced a future that was too grey to even see where it might end up. She thought of Paddy's words – Richard Blair, he was an investment banker now. The fortune that it would take to save the mills would probably be little more than loose change to him.

Miranda sighed. She couldn't go to him, cap in hand. It would be like admitting Paddy had failed and whatever mess they'd found themselves in, Miranda was quite certain that it was one her husband could have dug them out of, if he'd just had time. It seemed to Miranda there was only one man she could ask for advice and so she set off walking to the village.

Stephen Leather had just returned to Ballycove to take on his father's practice. He was young and hungry, but the fact that he'd returned meant something. He had an affinity to this place, Miranda suspected, perhaps to the mills also. He certainly had great time for Paddy for as long as she could remember.

'Ah, Miranda,' he greeted her as though she was a welcome diversion on a stuffy morning. 'Come in, come in. Would you like some tea or…' He smiled at her. It was what everyone did these days.

'Ah, Stephen, I'm afraid tea isn't going to go very far on sorting out my problems as you well know,' she said gently, hoping that it might cut through the formal niceties and move them onto ground that was more firm.

'Of course. Tell me, what can I do for you?' He sat across from her, the wrong side of his desk, but she presumed that was as much because she'd caught him unawares. Whatever the reason, it set the tone for their meeting and Miranda hoped it would set the tone for their lifelong business dealings.

'Well, you know about the army contract?' she asked. Miranda thought everyone in Ballycove knew about the army contract. At first they believed it would be the great hope that would bring the village great prosperity. Now, months after delivery with no sign of payment, it looked likely to do the reverse. They were sinking fast beneath a crippling overdraft and Miranda knew they were within a whisper of having the banks foreclose if she did not get some payment in soon. Stephen nodded solemnly and she went on, 'Do you realise that they haven't paid a penny to the mills yet?'

'I knew it wasn't going to be straightforward, not with… Well, there's a rumour doing the rounds and it's churning out stories, mainly about the Four Courts…'

'What have you heard, Stephen? I need to know if I'm going to save the mills.'

'Well, I'll tell you what I know, but I'm not so sure that it's going to be of any help. It's not gospel, but these things usually have some roots in the truth,' he said mildly.

'It can't hurt. I have to take some action; otherwise, we'll be meeting again to wind up the mills permanently.'

'It's that bad?' he asked solemnly.

'I'm afraid it is.'

'In that case.' He walked to the sideboard and poured them both a generous measure of port. 'You might need a drink for this.' He placed the glass on the desk before her.

'Apparently, your payment has got caught in the crossfire between government departments, or at least that's what some of our great and good want people to believe.'

'The great and good?'

'Don't forget, we have a general election coming up this year and at the beginning of next year we'll be seeing the end of the presidential term, which means that the office will be open for someone new to run.'

'I don't see how this could have anything to do with my payment for the mills,' Miranda said.

'Don't you? Have you heard who's in the running – or rather who wants to be in the running to be Ireland's first woman president?'

'No, I didn't even know that anyone was thinking of running for it,' Miranda said mildly amused, but of course, if they could have women in the government, why couldn't there be a woman in the Phoenix Park?

'None other than Sile Dempsey – she's a bigwig in legal circles, no reason for you to have ever heard of her, but there's one thing that you might find interesting about her...' He smiled now, a gentle lopsided smile that might have been playful, but Miranda was too upset to notice. 'Her husband just happens to be the Chief of Staff in the Irish Army.' He shook his head. 'I'd say, the last thing he'd want is any kind of scandal around payments or money going missing or worse, being implicated in the closure of a factory and the loss of jobs, wouldn't you?'

'You could be right.' Miranda began to cheer up a little; it seemed there was the narrowest chink of light shining into her world all of a sudden. 'And this Sile Dempsey, she works in Dublin?'

'You'll find her in the Four Courts most days, but if she wasn't there, for any reason, there's a good chance—' he leaned across the desk, took up a black diary and flicked through it until he came to a note written in the most illegible writing she'd ever seen '—you could find her here.' He scribbled off the address, folded it and handed it to her.

'Thanks, Stephen,' she said, then sipping the drink he had just poured for her.

'You're not alone, you know that, Miranda. There are plenty of people around this village who'll help you if you ask,' he said draining his glass. 'Paddy was a good man, he helped out more people in the village than you might realise and they want you to make a go of those mills.'

'I appreciate that, Stephen,' she said. She felt decidedly better in herself, whether that was down to the port or down to the corner of paper she had tucked deep into her purse.

Miranda had never been in the Four Courts before. Of course, she'd passed by them; you couldn't not notice them. They were, apart from being the centre of the Irish courts system, one of the most iconic buildings in Dublin. It seemed, when she arrived, that everyone was on their very best behaviour. Men and women in their Sunday best seemed to be holding their breath until they managed to get out the vast doors again into daylight. Dotted about, in various corners, barristers stood in hollow groups, wigged and gowned and oblivious to the discomfort of just about everyone else around them. Miranda made her way towards the smallest and least intimidating of these groups. It seemed they were all men and she had a feeling that if Sile

Dempsey were here, she would spot her as the only female in the inn.

The elder of the group eyed her speculatively, unsure if he could mark her out as a customer or some kind of clerk. He pointed her in the direction of the open courts and told her she would find Mrs Dempsey there, if she waited long enough for sentencing. Then he guffawed with his colleagues at some in-joke that she couldn't care less for.

Miranda sat to the side of the courtroom entrance and as luck would have it, the judge called a break within a few minutes of her arrival. That's when Sile Dempsey made her way from the courtroom under a stack of battered files, her expression set in something inscrutable.

'Mrs Dempsey,' Miranda called her as she passed.

'Yes.' She looked across to Miranda and like her colleagues before her, seemed to gauge her with only a limited set of possibilities. 'What is it?'

'I need to talk to you,' Miranda said. She had been thinking about this conversation for the whole train journey to Dublin. Should she appeal to the woman's better nature? Would she explain that the mills were vital to the local economy, that she was a widow, trying to keep her family with food on the table?

'Well, make it quick, I have to be back in court in a few minutes.' Her eyes were hard and her lips, when she spoke, hardly moved. Miranda had a feeling it was a long time since they'd experienced laughter, much less empathy.

'Of course.' There was no better nature here. 'I'm here to talk about your ambitions for the presidency,' Miranda started bravely and was rewarded by an abrupt halt to the other woman's walk.

'My ambitions are hardly any concern...' Sile Dempsey turned to her. She considered her for a long few seconds and Miranda held her glare and gave back more in spades. Perhaps she believed that she'd chewed up bigger and better than Miranda in her day, but if she had, she still wasn't sure of the steel that held firm in Miranda's eyes. 'I don't know what you mean,' she settled on then, but she stood facing her, waiting for what might come next.

'It's like this. My factory is owed over twenty thousand pounds by the Department of Defence. If I do not receive payment by the end of next week I will be going to the papers and telling them about the...' Miranda paused '... irregularities, in your husband's accounting practices as the head of the Irish Army.'

'That's slanderous and you must know that you can't just decide to blacken someone's reputation, particularly someone of such good standing.'

'I think it's only slanderous if it isn't true.' Miranda lowered her voice. 'I've had good legal advice and plenty of documentation to back it up. Either way, the scandal it will create will be enough to block any political party considering you for office.'

'Oh, please, are you trying to blackmail me?' She looked scornfully now at Miranda.

'I'm not trying to blackmail you at all. I'm asking you, for the benefit of a whole community, to ask your husband to release the money that is rightfully due to my company.'

'And if I don't...' Sile Dempsey asked contemptuously, looking Miranda up and down in a way that let her know that she wasn't quite good enough for these salubrious surroundings. Miranda didn't flinch; at this point she didn't care what anyone thought of her. For now, all she cared about was the mills. If she could pull them through successfully, she would consider fancy suits and shoes afterwards. 'Fine, if you're owed it, I suppose.' Their eyes were locked now and Miranda could sense the danger that this woman could pose if you stood on her toes. 'I'll have a word, but if I ever see you in these courts again, I'll personally make sure the only way you leave will be in a custody vehicle.'

'Fine. I'll need that cheque by the end of next week,' Miranda said evenly and then she turned on her heels and walked away as cockily as her nerves would allow.

To Miranda's greatest relief, the cheque arrived three days later with a note from the Chief of Staff thanking her for her great patience and wishing her well.

Funny, but after Paddy died, part of her expected Richard would return to Ballycove, while another part of her knew that it was all too late for them. When he had come back, one summer, for a moment their eyes had met, a lifetime of what-ifs passed between them, but it was not their time and they both knew it. He'd come back to take care of some family business that had something to do with the Hall, but no-one in the village was quite sure what.

Richard and his son travelled back; perhaps they thought they'd stay in Blair Hall, but by then, it had been empty for over a decade and it would take more than an airing and a fire in the grate to welcome them. Richard had arrived without fuss, his little boy, a miniature version of himself in tow. They'd walked into the mills, perhaps expecting to find Paddy Corrigan bent over a machine or studying lists of orders and invoices. Instead, he found Miranda. Her fingers were covered in red dyes that she hoped to get just right and at her side a little girl who seemed every bit as intent on the job at hand.

In every other way, it seemed that neither of them had changed so much from who they were all those years ago.

'Oh,' was all Miranda managed at first.

'Oh, yourself, that's a fine how do you do after all these years.' Richard smiled at her and in that moment the years melted away as if they were nothing more than the flushing through of the river at the back of the mills. 'How have you been?' he asked gently. His father or perhaps, more correctly, Edwin's secretary, sent a card when Paddy died, but there had been no word from Richard.

'Busy, I've kept moving and I've lots of help.' Miranda smiled down at Callie.

'She's the image of you,' he said wistfully, perhaps remembering all those years earlier. 'They could be us all over again,' he said nodding to his own boy, who was his father's image. David shared something undeniable in his expression that captured all the Blair charm in one small flicker.

'Callie is my youngest and she's eight,' Miranda said, placing her hand gently on Callie's head. 'Callie, why don't you bring…'

'David,' Richard supplied.

'Why don't you bring David up to my work room and show him what we were working on earlier?' She winked at Callie. 'I have a stash of homemade toffee – we made it this morning as a treat.'

'My grandmother loved this place,' Richard said then, looking about a little wistfully.

'The mills? Did she?'

'No, maybe not the mills so much as Ballycove and everything about it.'

'Well, she was good to people. It's only now the villagers realise what it took to keep this place going.' It was true, Miranda wondered how on earth they'd managed to crawl along on what was made and sold over the years before Paddy took the place in hand. 'It's strange to think that's the last connection with the Blairs in Ballycove now,' Miranda said a little sadly.

'I wish it hadn't been, you know that. I would have loved to...'

'What?'

'Well, if things had been different...'

'Don't,' Miranda said, resting a hand on his arm and then withdrawing it quickly when she felt the tension that it drew up between them. 'It was all a long time ago now, wasn't it?' She smiled then, a light airy smile that meant nothing but it moved them away from the unsaid words that hung about them still.

'I'd have come back for you,' he whispered. The words were hardly a croak. 'You must have realised I'd never have left you, not unless I didn't have a choice.' He shook his head sadly.

'Good God.' She felt the words leave her; in a breath she couldn't control any more than the years that had wasted between them. 'If I'd known, Richard, if I'd only known.' She shook her head sadly. Then she looked up to see Callie and David rushing along happily towards them, chewing lazily on the sticky toffee. 'But then, maybe...' She was thinking of Paddy, of Constance, of their children – she couldn't do something that would hurt so many. 'My life is here with my children and I have the mills; that's enough for now...'

'I know. I wouldn't swap David either,' he said as he swept the little boy up in his arms. 'But if things had been different...' He caught her eye and there was no mistaking the emotion there.

'Yes, Richard. If things had been different,' and she knew that there was no turning back the clock now – too many people had entered their lives for it to ever be the same again. She watched Richard Blair walk away from the mills that day and felt in her heart this really was goodbye.

37

Miranda loved nights like this and they happened far too infrequently for her liking these days. Her kitchen filled with the people she loved, everyone sitting together to eat and drink and be merry. It felt as if the whole cottage had sighed into life again, with huge waxy candles burning brightly and the aroma of fresh flowers permeating every corner.

Miranda had gone into the garden in the afternoon and selected the biggest, brightest blooms – in the kitchen ornate old vases stood in corners filled with larkspur, cornflowers, irises and violets. The porch had an ancient copper jug filled with sunflowers, dog daisies and zinnia. Their tangy fragrance welcomed David who arrived a little early, but with offers to help with anything he could. Simon had already set up enough comfy chairs on the veranda so they could have after-dinner drinks looking out across Ballycove and the river as it turned to inky black beneath them.

It turned out this was a celebration – she was going to be

a grandmother., She still smiled as she hugged the secret to herself. Callie had told her in the afternoon. She'd sat her down with a cup of Earl Grey and it felt as if Miranda's whole world had shifted closer to something she'd long thought would never happen.

'Pregnant?' she'd repeated, although she knew, she'd already said it twice. She'd thrown her arms around her and they'd cried, tears of joy. 'But how? When?' And she knew none of that really mattered. 'Oh, don't mind me, none of that matters. All that matters is when you're due and well, I'm going to be a grandmother…' she said softly, liking the sound of the title as it fell from her lips.

'I know, isn't it amazing?' Callie whispered, as if to say it too loudly might break the magic. 'I thought we might tell the family this evening, after dinner…'

'How perfect,' Miranda said, loving the idea of holding this precious news close to herself for just a little longer. 'I feel as if I could do a jig, I'm so excited – isn't it crazy?' she confided.

'I felt exactly the same…well.' Callie laughed then and Miranda wondered how had she not noticed her daughter was blooming. 'I still do…'

'Oh dear, and there I've been letting you work like crazy in the garden and here…' Suddenly Miranda felt a little flustered by it all.

'Stop it now, I'm a perfectly healthy woman going about and doing normal things.'

'Are you?' Miranda asked. 'Healthy, you know – you're not as young as some who'll…'

'Yes, I am. I've had it confirmed at the doctor's today: blood pressure and everything else is just as it should be.'

'Oh, you clever, wonderful girl.' Miranda threw her arms around Callie's shoulders once more. 'I can't tell you how happy this has made me.'

'I think I can guess.' Callie laughed then she looked at her watch. 'I'd better check that everything is behaving in the stove.'

Ada and Anthony arrived exactly on time and Miranda shared a smile with Callie. It was no less than they'd expect from Ada. Tonight, Miranda thought her oldest daughter looked drawn, as if she was carrying a weight of worry on her narrow shoulders. Her black woollen dress added to the sense of gauntness about her and accentuated the dark circles beneath her eyes. She was not happy to see David had arrived before her and pulled her mother aside to whisper, 'What's *he* doing here?'

'David is my guest. I didn't realise I had to run a list of invites past you,' Miranda retorted. Really, sometimes Ada was too much. Miranda watched her dance around David as if he might have leprosy, and yet there was something odd in how she looked at him. Miranda found herself wondering exactly what her oldest daughter thought of David Blair.

Ada was blessed with flawless, almost porcelain skin, so very different in every way from the rude health exuded in both Callie and Miranda who spent most of the year tanned and always glowed as soon as they hit the fresh air. She was quiet too, perching uncomfortably on the edge of her seat and sipping a little too quickly the pre-dinner gin and tonic Simon handed her.

Callie had spent the day cooking; she'd pulled out old servers that Miranda hadn't used since they'd all spent

Christmases together many years before. There was something almost romantic about seeing the old platters produced for the evening. They too had been an heirloom belonging to Mrs Bridgestock, although never in Miranda's memory had the old girl had any occasion to use them. Miranda loved them, they were gaily patterned, chunky and solid and at a guess, she'd put them at over a century old, making her feel like quite the young thing when she sat down to dine. Tonight, they were filled with the brightest and freshest vegetables from Miranda's garden. Callie had selected a colourful array to go along with a succulent salmon and crayfish pie that she seemed to throw together in a flash. The evening flew by, with warm stories and a chance to catch up.

'So, what are your plans, Callie?' David asked, then he looked around the table at the other obviously interested expressions. 'Or am I not supposed to ask?'

'Well, that's a good question.' Callie laughed and topped up Miranda's glass beside her. 'I'm officially finished at Theme, as of this week. The severance package I negotiated has been honoured and so I'm…' She smiled now. 'Well, I'm as free as a bird.'

'Must be nice to have all that money just to sit on,' Simon drawled.

'It's start-up money, that's all,' Callie said and she exchanged a look that seemed to silence Simon. Miranda wondered if perhaps he'd already tried to talk her into some new scheme. At least, she was fairly confident; she didn't have to worry about any of her daughters becoming embroiled in Simon's business escapades.

'I still can't see why you left at all, when everything

seemed to be so perfect...' Ada said sharply into a silence that cut around the words with the precision of a fine, expertly handled blade.

'Sometimes,' Callie said coolly, 'you're just ready for a change.'

'Hmph.' Anthony reached forward and placed his arm around Ada's back, but she shrugged him off – there was no missing the hurt in his expression.

'It seems like a very generous *change* package to me,' Simon said softly, exchanging a look with Callie that communicated he knew far more than she wanted him to. He'd been in foul humour since they'd talked about the Mullers. Part of Miranda wanted to just buy his share of the mills, but she knew that would only create a bigger headache for her when it came to sharing things out between her daughters.

'So, now you're listening in on conversations,' Callie said. 'If you must know, all of you—' Callie nodded towards David '—I've been having an affair with Dennis Wade for years. It came to an end this year and with it, I felt it was time to move on, both personally and creatively.' Callie looked about the room and Miranda noticed the tiniest smirk curl at her lips. Between Ada and Simon, she had both shocked and surprised them. David looked bemused and Anthony – well, Miranda wasn't entirely sure if he even registered what she'd just said.

'Well then, lucky for us,' Miranda managed brightly. Whatever her views on the rights and wrongs of having an affair with a married man, Callie was her daughter and she would support her whatever she had said. Only one small thought bothered her: was Dennis the father of her grandchild? And if he was, what would that mean? Miranda reached forward and placed her hand across Callie's. 'I'm just glad you're here, darling.'

'Thanks, Mamma,' Callie said, 'it's a new beginning, the start of something completely different.' She placed her hand across her stomach, and smiled contentedly.

'So, you'll start something new?' Ada asked with a glimmer of curiosity that mightn't stretch to optimism, but at least it was pleasant.

'Perhaps.'

'I'm sure you'll have offers from all over the world to work your magic on other knitwear labels,' Miranda said easily and it was true. Once the fashion world realised that Callie Corrigan was no longer with Theme, there was every chance that their competitors would want to employ her.

'I'm not sure I'd want to go back and do the same again. It would be like travelling the same road, just with different people. I think I'd like to do something new and of course, London is completely out.' She stroked the stem of her wine glass. 'That's part of the exit agreement – the last thing they want is to be paying me bonuses when I'm working for the competition on their doorstep.'

'Won't you miss it?' Anthony asked. 'I mean your whole life, your lovely home and all your friends... I can't see Ballycove measuring up to all of that.'

'I don't know. I think I'm ready for something different, something completely different.'

'Well, there's always the catering industry.' David was laughing now, waving his hand across the kitchen where the bouquet of fresh cooking wafted aromatically in the air.

'Much as I've enjoyed tonight, I think I'll stick to the

woollen industry; it's in my bones. I've always loved the mechanics of the machines, the crash of the looms and the wash of the dyes. I've done the fashion scene, up to my neck in the glitz, now I want to work with people who are solid, who have weaving and wool in their family trees, going back and forward as far as they can see.'

'So, you're coming back to the mills.' Ada's voice was a bitter murmur.

'Not necessarily and certainly not to take on a role as things are now, but I'd like to do something different and who knows, if I can make my own mark, perhaps we can work together, Ada…'

'I see,' Ada said and she gulped down a large mouthful of wine before reaching to top up her glass. Her expression was unreadable and Miranda decided that now was a good time to change the subject.

'You've outdone yourself this time,' she murmured to Callie. 'I don't think I've ever eaten such a delicious meal.'

'Oh, Mamma, it's all down to your tardy stove and the masses of herbs to choose from in the garden. You really have everything on hand to cook the most wonderful food.'

'Well, I think any five-star hotel in the country would be proud to put up that dinner for their most esteemed guests.' Tony held his glass up in her honour; he was changing before Miranda's eyes. From the lazy waster she had always assumed him to be, he was turning into the most devoted husband. She could see it in his eyes, the solicitous way he moved around Ada and deferred to her every word. Miranda thought it was touching, if such a pity that Ada didn't seem to notice.

Tony rang Miranda every other day, worrying about

Ada. So much so that she'd been relieved that they had come along tonight. He had been expecting Ada to cry off, but they'd arrived dolled up to the nines and bang on time. His expression when Miranda greeted them at the door was like one of bewilderment, because presumably coming had all been down to Ada. 'To Callie,' he toasted, 'for the finest cooking this side of the Shannon,' then he looked across at Ada who for once didn't seem to mind that he had complimented Callie.

'It was a lovely meal,' Ada said tightly and Miranda couldn't help but notice the deflation in everything about her daughter. Gone were the characteristic snippy comments; in fact, she was almost a trance-like version of her usual self and for a moment, Miranda wondered if she hadn't taken some kind of medication to blunt her usual biting verve.

'I just hope you've left room for dessert,' Callie said brightly as she set aside her napkin to check on a succulent apple crumble that she had popped into the oven just as their meal had begun. Miranda watched her youngest daughter, so different here in worn-out jeans and a simple white shirt that she somehow managed to make look elegant without any adornment; still she was a million miles away from the Callie Corrigan the world thought they knew.

'Oh, God,' David groaned loudly, 'she's trying to kill us with kindness.' Miranda watched as he patted his flat stomach. He had settled in at her kitchen table as easily as any of her children and in some way it was almost impossible to think of a time when he hadn't been here with her.

There was a simmering connection between him and Callie. You couldn't miss it if you tried. Ada recognised that connection too and it was all too obvious that it had rattled her more than she probably realised. She hardly spoke to David all evening. It was as if she was embarrassed to even meet his eyes. Poor Tony. Miranda wondered if he even realised; but of course he did. It was why he called Miranda every day, not checking up on his wife, so much as checking in to see if Miranda had noticed what was too painfully obvious to him. Dear Tony.

Miranda wasn't blinded either to the seething jealousy that lurked behind Simon's eyes when he watched David Blair, but she had decided many years ago that she was not going to allow her children to control who was welcomed to Bridgestock Cottage or indeed, as they were learning these past few weeks, who was welcomed at the mills. She smiled then, catching David's eye. She wouldn't be without him for the world now. He was solid and loyal, the kind of man she'd always hoped Simon would become.

'I may have to cry off...' David was saying, but then his smile grew wider as the steaming pie was placed before him. Callie placed a large bowl of cream and breakfast dishes in the centre of the table. Miranda knew none of them could resist the aroma of apples and cinnamon still sizzling on the table before them.

'Come on, dig in,' Callie said as she dropped into her seat. 'David, you can do mother, since you've decided not to have any.' She laughed easily at his expression and handed him a bowl to help himself. 'It's only fair since Simon is going to be cleaning up after us tonight,' Callie said eyeing her brother meaningfully.

'Well, whoever is clearing up, I think we should all raise a glass to you,' David said and for a moment, it felt as though everyone was intruding on something very intimate between them as their eyes locked across the table.

'Get on with it then,' Simon said, tapping his glass slowly with his knife.

'To Callie, the best thing ever to come out of London and we are very lucky in Ballycove to be getting you back,' David said softly.

'The story of my life...' Simon said with mock sadness. 'Callie sweeps off into the sunset – well, rides out of London in style – while I return from Dublin without any glory only to wash the pots and pans.' Everyone except Ada laughed.

'Hardly.' Ada was regaining some of her usual fire. 'I think you're mixing yourself up with my lot in life, dear brother,' Ada said and now Miranda thought she could hear the slur of just a glass too much wine on her daughter's lips.

'Oh, Ada, he's only joking,' Callie said softly, passing along the bowl of freshly whipped cream to her sister.

'Really, well, here's the thing. I'm not joking. I'm sick of all this happy families and everyone pretending that everything is just fine. It's bloody not fine, none of it is fine and you may put up a wholesome meal and act like Julia Child, but we all know that since you came back here, we've all been pushed aside to make way for the great Callie Corrigan.'

'Ada, really, I don't think you mean any of that...' Miranda said, but she caught a look in her daughter's eye that made her stop, because there was a rage burning within Ada that was fuelled by something more than the familiar jealousy she'd witnessed so many times before.

'And you, Mother, yes you – well you might be sitting there, holier than thou, but don't you dare think my father didn't see clear through you and so do I now.'

'Ada,' Callie shouted at her sister and David had the good grace to push his chair back from the table, perhaps wondering how best to make a dash for it.

'Don't you dare leave,' Ada flashed at him. 'Don't you dare, this has as much to do with you as it has with anyone else here. I've seen you, both of you.' She pointed towards David and Callie. 'It's disgusting, that's what it is. If only you knew the truth, but you…' Her voice was cracking as her gaze darted towards Miranda. 'You knew, you've known all along and yet you sit there with…'

'Please, Ada.' Tony tried to cover her hand with his and Miranda thought the action so far out of the range of their relationship that she had to choke down a hysterical giggle.

'*Please, Ada? Please, Ada* – please what, Tony? As usual, you haven't got a clue what's going on here.' She met Simon's eyes for a moment. 'And neither do you, for all your sly manoeuvrings.' Ada stood now, like some grotesquely terrible Inspector Clouseau, bringing together the final denouement of a difficult and long-running investigation. 'Our mother…' A tear scudded from her eye and she wiped it away ferociously, as though it was a traitor in the moment she most needed support. '*She* was trading love letters with Richard Blair well into her marriage to our father, right up until you were born, Callie.'

'I…' Miranda felt as if the air had been throttled from her chest. Richard? What on earth was Ada talking about?

'Oh, yes, Mother. I can see clear through that saintly charade you've been carrying about with you all these years. And our father could see it too. He'd kept one of your lover's letters, hidden away so you'd never know, but he knew. He knew that right on your wedding day. You looked off into the distance for Richard Blair – I'm right, aren't I?' Ada was shouting now, hysterical.

'It's not what...' But Miranda couldn't find the words to mend whatever damage had been caused here tonight, because for now, she was in shock. It felt as if nothing that was said over the next hour would even penetrate her brain, never mind allow her to make any kind of defence. 'Richard?' Her eyes slipped to David now and suddenly it all made so much sense. 'Richard was...'

'Oh, please...' Ada was shouting now, hysterical. She jumped up from the table, darted to the far end of the kitchen bringing back the soft linen clutch she'd left there. 'Do you want to hear the rest of it? Callie – do you want to hear why David Blair has come here and taken up position at our mother's side?' Her mouth turned into a miserable thin line, narrowed by the most fowl bitterness. She pulled out an old-fashioned envelope, light blue, not unlike the kind Richard had used all those years ago. Miranda found herself staring at it, then she reached forward, placed her hand on the envelope, traced her fingers along his familiar seal. Ada was crying now, tears flooding from her sunken eyes, but she straightened out the old-fashioned sheet of notepaper and began to read in a wobbly voice.

London.

My darling Miranda,
I can't quite believe that after all of these years I am writing to you again. Please listen to what I have to say.

374

My heart has never stopped loving you. Circumstances and I fear perhaps my father have come between us over these missing years.

I have wavered about contacting you, knowing that you are married to Paddy, knowing that I am married to Constance. The practical side of me sees that to go back now, to change things to how they were surely meant to be would be the most difficult thing, and yet I feel that going on without you is almost impossible.

I so wanted to take you back to London with me last July. I wanted to march up to Bridgestock Cottage and make my case, convince you that there is still a chance. I've been sorry since that I wasn't brave enough to turn convention on its head and follow my heart. I think, if we could meet, if I could explain to you, instead of to Paddy – well if only…

The child you carried could have taken my name; we could have made good lives for ourselves together as a real family.

Paddy asked me not to reach out to you. He promised me he would give you a good life and that you were happy, but I can't imagine either of us being happy apart.

Say you will think of joining me in London, I beg of you. Bring the child and we will make up our own little family. The baby could be a Blair, a sibling for my own son, David. There could be nothing wrong in something that has always seemed so right to both of us.

I await your answer with the deepest of hope, my darling Miranda.

You are in my heart forever,
Richard.

'Oh dear God.' Callie seemed to fall back into her seat.

'No, no…' Miranda cried. 'It's not what it seems, not…' but then a crushing pain in her chest seemed to flatten any words from her. Her lungs it seemed could not quite reach far enough to supply the air to breathe. She raised a hand to her breast, but she knew it was too late. Around her, she watched as shocked faces turned to expressions of panic.

'Mamma, Mamma.' Callie was beside her, loosening her blouse, shouting at the others to call an ambulance, whispering all the time in her ear. Miranda could hardly hear the words but she could make out the faint whisper of her daughter's love on every ragged breath, and then it seemed that whatever funny turn had stopped her breathing began to pass, and even if she was upset, she knew she was not having some kind of attack.

'It's okay, I'm fine,' Miranda said stoutly, looking across at Ada. She pointed to the letter. 'I believe that is mine,' she said before taking it and reading it slowly, softly to herself. She did not realise she was crying until her tears reached the paper and then she brushed them off impatiently. Eventually, when she had begun to recover herself and managed to pull herself back into the present, she looked up at the five bewildered expressions on people who were stunned into silence. Even Callie and David had been knocked back into their seats by the venom of Ada's words and implications. Miranda smiled then as much as her emotions would allow. 'This is a very old letter, dating back to a time, long ago…'

'Oh, Mamma,' Callie said softly.

'It seems she really was no different to you, after all, Callie.' Ada spat the words out, a volley of venom directed at the sister who for so long she could never get the better of. 'Carrying on with a married man, when you had a family and a husband here too...'

'Stop it Ada,' Anthony said in a voice that was so low Miranda had to check that he'd actually spoken. He put his hand on his wife's arm and somehow it managed to restrain the flow of malice from her.

'Yes, it was probably sent just after you were born and before your father passed away, but it isn't what it seems.' Miranda sighed, feeling the weight of a lifetime of misunderstanding between them all. 'Richard and I were... well we were very young and I never knew why...' Miranda smiled then, thinking of Paddy, her great love, it turned out in the end. 'When Paddy was dying, he told me about this letter. He told me that he had spoken to Richard and they had made an agreement of sorts that nothing more would be said, but Richard sent this and Paddy never passed it on to me.' She smiled sadly, then looked at David. 'I felt a great deal for your father once, but I would never have considered hurting Paddy for anything or anyone.'

'And the photograph...' Simon's voice was drier than she'd ever heard it before. He was holding the small faded photograph in his hand. Miranda remembered it well, hadn't thought about it in years, that one image that seemed to capture so fully a moment of longing for what was outside that church before she finally let Richard go.

'Ah, yes, well, I loved your father very much and yes, on that day, the day of our wedding, I did think of Richard as I arrived at the church, but from the moment I began to walk up the aisle to Paddy, I knew that I was making a commitment to him. He was a good man, the best man I could have married and while it makes me sad – the notion that somewhere along the way, Edwin Blair probably did come between us – still I know that everything turned out just as it was meant to.'

'Did it though?' David whispered. 'I know you've always had a huge place in his heart. I think even my mother knew it. Although he was a good husband and father… there was always a wistfulness about him when he talked of here and when he talked of you.'

'And I have felt that same nostalgia at different times too, but when you were about eight, I met you both, here in the mills. I'm not sure if you remember that day. I was a widow at that stage and it would have been easier… if… but time had passed. Our time had passed and we've both had good lives.' Miranda looked around the table now at her family and David, then she smiled at Callie and said softly. 'You are Paddy Corrigan's family, everything about us is exactly as it was meant to be.' She'd always known that. There was a certain peace in saying it aloud.

'Well I really can't believe you're all going to sit here and…' Ada got up from her chair, flustered and perhaps embarrassed at the way she'd behaved.

'It's an understandable mistake to make, but I've done nothing to hurt your father or David's mother, Ada. I do wish you'd brought the letter to me when you found it; after all, it did have my name on it…' Miranda said softly. 'It certainly could have spared us having this dramatic end to such a lovely evening.'

'Oh, Mother, you just haven't got a clue, have you? You think it's okay to wave off a love letter during your marriage to our father and then ensconce your lover's son at the helm of our mills… It's not a mistake, it's downright callous,' Ada said and she stalked to the door, an embarrassed Tony in her wake, trying vaguely to apologise on her behalf, but knowing his place was at her side. The cottage seemed to rattle on its ancient foundations when Ada banged closed the front door behind her and Miranda let out a huge tired sigh. She took up the letter and folded it carefully. She would allow herself to reminisce and maybe cry just a little more in the privacy of her own room later.

38

Ada

Ada shivered on the car journey home, so much, her teeth began to chatter. It was possible she had become cold to her very core and it felt as if she might never get warm again. Tony fiddled ineffectually with the heating dials, but he could not get the car warm on the drive home from Bridgestock Cottage that night.

'Oh, Ada,' he murmured over and over on the journey, but Ada was a sobbing, blubbering mess in the passenger seat next to him. Their house, when Tony let them through the front door, was cold too, but this time Ada recognised the chill for what it was. Emptiness. Not just the kind of bleakness that comes without people to give a house life. This was a starkness that was born from two lives that had spiralled away from each other to such an extent that they may as well have been living on different planets. Their *home* was overflowing with the sort of loneliness that marked it out as crammed with lives that were unfulfilled.

'I don't think I can do this any more,' Tony's voice

scratched against the surface between them, but it sounded as if his words came from deep within. There was no stemming the hurt within them. He stood there, in the near darkness of their familiar hallway, tears streaming down his face and yet he wasn't crying; perhaps things had gone too far for that.

Ada couldn't think of what to say to him. She was his wife, of two and a half decades, and it felt as if they were complete strangers and perhaps they both knew with certainty that this life they were living had suddenly, abruptly come to an end.

'I'm going to bed, Tony,' Ada said and her words echoed behind her as she climbed the stairs with steps that seemed heavier than she'd ever heard before.

'No,' he said coldly and she froze mid step. 'We have to talk.'

'I was drunk,' she said, not turning to even look at him, completely embarrassed and deflated having volleyed out the last grains of dignity she had left in David Blair's eyes.

'That's not good enough and it doesn't cover what's really wrong here,' Tony said coldly. 'Come down to the lounge, now. I need a drink and we have to set things straight, once and for all.' He said the words with a kind of finality that shook something deep within Ada. Tony had always been a beer man – truthfully, he would prefer a cup of tea, but he knew that what lay ahead required something stronger than a Ceylon brew. He poured a large tumbler of his wife's whiskey and for once, he didn't offer anything to Ada, so she sat, rather meekly on the end of the sofa, shivering cold and becoming more depressingly sober by the minute.

'I didn't know, Tony, I really thought...' She had cried

so much now the only make-up remaining on her usually pristine complexion were long dark streaks of mascara smearing down her cheeks. 'And then, there was that moment with Callie and David talking and they just seemed to take up the whole kitchen with a shared glance... and I...'

'Oh, let's just cut the bullshit, for once in our relationship, Ada. I'm going to get to the core of it. I'm not perfect, I've never been the perfect husband and maybe I've gone about things the wrong way these last few weeks. I've tried to win you back with small gestures and perhaps we both knew it was too late, but tonight... tonight was inexcusable.' He shook his head and it felt as if the silence between them weighed a dark and heavy tonne. 'You had every intention of throwing that letter in your mother's face at some point. Maybe not tonight, but some day and it would have been soon, because we all know that it's much too hard being a judgemental cow to keep something like that in.'

'Anthony,' she breathed, but she didn't argue; perhaps she knew there was no point, or maybe she realised that it had been coming a long time and it was better to take her medicine while it was being delivered here, in the privacy of her own home, rather than as she'd done to her own mother: humiliating her in front of others.

'No, Ada. This wasn't about looking out for Callie or for David; this was about you. I've seen the change in you, these last few weeks; you couldn't hide it, not even if you tried.'

'I really don't know what you mean.'

'Oh, come off it, Ada,' Tony sighed. 'We can't move from this spot until we at least have enough respect for each other to talk with a grain of honesty.' He looked at her now with a lot more tenderness than she knew she deserved. 'I mean our marriage, Ada. You are slowly destroying us and… soon, there will be no coming back.'

'I certainly am not. I've been a good wife to you, better than any other woman in the whole village, keeping you here and…' But her voice faltered because they both knew that things between them were very different to how they might look on the outside. Ada might pay all of the bills, but she needed Tony to keep the show on the road. He calmed her and she knew that without his gentle presence urging her to see the good, she might have long ago lost all faith in everyone around her.

'You've been like a giddy schoolgirl since you laid eyes on David Blair and if you set out to do anything tonight it was to make sure that Callie didn't swipe him from under your nose…' Tony said coldly, but when Ada looked into his eyes, she could see the pain she'd caused there too clearly. 'Can you at least admit that? Here, between us, you've been falling in love with him, since he arrived, and I've become little more than a housekeeper to you, Ada, and that's just not…'

'I…' Ada dropped her head into her hands. It was true, every word. As usual, Tony had seen exactly what had been raging through her and he'd stood by, waiting, looking out for her, hoping that she would see sense before it was too late. 'Oh, it was so stupid of me. How could I have been so callous and stupid?' She was talking to herself, more than to Tony.

'I've given you everything I could, Ada. I've kept the show on the road while you had your chance to go out and make a go of things. I've been the one making sure the washing machine is emptied, that we have clean clothes to wear first thing on a Monday morning, I've been the one...' he stopped, as if the effort to continue was too much. 'And you...'

'I'm sorry... I've been a terrible fool.'

'You have just used me, Ada. You've treated me as if I don't matter to you and that's just not... well, it's not even decent, never mind anything else,' he muttered and slugged back the whiskey.

'Have you... have you finished with me?' she asked timidly, expecting the worst but being nowhere near contemplating it because to Ada, this was coming out of the blue.

'I'm finished with this half-life I've been living...' He shook his head sadly. They sat for a long time, listening to the whisper of the trees outside, the creaks and murmurs in their tight little house. It seemed as if even the smallest squeak would raise the dead, so silent was the air between them. 'Are you still in love with David?' Anthony managed to whisper eventually.

'No.' Ada's voice was gravelly, earthy in a way that made it sound as if it might have come from someone else. 'No, Tony, you have to believe me.' It was the truth, so easy to see in the face of perhaps losing the one man who truly understood her and whom she loved, even if she'd lost sight of it for a while.

'But you were?'

'I was infatuated, carried away in a kind of silly madness, but it meant nothing... I don't think I really thought about what would happen if... I mean, Anthony...' Her voice croaked now, as though it had soaked up all her emotion and run dry. 'I couldn't ever imagine being… with anyone but you – you have to believe that.' She was pathetic – she knew that. It was beyond embarrassing. She'd made a complete fool of herself, but worse, she'd betrayed Tony, who was never anything less than loyal, loving and supportive since she met him. She had acted like a love-struck teenager, over a man who'd never given her any cause to think he wanted anything more than a professional relationship – and why? To somehow bolster herself because she couldn't face the fact that things she needed to change were so much closer to home. 'I'm so sorry.' She hung her head, filled with shame and emptied of any shred of pride. All she knew now was that she loved Tony far more than she'd realised and she didn't want to mess this up too.

'Oh, Ada… I don't know what to believe any more. I'd never have imagined we'd be sitting here tonight, the two of us, talking like this and feeling as if it was all finally over between us…'

'Anthony, please, don't say that.' She rushed to his seat, knelt before him, grasping his hands desperately, knocking the whiskey so it fell to the floor, seeping into the carpet and she realised, for the first time, that it didn't matter. 'You can't give up now. We've been married for twenty-five years. I couldn't imagine not having you here!' She looked around her, as if the living room furniture would be incomplete without him.

'It's not enough, Ada. I'm sorry, but it's just not enough, it never has been. I just haven't been able to say it before.'

'Well then, what, what do you want me to do, please? I'll do anything; just tell me you still love me.' She was hysterical now. She could feel panic overtaking her, as if it was stealing the very breath from her lungs. Losing Tony, it was the one thing she'd never really thought of. God, how crazy was that? For all her plans and dreamy ideas, she'd never really considered what her life would be without Tony. Now she knew, in one doubling whack she would rather die than lose him.

'Ada...' the word was more a sigh, a deflated noise on the cold air between them.

'Please, anything, I'll walk away from the mills this minute if it will convince you that I mean it. We could go away, just the two of us...We could travel, go to all those places we should have gone when I was so wrapped up in the mills...' She was in fight or flight mode, could hear her voice rising higher as she spoke. 'Or move, completely away from here, somewhere warm...' She was almost becoming animated, lost in the notion that there were possibilities she'd never yet thought of. 'Don't laugh, but we could move to Australia? We could go to the furthest end of the earth and start again. I'm sure we could make a good life there; you'd like it. Barbecues and football and...'

'Oh, Ada. That's not what I want,' he said softly and she felt his body fall into a limp and helpless form as if she had somehow drained all the vitality from him. She knew, in that instant, the mills meant nothing to her, not in the face of losing him. 'Listen to me.' He placed his hand on her head and he waited until she looked up at him, a sorry, pathetic reproduction of her normal self. 'Listen carefully. I don't want you to stop doing the things you love; I just want you to make room for me...'

'But the mills, honestly, if it came to picking between you

and the mills, there would be no choice…' She was crying now, but smiling too, perhaps sensing that there was some hope of a future, maybe a better future than before.

'It wouldn't be much of a love if I asked you to give up what you have put your life's work into; but Ada, you have to see that the way you've been around Callie and Miranda and the future of the mills, it's…' He shook his head. 'You have to let Miranda make up her mind about what she wants and accept it gracefully.'

'No, Tony, no, I don't have to accept that at all,' Ada said carefully and for the first time in her life, she felt something close to power in her ability to shape what would happen to her own future. 'I just have to let them go. Maybe I needed to make a complete fool of myself to see, maybe we needed to have it out like this for me to understand what's important.' She laughed then, a burst of sound that wasn't so much hysterical as it was perhaps utter relief. She shook her head with certainty, as if something had been agreed, silently, between them.

'What?'

'My mother always said, bricks and mortar, they're not worth getting sentimental over and I've always thought those were just empty words. I can see now, really see, she actually meant it. The mills have always been about people for her. I just didn't understand… people like the old man who's been there since before I was born and I hardly have time to say hello to him…'

'Stop it,' Anthony said. He was rubbing her hair now. It was already a tangled mess, but somehow the stroking of it seemed to calm them both down. 'You didn't know.'

'No, I didn't and that's the thing. Mother was right, all

along.' She smiled now. Her eyes were red and tired but they'd never seen more clearly. 'I'm going to…'

'What?' he asked, unable to read the smile that was lighting up her expression.

'I'm going to be free, Tony, content to live a happy life with you, without the weight of the mills constantly on my back, if you'll have me.' She stood before him, put out her hand to pull him off the chair.

'*Have you?*' he repeated her words softly and they both knew that the playfulness in his voice was something that had not been there in far too many years. 'I'm never going to let you go again,' he said and he followed his lovely wife upstairs to begin their new lives together.

39

Callie

It was the thud that woke Callie. She pulled a large jumper over her pyjamas as she climbed out of bed. It couldn't have been Simon as he had set off after dinner. She assumed he had managed to talk one of those girls in the mills into a date of some sort. It was unlikely, knowing Simon that he would be back before breakfast. The scratching noise sounded again.

It could only be from her mother's room. She heard a sort of scrabbling, as though there might be a mouse at play in the wardrobe trying to get out. It really wouldn't surprise her; Bridgestock Cottage was old and easy-going. Her mother might have set a trap if she saw a mouse, or then again, it could be something she planned to get around to.

Something stopped Callie in her tracks then. It wasn't a sound exactly, but it was a troubling sense, as though she'd crossed a trip wire and it set something off deep in her awareness. She lightly tapped on her mother's door then poked her head into the darkened room. She heard a murmur come from the bed, as though her mother called her, but from very, very far away. Callie moved fast, intuiting that something was not right. The glass upturned on the floor, a pool of water beneath her feet, were enough to send a rivulet of panic through her.

'Mamma, are you all right?' Callie asked when she switched on the light, but of course she wasn't. She was lying in the bed, having some kind of funny turn. Callie ran to her own room, pulled out her phone and called up the ambulance, telling them to come as quickly as they could. 'Can you tell me, Mamma, have you any medication I can give you? Is there anything I can do?' She felt the quilt cover, wet against her mother's skin and began to pull it down, drying off her neck and shoulders. 'Here.' She placed her own quilt up around her mother having grabbed it from her room, and tucked her in to keep her from getting cold, then she heard the ambulance siren outside.

To Callie what happened next was a haze of movement around her. One of the attendants moved her gently towards the door and soon they were transferring her mother to a stretcher and slanting her down the narrow stairs of her lovely home. Callie scrabbled about to find her car keys, but she caught the ambulance up before they left the village.

It felt like the longest night of her life, sitting in the hospital waiting room while they took care of her mother. Her back ached, which she figured had more to do with being pregnant and worried than it had with the uncomfortable seating. At five o'clock in the morning, she wondered if it was too early to ring Ada. She decided against it, would leave it until after eight at least. What was the point of both of them sitting here mindlessly browsing out-of-date magazines?

'Callie Corrigan?' The doctor looked as wrecked as Callie felt. At least he wasn't wearing pyjamas underneath his scrubs though, she hoped. 'I'm Dr Brennan.' He held out a firm and perfectly manicured hand. 'I've been taking care of your mother. We are moving her to intensive care.' He sat down beside her, elegantly for his large frame. 'I have to tell you, that we've been here before.' He smiled then. 'But of course, I think that was with your sister.'

'Yes. Ada,' Callie said. 'You took care of Mamma the last time this happened?'

'Last time, it wasn't so severe. I had hoped that we would be able to keep her well with just medication, but now, I'm afraid it looks like we will have to take more serious steps.'

'But she's going to be all right?'

'She's not young, you know that?' His voice was gently leading her to where he needed to take her. 'She has heart valve disease. I did explain to her that she needed to reduce her stress levels, think about taking things a little easier.'

'You probably knew her well enough to know how much heed she'd take of that advice.'

'But she was thinking of cutting back, she told me so herself.'

'Yes, but it hasn't been straightforward for her.' Callie looked down now at her hands, examining them too closely so she might put aside for now the fact that she hadn't made things much easier for her mother in the last few weeks. 'I suppose, we should all have rallied around and helped her more, really.' Callie bit her lip. The truth was that each of them, in their own way while encouraging Miranda to take things easy, had only been thinking of themselves.

Why even she, Callie, could admit that gardening and

cooking were her ways of pretending to help, when in fact, she had probably worried her mother sick with her abrupt arrival and dearth of information about what had really happened in London. Miranda was nobody's fool and Callie knew she worried about them all, even more when it seemed that their worries were too huge to share. The only decent thing she'd done was to share the news that she was going to be a grandmother and even then she'd kept that from her for quite a few weeks.

'And you didn't?' He wasn't judging her.

'No. I suppose we didn't see it like this. We just thought... well, I just thought...' What had she thought? The truth was, just like Ada and Simon, Callie knew she'd only thought of herself in all of the plans for the future of the mills.

'Well, perhaps after her surgery you can put that right?' Dr Brennan said then and he stood over her. 'You can visit her, if you wish, but don't disturb her. She really needs to rest now.' He looked at his watch.

'Surgery?' Callie echoed, fixated on the first part of his sentence.

'She will have to have some repair work to the heart arteries, perhaps some support in keeping them open. It is a standard enough procedure, but your mother is not young and she has already put her body through much stress and trauma with this attack.'

'Oh...' It was all Callie could manage.

'You can follow me, now, if you wish to see her,' he said leading the way towards Miranda, and Callie knew it really was time to help her mother in any way she could.

40

Miranda

When Miranda woke, it took too long to figure out exactly what had happened. She was in hospital, a darkened room with beeps and buzzers and not a flower in sight. Of course, that meant she must have lived, she thought, and might have laughed but her chest felt as though it could collapse if she made a sound that wasn't vital.

'Mamma,' Callie whispered by her side. 'It's okay. You're fine, you're in the hospital, they are taking really good care of you, so…' Callie tried to smile, her lips turned up for sure, but her eyes held the kind of concern that Miranda hadn't ever wished to see in any of her children.

'How did I…' She pointed towards the water and Callie obliged with just a sip. God, it felt as though she'd walked through deserts before she woke, so parched was not just her mouth, but her whole body.

'It happened in the night. I heard something and I checked on you and then it turned out you were having a heart attack. They've given you medication to stop any damage.' She cast her eyes towards a drip next to Miranda's bed. Callie placed her hand gently on Miranda's face. 'Oh, Mamma, I'm so sorry.'

'Why?' Miranda wasn't sure what they were talking about now. 'What happened?'

'I'm sorry for everything.' Callie began to cry and then she told her about the operation and what the doctor had said.

'The mills?' Miranda finally managed, because if she was here and Callie was here, it begged the question who was running the mills?

'I'm afraid I took an executive decision in your absence,' Callie said gently. 'I had to– you've been here for three days, resting,' she clarified.

'I see.'

'It's been like a vigil, even David took his turn to watch over you.' Callie smiled now; perhaps she knew Miranda would like that.

'Oh?'

'I asked him to step into your shoes. He's doing a magnificent job of it; you have nothing to worry about.'

'David.' Miranda sank back in the pillows and somehow she felt Callie was right. 'David.' His name floated on her lips once more and she closed her eyes. 'I'm so, so very tired,' she said as some of the fog began to clear from her mind. 'You like him?'

'I do. In fact, not only can I see why you wanted him to work in the mills, I'm wondering why on earth you didn't just appoint him as your second-in-command until you retired.' Callie smiled.

'You know, I couldn't do that. Not really... not with Ada,

it would have broken her heart, and Simon, and then, not knowing what to do for the best with you, it just all spun away from me so I couldn't see what was the right thing to do.' Miranda felt a tear fall gently down her cheek. 'Now, I really do feel like a little old lady.'

'Oh, Mamma, there's nothing wrong with that.' Callie bent forward and kissed her gently on her head. 'No-one could have made that decision these last few weeks. I'm sorry, I never realised how awful we were all being about everything.'

'You weren't. Not really, I mean, I could always see Ada's point of view. She's been loyal and hardworking and to be fair, she's done a lot of good at the mills. As to Simon, well – he was just being Simon.'

'And me?'

'Ah, Callie. You know if I could have asked you to take them on, I would have, but your life was in London, not here…' Miranda smiled sadly.

'What if it was here, though, what then?' Callie asked gently. 'I might enjoy being part of the mills, you know, if it was something that I thought would work…'

'Callie, Callie.' Miranda looked at the clock on the wall opposite. Down the corridor, she could hear the dinner ladies making their way with a trolley that refused to keep the centre ground. 'God, I'd have given anything to have you there with me these last few months.' She looked at her daughter. A sliver of golden sunlight breaking through the blinds behind her reminded her that they had lots to look forward to. She was going to have a grandchild and now, maybe Callie back home in Ballycove too. 'Oh, Callie.' She felt the tears glisten in her eyes.

'What is it?'

'I'm just so happy you're here now...' She glanced towards her daughter's tiny baby bump. 'I'm just so happy we're all here.'

It would take weeks, the infuriating, but charming Dr Brennan told her when he came to visit her on his rounds the following day. He smiled at Callie as he'd never smiled at Ada and Miranda caught her daughter's blush and wondered at how sometimes the most unlikely things can work out better than you think.

'But you have, I think, good support around you this time,' the doctor said smoothly.

'I've always had that.' Miranda was too proud to ever say otherwise. But of course, she knew he knew the truth of it. She probably wouldn't be here if it hadn't been for all the to-ing and fro-ing about the future of the mills.

'So?' She rounded on Callie then. 'Tell me, how is everything really?'

'Really, it's better than any of us could have predicted. Ada was here earlier. She's so sorry, Mamma. I've never seen such a change in someone. It's as if, well, it's as if she's a different person.'

'So, it took me having a heart attack to make a difference to her,' Miranda muttered sadly.

'No, do you know, I think it's something else, something – it's enough to convince me of magic.' Callie laughed.

'Go on, I could do with a giggle,' Miranda whispered.

'She came as soon as I called her to tell her you were here, but it's like she's different, really different. She walked in here with Anthony, and I swear, they were like a courting couple.' Callie shook her head happily at the memory. 'But,

Mamma, more importantly, we talked, we really talked and she says she's learned a terrible lesson, that she thinks she's been so lucky to have found out... well, she says nothing is more important to her than family and she wants to step down from the mills to enjoy life. She wants to take early retirement and travel with Anthony. She mentioned France and Australia. Honestly, Mamma, you could see the difference in her eyes. It's as if the worry and the bitterness have been completely rubbed out.' Callie's expression was so animated. Miranda tried to sit up, to be sure that she had heard correctly.

'So, she's actually leaving the mills?' Miranda sighed, not entirely sure that was what she'd wanted for her daughter. 'Please don't tell me she feels pushed out or that I didn't want her there or that I chose...'

'Shh, Mamma, none of those things. She said that she and Anthony spoke long into the night and it seems he's convinced her that now you can choose who's going to take over the mills it is giving her some breathing space.'

'Well, I never expected that...Good man Anthony; he really is full of surprises.' Miranda was more pleased for her daughter, but it was a cautious feeling, until she saw for herself that Ada was not bruised – the last thing she wanted to do was hurt her daughter.

'You could be right there. From the looks of the pair of them today, I'd say they did a lot more than talk into the early hours of the morning.'

'I'll have to organise something. I'll have to think about a retirement...' Miranda felt her head swim at the notion of sorting out some kind of generous finishing-up payment for her daughter.

'For Ada.' Callie laughed. 'That's a hoot, Mamma. Don't you know, Ada will have that all worked out already; no doubt she's been planning her retirement package since she made her confirmation.'

'True, you're probably right.' Miranda shook her head and smiled. 'Well, I have to say, I'm rather looking forward to seeing her now and Anthony.' It was nice, Miranda realised, because when she was in hospital before, she honestly dreaded Ada's visits. She would sit sternly at the end of the bed, forcing small talk and wrinkling her nose at things that she knew nothing about. 'And you, Callie, what about you? If Ada has her happy ever after, surely you too...'

'Oh, Mamma, I think I've found my happy ever after right here.' She rested her hand across her baby bump.

'But London...Dennis? I assume he's the father, surely, he'll want you to...'

'Yes. Dennis. I should have told you, but it was all such a complete mess and I really didn't want you to worry, but I realise now that you probably worried more by not knowing.'

'You know me too well,' Miranda shook her head.

'Dennis's wife owned Theme – that much you did know? Well a few weeks ago I found out he was not just having an affair with me behind her back, he was also cheating on me.'

'He sounds like a swine.' Miranda stopped herself. This was the father of her grandchild; still, she was glad Callie was here and he was a long way away in London. 'I'm sorry, Callie.'

'No, nothing to be sorry about, really. It was a total

cliché, younger version of myself, but it hurt and then, somehow, his wife must have got the wrong end of the stick. She realised he was having an affair and assumed I was the new object of his desire.'

'Gosh, he's a right one…' Miranda shook her head.

'Yes, well, it turns out she was a mile behind the times, because I would say he was about to throw me over for this new girl. When Veronica called me to lunch, I knew the game was up, what I didn't expect was the generous exit package she offered to get me out of London.'

'So, you took the money and ran back here.' Miranda was smiling. In some ways there was a messed-up sort of justice in it all. 'Are you going to tell her about the new girl?'

'I think she'd rather hear it from Dennis, so I've given him an ultimatum of sorts. They've paid me ten million pounds not to work for a direct competitor in London. It's really only bonuses for three years and a severance package based on my benefits, but it's a huge chunk of money. All the same, I know that if she realised that I was not the competition it wouldn't have been nearly so generous.'

'She doesn't sound like the warmest person you've met in London.'

'No, but could you blame her? After all, I'm not sure I'd have been any better after I saw Dennis with his younger lover,' Callie said sadly, but then she smiled. 'Those are worries for another day. I've got the best possible thing out of the whole mess right here.'

'You certainly have.' Miranda would not press her daughter any further. Callie would do the right thing; she knew that now.

'I've been thinking, these Germans…'

'I haven't even thought about their offer, to be honest with you. Now, they would happily pay out a couple of million from what I could gather...'

'Yes, Simon is very eager to sell...' Callie had a familiar glint in her eye. 'How would you feel about me buying his share? I'd offer him a fair price and it would give me a forty percent share in the mills as well as giving him what he wants.'

'Hard cash?' Miranda sighed, imagining her profligate son wasting every penny on the high life and disastrous business deals. 'It's sounds more than fair...It would certainly make things straightforward for everyone.'

'Well, I'll have a chat with him; maybe offer him half first and then half in two years' time...' Callie had planned all of this already. They both knew that Simon would fritter away every penny, but a year or two of living on the breadline might just make him more prudent. 'Now, he won't be receiving dividends any more so...'

'Callie, he's over forty years of age. It's time for him to stand on his own two feet. If lying here is making me see one thing it's this... I won't always be here; the mills will go on without me and all of you will get on with life when I'm just a memory.'

Callie was right about Ada. She arrived to visit Miranda every day and it seemed that her smile grew wider, her eyes lost their tired and empty expression and there was a vivacious lilt to her words when she enquired not just about Miranda but about the other patients in nearby wards also. On that first afternoon, Miranda noticed immediately her daughter was wearing jeans – she couldn't ever remember Ada wearing denim.

'You seem... different.' It was, Miranda felt, a little like that vast elephant in the room that everyone tiptoes around and yet it seems no-one is brave enough to admit it's there. It seemed that everything about her daughter had become the antithesis of what she'd always been. There was no briefcase, no pearls, and no tweed. Instead, she wore earrings that might have been picked up on a market stall and the scent of lavender instead of expensive French perfume was unmistakable. On her feet she wore trainers. Miranda tried to imagine her going into a shop to buy them. They were brand new and as far away from her usual kitten heels as it was possible to imagine.

Miranda felt a rush of love for this daughter who had taken so very long to grow into herself, but it seemed as if the transformation was happening before her very eyes now.

'I am,' Ada said proudly. 'Callie has told you that I'm stepping down from the mills.' Even the warmth in her voice, enveloping her sister's name, marked out a huge change in her.

'Why the sudden decision?' Miranda asked carefully, because this was Ada and she'd spent a lifetime choosing her words; she didn't expect a complete sea change.

'I had a wakeup call. I behaved abominably that night. Even if you hadn't ended up here, I knew that, well, I had crossed a line. In my heart, I had let something eat away at me and it's been slowly gnawing through me for years. That night it all just sort of flooded out of me. Later, when we got home, it took Anthony to tell me that he wasn't going to hang around any longer, to make me realise what I could lose.'

Ada's eyes dropped to the floor, perhaps she was still embarrassed about how she had thrown a letter that was private and innocent in her own mother's face. 'You see, Mother, after all is said and done, I've always loved Anthony. I might have lost sight of him in my quest for control of the mills, but I never forgot how much I needed him and how much he meant to me. That night and in the weeks leading up to it, somehow, I lost my way.' She raised her head now and looked at Miranda. 'I convinced myself that I was falling in love with David Blair – please don't laugh, I know that sounds ridiculous...'

'I would never laugh at you Ada, even when we had our worst rows; all I've wanted is for you to be happy. I just always believed that there is a difference between getting what you think will make you happy and actually being content with the many blessings you already have,' Miranda said softly.

'And I suppose that's one of those things that I couldn't understand. You and Callie, so content to sit on the garden swing wrapped up in a woollen blanket or sweep leaves and then sink down with a hot cup of tea and a natter. I had forgotten how to be happy – just with the little things...'

'Forgotten?' Miranda said faintly.

'Well, maybe I never learned it, but I'm learning it now. I think...'

'What, darling? What do you think?' Miranda wanted to cry, but it was Ada's new-found humility that moved her so much and she wasn't sure it was sadness, rather a release of emotion that she had never expected to feel.

'I think that almost losing Anthony, or feeling that he might leave me, well it was like the wakeup call I needed. Suddenly, I realised that no job in the world could make up for that. And then, it dawned on me that I'd sacrificed so much and nobody expected anything like that from me, I just didn't know what else to do… and you'd have never signed it over to me. I could see that, especially once Callie came back.' A small tear scudded down her cheek.

'Oh, Ada, please don't…' Miranda reached out and touched her daughter's arm. 'You've done a brilliant job at the mills. You've been as much a part of their success as I have. I've always known that, even if I didn't really say it to you.'

'Thank you, Mother, that means so much, it really does. I suppose we've both played our parts and perhaps brought them as far as it's taken us to let someone else take care of the next part of their journey,' she said softly and Miranda knew that she was hearing the absolute truth of how her daughter was feeling.

'And you're not upset, or feeling that I've…' Miranda couldn't put it into words, but it was that she'd favoured Callie over Ada – because she wasn't sure she wanted to look too closely at the truth of that.

'No, really, I'm not upset about any of it now. I can see, you were right: it wouldn't have made me happy. I would have just stepped into something that would have made me more unfulfilled than I already felt. I'm not cut out for it. Finally, I understand that, you know? When you used to talk about relationships and community, I never really got that. It sort of never seemed important, but then, when I saw the pain I had caused Anthony… Well, it was like something sort of clicked into place and I…'

'Go on?'

'I just knew.' Ada smiled and it was a warm and genuine movement that enriched all of her features, so it seemed to raise her up inside herself. 'I just knew what I had to do.'

'We'll have a party,' Miranda said then, 'something to look forward to, to thank you for all those years and, of course, you'll still be a director.'

'Oh, Mother, we're having a party already. Have you forgotten the anniversary of the mills is being planned? It's going to be the most marvellous shindig ever!'

41

Apparently, Ada was going to help him invest the money wisely. Well, Simon had been clear from the outset, he was not going to stash the payment for his share in the mills into some fusty old account that might be worth nothing after a couple of decades. No, Simon had his own ideas.

Callie was true to her word. She had everything drawn up by Stephen Leather – their family solicitor – so it was all above board. They'd even tripped down to the old man's poky offices on the main street to sign up the agreement. The Mullers would never have come up with such a generous amount and Simon knew Callie had offered it to him so they just wouldn't get a look-in. His mother was pleased as well, although she did take the time to explain to him that if he accepted the offer, he was no longer going to receive his annual payment in dividends.

Simon agreed, knowing that by removing him from the mills, going forward had just been made easier for his mother. The fact was, he was just so delighted to free up his cash; he hadn't thought about dividends or any of the other ties to the mills. Now it dawned on him, he would not have to attend meetings or pretend to be interested in yarns or this year's colours or the price of wool in the end-of-year accounts. Two million euro for just his share, to be paid in two instalments. The first, immediately on signing, would be transferred into his bank account and the remainder twenty-four months later.

Simon woke up in Bridgestone Cottage the following morning feeling as if something had just fallen right in the world. He was officially a millionaire and it felt good. He whistled tunelessly while he made breakfast, set the table with coffee and toast and some fried bacon for both himself and Callie. When his phone rang, it startled him. It was much too early for any of his friends to call making plans and the number was one he didn't recognise. Dublin, but still – no-one ever called him before eleven in the morning.

'Simon…' The voice on the other end of the line sounded as if the melody had been lost from it. 'I haven't heard from you and I wondered if there was any news.'

'Gabby,' Simon whispered her name and suddenly he felt an overbearing sense of guilt. He had used her. 'I was going to ring you later today…'

'I'm sure…' They both knew she was quite sure he'd never have picked up the phone. 'You've high-tailed it out of Dublin and every penny I put into that… that… scam… well, I might as well have chucked it into the River Liffey.' There was an emptiness to her voice. Simon knew that although it was a lot of money to most people, a couple of hundred thousand to Gabby could be written off as a bad debt.

'I'm sorry, Gabby,' and he was, because for just a moment, he could imagine her, sitting there, in her little office in the attic of the building that her family had owned for generations. The jewellery shop three floors below would seem like another world. Gabby had let out every other inch of space to professionals willing to pay premium prices for a rental slice of one of Dublin's most sought-after addresses. Gabby was not poor, but she was lonely and maybe, over the last few weeks before he left Dublin, maybe she'd been the best friend he'd had. 'Listen, I'm coming to Dublin at the weekend. Say you'll have dinner with me, my treat?'

'I don't know, Simon. I mean, you've really let me down – you know, over this investment thing and then scarpering out of Dublin, just like that. I'm not sure I should.'

'Gabby.' Simon paused, because he wasn't planning to say what he said next, but he knew he had to say it. 'Listen, we've come a long way and I know I've been a terrible fool. I mean, I've just bounced from one awful decision to the next but...' He took a deep breath, knew he was, maybe for the first time in his life, about to do the right thing. 'I've managed to sell my share of the mills and I'd like to try, at least try and make it up to you...' The words flooded across the line into silence on the other end and he imagined her, examining the large emerald she wore on her right hand, maybe patting down her hair in some nervous movement.

'What exactly are you saying, Simon?'

'I'm saying have dinner with me. I'm saying take a chance on me, but maybe...' He smiled then, a feeling of happiness washing over him. 'Well, maybe don't take an investment opportunity with me again, but, well, we could start with dinner…'

'I…' She stopped for a moment, then he heard something light enter her voice. 'Simon Corrigan, yes, I think I would like that very much.'

Epilogue

It was with a strange mix of pride and disappointment that Miranda Corrigan looked about the assembled family, friends, neighbours and colleagues. They were gathered in what had once been the machine room – a long hangar that when Miranda first came here had thundered out a fierce noise, echoing loudly the looms that stretched along its middle. That was over sixty years ago. More often now, she felt herself hit with a wave of nostalgia for those days; perhaps it was the planning of this anniversary celebration for the mills, uncovering memories that had long ago been stored away. It filled Miranda with a sense of wistfulness that she was, as a practical woman, quite unused to – and she was not at all sure that it suited her.

'Here, Mamma, are you ready?' Callie, her youngest daughter, handed her a glass of cool champagne and nodded towards the little platform they had borrowed from the nearby deanery. It too had looked tired and worn out, but old Bert Hannigan took it aside so now its walnut gleamed with a high polish that shrouded any flaws drawn in over the years.

'Is everybody here?' Miranda looked about, but while she had once been a tall athletic woman, the years had pushed her down, so she no longer had the advantage of being able to see with certainty the turnout in the room.

'Well, if they're not, we'll have trouble squeezing in very many more, so I think it's probably best to begin.' Callie squeezed her arm encouragingly. She was still the same little girl she had always been to Miranda, although life had scratched out the finest lines about her pretty face. She was no longer a young woman, even if her energetic thirst for life and guileful grooming fooled you into knocking a decade and a half off her real age.

Tonight she was wearing a beautiful gown, white silk with a tiny golden fleck, hardly noticeable until she caught the light, and then it seemed as though she was ethereal. It worked well against her soft skin, warmed olive from time spent between the garden and walking across fields with a rescue dog she'd adopted only a week ago. Callie, her darling Callie, there was a time when Miranda worried about her youngest daughter – well, it's what you do, isn't it – worry about them until they settle down with some nice young man?

Callie had no intention of settling down with anyone other than the baby she was due to deliver in a matter of weeks, but she was the happiest Miranda had ever seen her, so perhaps all that worrying had finally paid off. The news that there would be a new generation of Corrigans in Ballycove was something that had lit Miranda from within. If she was honest, it was what she'd wanted more than an immediate successor in the mills, although she was fairly certain that none of her children would believe her if she told them so.

Now she worried less about any of her family – it was

time for them to take the reins of their own lives and she was sure they had, apart from their expectations around her and the mills.

The podium was at the furthest end of the room and Miranda enjoyed walking through the well-wishers gathered thick along the way. They had cleared back the stock that normally filled this place. The mills, to survive, had undergone a gradual lifelong renovation. Smaller, faster looms freed up over eighty percent of the building now; the old machine room had transformed into a grand shop floor, its laid-back elegant ambience enhanced by the original high oak exposed beams, and flag-stoned floor buttoning in the authenticity of the place. Tonight, it glowed with sparkling twinkly lights, draped along the awnings that overhung various displays and newly installed sections to cater for refreshments, finger food, champagne and punch.

'Well, Bert, you've done us proud.' Miranda stood beside the man who'd been here just a fraction longer than she had. Bert Hannigan had joined the mills as a ten-year-old messenger boy almost seventy years earlier. Back then, he had been thrilled when they let him have a huge bicycle that dwarfed him, so he had to ride it with one leg under the cross bar and stopping meant slowing down, so he could find a wall to lean against before dismounting.

'Ach, Mrs Corrigan, sure all I've done is spit and polish,' he said shyly, his attention drawn to the glass in his hand. He was a shrunken foreigner on his own home turf tonight. Cast off in a sea of black tie, shiny-faced whippets, old Bert had made an effort, but it amounted to his Sunday best, dry-cleaned for the occasion. At his neck, with some aplomb, he wore a tweed bow tie that Miranda had pressed into his granddaughter's hand a week earlier when she called in to pick him up. 'And I enjoyed it – sure it's a great honour to be here, when you think of all the people who have passed through this place over the years.'

He smiled sadly, his hooded blue eyes moist with memories of the many friends they'd lost along the way. Bert's wife had worked here too. Glenda Fish had been a snippet of a thing when he married her – blonde and green-eyed, they'd made a lovely couple.

Bert believed he'd won the lottery in life, to have Glenda as his wife, their only son married and settled in a little bungalow down the road from them. Miranda found a photograph of them when they cleared out the old pantry to make storage room for tonight. It was hard to believe that Bert was once dapper, a neat man with fine features and skin that stretched across his cheekbones like soft silk. Miranda had stood for ages studying the photograph, because somewhere along the way, while they hadn't really noticed, Bert had turned into the man she knew today. He was an old man, a really old man, with thinning snow-white hair, skin that fell in folds around his eyes and mouth, and his once straight back now hunched as though he no longer had the energy to pull himself level with the world. It saddened Miranda to think that time had passed so quickly.

'What do you think of the champagne?' She dropped her voice; they were after all from the same stock, co-conspirators in a modern age that tried its best to relegate them.

'Not for me, but I'll have some to be social mind.'

'Prefer the black stuff from the "Squealing Pig"?'

'I'll be clearing out my palate with a half one, just as soon as we've finished here.' He smiled now at her. No matter that she had risen to the most important position in the mills and he stood squarely in what was considered the lowest, they were friends for too many years for that to make a difference.

'I'd be tempted to join you, if it wasn't for…' She nodded back to the podium. They both knew her night would go on until everyone left the mills.

'Well, don't let them keep you up too late,' he said gently.

Across the room, Miranda saw Simon. He had caused her more worry than her two daughters put together, but tonight, when he introduced her to Gabby, she had a feeling that somehow, he had managed to grow up. Simon had brought home very few lady friends over the years, but she knew he had dated a string of heiresses – assumed that they would have as much interest in the mills as Simon would – which was very little. Gabby, on the other hand, looked about the same age as Simon. She was not a stunner, but she had intelligence about her that Miranda liked immediately. She was not some slip of a thing that Simon would run rings around, nor was she likely to be taken for a fool a second time round, but he seemed to hang on her every word. Perhaps as unlikely as they may seem, they could yet be a very happy couple together. Miranda did hope so.

Her recent health scare had taught her a valuable lesson. Hope was the best she could do; worrying was just for people who didn't know any better.

'Ah, Mother, there you are, the woman of the hour,' Simon said air-kissing her. 'It's a lovely party.' His voice held warmth that went deeper than his usual affable charm.

'You're enjoying the champagne.' She nodded at the chilled glass in his hand.

'Oh, yes, of course, the very best. I wouldn't have expected you to put up anything less.'

'Well, I'm afraid, Simon, that I can't take the credit for that. Callie organised the refreshments, one champagne is the same as another to me.' She looked around for Gabby.

'Ah,' he said smiling, 'Gabby went to the bathroom. I think she really wanted to take a look around the shop floor. She's grown up in the jewellery business, owns a nice shop just off Grafton Street.'

'I like her, Simon. I do hope that...' Her words petered off, because she wasn't sure how to finish the sentence delicately.

'I won't hurt her, Mother, if that's what you're worried about. We're old friends and I've already talked her into one bad investment, so she knows what I'm like, but...' He laughed now, a sort of incredulity in the back of his throat. 'We sort of fit together, in some funny way...'

'You're serious about her?' Miranda thought this could be the best news of the evening.

'Actually, yes, I think I am.'

'I'm so pleased,' she said, squeezing his arm when she spotted Gabby weaving her way back to them.

'It's a great party, Mrs Corrigan,' Gabby said brightly.

'Yes, it is, isn't it, and you must call me Miranda, dear,' Miranda said as she moved off towards the podium. She stood for a moment, in the centre of the great room, enjoying this special occasion. Everyone here was a friend and Miranda knew she was blessed to have many good and lifelong friends. There were people here who had sacrificed much for her and her belief in the mills. People who had taken wage cuts and believed in her ability to bring them through. The fact that they all stood here tonight, celebrating the thriving force that the mills had become, was testament to their faith in her as much, she felt, as her ability to make it all such a wonderful success.

Of course, she had a relationship with every person in this room. The mills had over the years managed to stretch far enough to pay unforeseen medical expenses, roof houses badly damaged in an obliterating storm and take care of a hundred and one other little tragedies in their small town. They pulled together the entire community around them so they remained at the centre of Ballycove. The mills were more than just a factory, but rather they were a symbol of all that people were most proud of.

And that was what gave Miranda the most pleasure here tonight. The fact that in some way, she'd managed not just to save the mills, but also to carry on the kind of ethos that would have made Paddy proud. It was worth more than any balance sheet figures at the end of a lifetime's work.

It was something she'd spent years trying to convince Ada of; Ada was her eldest daughter and Miranda had adored her from the moment she arrived in her delicate perfection. Such a placid child, she'd never really shone in her own right and in many ways Miranda supposed that suited her. Callie was the star, Ada was the dutiful daughter, the one who stayed in Ballycove and worked in the mills and now… Miranda sighed because she was not sure what to do now. The simple fact was that Ada would not be here any longer. She was embarking on a new life and in two days' time, she would be leaving Ballycove with Anthony to travel to places that Miranda had never even dreamed of seeing.

'Mother, you must be pleased.' Ada was at her elbow

and it seemed over the years she'd never really moved away from her. It was unexpected, Miranda thought, this notion of missing Ada so much before she'd even left.

'Of course, it's a lovely evening, quite the social event of the year, I'd say.' Miranda smiled. 'Still, we have another piece to get through and then I shall really relax and enjoy myself.' Miranda nodded towards the podium. She checked her watch. It was almost eight o'clock, time for her to get her speech over with and let the band really get into full swing.

'You're going to be wonderful,' Ada whispered and kissed her mother gently on the cheek before turning back to Anthony.

'Well, we'll see,' Miranda said lightly. Some of her confidence had deserted her since she returned from hospital. She'd all but given up her job in the mills. Of course, she turned up there, occasionally, to walk about and check in with people and the anniversary celebrations had managed to capture her imagination, but she really was pulling away. Perhaps, they were pulling away from her too. Callie and David were, she had to admit, a fantastic team and she knew the mills were in good hands. She sighed then, because rather than feeling as if the jigsaw had been completed, the notion left her feeling rather redundant.

Apart from it being a great honour to stand as the head of the mills on the event of their anniversary, Miranda had things she wanted to say. Even now, tonight, amongst the glitter and sparkle of these celebrations, Miranda could not lose sight of the journey it had taken to arrive here. She held her long skirt just a little up to negotiate the half dozen steps more safely to the podium, looked back across the room, catching David Blair's eye. He understood this would not be easy and part of her felt that he was rushing his youthful strength towards her in a great push of courage and support.

On the second step, Miranda felt herself go a little light-headed as though she might faint, but she placed her foot on the next step up. Her speech would take no more than a few minutes and if her blood pressure was going to play up, it would bloody well have to wait its turn until this was over. Then, it seemed in an instant she was standing at the podium, looking down on the assembled crowd who were oblivious to her bird's eye position. From here, it was as if she was watching them from another plane. Their voices high and laughter blending beneath the low sounds of a band Callie found weeks before who would set exactly the tone for the evening. She watched them for a few moments, people she'd known for years, talking and celebrating, and she might have been looking down on them from heaven. In her heart, she felt a lightness overtake her, a whispering in her ear, as if Paddy stood at her shoulder.

She waited a bit longer, committing the mill floor, the decorations, the faces, sounds and familiar aromas to her memory, feeling that in some way, as each breath was taken, it slipped a little further from her with every passing moment. Then, a hush came over the room, as though they knew she was watching them, and slowly, like an uneven Mexican wave, all eyes turned towards her, waiting for what she might say to them. She waited, still, enjoying the silence that was spreading about the gathering like a virus, infecting conversation and laughter until it drew it up into an arrested hush. Then, as if to spur her on, the microphone let out an elongated whine. It was time to speak and for a moment, Miranda wondered if she'd have the courage to deliver the words she'd planned for weeks.

'Good evening,' she said to start and felt a jangling of nerves that had nothing to do with standing before people. 'You're all very welcome...' Miranda had already learned off everything she was going to say this evening. She'd gone through it time and time again. She could probably recite it backwards if she tried. Callie and Ada had helped her write it, well most of it. She drew her breath in. She didn't have to actually make the speech to the very end, but she intended to. This was her chance to put things straight and she had every intention of marking out the start of the next hundred and fifty years in the mills' history with naming her successors before her speech was done.

At the end of the speech, the rousing applause made her light-headed. Miranda knew she needed fresh air. David and Callie having stood beside her for her final words at the podium joined her back down onto the main shop floor.

'I think I'd like some fresh air,' she whispered to Callie as they made the final step. They walked out into the balmy evening and Miranda batted Callie away; she just needed a few minutes' peace and quiet to gather herself. She would sit here and then perhaps in a moment or two walk along the riverbank. That was her plan at least, but then her eyes began to feel so heavy and when she woke, the evening sun had begun to dip far off into the west. She gathered up her long evening dress and the heavy shawl Callie had insisted she wear if she was going outside for any length of time.

Her thoughts raced, remembering how it felt to look

down on all the people gathered to celebrate the mills. She thought of Ballycove now, a riverside village, nestled beneath green and grey rock hills, the sea whispering on warm sunny days against grey shingle that flashed surprising light when water and sun chose to pick out rocks and glassy stones occasionally.

To the unpractised eye, Ballycove may appear to be no less and no more than a hundred other tiny villages dotted about the Irish coastline. It had all the necessary amenities – small family-owned shops, a post office, a 'big house', a gushing salmon-filled river and, of course, the woollen mills. It had sun and cool breezes in summer, rain and hardy storms in winter. One year, not that long ago, it even had snow settled on the river's evergreen banks. This had happened only twice in Miranda Corrigan's memory, but still she remembered it on the warmest of days. There was a caravan park for the holiday-making families and a little guest house that did Sunday lunch – beef or salmon, on old-fashioned plates with warm white wine from the bar next door. There were two bars, well three if you counted McGinnity's, but no-one ever did. Mrs McGinnity still opened her front door and served up stout or beer to the few elderly locals who knew the difference between mixed and special and remembered a time when you never ordered a pint without a half one on the side.

Mostly, Ballycove was a village of familiarity. It had the age-old charm of everyone knowing everyone. Still no-one wanted to pretend they knew half of each other's business that they couldn't help but know. If not exactly the valley of the squinting windows, certainly, there were a number of locals who could be relied upon to stoke the fires of gossip and ensure that private family affairs were kept anything but secret.

Miranda walked along this road, most days. It was more than just a way to keep her heart ticking at a normal pace. Even the occasional sighting of a fox or stray squirrel was only part of the allure. For Miranda, this place was all about her memories. They were a mixture of good and bad, but mostly happy times spent along the riverbank. Tonight promised to be one of those magical ones that could stay with her for what remained of her lifetime.

In the distance, she saw a vaguely familiar figure. Instead of lying on the grass as he would have once done, Richard Blair was sitting on a park bench that Miranda had donated to this walkway. It held an inscription to Paddy and when she sat on it herself, she thought of days when they had ambled here together. Paddy Corrigan filled her with the best stories and sometimes, if she was still enough, she heard him whisper to her once more on the breeze.

'Ah, my dear Miranda.' Richard Blair stood before her. 'I've been waiting for you for a very long time.'

Acknowledgements

In writing this story, I have the following people to thank for helping me make it into a book…

The Aria Girls – my lovely editor Hannah Smith and her fantastic team – Vicky Joss, Nikky Warde, Geo Willis, Rhea Kurien, Helena Newton, Sue Lamprell and David Boxell.

Extra special thanks to my agent for all her hard work on my behalf – Judith Murdoch – I count myself very lucky to be a J girl!

My family – Cristín, Tomás, Roisín, Seán and James (Mr H) – my loudest cheerleader! Bernadine – my go-to woman on that critical first draft and Christine Cafferkey for continuing to keep us all between the ditches!

About the Author

Faith lives in the west of Ireland with her husband, four children and two very fussy cats. She has an Hons Degree in English Literature and Psychology, has worked as a fashion model and in the intellectual disability and mental health sector.

Hello from Aria

We hope you enjoyed this book! If you did let us know, we'd love to hear from you.

We are Aria, a dynamic digital-first fiction imprint from award-winning independent publishers Head of Zeus. At heart, we're committed to publishing fantastic commercial fiction – from romance and sagas to crime, thrillers and historical fiction. Visit us online and discover a community of like-minded fiction fans!

We're also on the look out for tomorrow's superstar authors. So, if you're a budding writer looking for a publisher, we'd love to hear from you. You can submit your book online at ariafiction.com/ we-want-read-your-book

You can find us at:
Email: aria@headofzeus.com
Website: www.ariafiction.com
Submissions: www.ariafiction.com/
we-want-read-your-book

 @ariafiction
 @Aria_Fiction
 @ariafiction

Made in the USA
Coppell, TX
05 May 2020

24565320R00243